The Empyrean Quest

A Journey of Discovery

Don Horsfall

The Empyrean Quest

First published in Australia by Don Horsfall 2018
www.donhorsfall.com

 A catalogue record for this book is available from the National Library of Australia

ISBN: 978-0-9876443-0-5 (pbk)
ISBN: 978-0-9876443-1-2 (ebk)

Typesetting and design by Publicious Book Publishing
Published in collaboration with Publicious Book Publishing
www.publicious.com.au

THE POWER
OF COMMITMENT

The following words on **commitment** – by W.H. Murray, The Scottish Himalayan Expedition, followed by Goethe's couplet – have always been important to me. They tie in with the theme of the novel as it relates to commitment to oneself/our inner truth, and the power of creation that comes from pure, focused intent.

Until one is committed there is hesitancy, the chance to draw back.
Concerning all acts of initiative (and creation) there is one elementary truth, the ignorance of which kills countless ideas and splendid plans:
That the moment one definitely commits oneself, then providence moves too.
All sorts of things occur to help one that would not otherwise have occurred. A whole stream of events issues from the decision, raising in one's favour all manner of unforeseen incidents and meetings and material assistance which no man would have dreamt would come his way.
I have learnt a deep respect for one of Goethe's couplets:

Whatever you can do, or dream you can, begin it!
Boldness has genius, magic, and power in it
(Johann Wolfgang von Goethe).

FOREWORD

BY DR JOHN DEMARTINI

Have you ever questioned your life's direction, wondered about your purpose for being here or why you have had to go through and endure what seemed to be emotional hardships? Have you ever found yourself repeating the same patterns and behaviours, stuck in a cycle, attracting the same drama in your life? If your answer is yes to any of these defining questions, *The Empyrean Quest* has come to your awareness for a reason.

Author, Don Horsfall, has been a student of mine for many years. His life demonstrates an unending thirst for knowledge in the area of human development. During one of my intensive ten-day courses in Houston, Texas, Don was struck by a desire to share some of the life-changing concepts we were discussing. *The Empyrean Quest* was the result of that spark of inspiration.

Whilst this book has been crafted as an engaging work of fiction, the compelling storyline has, throughout its pages, thoughtfully threaded universal laws that exist all around us and affect every aspect of our lives. The irony is that these truths are known by very few.

As you take this journey of discovery, I am confident you will find it thought-provoking, confronting and challenging to many of your previous, or possibly entrenched, beliefs. For many, it will hold valuable clues to leading a liberated, emotionally balanced life, revealing critical insights that shape our very existence.

Dr John Demartini
Founder of the Demartini Institute and international best-selling author of *The Values Factor*

Contents

PREFACE

The Empyrean in Greek mythology is the ultimate source of pure light at the centre of all creation. The implication by ancient philosophers, by its very suggestion, is that we are all on a journey back to the Empyrean, the source. Do you believe that there is a purpose to your life? Is there a reason for all of your experiences that is ultimately helping you on the way to somewhere? Or do you believe that life is just happening to you randomly outside of your sphere of influence and at the end, there is nothing? If you subscribe to the latter, perhaps the adventure story that follows may be just a worthy read. For those of you who intuitively seek answers to life's mysteries, this literary adventure may resonate with something inside of you, awakening a knowing within and igniting further inspiration for your journey.

What is the underlying purpose of your life then? Are you looping around and around doing the same things, stuck in a rut, striving but never arriving? Have you ever wondered what lies just beyond your horizon, but are afraid to venture there? How much then do your beliefs restrict your human potential and ultimately, your evolution as a soul? The easiest task for mankind is to deceive ourselves. It seems we are ever willing to believe what we wish to be true in order to justify our existence. This is not a new concept. It was attributed to Demosthenes in 384–322 BC. What if your life experience is a manifestation of your limited thoughts and perceptions? After all, our history is rich with great achievements, breaking down previously unshakable beliefs which have led to new discoveries. Columbus discovered that the world was round when all but a few believed it was flat. Voyager has revealed an expanded Universe that was always there; we just could not see it. What if there was an expanded Universe for you to explore, hidden in plain sight?

We as individuals are often restricted by what we see and believe, enshrined in a mist of deception based on our own perceptions. It's our obsession with what we believe to be unquestionably true that are the boundaries of our world and that keep us confined, blinded to the reality of what is there and has always been there, just beyond the horizon. Just as the hand held before the eye can hide the tallest mountain, so the routine of everyday life can keep us from seeing the vast radiance and the secret wonders that fill the world (Chasidic saying, eighth century).

Most of us live in a bubble, a dream state, day in, day out, doing the same things, doing life, not living life. We are stuck in animal level behaviour, driven by wants and desires and prone to reaction. It's superficial and material by nature, chasing the next pleasure and trying to avoid any pain. We are slaves to our ego which is obsessed with external validation, always measuring ourselves against others. We believe life is happening to us and our existence is dominated by external influences. We dismiss the ever-present messages of the higher mind and soul that are connected to our true self and the collective wisdom that flows to us. We only reach the edge of our current known existence where real expansion exists when we create some trauma or event that shocks us out of our comfort zone. These are our own creations, perfectly designed to provide equal challenge and support for the expansion of our soul. When we finally see the hidden order, it's liberating to learn that nothing is good or bad, black or white. The evidence for every aspect of our existence lies in the laws of physics, which demonstrate that everything is always in perfect balance. Like a magnet, we have two perfectly balanced opposing energies that can never be separated. It's only our lopsided perceptions that create imbalance in our emotions and thinking. Once we are aware that this is a perfect design, necessary for our own evolution, we see the perfection to life. We understand that all our experiences, which prompt us to feel heightened emotions, are perfectly designed as a guide for our soul. For some, this realisation can create sudden and lasting expansion and liberation. Others may not seek to understand why they are unfulfilled, always lopsided, attracting drama in their life. They are destined to repeat the same patterns over and over.

As we grow and expand into ever-increasing realms of knowing, we see the order of things guiding us to our divine course with an expanded vision. Eventually, we will no longer need to engage in the emotional constraints and games of our conditioning, patterns and beliefs that have kept us stuck, looping in a restricted world without purpose. We will have an unwavering belief that all is in perfect balance in every situation. The exciting part for us all is that the soul journey has no end. We continue to bump into the edge of our known reality at each new realm of existence, creating new and challenging situations that are for the benefit of our expansion. That is the endless evolution of the spirit and the essence of creation. Many speak of creation as if it were over. Creation is taking place every moment of our lives. Einstein famously said, *"Everything is energy and that's all there is to it. Match the frequency of the reality you want and you cannot help but get that reality. It can be no other way. This is not philosophy, this is physics."*

When we can accept that we create every experience in this life, both good and bad, for our eternal soul's expansion, we realise that the problems we attract are *on the way* not *in the way*. What other purpose could there be for your many life challenges but to evolve through experiential learning?

I offer this book as part of my life's purpose in building a bridge of understanding between our human behaviour and emotions, and the universal laws that govern our existence for the ultimate benefit of our higher mind and soul, based on my own learnings, beliefs, philosophies, and knowing. My goal is to light a spark of inspiration, leading to an enhanced ability to challenge your perceived limits, alleviate unnecessary emotional suffering and break free from the mist surrounding you that blinds you to the possibilities. May you discover the perfect balance in all things and the truth that is there right in front of you and has always been there. These themes are threaded throughout the adventures about to unfold in the pages ahead. Enjoy the journey.

Don Horsfall
Author

GRATITUDE

I have eternal gratitude for:

My parents Bas & Barb, who gave me life, unconditional love and support based on a framework of dignity and respect for others, gratitude for the world as it is and encouragement to explore the possibilities.

My wife Bron, who has supported me, challenged me and loved me as we share this amazing journey together. She is the wisest woman I know.

My children, Justin, Brendan and Leah, who continue to be amongst my greatest teachers. They are an inspiration to me and my ongoing evolution. I am so proud of you all.

My amazing groups of friends, who continue to support me unconditionally through the peaks and troughs of life and have stayed the course. Thank you for being there.

INFLUENCES

Dr Murray Banks, Author, Comedian, Clinical Psychologist and Professor of Psychology at Long Island University, who was one of the most sought-after public speakers in the United States in the 1950s and 1960s. He followed his passion for comedy and live entertainment, spreading common sense information on mental health. At an early age, I listened to his recordings with my father and was taken by the life messages he provided in a humorous way, which helped shape my early philosophies on life and sparked a passion for human dynamics that is with me to this day.

Graham Hart, former Chief Executive of the Bank of Queensland in Australia, who believed in my potential and provided career opportunities that led to my eventual appointment as Head of Human Resources. He became an early mentor for me in human dynamics in a corporate environment and encouraged me to undertake tertiary education. He taught me the inherent value of people and the importance of harnessing the collective potential of all towards a common goal.

Murray Masarik and Denise Holmes-Masarik, who were a significant part of my learning as a life coach. Their inspired work at Real Education enabled me to spend a decade healing and helping thousands of people through their life-changing workshops. It was through the intensity of this work and my total immersion that I developed an in-depth knowledge and understanding of human dynamics and the patterns and beliefs that control most of our behaviours. I am forever connected to you both and your work.

Dr John Demartini, who, through his dedication as a polymath, has tirelessly studied every 'ology', every religion and the theories of the past masters in a lifelong search to uncover some of the mysteries of life with a view to unlocking the secrets of the Universe. He continues to inspire me by living his life's purpose passionately through the sharing of his knowledge and philosophies. His ground-breaking work in human dynamics underpins many of the themes threaded throughout this book. Having worked with tens of thousands of people, he has consistently demonstrated that the laws of universal balance apply equally to the human condition. Dr Demartini has unlocked considerable knowing within me and inspired me to write this book.

My purpose, in turn, is to inspire readers in transitioning from their emotional and behavioural-based existence (an essential path for our evolution) to universal knowledge, purpose, creation, love, and the equilibration of the higher mind and soul to bring them to absolute synchronicity.

The well-known saying, *When the student is ready the teacher will appear,* has been incredibly true for me in my life's journey.

I am eternally grateful to you all.

CHAPTER ONE
Living the Lie

It was early December in Sydney, Australia and the summer heat was oppressive, creating an uncomfortable sticky atmosphere matched only by the tension of the crowd gathered on the steps of the Supreme Court. Thirty-two-year-old Beau Sterling, senior partner of one of Australia's most prominent law firms, Sterling and Finch, had created an enviable record for winning the tough cases and today, he would need to be at his best.

He sensed the overriding presence of his father, Jack Sterling, standing at the top of the stairs keeping a watchful eye on proceedings. Jack was a second-generation managing partner of the firm Beau's grandfather had founded in 1942. The firm had progressed slowly but surely during its first fifty years, reaching prominence under Jack's leadership after he took over from his father, Basil Sterling, in 1996.

Jack was of average height and he had a powerful stocky build. He had grey hair and sported a trademark thick moustache. He was an uncompromising man in every aspect of his life and a ruthless court performer. He had built the firm's reputation by winning over many years and had represented some of the most prominent clients in the country. He demanded no less from his son.

Beau, a strikingly good-looking, tall, athletic man with thick, dark, wavy hair, grey-blue eyes, a square jawline, and an olive complexion, had spent his life trying to live up to his father's expectations. He had an imposing presence in his own right. He was, however, very different from his father, possessing a sensitive, caring and compassionate nature. He could not remember a time when he had not been accountable to his father for his every action. He was, after all, being groomed to be the next managing partner of Sterling and Finch.

Beau pushed his way through the crowd with the help of four police escorts and reached the top entrance to the courthouse.

'Morning, son. I hope you're ready to go. They'll throw everything at this case to put McFarlane behind bars. This one is political, and they want him out of the way. Stay alert. I could have a late development for you.'

Beau looked at his father, wondering what he had up his sleeve this time. Based on the overwhelming evidence, the case was looking very much like a conviction for his client. The weight of expectation sat heavily on Beau and he felt sick. He could not contemplate what might happen if he didn't pull a rabbit out of the hat today and get his client acquitted. After all, everyone knew that Dan McFarlane, the head of the Transport Workers Union, was a feared underworld figure.

It was common knowledge he had been involved in the illegal movement of stolen goods, money laundering and stand-over tactics in running non-union privateers off the roads. Beau's final strategies and closing argument could be the deciding factor before the jury retired to contemplate his client's fate.

The union had called for a blockade in support of their leader and over fifty trucks had arrived in the inner Sydney streets. They created a gridlock, causing mayhem for morning commuters trying to get to work. The police were powerless to stop the trucks and were doing their best to control the increasingly vocal protesters chanting for McFarlane's release outside the Supreme Court.

Beau sat in the lead defence chair as McFarlane was led in by two prison guards. He was an intimidating man, dwarfing the guards either side of him who looked to be extra-vigilant given his reputation for violence. He had used his size and bullying tactics to rise in the ranks of the union. His ruddy complexion indicated a hard-living man who did everything to the extreme.

He gave Beau a menacing look as he sat down next to him.

'You'd better be on form today, Counsellor,' he quipped threateningly in a broad Irish accent. He seemed somehow unconcerned, however, almost nonchalant. It was the look of a man who had an ace up his sleeve.

Beau did not respond and nervously ran through his tactics for the day. He wondered, deep down, what the hell he was doing there. His father interrupted his thoughts, leaning over him, whispering in his ear. He looked up at him, confused, wanting to question the information passed over, as his father slapped him on the back in a gesture of support loaded with expectation. Beau's concentration was shattered by the booming voice of the clerk of the court.

'All rise, the Honourable Judge Hayden Blunt presiding.'

The crisp crack of the gavel sounded the start of proceedings.

'Are you ready for your closing arguments, Counsellor?' the judge prompted.

Beau looked at the judge and affirmed, unconvincingly he thought, 'Yes, your Honour, however, before I proceed with my closing arguments, I call retired federal police officer Bill Wilson to the stand.'

'Objection!' came the cry from Mr Bailie for the prosecution. 'This witness is not on our list, your Honour. We haven't had a chance to depose him.'

'Will both counsellors approach the bench?' the judge demanded, losing patience. 'What are you trying to pull, Mr Sterling? You'd better have a good reason for introducing a new witness at this late stage.'

'Yes, your Honour. Mr Wilson is a federal police officer and was involved in the search of the union offices and the seizure of documents used to incriminate my client. He is a rebuttal witness. We have only just located him, your Honour. We will be alleging that the search was illegal.'

'We have already heard from a number of arresting officers, your Honour,' protested Mr Bailie for the prosecution. 'This witness will add no value to the proceedings.'

Beau looked at the witness who was now standing at the rear of the court. He appeared scared, looking around nervously, trying to avoid the glance of McFarlane. He had disappeared after resigning from the service just after McFarlane's arrest.

Judge Blunt looked towards the witness and finally determined. 'I will allow a little latitude, Mr Sterling; however, you had better get to the point quickly or I will throw it out.'

'Yes, your Honour.'

Over the next twenty minutes, Beau interrogated the witness over procedural irregularities and at each turn, the prosecution tried to dismiss his arguments due to inconsistencies. The witness contradicted previous witnesses and admitted personally to shortcuts and misrepresentations in providing false affidavits to obtain warrants used to search the union offices. Finally, he was dismissed and allowed to stand down.

Judge Blunt sat for some time with a sickening knowing that someone had got to the witness, contemplating the ramifications of what had transpired.

'Both of you, approach the bench.'

Obviously frustrated, the judge covered his microphone and leant over to address the prosecution.

'Mr Bailie, I have no choice but to agree with Mr Sterling's argument. The search was indeed illegal based on the evidence of Mr Wilson. While I cannot go on record, however, I do find it interesting to say the least, Mr Sterling, that the witness has just now decided to reveal his role in procedural inadequacies in obtaining warrants for the search,' he said, looking directly at Beau. 'Nonetheless, the documents seized in the raid on the union office are the foundation of your case against the accused, Mr Bailie, and as such, I have no choice but to rule the evidence obtained in the search as inadmissible. Unless you have new evidence to introduce at this stage, I will dismiss the case here and now.'

The prosecutor stared at the judge in disbelief.

'Your Honour, you can't do that. You know what's going on here. Based on the evidence, his guilt is undoubted. You can't let him go just like that.'

'Mr Bailie, my hands are tied here. If your office and the federal police can't establish a lawful search and seizure, you leave me no alternative.' He waved both parties away back to their respective docks. The gavel sounded again to bring the muttering in the room to an abrupt end.

'Based on the evidence I have heard this morning, I have no alternative but to dismiss the prosecution's case. I thank the jury for their service.'

Judge Blunt looked for an age at McFarlane and eventually, with contempt in his voice, announced, 'Mr McFarlane, you are free to go.'

The room erupted as the judge stood and was escorted from the courtroom. Word filtered to the protesters outside and was received with a resounding cheer. McFarlane stood and extended his hand to Beau, who was still seated deep in contemplation. He was surprised that the witness had come forward so late in the trial and knew the union heavyweights had got to him in some way. McFarlane had the calm demeanour of a man without concern. Beau felt dirty and disgusted in a system that allowed criminals to walk free, and for the part he had played in making that happen.

'Outstanding, Counsellor, outstanding,' McFarlane said with a broad smile.

Beau shook his hand even though it repulsed him. He then looked to his father for a hint of approval, knowing deep down that Jack Sterling would never go out of his way to acknowledge him, even after today's notable performance. He looked to the back of the room to see his father leaving. He wondered what part the old man had played in the whole farce, given his firm had been representing the union for years.

Beau left the court to face the press gathered in a pack on the steps outside the courthouse. He was more depressed than he had ever been, stuck in a system he despised and on a career path that had been laid out by his father from the day he was born.

CHAPTER TWO
Living the Dream

There is nothing quite like the wide expanse of the Southern Ocean. Her azure depths are alive beneath the white foam caps, constantly moving, seemingly harbouring a mysterious life force within. She has many moods and when the great southerly windstorms arrive from Antarctica, there are few more hostile places on Earth than the Southern Ocean's infamous Bass Strait. Spanning mainland Australia and Tasmania, it is one of the most feared passages for all who travel by sea.

It is also a playground for the rich and famous who, each year on Boxing Day, test their skills against the elements in one of the great blue-water ocean yacht races of the world, the 'Sydney to Hobart'. *Litigate*, the sixty-five-foot ocean racer, was making good progress, leading its class and running fourth overall for line honours. Beau was in a pensive mood, contemplating his future and daydreaming about life, feeling unfulfilled and empty and still rocked by the events that had unfolded in court earlier that month. He was on a predestined course, unconsciously living day to day. What was he really meant to be doing? Was this the life he was destined to live? His only outlet was on a yacht with the wind in his hair, challenging himself against the elements.

The southerly, as predicted, arrived on time and the next twenty-four hours were going to be an uncomfortable slog to the mouth of the Derwent River and the finish line at Constitution Dock, Hobart, Tasmania.

Jack Sterling was at the helm of his beloved yacht. He had a keen eye on his nearest rival two nautical miles astern. At sixty-three, he had lost none of his competitive spirit and was barking orders as he drove

Litigate up close to the wind. 'I want more tension on that headsail now! Get all available crew onto the rail. It's going to be a long night! I'm not accustomed to losing and I'm not about to start now.'

Jack was wringing every ounce of performance from *Litigate*. The yacht groaned and creaked as she drove through the increasing swell, now building to four metres. Green water flowed over her decks, and she rose and free-fell into the next trough with earth-shattering thuds. The salt spray lashing across Jack's face stung. Beau knew he loved every minute of it. Pushing his yacht to the brink of its potential was typical of Jack. He looked across at Beau, tactician on *Litigate*, and demanded an immediate update on their progress.

'The main sail's trimmed and boat speed has improved one knot, Skipper.'

Even now, in this hostile place, he was still under the watchful eye of his father, he lamented. He wondered how he had ended up on this path and whether he could ever be good enough in his father's eyes. He was grateful for the amazing opportunities he had been provided, but they came at a price. As he stared into the indigo blue of the ocean swell, he felt trapped and obligated. It was as if his life was a movie and he was just acting out the main character. Did he really have a choice? He dreamt of escaping and having the freedom to explore the world, to choose his own path.

Beau looked around at the rest of the crew, ten in all, decked out in their royal-blue *Litigate*-branded all-weather jackets. With all their experience and independent success, there was not a man amongst them who would question the great Jack Sterling. Beau had to admit he was not in that category either. His father's power over him had always been tangible and whenever he found himself in his father's presence, he felt like a little boy again. His only sibling, his brother Leon, was estranged from his father since he had announced at the age of fifteen that he was gay. He'd had little contact with the family since leaving home, largely due to his father's rejection. He lived in the seedy area of Kings Cross, inner Sydney, and had become lost in a world of drugs and prostitution. Jack could not bring himself to deal with his son's choices and so he had disowned him. He never spoke of him and forbade others from doing so. In spite of his father's wishes, Beau occasionally did try and contact Leon. His attempts were more often than not met with rejection, although Leon occasionally uninitiated contact with him, desperately seeking money. This left Beau in the impossible position of trying to support his brother financially, knowing if he did, he would no doubt be feeding his drug addiction. The only legitimate heir to the family law firm, Beau felt the constant weight of expectation that went with it.

Beau had always been privately uncomfortable with his father's tyrannical leadership style. He had certainly been a victim of it throughout his life and it was obvious to him the damage it could do to good people with good intentions. Jack was always right, and heaven help those who questioned his decisions. Beau preferred consultation, encouragement and acknowledgement and found they were more effective in getting the best out of the men onboard. He had learnt these values from his mother. Beau knew that his father thought him weak, and that he was on a mission to toughen Beau up and prepare him to take over the reins at the firm eventually. No wonder his beautiful mum, Barbara, an evolved and wise woman, vibrant and constantly searching for the wonders of life, had left Jack. She was the strong one and had chosen not to tolerate his father's abuse. He was impossible to please, always striving for more and not caring who he had to step on to get it. Beau had long been convinced that she had done the right thing leaving him all those years ago. His father still blamed her for breaking up the family.

Beau was more like his mother in temperament as well as looks, with her dark olive complexion from her Sicilian ancestry. He recalled how enchanted he had been at the mystical stories she shared with him when he was growing up. It was her way of encouraging Beau to keep searching for answers to life's mysteries and creating more potential to live an inspired life. She knew intuitively that Beau wore the expectation of the Sterling legacy and had subtly encouraged him over the years to seek his own path without rocking the boat too much. Beau craved his mother's free spirit and her calm, centred wisdom. He wished he had her strength of conviction to follow what truly inspired him, but the Sterling dynasty was all-powerful and all-consuming.

Jack's tolerance was decreasing as the wind pressure increased. He was again barking orders at Beau, which shook him out of his daydream.

'Beau, I need that headsail trimmed now. We're losing speed again. Keep your eye on the ball. Another mistake like that and *Genesis* will sail right over the top of us.'

'Sorry Skipper, it won't happen again.'

'It damn well better not. Sort it out or I'll replace you with someone who can do better.'

As the night closed in, their relentless progress smashing through huge swells was taking its toll on the entire crew. It would be all hands on deck tonight and with any luck, they would be closing on the mouth of the Derwent River and the finish line by daybreak. Jack remained intensely vigilant of the lights of the yachts bearing down on them from behind and their position relative to *Litigate*.

'That damn *Genesis*, we just can't shake her. Stuffed if I know how she's keeping up with us. We're a much bigger yacht. She shouldn't be keeping pace with us. Beau, we have to find more boat speed. Check the settings again.'

'Will do, Skipper,' Beau replied.

'Once you've done that, come and take the helm for a short shift. I need to get a few hours' rest if I'm going to take her to the finish line in the morning.'

'I'm all over it, Skipper,' replied Beau, relieved he was going to have some time at the helm without being under his father's watchful eye. Beau prided himself on his capacity to skipper *Litigate*, which he had done many times over the years. In fact, he was convinced that he could make ground on *Genesis* while his dad slept. Surely the old man would acknowledge him then. Beau loved the feeling of the sixty-five-foot yacht in his hands. She was so responsive to the slightest movement of the helm, and he could feel the ocean's movement beneath him. It was the one place he felt truly free and connected to the environment around him. It was hard to explain when it happened, but he knew he was connected to the whole world and everything in it, completely focused and in flow.

An hour into his shift, Beau realised he had been daydreaming again but somehow, he was still connected to the feel of the boat. He had experienced this before and found he often solved many of his problems when he was lost in this daydream state. It was as if he travelled somewhere else in his thoughts and it provided clarity and perspective. Time stood still. He snapped back to present time and looked to the rear. The lights of *Genesis* were barely visible. He was one with the ocean and *Litigate* was gliding through the huge swell like a knife, skating down the back side of the waves and reaching twenty-five knots on the satellite navigation system. The crew was switched on and focused, casting broad smiles towards him in spite of their obvious discomfort due to the cold and stinging salt spray lashing them each time the yacht pierced another wave. They sensed the pure boat speed they were achieving and apart from that, they were relishing a brief reprieve from the constant pressure of Jack's huge presence and his demands for perfection.

Without warning, Beau's intense focus was fractured by a massive thud.

'What the hell was that?' he yelled to anyone who could hear him.

'Beau, I think we hit something big,' replied Sandy, a regular crew member on *Litigate*, who was sitting on the high side rail.

'Hit something? What could we possibly hit out here?'

In an instant, Jack arrived back on deck and critically surveyed the scene, assessing the crew and the boat speed, which had slowed considerably.

'What in God's name is going on?' he demanded.

'Look, out the back!' cried Sandy. 'A sunfish, we hit a sunfish.'

As the crew looked back in the lee of the boat trail illuminated by the deck lights, the massive side of the sunfish was turning, protruding above the water.

'I have never seen one in all my years out here,' commented Sandy. 'They're enormous sea creatures that can grow to four metres long and weigh up to a ton.'

'Well, that's a first,' commented Beau, clearly shaken.

Jack raced up and pushed Beau out of the way, grabbing the wheel.

'That would be your style, Beau. You've got the whole of the Southern Ocean out here and you had to go and hit something. I want a damage report right away. Two of you get below and tell me if the hull has been breached.'

'On it, Skipper,' replied Sandy, who was already heading below, closely followed by Beau. There was that familiar 'not good enough' feeling again, which had been the story of his relationship with his father. The old man has to blame someone even for a freak incident of nature, he thought. They searched from stern to bow and after careful inspection, it seemed they had avoided any structural damage.

'Boat is intact, Skipper,' informed Beau as he returned on deck.

'She's not so light in the steering. We may have some rudder damage. In any case, we're not sinking so let's get her back up to speed. We've got a race to win.'

Jack now had time to assess their position relative to their nearest rivals.

'It seems *Genesis* couldn't maintain her speed after all,' Jack said, giving no credit to the effort of Beau and the crew in his absence. 'Beau, you look shot. Get below, sort yourself out and come back in an hour or two ready to do your job.'

Beau, still reeling from the shock of the collision, quietly withdrew below decks for some well-deserved rest and some space away from his father. He climbed into his makeshift bunk and his thoughts immediately turned to the huge argument he had had with his fiancée, Liz, when he'd left for Sydney Harbour and the start of the race on Boxing Day morning. Liz had known that Beau wanted to compete in the Sydney to Hobart, as he had done every year for the past twelve years, but she'd expected he would do as she wished and stay home. After all, they had invitations to some of the more prominent parties in town and she could hardly go without her fiancé on her arm. Beau was not at all into the social scene. Liz Weir, at twenty-nine, was a strikingly beautiful, five-foot-ten ex-model with long blonde hair. She had made her mark in the fashion industry, predominantly funded by her father Kerry Weir's money. She knew all the right people and moved in the upper echelon of Sydney's social circles. Kerry Weir was a prominent mining magnate, as well as the lifelong friend and an important client of Jack Sterling. He had been an influential figure in Beau's upbringing, with the families having holidayed together each year, in addition to their many regular social gatherings.

Beau and Liz had more or less grown up together. Beau had always thought that their coupling was inevitable, sanctioned by the two families. He had a deep care and love for Liz. However, he had always felt there was something missing in their relationship. It lacked a spark and the passionate intensity that he craved in his partner. Perhaps that was a fantasy and an unrealistic expectation, he thought. Liz's family lived in a magnificent mansion overlooking the water in the well-to-do area of Sydney's Rose Bay. Liz at times displayed all the characteristics of an only child, spoilt by her parents. Anything she wanted she received. Beau thought how glad he was that he had asked his best mate, Damion Carter, an up-and-coming Sydney barrister, to accompany Liz to some of the many boring socialite parties while he was away. After all, Damion was into that sort of thing. He would do anything to network and build his profile.

Damion had graduated law school with Beau. Like Beau, he had an athletic build, and was lean and tall. He had thick blond hair and a tanned complexion. He was the ideal chaperone and he revelled in his capacity to attract the attention of the opposite sex. Unlike Beau, Damion was single and was considered quite the playboy in the Sydney social scene. He took any opportunity to meet beautiful young rich girls and had always envisaged a life at the top end of the social level. Beau enjoyed his company immensely and they had a competitive rivalry in all things sport, from their weekly squash games and regular golf games to sailing races on Sydney Harbour.

Beau's thoughts turned to the days ahead. It would be another five days at least, favourable weather permitting, before Beau could try and mend the rift with Liz. He knew that his father wanted him to skipper *Litigate* back to Sydney after the race. Jack was due in court in Sydney on the 3rd of January for a high-profile case and would be leaving straight after the New Year's Eve celebrations on Constitution Dock. Normally, Jack would have done anything to get out of the court appearance, as he loved the trip back to Sydney on *Litigate* and treated the race and the return trip as his annual holiday away from the firm. This year, duty came first and he would be unable to skipper *Litigate* back. A wave of exhaustion came over Beau as he lay in the hammocks below deck. Even with the constant pounding of the waves on the hull, he drifted off into a deep sleep.

Beau was awakened suddenly by the painful jabbing of a finger in his chest. 'Beau, wake up! We're entering the mouth of the Derwent River and your old man wants you to get back to your position as tactician.'

As Beau cleared the sleep from his eyes, he recognised old Jim Banks with his matted grey hair and his skin turned to leather from years of sun exposure. Jim was the Vice-Commodore of the Royal Sydney Yacht Club and a permanent crew member on *Litigate* for the big ocean races, even though he raced his own yacht in local regattas. Beau was not sure if Jim was on board through his friendship with Jack, or whether it was Jack's generous donations as a benefactor of the RSYC. In any case, Jim was by far the most experienced yachtsman on board and a great asset to the crew.

Beau came through the hatch on deck and noticed that it was early morning and the seas had abated. There was a beautiful soft light dawning on the day and a gentle swell assisting from behind *Litigate*. She had made it through the night without any significant damage and although the crew was exhausted, they were running on adrenaline. They were still leading their class. He gained his bearings and noticed that *Genesis* was only half a nautical mile astern on the starboard side. He wondered how they had made so much ground overnight.

'Hey Skipper, how did those bastards get so close to us?' Beau asked.

'We lost sight of them through the night and it would appear they tacked offshore to open water and found more wind over the last few hours once the storm cleared,' Jack replied. 'We've been drifting along slowly on this light breeze during that time.'

'Well, we've sure got a race on our hands now.'

'You're damn right,' replied Jack. 'So wipe that sleep out of your eyes and get to your station and see if you can pick where the wind shifts are coming from. I want to know which side of the river will be favoured. *Genesis* is much lighter than us and in these lighter winds, she has the advantage. Jim, give him a hand.'

'Sure thing, Skipper,' replied Jim. 'There's no way we're letting her past. This river is tricky and it takes years to understand her currents and wind shifts. Forty years in my case. We'll bring her home, Skipper.'

Beau was angry with himself for having slept so long. It was just another reason for Jack to view him as soft.

'Take her over to the right bank of the river, Skipper!' shouted Jim. 'We've got an incoming tide and the currents are faster there.'

The wind was now light from the northeast and *Litigate* was definitely losing ground to *Genesis*.

'Okay, it's time to fly the big spinnaker,' commanded Jack. 'We'll need as much sail area as we can get.'

After much urgent action on the foredeck, Beau, fearing it had taken far longer than his dad would have liked, finally confirmed, 'Spinnaker set, Skipper.'

His dad acknowledged with a disapproving shake of the head.

'Boat speed is improving, Skipper,' Beau announced, trying to relay something positive to his father. '*Genesis* is now only half a nautical mile astern to our port side.'

'Yeah, I can feel her breathing down our necks. If they come up too close on our stern, she'll take our wind and sail right over the top of us. I'm changing direction, thirty degrees to port. We need to keep that big spinnaker full if we're going to have our nose in front at the finish line.'

Litigate lifted on a slight gust and with a full spinnaker powered ahead, only to be caught again as *Genesis* surged on a fresh gust coming from behind her. *Genesis*, now just a hundred metres behind, tried to cover and follow *Litigate* but she could not match the speed of the big yacht once the wind gusts filled her sails. Just when the finish line was in sight, a mere three hundred metres away, the wind dropped to almost nothing. *Litigate* still had a good one hundred and fifty metres on *Genesis*. Another gentle gust came through from behind the fleet and *Genesis* picked up the first benefit and closed to fifty metres behind *Litigate*. With thirty metres to go to the finish line, *Genesis* drew alongside *Litigate* and then slightly ahead just as *Litigate* gained the benefit of the same gust. Jack was now almost hoarse from yelling orders at the crew, tinkering with every setting in an obsessive need to win. Just as it looked hopeless, the spinnaker filled and the big yacht gently but surely accelerated again. The crew were all on a knife's edge. After many intense days of nonstop sailing, it came down to this moment. With ten metres to go, both crews were yelling instructions, trying to wring every ounce of boat speed possible in the light conditions. The boats were side by side as the finish line approached. Jack was so focused, he was unaware that they had crossed the finish line. He was woken from his trance by the finishing gun. As he looked up anxiously, he saw the jubilation of the forward deckhand some fifteen metres away. They had just stolen victory from *Genesis* by a couple of metres. The crew burst into a spontaneous celebration, knowing they were first in their class again. It was going to be a wild night at Constitution Dock tonight. Jack looked across to the skipper of *Genesis*, a great mate and rival from the same sailing club in Sydney, and doffed his cap in acknowledgement of another well-fought battle.

Constitution Dock in Hobart on New Year's Eve is one of the most festive, celebratory places on Earth to see in the New Year. Just completing the Sydney to Hobart yacht race is a victory for many, and the relief spills over into a huge celebration, with all the boat crews joined by people from all over Australia and the world looking to share in the festivities.

Jack was holding court on the deck of *Litigate* where the beers were flowing, as were the tall tales of this race and many others. He looked across at the super maxi yachts tied up further down the marina. Between eighty and a hundred-foot long, they were the masters of the sea, incredibly quick and powerful and able to handle all conditions. Just one mast on those majestic yachts was worth $300,000. Although he was proud of his class win, Jack knew he would never achieve line honours in this race unless he was skippering one of the super maxi yachts. They were the toys of the mega-rich and Jack was not in that class, yet. One day, I'm going to win line honours in this race if it kills me, he thought.

'Beau, I've got to go and make a quick call and confirm my flights for the 2nd of January,' informed Jack. 'I also need to check in with Jeff Graham, second chair for the court case on the 3rd, to make sure that everything is in order for the trial. I'll be back in a moment.'

Beau was not listening. He was preoccupied with thoughts of Liz and what he would say when he had the opportunity. He felt an increasing urgency to get home and put things right. He was not in a celebratory mood at all, even with the great achievements of the past few days. He decided to go and find some quiet space to call Liz. He walked along the dock amid the hustle and bustle of excited revellers dancing and laughing and singing. He felt somehow separated from the festivities, as if in a different world. There, but not a part of it. For nearly twenty minutes he wandered, gathering his thoughts and leaving the excited energy of Constitution Dock behind him. He sat on the headland at Battery Point, overlooking the beautiful mast lights of the yachts shimmering on the harbour like a night sky full of stars. With a great deal of hesitation, he called Liz.

'Liz, it's Beau. We won our class.'

'Really? That's great,' said Liz condescendingly.

'It was incredibly close. We just snuck our nose in front on the finish line. How have you been?'

'Fine, thanks. Just the usual parties and cocktail functions, you know how it is. When are you coming home?'

'Dad wants me to bring *Litigate* back to Sydney, which will be another three or four days at least,' Beau replied.

'How incredibly boring. Can't you just ask him to get someone else to bring the boat back?'

'You know Jack. Do you really think that's an option for me?'

'Sometimes I wish you would just stand up to him, Beau, and tell him what you need to do. You're like his puppet, catering to his every wish. I'm sick of it.'

'Don't be like that, babe. At this stage there's no one else to take the boat back. Jim is the only other crew member who could skipper the yacht, and he has to fly back to Sydney with Dad due to prior commitments at the yacht club.'

'Just do what you've got to do then. Obviously, your father is more important to you than I am.'

'Don't say that, babe, you know it's not true. I'll be back by the 5th or 6th, I promise.'

'Whatever,' Liz said. She seemed to revel in her ability to make him feel guilty.

'I love you and miss you, babe.'

Beau sensed that Liz had hung up before he could finish saying goodbye. The conversation only served to confirm Beau's fears about their relationship. He felt that between his father and Liz, he was being pulled apart by two powerful people and he was not sure which way to turn. In any case, there was nothing he could do right now. He would have to wait until he got back to Sydney to resolve his relationship problems with Liz.

Beau returned to the boat where Jack was still holding court telling tales of races past. As he climbed aboard, Jack announced excitedly, 'Hey Beau, the case has been adjourned for two weeks. I can sail *Litigate* back to Sydney after all. Isn't that great news?'

Beau thought for a moment and realised this could be a perfect opportunity.

'That is great news, Dad. I know how much you love to do the return trip. Do you mind if I head back to Sydney and leave you to it? Liz isn't too happy with me at the moment and I'd like to get back as quick as I can.'

'Under the thumb, hey?' said Jack, encouraging the rest of the crew to join in his attempt at humiliation.

'You know how unhappy she was about me doing the race this year. I'd just like to get back as soon as possible,' replied Beau.

'Go ahead if you must. There are enough of the boys here that want to crew the return journey and we only need one skipper, so you're not really required.'

Beau knew his father was having a dig at him, but he did not care. He was relieved that he could arrange an early flight back to Sydney and surprise Liz, demonstrating his commitment to her in an effort to put things right.

The celebrations went on late into the night with the thousands of New Year's Eve revellers enjoying the fireworks, music and atmosphere at Constitution Dock that evening. Shortly after the stroke of midnight, Beau crawled into his bunk, exhausted, and crashed into a deep sleep.

CHAPTER THREE
The Wakeup Call

Morning dawned and Beau awoke with bodies scattered around the cabin. The empty bottles lying about on the floor were the only remaining evidence of the celebrations from the night before. Beau decided to pack his bag and leave for Hobart airport to arrange his flights back to Sydney before the others awoke.

As he left the yacht, he could not help but marvel at the pristine day with the sun-drenched yachts all gleaming as they lay idle in the harbour. The early-morning shuffle of people going about their day created an energy all of its own. He loved the life around the marina and the freedom of being a part of it.

He decided to stay at the airport on standby for the next available flight. Even though it was New Year's Day, as fate would have it, there were cancellations. No doubt some who were yet to recover from the New Year's Eve celebrations. Beau took his seat on a direct flight to Sydney, arriving at 3 pm. During the flight, he rehearsed what he would say to Liz that afternoon in an attempt to reconcile with her. He was looking forward to surprising her at their luxury apartment on Sydney's Darling Harbour. In the forty-five-minute ride from the airport, Beau became increasingly anxious about how he would be received by Liz. He called her at their apartment just to check if she was home. If she answers, I can pretend I'm still in Hobart, he thought. The phone rang out. She's probably at her mother's New Year's Day garden party in any case. Her mother, Julia, was famous for her extravagant lunches, and her New Year's Day bash was one not to be missed by the glitz and glamour set of Sydney. Beau had spent many a lunch on the lawn overlooking the harbour, being paraded before Julia's friends and acquaintances, as she proudly explained that he was the future managing partner of Sterling and Finch.

Beau paid the cab driver, grabbed his bag and fumbled for his keys. The apartment was one of the many perks of his relationship with Liz. It was ideally positioned on the fringe of the Sydney CBD with views overlooking the harbour. He felt truly blessed to come home to this beautiful place on one of the most stunning harbours in the world. Beau noticed Damion Carter's Porsche parked in the apartment complex carpark. Damion, as a young barrister, loved the flashy toys even though they stretched him financially at this stage of his career. He subscribed to the 'fake it until you make it' principle. They must have returned from a party for Damion to still be parked here, Beau thought. He was glad his mate had taken up his offer to escort Liz to some of her famous socialite functions. Perhaps she won't be so upset with me if she's had an afternoon of Champagne and idle gossip, he thought. I'll offer to make her a nice dinner and chill down a bottle of her favourite Moet. I'm sure that given my time away, Damion will understand and graciously exit for the evening.

Beau caught the lift up to the top floor. The building was four floors high and boasted some of Australia's rich and famous on its tenancy list. Liz had fallen in love with the property and her father, in typical fashion, had helped to secure it as her twenty-first birthday present. Beau struggled through the front door and into the entry, throwing his things into the walk-in coat cupboard. I'll sort it all out later, he thought. 'Hi guys, I'm home!' he yelled, wandering into the large expanse of the open-plan apartment. No answer. They must have decided to have a few drinks and catch a cab. Perfect, he thought. I'll cook an intimate dinner for two and surprise her when she returns. Keen to get some food ready and make sure the Champagne was chilled in case Liz came home soon, he walked into the huge kitchen with panoramic views of the harbour and opened the fridge door. He carefully selected all the necessary ingredients for his signature dish, fresh pasta, chorizo sausage, basil, wilted spinach, heirloom tomatoes, and lots of garlic. He knew how much Liz loved it when he cooked, particularly given she rarely did. He placed a bottle of Moet on ice, put on some music and surveyed the room. Of course, incense. She loved incense. All was set for a great intimate dinner.

Beau walked down the hallway towards his bedroom for a quick shower and change. Afterwards, he felt relaxed and fresh with clean clothes and a shave after six days of growth. As the afternoon drifted away, there was still no sign of Liz and Damion. He settled on the couch to watch some sport to pass the time and before long, drifted off into a deep sleep after his long day of travel and the pure exhaustion of five days on the ocean with very little sleep.

Beau awoke suddenly and looked around the familiar environment of the apartment. For a minute, he thought he was still on *Litigate*. He could feel the gentle rocking motion of the boat, as his inner balance was still to settle down. He looked at his watch and realised it was 8:30 pm. He called out to Liz expecting her to be home but there was no answer. He decided to call her on her mobile, having given up all thoughts of a surprise dinner. He just wanted to see her and find out when she was coming home. The call went straight to her message bank. 'Call me back as soon as you can, babe.'

Beau wandered into the bedroom to see if Liz had arrived home but had left him on the couch to sleep for the night. No sign of her there either. Still exhausted, Beau slipped into bed and drifted back into a restless sleep.

In a half-sleep, half-awake state, Beau experienced some very weird dreams. He was at one of Liz's fancy parties. Damion was there holding court, telling tall stories and laughing with a group of people including Liz. He found himself thinking, is he trying to impress her? In his half dreamlike state, he dismissed the thought as ridiculous. What a crazy notion. He had never contemplated such a bizarre thought before. As the laughing got louder, Beau gradually came to the realisation that he wasn't asleep anymore; he was very much awake. The laughter was coming from the lounge room. Beau slowly peeled himself out of bed and followed the noise to the lounge room. He listened intently, almost challenging his own reality. Am I imagining this? Am I still dreaming? As he approached the lounge room, he noticed clothes strewn across the floor from the front door to the lounge area, as if thrown off in urgency. Beau stepped further into the room and there, right in front of him, was the image that would be etched in his memory forever. His fiancée Liz, and his best friend Damion, naked, in a passionate embrace right in front of him on their imported leather couch.

'What the fuck are you two doing?' Beau demanded, his presence clearly startling Liz. She quickly rolled off the couch naked, grabbing for any clothing she could find within arm's reach to cover herself up.

'Beau, you're home.'

In shock, Beau found himself struggling for words.

'It would seem so,' he stuttered.

'Beau, this has never happened before. We had a lot to drink,' exclaimed Damion.

'You're supposed to be my best friend.'

Beau was barely able to contain his emotions. He could feel the tears welling in his eyes as the enormity of what he had just witnessed began to sink in. Liz ran past him to the bathroom, pale from the shock of being so completely discovered. Damion quickly pulled on his pants, grabbed the rest of his clothes and moved towards the front door. Beau called after him, half crying and half screaming. 'That's right, run, you bastard. I'll deal with you later.'

Beau contemplated his two closest friends in the ultimate betrayal. How could this have happened? How did I not see this before? How long has this been going on? There were so many questions he needed answers to. He walked into the bedroom en suite to confront Liz who was sitting on the floor, head between her knees, sobbing uncontrollably.

'No wonder you didn't care if I came home or not.'

She did not respond or even look at him. Somehow he felt sorry for her in this pathetic state. In the same instant, he thought, wait a minute, I'm the one who needs the sympathy here. So many conflicting emotions were running through his mind. He knelt down beside her and put his hand on her shoulder to try and get her attention. She looked up at him and he saw that she had blood streaming from a gash on her eyebrow. A bruise was already appearing around a sizeable lump.

'What happened? he asked with concern.

'I slipped in the dark and hit my head on the vanity,' she said, distressed.

He couldn't be angry with her in that moment and raced off to the kitchen to get ice and a washer for her injury. Returning, he sat down next to her and held her head against his chest with the compress pressing on the side of her face. She cried uncontrollably, prompting years of emotion to well within him. They both sobbed and held each other for what seemed an eternity. After a considerable time, both exhausted from the emotion, Beau realised this was a cathartic moment in their lifelong relationship which, in an instant, had changed forever.

Beau awoke as the daylight streamed through the bedroom window after a night of tossing and turning. The room seemed familiar, but he soon realised as he looked around that it was not his room. A feeling of absolute devastation flowed through his body as the events of the night before flooded back to him, like the recollection of a nightmare, except this nightmare was real. He recalled he had decided to sleep in the spare room as he could not be in the same bed as Liz. He also remembered how much Liz had tried to apologise and convince him to stay with her for the night.

Even in their emotional state, she had attempted to seduce him in a desperate act to minimise the fallout of her actions. The last thing she could afford was to be known as a cheat. Everyone loved Beau and she would be harshly judged by the social set in Sydney if she couldn't rescue this disaster. The truth was that Beau was the ideal husband, adored by all, future managing partner of one of the country's top law firms. She loved Beau but she knew that she was 'in love' with Damion. She just did not get the same passionate, sexually charged feelings with Beau. Liz had been fighting this feeling for years, as had Damion. She thought of the numerous times Damion and she had successfully enjoyed each other's company without detection. Perhaps they had become complacent. Beau would be destroyed if he knew how long they had been meeting behind his back, she thought.

Beau walked out from a quick shower and tried to regain some clarity and rational thought. He always felt more centred around water, even under the shower. He walked into the kitchen where Liz was preparing a cooked breakfast. She had a large bruise over her left eye which had now turned black. She could barely look him in the eyes as she said good morning and passed him a cup of coffee. He noticed she had gone to great trouble to prepare their breakfast.

'I'm not hungry,' he said as he sat down on the stool facing Liz.

'But I made you your favourite, Beau.'

'Didn't you hear me? I'm not hungry.'

Liz's eyes filled with tears. 'Yes, I'm sorry, I did hear you. I was just checking with you.'

Beau was upset that he had snapped at her like that. It was not in his nature. But perhaps understandable under the circumstances, he thought. Why shouldn't I get angry at her? I'm sick of being the nice predictable Beau, trained to be the polite accommodating good boy. Fuck that! His newfound expression helped to release some of his suppressed anger and empower him. He did not understand it, but he liked the feeling of freedom.

'Beau, we need to talk about last night,' said Liz sheepishly.

'Damn right we do.'

Liz grabbed her coffee, came around the front of the kitchen bench, took Beau by the hand and led him to the outside patio overlooking the magnificent Sydney Harbour. At this time of the morning, the harbour was bustling with all manner of boats going about their daily activities, the iconic Sydney Harbour Bridge dominating the landscape. They sat on the deck lounge and Beau stared blankly out to the water without really seeing anything of the magnificent January day. Liz turned towards him, grabbed his hand and said, 'Beau, I'm sure you have a lot of questions but I just wanted to say before you speak that last night was a huge mistake. We were both drunk and it just sort of developed. I love you and always have.'

'It didn't seem so last night.'

'I understand. I can't imagine how hurt you must feel right now.'

'No, you can't,' Beau said curtly. 'I just can't believe it. You and Damion.' He was bewildered. 'I asked him to take care of you while I was away. It's like sending a wolf to look after the sheep.'

'It's not all his fault, Beau. I'm equally to blame.'

'You got that right,' he replied. 'How long has this been going on between you two?' Beau wasn't sure if he was ready for the answer.

Liz looked out across the harbour and contemplated her response.

'We've been close for a long time, Beau, and our feelings for each other seemed to change recently. It only became physical last night for the first time.'

'Are you telling me that you haven't been intimate with him until last night?'

'It's the truth, Beau. You have to believe me.'

'Why should I believe you?' dismissed Beau. 'I don't know what to believe anymore.'

'I don't want this to end our relationship, Beau,' Liz pleaded. 'We are so good together.'

'Do you want to be with him?' Beau asked again with tears welling in his eyes.

'No, Beau, I want to be with you. He's been a great friend to me and he listens to my problems. I guess we got too close.'

'You think? He's supposed to be my closest friend. I need time to think, Liz. I can't promise anything at the moment.' He let go of her grip. 'I'm going away for a few days to get some space to think.'

'Where will you go, Beau?'

'I don't know.'

'Please keep this between us until we can discuss our future. Promise me you won't tell anyone.'

He got up and without further comment, packed a small bag and was gone.

Liz was left on the patio in tears, contemplating how she would tell her father. He'll be furious, she thought. He might even cut me off. It would be an immense embarrassment to the family. Hypocrite, she thought, given all the affairs he'd had over the years. Her mum seemed to turn a blind eye to them all, although no doubt she knew the truth. Liz decided to keep it to herself for now in the hope Beau would agree to give her another chance and tell no one else about her indiscretion. It could ruin everything she had worked towards over many years if she could not contain the damage and salvage their relationship.

Damion answered his phone the moment he saw Liz's number.

'Damion, it's Liz.'

'Hi, beautiful. What a mess, hey, I can't believe it.'

'We were so stupid to go back to my place. What were we thinking?'

'I know, but the damage is done now. How is he?' Damion asked.

'He's shattered, of course. How do you think he is? He's left for a few days, so he says. I've never seen him like this. I don't know when I'll see him again.'

'Right,' said Damion, 'we need to think. You told him it was the first time, I hope?'

'Of course I did, I'm not stupid!'

'I know, I know, settle down.'

'You're single. You don't have to face the shame and judgement of it all,' said Liz. 'I need to see you, Damion. Can you come over?'

'That's not a great idea, babe.'

'What about your place?' she asked.

'He may be checking my place. Perhaps we need to lay low for a while?' Damion was confused, wondering how he could put the pieces back together.

'For how long?' protested Liz.

'As long as it takes for me to get clear on what to do next,' said Damion firmly, not giving Liz a chance to negotiate a different solution.

'Well, it has to be that way I guess.'

'I'm here to support you as much as I can through this, babe. We'll talk on the phone in the meantime and in the next week or two, we will find a chance to be together,' he said, trying to console her.

'I love you,' she said in tears as she hung up the phone. It's ironic, she thought. Her life had been perfect when she'd had Beau as her public stable life partner and Damion as a secret passionate lover. She'd had it all, at least for a short while. I guess that was never going to last, she lamented.

Liz was shattered at the thought of not seeing Damion for a couple of weeks. She was seriously infatuated with him and would miss their passionate connection. Sex with him was the most erotic, raw and passionate she had ever experienced in her life. Beyond that, they had a deep connection and could talk for hours on any subject.

Liz was standing in the bathroom inspecting the now dramatic black eye and lump over her left eye. I look like a battered wife, she thought. Then it struck her, a way to save face.

'Hi Dad,' she said, crying into the phone. 'I need to see you. Can you come right over?'

'Of course, baby, anything for you.'

Within half an hour, Liz was in her father's arms with tears rolling down her face.

'And then he got really angry. He demanded to know where I had been when he was away. I think he'd had a few to drink. He's so possessive when he gets like that. You don't know who he becomes behind closed doors. In a fit of rage, he struck me across the face with the back of his hand. He scares me when he's like that, Daddy.'

She was pulling the little girl act with her father that she had perfected years before. Even down to the child-like inflection in her voice. He was powerless when she turned it on and he believed anything she said.

'Right, I'll have a domestic violence order against him before the sun sets today. No one touches my little girl and gets away with it. We will press charges as well. When I'm finished with him, he'll be rotting behind bars.'

Liz sensed she might have unleashed a monster and tried to rein it back in.

'I don't want him to go to jail, Dad. Please don't involve the police. I just need him to stay away from me.'

'Whatever you want, baby,' Kerry replied, rocking her as if she was an infant. As his only child, Liz was everything to him. 'I'll give Jack a piece of my mind too. He raised the son of a bitch.'

Liz knew she had started something that now had a life of its own.

CHAPTER FOUR
The Safe Haven

Beau had been on the road for a good hour and a half as he approached the foothills of the Blue Mountains outside of Sydney. His mother had moved to this calm and beautiful place with her partner a few years after she had left Jack. They lived a simple life. His mother had pursued her passion for art and spiritual growth and Scott, her partner, found it the perfect base for his writing. Scott contributed weekly articles and feature pieces to a number of prominent business publications. He was independently wealthy as a property developer and the writing gave him purpose.

Their home was perched on a rock escarpment with panoramic views over the valley. It was constructed of red cedar timber and glass and architecturally designed to take in the majestic vista. As Beau pulled into the driveway, his mother rushed to him, embracing him as if she had not seen him in years. She had always been incredibly supportive and given the trials and tribulations she had endured during her life, Beau knew this would be the ideal sanctuary for him.

'How have you been, Mother?' Beau asked.

She held him in a tight embrace as if she would never let him go.

'I'm great.' Her voice was always genuinely uplifting. She grabbed his shoulders and gently separated from their embrace, looking him directly in the eyes. 'What's wrong, Beau? There's something wrong.'

She always knows when something's wrong, Beau thought, as they walked up the driveway.

'I'm okay, Mum,' he said, masking his true feelings.

'It seems like we need to talk,' she said, as she grabbed his hands and led him into the house.

Inside, Beau walked towards the veranda and greeted Scott, who was already preparing a bottle of red wine, glasses and a cheese platter in anticipation of a long afternoon. 'Hey Beau!' Scott replied. 'Congratulations on your race win.'

Beau had called his mum on the way to ask if he was welcome to stay for a few days. Right away, she'd known something was wrong. Beau sat at the large outdoor table and took in the magnificent view of the Blue Mountains before him. A haze had settled over the valley floor and it gave the mountains a subtle, ever-decreasing colour of azure as the ridges folded away into the distance.

'What's going on, Beau?' his mum asked in her compassionate but knowing way.

'Liz and I are having some time out,' he replied, looking down in an effort to avoid eye contact.

'What happened?' she asked. Beau had been put under extreme pressure by his father and Liz's family to form a couple right from when they were children. At no time had she encouraged the relationship. Although she had never said so to Beau, she felt Liz was pleasant but superficial and materialistic and that she lacked emotional depth. How could she not be with a father like Kerry Weir? she thought. Beau, on the other hand, was extremely sensitive and caring. It seemed he made all the compromises in their relationship, suppressing who he really was. Deep down, Barbara had always hoped that Beau would see the relationship for what it was. He deserved more. 'I get the feeling this separation wasn't necessarily your idea. You seem to be in shock.'

'It only happened last night,' Beau said as he shuffled in his chair.

'So tell me what happened. Take your time and tell me.'

Over the next twenty minutes, Beau outlined the emotional rollercoaster of the past twenty-four hours. His mum listened intently, as did Scott, and they sensed his grief, anxiety, anger, and confusion. Interestingly, Barbara also sensed a certain resignation, almost as if Beau felt this day had been inevitable.

'Where is Liz, Beau?' his mum asked.

'She's at the Darling Harbour apartment, I guess, unless she's consoling herself with that traitor Damion.'

'Things happen for a reason, Beau. What are you going to do?' she asked.

'I have no idea. What do you think I should do?'

'It's not up to me, Beau. Only you can decide if this relationship is right for you.'

'Your mother is right,' chimed in Scott. 'It might be best to give it a day or two, allow the reality of your situation to sink in, and make a clear decision in the light of day,' he added.

'Stay here with us for a while and get your head clear,' his mother pleaded. 'This is a big decision and you'll want to sleep on it to make sure you're responding rather than reacting.'

Beau agreed to stay, as he always found his mum's home a place of calm reflection. That had more to do with his mum than the place itself. The night drifted on and no more was discussed about the situation. Barbara and Scott purposefully kept the conversation light. They sensed he had been through so much emotion that he was exhausted and needed downtime without dwelling on the stark reality of his dilemma. They encouraged Beau to tell them all about the race and his experience crossing Bass Strait, which he did in a distracted, semi-present manner.

Eventually, his mum said goodnight, tactfully giving him the space he required. 'Scott and I are off to bed.'

'See you in the morning, Beau,' Scott said.

'Yes, good night guys,' replied Beau, as he sat staring out into the night. 'Thanks so much for your love and support.'

Beau's mum gave him a long hug and poured all her love and compassion into him. He felt overwhelmed by the pure energy of it. It brought tears to his eyes. Words were unnecessary. She had a wisdom she could not describe and a way of understanding. She was a very special person, an angel on Earth, he thought.

As he sat alone on the veranda, Beau tried to ignore his faint inner voice telling him this could be the 'out' from his relationship with Liz. The thought was quickly overridden by the love he felt for her. But was it the right sort of love? His thoughts drifted back to his time on Battery Point in Hobart where he had recognised a lack of passion in their relationship. HeeH surrendered to the fact that he would not get much sleep with so many thoughts flooding his mind in what seemed like a battle between two opposing forces, tearing him apart.

Beau was awakened the next morning by the familiar voice of his mother.

'There's a hot breakfast waiting for you in the kitchen, Beau. I cooked your favourite, spinach omelette and crispy bacon.'

'Thanks, Mum,' replied Beau in a semiconscious state. 'I'll be right out.' He remembered crawling into bed sometime in the early morning, mentally exhausted and no closer to any clarity in his relationship with Liz. He glanced at his watch and was alarmed to realise it was 10 am.

'Why did you let me sleep so long?' he called out to his mum.

'You needed to rest. In any case, sleep is the best thing you can do for stress. Your subconscious works on your problems. You need your sleep.'

Beau took a quick shower and stood under the hot water pouring over his head. He lost track of time as his mind drifted off, churning through everything that had happened. A shower was always therapeutic. Following a hearty breakfast, Beau and his mum took a stroll down a winding pathway along the escarpment ridge to a place twenty minutes from the property. His mum often walked to this spiritual place where the rock ledge extended out, suspended above the valley floor half a kilometre below. The mountains lay before them, extending off into the far distance, their blue-tinged craggy ridges seemingly whispering a song of pure serenity. The two of them sat there for an age, taking in the majesty that surrounded them. The air was sweet and clear.

Beau's mum finally broke the silence and asked, 'What's next for you, Beau?'

'That's the million-dollar question,' replied Beau, staring into the distance as if seeking some divine intervention.

'I feel I need to ask you a question.'

'Sure,' Beau replied, a little reluctantly. He knew how insightful his mum was and how she could always see right through him to the core of his issues.

'Whose life do you think you're living, Beau?' she asked.

'What sort of a question is that?' Beau responded, not really understanding where his mum was heading.

'Many of us spend a great deal of our life making decisions about our life's direction based on what someone else wants us to do, not necessarily what we should be doing for our own higher good.'

'I don't think that applies to me. I'm in control of my own life, no one else.'

'Is that so?'

Beau looked at his mother, knowing that she was unconvinced by his answer.

'Who wanted you to become a lawyer, Beau?'

'It was always one of the options, I guess,' he replied unconvincingly.

'I recall a little boy who loved helping others, and was fascinated by the ocean and the outdoors. Seems to me, spending your life locked in a room preparing arguments for rich clients is more your father's game than yours. Who is influencing decisions regarding your life, Beau? Before you answer, I want you to search for your absolute truth. Did you do law for yourself, or did you do it to gain your father's approval?'

The faint traces of tears welling in Beau's eyes were evident as his truth revealed itself. 'Seems I spent my whole life trying to be good enough in Dad's eyes,' he stated as a wave of realisation came over him. 'I have never been good enough for him.'

Beau felt his mum's arms come around his shoulders in a supportive embrace. 'Even when you're sailing and you're the navigator, your dad is calling the shots. That's just your father's way, Beau. Based on his upbringing, all he knows is tough love. He loves you more than he can say but he has no idea how to express it. He is so proud of you yet he just can't bring himself to say it. He wasn't taught how to show love by his father, nor was his father before that. The Sterlings are a proud, stoic family. You remember your grandfather? Do you think your dad got much in the way of validation, or that he felt loved by him?'

'No, I guess not.'

'And so the generational legacy of emotionally constipated men goes on. It was one of the biggest issues between your father and me, which caused me to distance myself from him. That gave him the excuse to seek his female connection with others. Many others, as it turned out,' his mum lamented with a slight grin.

Beau sat for a long while and finally asked, 'Do you think I'm like Dad?'

Carefully choosing her words, she said, 'No you're not, Beau, and you're definitely not as driven to be powerful and controlling like your father is. If I can be completely honest, you're at times withdrawn and quiet. It can be difficult to read you when you seem lost in your own world. That can be hard work for a partner.'

'I don't want to be like that. Perhaps I pushed Liz into Damion's arms because she was craving more from me.'

'It's never only one person's fault when a relationship blows up, Beau. The gift is trying to understand what you did to contribute to it. That is where all the learnings are. Most people just blame, and that creates a one-sided perception, keeping them stuck in hatred and revenge. I started to resent your father's arrogance and control and so I withdrew from him emotionally and sexually. That caused him to seek his needs elsewhere. I know that now, however, it was not evident to me at the time.'

Beau thought for a long time about his mum's comments and searched his inner truth as to how he could have contributed to the relationship breakdown with Liz. 'I'm starting to realise how difficult it may have been being in relationship with me and not getting her emotional needs met. She did say that Damion listened to her. No doubt she was giving me subtle clues then. I'm still not sure if I want to be with her though.'

'Sometimes we subconsciously sabotage relationships to bring about their demise. It's not a conscious thing, Beau. At the end of the day, Liz made her own choices and she is responsible for them and for the impact they have on your relationship. Liz is a self-centred person obsessed with position and power. Her ego has control of her and she is driven by social status. Universally, she is in for a major correction in her life. This may bring down her "perfect persona" and she will be vilified by her own peer group for betraying you. They are a judgemental lot and regardless of how many of them are guilty of the same actions, they will join together to condemn her for fear of being vilified themselves. Aren't people funny? From all my years of supporting friends through similar situations, one truth has become apparent. Most have the same traits and none of them is beyond reproach. It's not about the sex when a partner strays into an affair, it's about the void, about what's lacking emotionally. Most of us feel the loneliness of not being loved in the way we need to feel loved. It does not mean we are not loved. It just means we don't feel loved. It's still worth qualifying, however, whether or not you're a good fit as a couple for the long term.'

'When I get beyond all the hurt, I'm left with that big question, I guess. I can't honestly say that I can commit to her as my future wife. I just don't know if she's right for me. Besides, I'm so angry with her right now.'

'Then that is your answer. Trust that. Resist the temptation to make a massive life decision one way or the other now, particularly when your emotions are running so high. Eventually, you'll have to decide because it's unfair to leave Liz in limbo, wondering if you're in or out of the relationship. If you're in, you have to be one hundred percent in. For now, it's fine to simply say, "I don't know" and leave it at that, Beau.'

That one comment from his mum provided instant clarity.

'That sounds perfectly right for me. I don't have to decide today or tomorrow. For now I just don't know! I've been going back and forth with the urgent desire to make a decision about my future one way or the other and I had lost sight of my truth. I just don't know right now. I'm confused and emotional, not in the best place to decide. I feel a massive weight has been removed from me.' Beau gave a huge sigh of relief.

'I recommend some time apart, Beau. Allow your anger to dissipate and spend some time owning what you need to about your part in the relationship breakdown. If you can't live without her, it will become apparent.'

Beau felt a deep appreciation for having his mum in his life, and he reached over and hugged her. 'You're right. I'm going to take some time to understand how I feel about what has happened and make sure I don't react too quickly.'

'One day soon, you will have a more definite knowing as to the right path for you. Don't make it about what she's done or what you've done because you have both equally created this situation,' Barbara said. 'Make it about your suitability as a couple, how similar your values are and your respect for each other. There is no forever in any relationship. Every day, you have to wake up and regardless of your challenges, choose to be in relationship one hundred percent, all in. If you're not prepared to do that, then get out of it. That is what will sustain you both in a long-term relationship. Project your life forward with honesty, and the right decision will feel lighter once the emotions you're feeling now have settled. Situations like this, life events, can lead you down a path of discovery. I have come to realise that there's a hidden order in things and when you gain awareness around it, all of life's challenges come into perspective. Don't miss the opportunity during this difficult time of seeking the answers to bigger questions in this life. I believe that we are here to evolve, little by little, after each cathartic experience, ultimately to take one step closer to the source of us all. Our experiences, which we attract into our lives, provide exactly what we need to grow and expand. Everything therefore is perfect. Our experiences are a feedback mechanism. It's only our perception that labels things good or bad. My favourite question is, what's right about this situation I'm not getting? Then sit with it until your higher mind brings forth the answer that was always there, hidden in plain sight.'

Beau sat in silence for some time before he spoke. 'That is pretty heavy stuff, Mum.'

'One has to be ready to hear the messages, Beau. They are always there but you have to be open to tuning in to them.'

'How do I do that practically though?' Beau asked with genuine interest.

'Understand why you created the situation you're in and own the part that's relevant to you. See that it is perfect for your ultimate journey. The soul only creates problems so that you may be challenged and supported, in order for you to learn and move to the next level of evolution with an enlightened perspective. This is a journey that has no measurable time. This is your path to your own evolution. It's no one else's.'

Beau took in all his mother was saying, thinking, could my whole life be a lie? Am I really, after all these years, living someone else's dream, engaged to a girl someone else wants me to marry? Just contemplating these questions rocked the foundation of who Beau thought he was, yet at the same time, he felt surprisingly liberated.

'Am I really free to live my life the way I want to?' he asked aloud.

'Of course you are, Beau; I just don't think you have ever allowed yourself to contemplate what you really wanted for yourself. Why are you here in this lifetime? What are you meant to be doing that will inspire yourself and others?'

With that, they stood up, hugged again and wandered back along the path towards the property, enjoying the silence, their connection and taking in the absolute beauty of the place and the day. Beau felt immense gratitude for his mother and her calm wisdom. At least one of my parents understands me and loves me for who I am and not who they want me to be, he thought.

The next day, Beau borrowed a backpack and trekked off to the valley floor to spend some time surrounded by the natural beauty of the mountains and the forest. In the past, he had gained great clarity of thought there. He departed soon after breakfast, his mother's words from the previous day clearly in his mind. He had done this trek many times before and he knew the area well. He spent a reflective day alone, contemplating the challenges in his life while wandering along the trails. The bush was full of mystical sounds. The birds, the wind gently rustling through the majestic gums and the rushing of the water as he walked past the familiar stream running along the valley floor. Beau was taken by the wonder of the way the light filtered through the treetop canopy, almost cradling him as he wandered. As the warmth of the sun lessened, he realised that it was at least early afternoon and time to head back. His thoughts had constantly been on the conversation with his mother the day before and he had become increasingly aware that he had indeed been living a life of seeking the approval of others, particularly his father's, and not necessarily a life driven by his own passions and desires. While he appreciated all he had learnt becoming a lawyer, he was starting to understand that he had followed his father's path out of some generational duty that he would inevitably one day take over the family firm. Somehow, he had unquestioningly allowed this vision of his father's to permeate his own path. His mother was correct in suggesting he had done it to gain the love and acceptance of his father.

Beau was less clear about his future with Liz though. He was still drawn between his undoubted love for her, a love that had developed since childhood, and her betrayal of him. Did he love her in a way that a husband should? He questioned his desire for her and recalled the many times he had been sexually attracted to other women in his life. Was that normal? Shouldn't I have eyes only for the one I love? Is that unrealistic? Why aren't I feeling as devastated as I should be? My future wife has chosen my best friend. Surely, there's an answer there somewhere?

On the trip back to the house, Beau recalled the clarity he had felt the day before, remembering his mother's words of wisdom. 'You don't have to decide now, Beau. If your answer is that you just don't know, then that is your answer.'

Beau arrived at the house after dark and was greeted by his mum.

'I was starting to worry about you. There's some dinner in the oven. I'm sure you need it after your long day.'

'Thanks, Mum, I'm absolutely starving. You're a saint.'

Beau spent another pleasant evening with his mother and Scott listening to their stories of overseas travel and adventures, before turning in early for some much-needed rest. The following day, he felt an urgent need to act on his newfound clarity. He hugged his mum and from a place of complete love and gratitude, thanked her for being there when he had needed her most. He gave Scott a quick hug, jumped into his car and headed towards Sydney and the rest of his life, whatever that might bring.

CHAPTER FIVE
Life Decisions

Beau arrived back at the Darling Harbour apartment around 1 pm to find Liz lying on the couch in a semi-dazed state. Obviously, she had taken some form of sedative and was barely coherent.

'Liz, it's Beau, wake up. Liz, wake up.'

'What, what? Oh Beau, you're back. Thank God. Where have you been?'

'Sorry, I should have called.'

'Yes, you should have,' she protested, dragging herself off the couch and quickly gathering her thoughts. She would not tell him about the domestic violence order for now. Not yet. That card she was keeping close to her chest. For now, it was all about keeping him in reconciliation discussions. That way, she could buy herself time. Time to think. Perhaps he had not told anyone and all this could be contained, she thought.

'I've been stuck here in this apartment, beside myself with worry about how you were and what you were thinking.'

'I've been thinking about a lot of things, Liz, including us, and more importantly about what I want to do for a change. I have had some big realisations about how I'm living my life. Things have to change.'

'What sort of things, Beau?' she asked, rubbing the sleep from her eyes. 'You don't mean us.'

'I can honestly say, Liz, I don't know about us right now. One of my realisations is that it's okay for me not to know the answers until the time is right for me.'

'That's not fair on me, Beau. I need to know what you intend to do. What's our future together?' she demanded, now very much awake.

'I can't say right now, Liz, that's my honest truth.'

'Well that's not good enough, Beau. You can't leave me hanging, waiting till you're ready to decide whether you want to be with me or not.'

'I understand it's difficult for you. It's difficult for me too. You're the one who thrust this decision on me by your actions. I need time to allow the emotions to subside in order to make a rational decision. I just don't have the capacity or the clarity right now to make such a big decision. My answer is that I just don't know. If that isn't good enough for you, then I guess you have to make your own decisions around that.'

'Snap out of it, Beau. You and I both know you're not going anywhere. You've got it too good. You're living in my apartment. You have a guaranteed future as managing partner of Sterling and Finch. Your whole future is laid out before you.'

'That's exactly the problem, Liz. My whole future has been laid out before me, my whole life, including you and me, married off at the age of ten. The only problem is that I didn't lay it out. I don't want to look back on my life and realise that I've been living someone else's dreams. I need to search for my own path, for what I'm meant to be doing.'

'Don't be ridiculous, Beau. Call your father. He's been ringing here for the last two days. He wants an urgent update on work issues. He has no idea you haven't been back to work yet.'

'Did he ask how we were after what happened?'

'Well, I haven't actually told him what happened. I just made an excuse that you were out for a while and would be back later.'

'So you're telling me that you haven't told him what's going on?'

'I think it's best if we sort ourselves out before we discuss things with our parents.'

'Yeah, I get it.' She just doesn't have the guts, he thought. In any case, Mum and Scott know the truth and I will tell whoever I want, when I want.

'You're not going to tell him any details are you, Beau?'

'I don't know what I'm going to say, Liz. Let's just say that I'm sure it will be an interesting conversation. I'm taking a month off work to get my head straight and decide my future.'

'I'm sure he's going to love that. He won't let you take a month off, Beau. You haven't had a month off since you started at the firm.'

'That's exactly why I'm due. It won't be so much a question as a statement. I'm taking a month off whether he likes it or not.'

'Wow, Beau, I've been waiting for you to stand up to your father for a long time.'

'I'm taking my life in my hands from now on and all of you better get used to it. I've allowed myself to be suppressed by dominant people, one of whom is you. That stops now.'

'Okay, Beau, I understand.' Given he was not reacting as usual, she skilfully opted for a change of tack. 'I respect you for that.'

'I'm going out for a walk, Liz. I'll be back late so don't wait up. I'll be sleeping in the second bedroom tonight. It would be wise for you to take some time to think about your future as well and whether you want to be in this relationship.'

'That's all I have thought about since you left, Beau. I love you. You know that.'

'I'll chat with you in the morning, Liz,' Beau responded, not wanting to be drawn into any further discussion. 'At this stage, I'm thinking of going overseas for a break. After that, who knows?'

Beau did not wait for a response. He moved towards the door and with a cursory, 'good night,' slammed the door behind him. Liz was left running over the conversation, concerned he would confide in his father which would force her to reveal her story. She was starting to regret the mess she had set in motion; however, it was too late to turn back now. She would bide her time and play the victim card when it was absolutely necessary. After all, it would be his word against hers.

Beau wandered along the waterfront near his apartment in deep thought. He passed a number of well-known restaurants with their maître ds out the front energetically trying to entice passers-by. It was a beautiful, lazy sunny afternoon and Beau decided to take a prime position at a fine-dining seafood restaurant, right on the harbour. He ordered one of his favourite bottles of Riesling and a fresh seafood platter in an effort to spoil himself and indulge a little. It was a perfect distraction from the constant chatter in his head. His thoughts kept oscillating over the pros and cons of the life decisions that confronted him. He was nervous about the conversation he would have with his father in the next few days when he returned from Hobart. He was committed to maintaining his new forthright manner; however, deep down he was dreading what would inevitably become a confrontation with his father.

The afternoon drifted by in a semi-dazed state that continued into the next few days. Beau did not attend work and avoided time in the apartment. He found himself predominantly alone for the entire time. His mood switched between excitement at the potential of his future, to despair and grief at the prospect of completely changing his life as he knew it. He felt clear that he needed a change in his professional life, although he did not yet know what he was passionate about doing. He just knew he was not passionate about practising law. He had a realisation that he had never stopped to think about it. Always busy, busy, busy pursuing success in life without having really defined what success was for him.

The following morning, Liz knocked on Beau's bedroom door, shouting, 'Beau, your father is on the phone! He's back from Hobart. Beau, are you awake? Your father is on the phone.'

Beau had been awake for many hours and was lying in bed deep in thought, as he had been every morning since that fateful night when his life was thrown into turmoil. 'Tell him I'll call him back, Liz,' he said, trying to maintain some control over the timing of things.

'Okay, if that's what you want but he won't like it.'

Beau didn't reply. He left the apartment as soon as he was showered and dressed. He had not had a meal there since coming back from spending time with his mum. He wandered along the waterfront as a light shower drifted across the harbour. Finally, after rehearsing every possible scenario, he called his father.

'Dad, it's Beau. How was your trip back from Hobart?'

'Hobart was ages ago. I've been trying to reach you. Where the hell have you been? Why haven't you been at work? There's a backlog here I can't jump over, and you're drifting around on an extended holiday.'

'I need to talk to you, Dad.'

'Talk to me about what? I just need you to get back to work and stop fooling around. As the future leader, you're hardly setting an example for the rest of the firm.'

'Sometimes life is not all about work, Dad. Liz and I are having problems and I need some time to sort myself out.'

'Well, you've had your time so now you need to get back to work. She's not still on about you doing the Sydney to Hobart race, is she? Buy her some flowers, take her to dinner and move on.'

'It's not as simple as that, Dad. I've been doing a lot of thinking and I need to talk to you.'

'Tell me now, for God's sake, and stop stuffing around.'

'I'll be in at work tomorrow and we can have a chat then, Dad,' said Beau.

'I've got a full day, so it needs to be early. Meet me in my office at 7 am sharp. You can have half an hour.'

'Fine, thanks Dad. See you then,' he said, greatly relieved he had avoided an immediate inquisition. He hung up the phone and a feeling of dread came over him. He was nervous about the meeting with his father the following day. I'll just need to stay true to what I need for myself and not be bullied anymore into doing what suits him, he thought, steeling himself.

The following morning, Beau made his way by cab through the relentless traffic to the heart of Sydney's central business district. He entered the magnificent foyer of Sterling and Finch's head office in Pitt Street, with its marble tiles and massive ceilings decorated with ornate chandeliers. He walked to the second bank of lifts which had access to the seventy-second floor, the executive floor of the five floors occupied by Sterling and Finch. The lift doors opened to the extensive reception area designed to intimidate opponents and impress potential clients. The firm's receptionist, Juleen, a veteran of twenty years with the firm, greeted Beau with her usual broad smile and offered to call him in his office once his father was free to see him. After shuffling some papers on his desk, Beau looked at his watch; 7:10 am. Typical of his father to keep people waiting, he thought. It was a ploy he had shared with Beau when he'd joined the firm. He believed it created a heightened level of nervousness and gave him an advantage in negotiations. Beau, who valued promptness and other people's time, just thought it was rude. The phone rang and Juleen, with some urgency in her voice, said, 'Your father will see you now, Beau. You've got twenty minutes before his next appointment.'

Beau walked down the long corridor to the imposing corner office with views over Sydney's central business district and glimpses of the blue water of the harbour in the distance. He knocked on the door and waited. Eventually his father said, 'Yes, come in. Come in, I haven't got all day.'

He opened the door and his father did not look up. The walk across the extensive expanse of the office was intimidating in itself.

'Finally, Beau, sit down. I've got some files here for you to look at,' his father said, dumping a heap down in front of him with a thud. 'The New Year has started off with a pile of work and I need you to take some of these cases off my hands.'

'Just wait one moment, Dad. Before we talk about the firm, I need to have a chat with you.'

His father looked up at Beau above his glasses as if to say, what now?

'I mentioned on the phone that Liz and I are having some serious problems. What I didn't tell you is that Liz has been seeing Damion behind my back.'

'Um, I see,' said Jack, as he sank back in his chair, arms folded.

'Well, son, these things do happen in a marriage, you know. What goes on behind closed doors in most marriages would surprise you. It's just an aspect of life that can create a lot of overreaction.'

'Overreaction?' said Beau disbelievingly. 'I don't think it's overreacting when you walk in on your fiancée and your best friend naked on the couch together, do you?' As he said this, Beau thought that his father would be the last person to have a problem with infidelity.

Jack thought about his response for a moment. 'I can see you're still clearly upset and I can understand that, Beau.' Jack allowed a little time to pass before he added, 'What I'm trying to say is, it's not something you throw your marriage away over. After all, I'm sure you have tasted a little fruit from other trees occasionally.'

Beau looked at his father, stunned by his suggestion. 'Actually, no I haven't. I'm not you, Dad.'

Jack gave him a glance that made it clear he did not appreciate the comment; however, he let it pass without a response.

'I've been giving it a lot of thought and at this stage I'm not sure what I'm going to do,' Beau continued. 'I had some time visiting Mum and it helped me get some clarity. I'm just not sure whether Liz and I are destined to spend the rest of our lives together. Until I'm clear about that, I don't want to make any big decisions.'

Jack thought for a while longer before he spoke. 'The best thing for you right now is to focus your energies and attention on your career. That way, you won't have time to dwell on all the negative emotions and get depressed. Just bury yourself in work and the rest will sort itself out.'

'I don't believe so, Dad. I know that's been your way of dealing with things. But it didn't work for you and Mum, did it?'

Jack sat back in his big imposing chair and gave Beau another displeased look without commenting.

'You see, I've been giving serious thought to my role here at Sterling and Finch. I'm not convinced that law is the right career choice for me.'

'Don't be ridiculous. You're a great lawyer. I've invested years in your development to make sure you're in the best position to eventually take over from me one day. Your future is assured here at Sterling and Finch.'

'I have no doubt that my future is very well laid out here, Dad. I just don't know if I can ever come out from underneath your shadow, even after you retire. No doubt you'll be a non-executive director and want to continue to have significant influence over the firm, even if I do get to run it one day.'

'Well, I do expect to have an ongoing role following my retirement, Beau, albeit as a non-executive chairman. You would run the firm on a day-to-day basis, however. And that's a good five years away.'

'That's my point. I'll never be my own man while I'm a prince in your kingdom. I have to break away and find out what I'm intended to do with this life. Above all else, I don't like being a lawyer.'

'Beau, stop all this esoteric bullshit. Your mother has got into your head again. You're a lawyer. You were born to be a lawyer ever since you were a little boy. That has been your dream.'

'No Dad, that has been your dream, not mine.'

With that, Beau stood up from his chair. 'Dad, I'm taking a month off to consider my future. I have plenty of leave owing to me and it's time I just took some time for myself.'

'That's not going to work for me right now, Beau. Look at these files. Who's going to do them if you don't?'

'I don't know, but you've got plenty of good quality lawyers at your disposal. I'm sure you'll find someone to take them on.'

'That's not the point, Beau. I want you to do them.'

After an extended pause, Beau looked his father directly in the eyes and said with a smile, 'I can't, Dad, I'll be on holidays in New Zealand. I've always wanted to do the Abel Tasman Coast track in New Zealand's South Island. I think this would be a great place for me to spend some time in nature where I do my best thinking. I'm leaving Friday morning.'

'So that's it then.'

'Yep, that's it,' said Beau, leaving no room for further discussion. Strangely, he felt comfortable stating his position so emphatically to his father. A comfort he had never felt before. Beau walked around to his father's side of the desk and held his hand out in an effort to connect with his father in some way. What he really wanted but had never received was a simple hug. It felt like an eternity but eventually his father, somewhat reluctantly, engaged in a handshake.

'I'll send you a postcard.'

'You do that.'

I'll let him get this out of his system and he'll be back, thought Jack. There's no way he'll turn his back on the opportunities I've given him and his obligations and responsibility to the Sterling dynasty.

CHAPTER SIX
Escape from Reality

Beau searched through his messages, noticing several missed calls over the last day or so. Clearly, Damion was keen to speak with him as he had left several messages. He was interrupted by the announcement, 'All passengers travelling on flight NZ 549 to Christchurch, report to gate thirty-six for immediate boarding. Please have your passports and tickets ready for presentation at the gate.'

As Beau was attempting to put his phone in flight mode, it rang. It was Liz.

'Hi Liz, I'm just about to board a plane so I can't talk right now.'

'Beau, I need to know, have you spoken to your father about us?'

There was a long pause before Beau answered, 'Yes, I have.'

Liz was in shock and her mind was racing. 'I thought we agreed we would wait until we discussed our future together?'

'No, that is what you decided, Liz. I need support right now and I'll seek it from whoever I need to. I won't be gagged. It happened, and it can't be undone. What's wrong with telling the truth about our situation?'

'So you don't want to discuss our relationship then?' she said, trying to paint him as uncaring.

'I'm so pissed off and angry at the moment that it would not be the best outcome for our relationship if we discussed it now. I need to be in my own space with my own thoughts to get clear on our future.'

'Well, I might not be here when you get back.'

'That's a chance I have to take, Liz. I have to go now, we're boarding. I do care for you, Liz, and I hope you'll be okay while I'm away.'

She was desperate to control the situation and knew now she would have to unleash her father to get her story out in the open as soon as possible.

'I think you're running away, Beau. Enjoy your trip.'

He hung up the phone reflectively and proceeded to board the plane.

Beau gazed out the window as the plane took off to the south over Botany Bay. It circled around towards the east, providing great views of the Sydney skyline. It truly was a magnificent city with the Harbour Bridge, and the Sydney Opera House perched on the edge of the shimmering harbour, one of the largest in the world. He could see the famous Sydney Heads, the entrance to the harbour. Only a few weeks ago, he had sailed through there in a frenetic race to round the first mark just outside as they set course for Hobart. It seemed like a long time ago with all that had happened.

The trip to Christchurch took two hours and Beau used the time to study maps of the area he was going to trek. Before he knew it, the plane was landing. He could see the majestic Southern Alps out of the window stretching to the south with permanent snow caps evident even at the height of summer. Beau collected his bags from the carousel, passed through customs and moved quickly to the line of taxis eagerly awaiting the daily Australian flight with its certain fares to the centre of the city. Christchurch was a popular destination for Australians during the ski season looking to take advantage of some of the world's best ski locations. Beau had been there many times before for exactly that purpose, as his favourite New Zealand destination, Queenstown, was only a few hours south of Christchurch. This time, however, he was heading north, to the top of the South Island and the start of the Abel Tasman Track.

Christchurch was a truly beautiful, quaint city resembling an English town. The shallow Avon River meandered its way through the heart of the city, framed by majestic willow trees and small, picturesque, arched bridges, a haven for birdlife and colourful fish. It was surreal, as if brought to life from a book of fairytales. Beau pulled up to his overnight accommodation, stowed his bags and decided to go for a walk around the centre of the city in the warmth of the midday sun. The town centre, bustling with life, was home to some beautiful old churches which stood in pride of place on the edge of the town square. There were buskers playing their instruments, and philosophers standing on soapboxes challenging the status quo and espousing all manner of conspiracy theories, actively encouraging those gathered to rally for a better world. There were food vendors enticing passers-by with the aroma of freshly cooked street food.

Beau had a sense of relief and calmness as he wandered the streets, taking in the energy and the movement of life around him. His phone rang and he could see that it was Damion again trying to contact him. He decided to answer the call as he knew it would play on his mind if he continued to ignore contact with Damion. 'This is Beau,' he said, acting as if he did not know who was calling.

'Beau, it's Damion.'

'What do you want?' Beau asked curtly.

'I've been trying to call you. Please don't hang up. I can understand why you haven't returned my calls. I'm not sure I would want to speak with me either in your circumstances.'

'What do you want?' Beau repeated.

'We go back a long way, Beau, and I just can't allow our friendship to end without at least making some attempt to save it.'

'Our friendship was over when you decided to seduce my fiancée after I had trusted you to take care of her.'

'I feel sick to my stomach that this has happened,' he pleaded. It was just a moment, you have to believe me.'

'Well, it was a very costly moment, you cheating prick. It has cost me my fiancée. I hope you're proud of yourself. I think it's the double betrayal that hurts the most. I'm not only dealing with the betrayal of my fiancée, I'm also grieving the loss of my best mate. You have smashed my world apart.'

'I know, Beau, and I'm just so incredibly sorry. I would do anything to unwind what I've done. I can understand that you may never forgive me, but I just wanted you to know how sorry I am and that I'll wait here for as long as it takes should you wish to try and salvage our friendship.'

'That's not an option for me right now, Damion. I'm not sure it ever will be.'

Beau hung up, tears welling in his eyes. Damion was more like a brother than a friend. His emotions fluctuated between grief and anger then back to grief. He was so confused and lost.

That night after dinner and a bottle of wine, Beau found himself sitting in a large plush room with red carpet, black leather chairs and soft lighting with three other men he did not know. A scantily clad young woman came up and sat next to him and said, 'Hi, my name is Belle, what's yours?'

She had an amazingly slim figure, long blonde hair, exaggerated makeup, and a heart-shaped tattoo just above her left breast. For reasons unknown to him, Beau replied clumsily, 'John, my name is John.'

'Welcome, John, where are you from? You're not from around here by the sound of your accent.'

'No, I'm Australian,' Beau replied awkwardly. He had never been to a brothel before in his life and was not sure why he was at one now.

'Well, handsome, if you need anything, I'm here to satisfy your every wish.'

Just as she left, another strikingly beautiful woman with black eyes and olive skin sat down next to him.

'Hi, I'm Anna, what's your name, handsome?'

'John,' Beau responded quickly.

'See anything you like, John?' she asked.

'You're all so beautiful.'

'Is this your first time, John?'

'No,' he stuttered, shifting in his chair.

'Then you know how it works,' she said. 'It's $175 for half an hour. Special requests and fantasies are $50 more. Pay the girl at the window and let her know your choice.'

Beau was shocked and confronted by her straightforward pitch. Awkwardly, he shuffled to his feet and said, 'I just need to go to the bathroom first. I'll be back in a minute.'

He walked straight past the bathroom door and left with a nauseous feeling welling up in his stomach. He just made it to the street before losing his dinner on the sidewalk. The cool evening Christchurch air brought him back to clarity and he wondered why he had ventured into such an establishment in the first place. Was he trying to get back at Liz? He had never had any interest in paying for sex. Did he just need some comfort from a woman? Feeling guilty, he quickly headed back to his room to call Liz, but reached her message bank. 'Liz, it's Beau. Just letting you know I've arrived safely.'

He hung up and wondered where she might be. He was feeling emotional, guilty and angry all at the same time. Why shouldn't I have sex with other women? She betrayed me first. As he lay in bed,

his thoughts kept looping around from one perspective to another. He realised that when he was off-centre like this, his emotional reaction to everything was exaggerated. He would overreact and get angry at people, even people he didn't know who were just serving him in a shop or checking him in at the airport. He did not like who he was becoming.

*

Liberated by Beau's absence, Liz and Damion had immediately headed off to her father's unused beach holiday home on the central New South Wales coast. They had been there together many times before and considered it a haven where they could plan how to handle the delicate situation they found themselves in.

There was no restraint as they entered the house, urgently tearing off each other's clothes, fumbling their way to the rug in front of the large open windows facing the beach. Naked, they spent a luscious afternoon indulging in each other, going through wave after wave of erotic passion. Like a drug, they could not get enough of each other. A life apart seemed impossible to contemplate, Liz thought.

'What are we going to do, Damion? I can't live another day without you.'

'Then don't, Liz, move in with me or I'll move in with you.'

'I would love to but it's just not that simple. My father is an old-fashioned man and he'll protect the family name at any cost. That includes cutting me off. It's just too soon. If you move in, everyone will know we were an item before Beau left me. And that leads me to something you need to know.'

'What do I need to know?' he asked urgently.

'I took out a domestic violence order against Beau. I used the black eye as evidence that he struck me the night he returned from Hobart.'

'You did what?' Damion stuttered in disbelief.

'I had no choice, babe,' she said, smooching up to him. 'I called Dad and he came over after you left. He asked me what happened to my eye and, well, I guess I told him Beau hit me. He went off his brain and the rest just took off from there.'

'That's unbelievable. Now I'm involved. Beau knows I was there. Remember?'

'Of course I remember, babe. Don't be angry with me. It happened so quickly. And then I couldn't control it. It just sort of got a life of its own.'

'Yeah, well lies have a way of doing that. Holy shit! What have you done? This will become very public.'

'It already has, babe.'

'Holy shit,' Damion repeated.

'I'll just deny any relationship with you and make sure everyone knows he's become an unpredictable abuser,' she added. 'After all, it's his word against mine. We were the only ones there that night. No one else knows about us. We need to be so careful. You haven't told anyone about us, have you?'

'Of course not. No one has any idea.'

'Great, then that is what we'll do. Then when he comes out with accusations, it'll be easy to convince people that I'm the one who's been distraught and he's making up stories because he'd been wanting to leave me for some time.'

'That's going to destroy him, babe. I'm not sure we want to do that to him.'

'It's too late. It's done. The hearing has happened, expedited by my father, and in Beau's absence, the order was granted. Don't worry; it's not like a charge or anything. It just paints him as a volatile, potentially violent man.'

'But that is just not who he is, Liz. It's so wrong.'

'Are you with me or not?' she challenged, looking directly at him.

Damion sat with his head in his hands and muttered, 'He's still my mate, even after what I've done to him.'

'Are you with him or with me, Damion?' she said again, forcing him to choose. 'Make up your mind.'

'I'm with you, babe, of course. You don't need to even ask me that.'

'Then it's settled. As long as we lay the foundations and stick to our story, we can pull this off.'

Damion left to travel back to Sydney due to an early court appearance the next morning. He was shaken by her capacity to go so far to save her reputation. *What would she do to me if I fucked up?* he thought. It was the first time he had witnessed this dark side of her nature.

*

Beau was up early and after a light breakfast, he caught a taxi to the train station for the eleven-hour trip to Nelson at the top of the South Island. The TranzAlpine train would take him from Christchurch on the East Coast to Greymouth on the West Coast through the famous Arthur's Pass. In Greymouth, he would connect with the West Coast bus service to Nelson. He was looking forward to this trip through the Alps. It was summer and there was no snow left on the mountaintops at Arthur's Pass. Each season, the rugged beauty of the Alps changed mood. Thick snow cover gave way to fast-running streams and lush green slopes in the lower reaches, and the mountains changed to craggy rock faces and dramatic vertical cliffs.

The train passed through a cutting, descending steeply to the West Coast of the country and into the sleepy town of Greymouth. Beau collected his bags and walked the two streets from the station to the bus depot where he boarded a bus for Nelson. There, he would meet the group he had booked the walking trek with. He took a window seat at the front of the bus behind the driver, and a young Australian woman who introduced herself as Jessie sat down in the seat next to him. She had a lean and muscular build and long brown hair, and her tanned skin indicated she had spent considerable time outdoors.

After their introductions, Beau learnt that she was one of the guides who would be accompanying him on the trek. Jessie said she made a point of returning to the region each year to support trekking groups. Beau quickly realised that she had led a remarkable life for her young years, travelling extensively throughout the world. He was excited by her descriptions of the area he was about to explore with their pristine beaches and crystal-clear bays. The time went by quickly during the trip north as Beau and Jessie exchanged stories of her travels and his sailing adventures. He enjoyed chatting with a complete stranger. It gave him a brief reprieve from the emotional turmoil of his life dilemmas. He was surprised when the bus driver announced, 'Attention passengers. We will be arriving at our final destination, Nelson town centre, in two minutes.'

Jessie said, 'If you would like Beau, you can collect your gear and we'll head off together to the tour bus that's taking us out to the national park headquarters at Marahau.'

'Sure, why not?' he answered, feeling out of his comfort zone and uncertain after his earlier enthusiasm.

In Nelson, Beau and Jessie entered the tour headquarters where a group of twelve trekkers and three guides had already assembled. There was an excitement and a buzz in the room as the group busily prepared themselves for the one-hour shuttle bus ride to Marahau. Taking advantage of the long twilight, there was still a three-hour walk ahead before they would reach their overnight destination. Beau introduced himself around without remembering many names of the people he met. There were three New Zealanders, five Australians, two Swiss, and one American, a diverse group that Beau thought would provide an interesting element to the trip.

They left their home base at the Marahau Information Kiosk along the Abel Tasman National Park Walkway on their way to Anchorage, passing through a magnificent beech forest followed by some open plains. Jessie was a great help to Beau during the trek, explaining some of the many wonders as they passed through the forests, and describing the unique mosses and vegetation. They even caught a rare glimpse of some of the unique native marsupials that lived in the region venturing out for their nocturnal scavenging. Finally, after an exhaustingly long day for Beau, they arrived at Anchorage, their first night's camp. That evening, the trekkers kept very much to themselves due to the late hour. They were just glad to get to their destination, grab some food and head off to their bunks for a well-earned rest.

Day two was a twelve-kilometre trek in the drizzling rain. They had to time their arrival at an estuary crossing, given that it was only passable two hours either side of low tide. After the crossing, they climbed steadily up and over low mountains and down through two valleys before reaching a suspension bridge above a beautiful inlet. Beau was sharing the day's walk with a New Zealander based in Auckland.

Cameron was a criminal lawyer, so they had much in common to discuss while wandering along the coastal fringe. They also discovered a common passion for sailing. Cameron was particularly active in the yacht racing fraternity on Auckland Harbour. Like Sydney Harbour, Auckland Harbour is one of the great blue water harbours of the world and has hosted two previous America's Cup challenges.

'Beau, why don't you come up to Auckland after the trek and spend some time sailing the harbour with me and exploring all the great little townships dotted around the foreshore?'

'I would love to, Cam,' replied Beau, who never missed an opportunity to sail and explore a new waterway. Beau was not sure what he would do after the ten days of trekking and kayaking, however, what he did know was that he would not be heading back to Australia anytime soon.

'Do you know any other people on the trek?' Beau asked.

'No, not really,' replied Cam. 'I did have a brief discussion with that American lady, Ellen. She's really fascinating, one of those people who seem to be able to see right through you. A bit freaky really. She's been travelling the world studying the origins of human development. A qualified psychologist and a Doctor of Philosophy no less.'

'What is she doing here then?' asked Beau, perplexed.

'I asked her that exact question. She's been studying the Maori culture and apparently, there are some Maori elders in this region she's hoping to chat to.'

'That makes sense, I guess,' said Beau, who had made a mental note to spend some time with her before the trek was through. 'She does sound really interesting.'

Their overnight destination was a hut at Bark Bay where they enjoyed a hearty meal of lamb stew and a few red wines, ensuring a solid sleep in preparation for the 6 am departure the next day.

Day three dawned with brilliant sunshine, a welcome reprieve from the constant drizzle of the day before. Beau had breakfast with a couple from Zürich who had just spent three weeks travelling the Queensland coast in Australia from Cairns to Brisbane. They were fascinated by the grandeur of the Great Barrier Reef, one of the Seven Natural Wonders of the World. They excitedly described their diving expeditions to the outer reef where they saw hundreds of different fish, beautiful coral gardens and inquisitive turtles that swam up to them fearlessly. Beau had sailed the area on many occasions and shared their enthusiasm for the Queensland coast, in particular his favourite destination, the Whitsunday Island group where one day he had always thought he would retire. 'There's no better sailing in the world than the pristine Whitsunday group of islands just off the Queensland coast.'

Beau found that as the days passed, he dwelt less and less on Liz and their problems. Being present and enjoying new people in the pristine natural wonders around him was the best way for him to gain perspective.

Day four started with another estuary crossing followed by a beautiful track that wound its way through tall forests, at times clearing out to majestic clifftops over the coast with spectacular views. After crossing some rocky headlands, they arrived in an old restored farm homestead for the evening. Beau noticed that there was a spare seat next to Dr Ellen Hass, the psychologist that Cameron had referred to earlier in the trek. He was reluctant to introduce himself and could not understand why. Was it what Cam had said about her? Finally, he walked up beside her and introduced himself.

'I've been meaning to catch up with you, Dr Hass. Do you mind if I sit next to you?'

'Oh, please call me Ellen,' she said, gesturing for him to join her.

'I'm Beau Sterling.' Beau extended his hand cautiously.

'Greetings, Beau Sterling,' she said with a smile. 'It's a great pleasure to meet you finally. We haven't had a chance to catch up with each other until now.'

'Just the way it's worked out, I guess,' Beau said. 'These trails are rather narrow and I find it difficult to talk with others unless they're directly in front or behind you.'

'You're the last one I have to meet on this trek, Beau. I've managed to spend some time with all the others except for you.'

'Is there any reason for that?' Beau asked, wondering if he had been avoiding her.

'Let's just say that I sensed you have a lot on your mind. Energetically, I decided to give you the space you needed. I trusted that you would find me when you were ready,' she said, enjoying another mouthful of her dinner. Ellen's presence was enhanced by her penetrating eyes. They were an unusual blend of piercing deep blue and an almost aqua colour that lit up when certain lights caught their brilliance. Her beautiful long glossy brunette hair reached the small of her back. Her face displayed wisdom beyond her years, and at the same time, she was unmistakably young and vibrant. Beau guessed she would be somewhere between thirty and thirty-five years but as a gentleman, he was not about to ask. She had an inviting smile and he could not help but feel awestruck in the energy of her presence.

'So, am I right, Beau, in assuming that you've got a lot on your mind?'

'Well, yes, you're right, Ellen. I've got a lot on my mind. In fact, this trip is meant to help me make some huge decisions in my life.'

'How will it do that exactly?' she asked.

A little intimidated by her directness, Beau said, 'I always think best around nature and given that I'm travelling alone, I have the opportunity to spend some time with my own thoughts.' He searched her face for a response and in the absence of any reaction, he added, 'To get clarity on the best course for me moving forward.'

After a period of contemplation, she responded, 'That can be a very helpful process, so long as you're not running away.'

Her head was tilted slightly towards him and she was searching his eyes out of the corner of hers. Beau felt uncomfortable, wondering what she could see in him.

'Do you think I'm running away?' he asked.

'I don't know, Beau, are you running away?'

'No, I'm not running away. I'm just taking some time out to explore my options.'

'That's great, Beau. That's what you should do then.'

In a strange way, Beau felt validated by her comment even though she had only just met him.

'Yes, that's what I'm doing then.'

She did not respond other than to smile softly at him, still searching his eyes. He was fascinated by her capacity to read people and understand exactly what was going on with them. He witnessed her during dinner engage in a conversation with a couple on the other side of the table who had been open in discussing aspects of their relationship. It was obviously a conversation that had started earlier in the day during the trek. In the process of unravelling their issue, she asked a number of questions, and in her answers, she explained the underlying dynamics that were affecting each of them. Beau watched this process with absolute fascination.

How does someone become that insightful? he wondered. Does she possess some clairvoyant powers? He was fascinated by her capacity to read people and make sense of their relationship dynamics. Perhaps it stemmed from his mother who was a particularly insightful woman in her own right, he thought. As he went to bed that evening, he could not get his short interaction with Ellen out of his mind.

Day five, the last day of the trek, passed without incident and Beau had a relaxing walk catching up with others in the group and reconnecting with Jessie, who had been busy spending time with all the guests equally, sharing her knowledge of the region and ensuring they travelled safely to each destination. Beau was delighted to learn that Jessie was a kayak specialist and would be guiding the next five days of the journey, travelling from bay to bay in ocean kayaks. During the meal that night, there were celebratory drinks to say goodbye to those who were not continuing with the kayak portion of the trip. Only four of the group were staying on, and Beau was pleased to learn that Ellen Hass was one of them. He was drawn to her energetically and knew instinctively that there was something she could teach him. Maybe she would have some insights into the decisions that weighed heavily on his mind? Apart from that, there was something incredibly attractive about her. He found she was entering his thoughts often, only to be consciously dismissed. The last thing I need right now is to get involved with someone else, he declared to himself. Beau made a point of catching up with Cameron to finalise arrangements for his visit to Auckland.

'I can't wait for you to show me around your part of the world,' Beau said, excited about the prospect of sailing Auckland Harbour.

'I've really enjoyed meeting you too, Beau,' Cameron said, giving him a firm hug. 'I'll see you in a week or so in Auckland.'

'It's a date,' Beau replied, slapping him on the back.

Beau enjoyed the last five days trekking in the remote areas, particularly as there was no mobile reception, leaving behind his other world and any chance his time out could be disrupted by Liz, his father or Damion for that matter. He did, however, miss his mother's consoling voice and was keen to connect with her as soon as he was able.

CHAPTER SEVEN
A Soul Connection

The kayak journey commenced the next morning with four others joining the group, along with Jessie and her guiding partner Jacob from New Zealand. They would all be travelling light for the next part of their journey, sleeping in two-man tents set up on the beach. Beau was paired up as a tent buddy with Jacob, Jessie was with Ellen and the other six were three couples who shared tents. The couples also had double kayaks.

Beau was pleased to learn that his kayak partner was Ellen, especially when he realised that Ellen was an expert in the art of ocean kayaking. With all her outdoors experience in remote countries, there was not much she could not do. It took a while for the inexperienced in the group to get the hang of paddling in tandem. Slow progress was made around the first few headlands, particularly with a one-metre swell rolling in from the Cook Strait between the Tasman Sea on the northwest and the South Pacific Ocean in the southeast, dividing New Zealand's North Island and South Island. It is twenty-two kilometres wide at its narrowest point and considered one of the most dangerous and unpredictable waters in the world.

Thankfully, they were not venturing far into the strait and would hug the coastline on their journey west. It was not long before they spotted one of the stars of the area, a herd of fur seals scampering over the rocks. They were oblivious to their new visitors only fifty metres away, and continued their playful games rolling around, wrestling one another and sliding in and out of the water with ease. The group hovered for some time just off the point, witnessing in sheer delight the amazing creatures.

As they travelled along the edge of a quiet secluded inlet towards their next evening's campsite, Beau asked Ellen, 'Why did you come on this trip?'

'The trek and kayak journey were the best way for me to connect with some Maori elders who live in the remote top part of New Zealand's South Island. I'm interested in their knowledge of tribal ways passed down from generation to generation, which could prove critical to our current understanding of human dynamics. If you go back far enough, all the indigenous tribes of the South Pacific region and on the other side of the Pacific Ocean are connected. From the Hawaiian Islands down to the Cook Islands, Samoa and Fiji, and extending right down to where we are now, the last country before Antarctica. I've been fascinated by their diverse cultures, but even more so by the similarities that exist within their rituals and spiritual beliefs.'

'Wow, that's fascinating,' Beau said.

'If you hang around me long enough, I have no doubt you'll hear more about the subject. It's all I think about and it's the driving force of my life. I've been looking to answer what I believe are the biggest questions that exercise the minds of scholars, both past and present, and that have been the focus of all religions since religions began. What is our reason for life on this Earth? What's it all about? Why are we here? Where did we come from and what are we meant to be doing? I believe many of the answers lie in our human evolution, in the common threads that exist between cultures, religions, races, and their link to universal laws. I've spent my adult life learning about what drives human behaviour. I studied psychology, philosophy, theology, and anthropology. I've devoted over a decade of my life to helping thousands of people deal with their emotional healing and understanding why they do the things they do. After all of my experiences, I've come to the conclusion that there must be more than these dynamics operating within us at a higher level. There are forces that exist at a subconscious level, a soul level, attracting us to the experiences we need to have in order to grow and expand. I'm convinced of that, and I've devoted my life to search for the answers. I believe there is no greater quest than to unlock the mysteries of life and our existence.'

'You sound like my mother. She's always been fascinated by the secrets to life, much to my father's disgust. She often talked about them when I was a boy and she related life lessons in stories that I could understand.'

'Really, Beau? That's awesome. I would like to meet her one day,' Ellen said.

Beau experienced one of those rare tingling sensations suggesting that this was fate rather than coincidence. He knew he had met Ellen for a reason. As the bow of the kayak hit the sand, Beau snapped out of his daydream. They shared the load, dragging the kayak up beyond the high-water mark, and unloaded the gear that was securely stowed in the storage compartments. The next hour was busy. They erected Ellen's tent for the evening, which turned out to be a comical exercise with both of them rolling around on the beach in fits of laughter.

'Well, I think it'll stand for the night,' Beau said as a parting comment, laughing. 'I'll catch up with you around the fire for dinner later on.' He moved off to his own tent, which Jacob had already set up. As he stowed his belongings, Jacob called from outside, 'I see you found our home for the night, Beau.'

'Yes, thanks for setting it up, Jacob, this will do fine.'

'I've hitched up a shower and screen over on the tree line, so feel free to have a wash when you're ready.'

Beau emerged from the tent, saying, 'That's awesome, thanks mate. It's exactly what I need before we settle down with a few beers to wash the salt out of our throats.'

'You're a man after my own heart, Beau. Sounds like a plan.' They gave each other a high five.

After a satisfying meal, the group sat around a fire on the beach enjoying a few well-earned drinks and sharing their various stories of the day. Beau was sitting next to Jessie, who had made a point of seeking him out during dinner. While he had not recognised it before, it was becoming apparent that Jessie was taking more than a passing interest in him. This realisation surprised him a little, as it had been some time since he had noticed the attention of other women. Was he putting out some sort of energy suggesting he was interested or available? he wondered. Now that he was aware, he noticed the subtle signals. The occasional touch of his hand, positioning herself so they touched shoulders and a flirtatious laugh at the comments he made. He was flattered by the attention but also uncertain about how to deal with it. Jessie was a beautiful young woman, vivacious and full of life. Why shouldn't he enjoy whatever experiences eventuated as the night unfolded? Again, he felt a battle within, just as he had done in Christchurch. Why is it I feel guilty doing to Liz what she did to me? he justified to himself. She changed the rules, I didn't.

The night drifted on comfortably and the wine flowed freely. Time seemed to disappear, as did the members of the group. Beau had not noticed that only he and Jessie were left, until he felt her hand slide down the inside of his left knee and on to his inner thigh. He was shocked and in unfamiliar territory, as Liz was the only woman he had ever been with. As Jessie leant over and kissed him on the side of the neck, Beau was intoxicated by the flush of warm energy that surged through his body. His excitement grew alarmingly and he turned his head and engaged in a long, passionate kiss. Embarrassed, he wondered if the others had left to give them some space, and found himself hoping that Ellen had not witnessed anything. Her passion rising, Jessie straddled him and grabbed his head and pulled it towards her as she continued to kiss him on the lips, nibbling his earlobe and neck. Beau grabbed her and pulled her towards him at the same time, moving her long hair to one side and exposing her neck. As he kissed her neck, he felt her hand guide his to her full breasts, heaving and seemingly bursting from the constraints of her clothing. In that moment, Beau whispered, almost to his own disbelief, 'Stop, please stop, I can't do this. Jessie, please, I just can't do this. I'm still engaged to be married.'

'What do you mean you can't do this?' she protested. 'You told me your relationship was over.'

'I know I did, and it may well be. It's just too soon. I'm supposed to be here sorting out my thoughts so I can make the right decisions.'

'Seems to me your thoughts were pretty clear just a moment ago.'

'I'm so sorry, Jessie. I didn't mean to lead you on, if that's what I was doing.'

She climbed off him, stood up and straightened her clothing before commenting, 'You might need to do something with that before you climb into your tent, Beau. Otherwise you'll scare the shit out of Jacob,' she said, walking away and chuckling to herself.

*

The next morning was a beautiful day, the wind having calmed overnight, and they made an early start. The conditions were glassy and Beau was looking forward to getting back on the water in the kayaks. He endured an awkward breakfast sitting opposite Jessie who, from time to time, gave him a look. He was unsure if it was a look of disappointment or just tiredness. Perhaps he was reading too much into it, he thought. She seemed to engage in normal conversation around the table and appeared unfazed by his rejection of the night before. Maybe it's affected me far more than it has her, he thought. I've been out of the game so long, I have no idea how these things play out. In any case, she's a great girl and I'll just treat her as I have from the start, he decided. With that, he finished his meal and on the way to the kitchen tent to clean his plate, he caught up with her and put his arm around her shoulder. 'About last night, Jessie, I'm just so messed up at the moment.'

'Forget about it, Beau, I get it. Don't sweat the small stuff, my friend. Let's have a great day out on the water and move on.'

Relieved, Beau realised that for Jessie, it had only been a bit of fun and was no big deal.

Ellen took the front position today in the kayak and Beau could not help but admire her easy paddling style. His main concern was matching the rhythm of his stroke to hers. She was setting a cracking pace, and she explained that she was meeting with the Maori elders around midday further along the coast. Jessie and Jacob were aware of this, and they would bring the rest of the group along later, she said.

'Beau, would you like to come with me and sit in on the conversation? Or would you prefer to stay with the kayak on the beach and wait for Jessie?' she said cheekily.

Beau was taken aback by her comment and guessed Ellen had seen him with Jessie the night before.

'No, Ellen, I'd prefer to come with you, thanks all the same,' he said, avoiding his desire to justify his actions of the previous evening. He was excited at the thought of joining Ellen after learning of her reasons for going. At first, he found it curious that he was so engaged in what she was doing. He had always found his mum's stories about spirituality and philosophy intriguing. How had he let this significant part of himself go unexplored? Being a lawyer tends to bash it out of you, he realised. Spending five years at university followed by ten years in practice, immersing myself every day in conflict, and at times defending the guilty certainly distort one's view of life, he thought. The material toys and benefits the position provided were undoubtedly an attraction as well, he conceded. He loved his nice cars, overseas holidays, yachts, and eating out whenever he wanted. Material things were awesome; however, they did not make his life happy, he now knew. There was something missing.

After securing the kayak in the tree line high enough to avoid the incoming tide, Ellen produced a detailed map of the immediate region. 'This is the valley we must go up, Beau. It's about five kilometres to the village.'

The two set off on what appeared to be a well-trodden path from the ocean, up through the heavily wooded valley. The path took a turn up the side of the valley and wound up steeply to a plateau at the top. Ellen led the way purposefully, focused on getting there. She looked back at him and urged, 'Keep up, Beau. We've only got a three-hour window before we need to be back on the beach to meet up with the others.'

As they entered a clearing, they saw a small community of modest houses that created a village feel.

They were drawn to a large structure on the other side of the common area which appeared to be some form of hall.

'Weren't these people once cannibals?' asked Beau.

'If you're not going to be serious, Beau, you can go back to the boat and wait for the others.'

'I'm sorry. I was only half serious.'

Ellen gestured for him to stop. 'Now I don't want to freak you out, but we're about to be approached by some tribal warriors. It's called a hongi, the traditional touching of noses. It's all part of their normal welcoming process. Maintain eye contact and do not speak.'

Beau was starting to wonder why he had agreed to come on this journey into the unknown. Just then, three Maori men moved forward and approached them. Beau froze, not knowing how to respond. The men walked right up to them, leaned forward and rubbed noses with their visitors. A woman began to sing, weaving her energy into the sacred space, making it safe for the two groups to meet. On and on she sang, the unfamiliar cadences creating a haunting spell. In her song she welcomed not only the visitors, but also all their ancestors, particularly those who had recently died. Ellen explained to Beau that the Maori culture had been welcoming people this way for as long as they had been in existence. Some of Captain Cook's men had shot the warriors during this welcome, thinking they were in mortal danger.

Relieved, Beau followed Ellen and the warriors into the main hall, which Ellen explained was called a *whare whakaminenga*, or meeting house. At the top of a raised section at the far end, three elders were seated. The aged man in the centre was obviously the leader. He stepped down from the raised platform and walked right up to Ellen, invading her personal space. He rubbed noses with her in a gesture of welcome, and then with Beau. Beau and Ellen sat on woven mats provided for them in front of the leader and the other elders. The leader introduced himself as Matiu. He introduced the elders on either side of him. His English was thick with his native accent. Beau noted that there was a young man sitting off to the side. Matiu proudly introduced him as his son.

Matiu then asked, 'Why have you come here?'

'I've travelled from America visiting many countries over the last five years, meeting with the traditional owners of the South Pacific lands. I'm researching your beliefs and how your communities have evolved,' Ellen replied. 'Thank you for agreeing to meet with me. This is Beau, a fellow traveller.'

'It's a good thing to seek to understand. If more of us sought to understand our differences, then there would be greater harmony between countries and even neighbouring communities. We have learnt to be grateful for what we have, without the need to take from others. At times, individual conflict can arise between people from our community and a member of a neighbouring community. There is some tolerance for allowing these conflicts to resolve themselves. If it escalates and spreads amongst other family members, then the elders from each tribe will meet and together we will decide how it should be dealt with. Even though we are all Maori people, we still protect our own.'

'That sounds like a very effective way to deal with your differences,' Ellen commented. 'There are many societies and religions around the world that still kill one another over a piece of land or differences in beliefs.'

'There is room for all, as long as one does not try to force their beliefs on others or take what is not theirs,' Matiu said.

The conversation flowed for over half an hour, guided by the same questions that Ellen had asked of all those she had visited in the previous five years. She then asked the question which was at the core of her search for the meaning of existence.

'May I ask, Matiu, what are your spiritual beliefs? What gods or god do you worship?'

Matiu's son Ropata answered. 'Our people have been influenced by the missionaries and have for over a hundred years adopted a Christian belief. If you look back to our ancestors prior to the missionaries arriving, we as a people worshipped Rangi, Father Sky, and Papa, Mother Earth. The marriage of these two celestial parents produced the gods and all living things on Earth. Christianity has changed that belief to one God who made heaven and Earth and all things. We have a great respect for all of the elements of the Earth and what they provide to us. There is a perfect balance between all living things, and we try to live in harmony. In the past we have worshipped the sun, the trees, the weather, the stars, and the moon, all as gods under Rangi and Papa.'

'Thank you, Ropata. I've come to learn from all the nations I've visited that there are many versions of universal creation. Ultimately, they are far more similar than they are different.'

'That is because we are part of the Malayo-Polynesian people who descended from South East Asia,' said Ropata. 'They were skilful seafarers, navigators and astronomers and they travelled great distances to unknown lands, just as Captain Cook did. That is why our spiritual heritage stretches from the Hawaiian Islands, Easter Island and down to New Zealand.'

'You're well versed in the history of your ancestors, Ropata. I also have a great interest in your heritage, which is why I'm here,' Ellen explained. Matiu watched on with great pride in his eyes as his son displayed his knowledge and education to Beau and Ellen.

'Matiu, if I may ask one final question? What do you believe happens to us once our time here on Earth has ended?'

Matiu pondered Ellen's question for some time and with a wry smile, asked, 'So, your search is for the ultimate mystery?'

'That is a big part of my interest, yes. I'm attempting to make sense of our existence and I intuit that the answers are all around us. It's just that we simply cannot see until we are ready to see.'

'You carry much wisdom for someone so young. As the chosen one for our community, I have a responsibility to pass down wisdom from generations past,' Matiu explained. 'That wisdom comes from many places. It comes from the stories of my ancestors. It comes from a place beyond here when I still my mind and listen to my inner voice. While I've been educated in the ways of Christianity, I have my own knowing on such things. After all, the book of Christianity was compiled by men, so blind faith may be unwise. I believe we are part of something greater than we can see, although we are not lesser. We belong to the far reaches of the heavens where pure light and energy live in eternal harmony and, in good time, the veil of this life will be lifted. If we truly listen to the messages, they are always there emanating from this place. Some call this source God, some Muhammad, and there are many other names. Who is right? Are we all wrong? As the legend is told by my ancestors, there is a mystical place, an island where the celestial descendants of Rangi and Papa live. They have chosen to return to this earthly place to assist others in their path back to the source. The legend goes that they will only appear when we are ready to hear their message. The messages cannot come through if we are in conflict with others and therefore ourselves. If we cannot forgive, if we are buried in grief, or if we do not listen to another's beliefs and maintain our own stubborn position, we are *toenga...*' Matiu looked to his son and spoke in his own language, gesturing to Ropata to give him a suitable phrase. 'We are out of balance, living in a fog of confusion until we shed the turmoil within. Until we are still and in touch with our inner spirit, messages from the source and our ancestors will not be heard.'

Ellen looked at Matiu with his long grey hair tied back, his prominent square jaw, piercing black eyes, and tribal tattoos adorning his face. She could not help but admire the immense wisdom and calming presence that he exuded. He is truly an ancient soul, she thought. 'I would like to thank you all for meeting with us today and we wish you peace and wisdom and love,' Ellen said, holding her hands together and bowing in a gesture of respect.

The Maori elders stood and held Ellen and Beau in turn by the arm, rubbing noses and blessing their path ahead in their language. Beau and Ellen started off briskly in an effort to make good time back to the kayak. They had a twenty-minute walk and an hour of kayaking before they reached their evening campsite. On the way down the path, Beau expressed his gratitude to Ellen for inviting him to meet with the Maori elders.

'That was an incredible experience. One I will never forget. I wish our so-called modern leaders would demonstrate that level of understanding and tolerance.'

'I know what you mean, Beau. It has been a common theme through all of my travels. I've been consistently inspired by meeting these great people. Did you understand the power of his last bit of wisdom?'

'I heard that he gets messages from somewhere, if that's what you mean?' Beau said, wondering if he was on the right track.

'That's part of it. He spoke of a mystical island where their celestial ancestors reside. I've heard this same description in many of the places I've visited. I first heard it as a young girl from a wise old friend who said he had seen it.'

'Are you seriously suggesting that this place, this lost dimension, actually exists?'

'That is why I've devoted the past five years of my life to it, Beau. I have recurring dreams about it. I can see it in great detail, although it's only a dream. Somehow, I believe it is out there if only in a metaphysical sense. Most would call me crazy; however, I believe that they are talking about a window, a portal to the next realm of existence. It's what I call my own personal "Empyrean quest".'

'What's an Empyrean quest?'

'In Greek mythology, the ultimate God source of pure light at the centre of all creation is known as the Empyrean. It's just a name from the ancient philosophers; however, it describes a concept that is evident in our everyday lives. It depicts the highest order a being can attain. Ultimately, the higher our vibrational frequency, the more we move towards pure energy and light, wisdom and love. I believe we are always connected to this source at some level in our continual evolution. The Empyrean is everywhere and its source exists in different realms. Some people experience it for fleeting moments. They believe they have tapped into a frequency outside of the physical world, and experienced a knowing they can't explain. I want to experience it, Beau. I'm convinced many of the keys to our existence can be uncovered in this place of pure centeredness, allowing us to ascend to a higher understanding.'

'So do you think Matiu is getting wisdom from the Empyrean?'

'I think we all are.'

'How do you connect with the Empyrean, Ellen? How do you find it?'

'You have to want to tune into it. Most of us go through life stuck in our own cocoon, limited by our beliefs and emotions. Matiu explained that when we are stressed emotionally, whether by anger, grief, hatred, envy…you name it, we are not open to receiving our own internal wisdom and guidance from whatever universal connections we may have. When you think about it, most of us are dealing with at least one emotional stressor most of the time.'

'Are you saying that there are spirits from above talking to us?'

'If you're asking me as a scientist, Beau, I don't have the physical evidence to prove it. Quantum physics has confirmed the existence of separate realms, bands of less dense energy fields above the Earth consisting of wave particles of light. These realms potentially contain information, so the theory goes. Just as our mobile phone transmissions hold information. The theory is demonstrated everywhere in our modern existence. They know this due to the variations in density and vibration. Most religions speak of these realms. My own personal belief is that we are tapped into something beyond us and the more evolved and aware we become, the more we tap into an energy source outside of our current frequency. Like tuning into a distant radio station that we could not hear before. Perhaps we're not supposed to know the grand design because in our ignorance, we make mistakes, learn and grow. If we truly understood the complexities of life, would we choose to have experiences that cause us pain, anger and hurt? Struggling through pain, anger and hurt and experiencing what brings us down and trapped in lower frequencies helps us understand what elevates us to higher frequencies. You must experience one to know the other. Matiu explained that their beliefs are passed down through ancient wisdom.'

'He did speak of an island where celestial divine beings of pure light reside, Ellen. So is that the destination of your Empyrean quest? To find this island they speak of?'

'I don't know if the island exists, or if it's more of a dream state once we achieve the right vibrational frequency. I've had glimpses of it in deep meditation. I don't know if it's real or imagined because as I come back into my body, I lose clarity. Sorry, I'm rambling.'

'No, please don't stop, Ellen, I'm fascinated. What started you on this journey? Was it the old man you spoke of?'

'Where I grew up in Florida, the old man I mentioned lived next door. His name was Captain Gill. Everyone just called him Cappy. He would have been in his nineties last time I saw him about five years ago. He was like a father to me. He was a mystical seafaring man and he used to tell me stories of great sea adventures to faraway places. One of his stories came from his time working on merchant ships. He spoke of a mystical island in the South Pacific with a massive active volcano at its centre. He said that he was shipwrecked on that island for two years. After much ordeal, he came across an evolved group of people living in a pristine valley. Their leader, who he described as the wisest person he'd ever met, shared many secrets about the mysteries of life. She was from a higher realm. He believed the island was a gateway to higher realms, guiding us on our soul's quest back to what he described as the Empyrean, our ultimate destination. Pretty heavy stuff, hey? Much of my inspiration came from the endless stories Cappy told me over the years. He is a very passionate storyteller and he captured my imagination when I was a young girl. I guess it started me on a journey to explore the mysteries of life myself and find my own answers. Sometimes, I thought it was just another fairytale. He made it seem so real though, and his eyes would light up whenever he spoke of it. Ever since then, I've secretly dreamt of finding his mysterious island.'

'Your own personal "Empyrean quest", Ellen,' Beau teased. 'You never know; perhaps you'll find your island one day.'

'Follow your dreams I say, Beau. That's why I've been island-hopping for the last five years.'

Beau had never contemplated such deep philosophical questions before. He had lived day to day, doing what he had to do, going to school, going to university, getting a job and enjoying his sport, the ocean and his friends. He'd had a basic religious upbringing at school; however, he had never harboured any strong spiritual beliefs.

'I guess I don't really believe in the God everyone talks about in Christianity, or any of the organised religions for that matter,' Ellen said. 'I decided that at a young age and trusted some inner knowing. The stuff they tried to teach us in religion at school just did not resonate with me. I've always been fascinated by nature, the planet and our solar system and beyond, though, and I'm not so naïve as to believe it all just appeared one day. Before it got here, what created it or even the concept of it?'

Beau was enthralled by their conversation, but it was cut short as they broke through the tree line to find that the rest of the group had arrived at the far end of the beach. They caught up with the group who had been having a well-earned rest under the tropical palms that provided a welcome canopy from the sun. They briefly shared their amazing experience before departing on the last leg of their journey. They spoke little during their final half-hour of paddling. Beau's thoughts turned to Liz, worried that she would be distressed without any word from him. He had been out of contact for so long. He would call her as soon as he could charge his phone and get reception when they reached Nelson the next day.

Beau sat next to Jacob on the long bus ride back to Nelson where his overnight accommodation in a motel and his bags would be waiting for him. They shared stories of their experiences during the trip, and Beau told him about meeting with the Maori elders. Jacob found it fascinating, being a born and bred New Zealander with some Maori blood. Beau noticed that Jessie had deliberately been avoiding him since his clumsy rejection of her at the campfire. Without explaining why he was interested, he asked Jacob if everything was okay with Jessie.

'She's fine, although I think she genuinely likes you, Beau. I'm aware that you and Jessie had a moment around the fire. In fact, everyone in the group is aware of it.'

'Are you kidding?' Beau felt exposed and foolish that their encounter was common knowledge. 'Did she say something to you?'

'She didn't have to. Several of us saw what happened from the tent site. After all, you guys weren't that subtle about it.'

'I feel so terrible, not so much for myself but for Jessie. The last thing I wanted was to create a problem for her with the others.'

'Don't worry about Jessie, she can look after herself. From what I saw, she was very much in the driver's seat.' He smiled.

Beau looked at Jacob and with a chuckle agreed, 'I guess she was.'

'So, what about you and the good doctor?' Jacob taunted.

'What do you mean, me and the doctor?' Beau protested.

'You guys have been hanging out quite a lot, and I just wondered whether something was developing. You make an awesome couple.'

Beau did not quite know how to respond to Jacob's comment except to dismiss it. In doing so, it forced him to consider whether something was actually growing between them.

'I just find her incredibly fascinating. I've discovered a real interest in her work.'

'Right, so it's her work you're interested in,' Jacob mocked.

'Her work, that's exactly right,' Beau replied, staring at Jacob intensely to put an end to the conversation.

It worked, because Jacob changed the subject. 'So, where do you go from here on your epic journey, Beau?'

'You know Cameron from the walking trek?'

'Sure, Cameron is a cool, fun guy.'

'He sure is. He invited me up to Auckland to do some sailing on the harbour with him.'

'That would be awesome. There are quite a few of the group heading that way.'

'Is that right?' Beau asked, wondering who they might be. 'Are you heading up there, Jacob?'

'No, Jessie and I have a few days off and then we head back on the same journey we've just done. We'll complete this loop five times this season,' he replied. 'Ellen mentioned she's heading up there,' Jacob revealed, watching Beau's reaction.

'Why is she heading to Auckland?' Beau asked.

'Why do you want to know?' Jacob taunted.

With a knowing smile, Jacob relayed the story that Ellen had shared with him. 'She's about to embark on a major ocean journey on her way back home to Florida via the Cook Islands and eventually through the Panama Canal.'

Beau quietly wondered why she had not mentioned it to him, but he responded, 'Of course she is. You wouldn't expect anything else, I guess.'

The bus pulled up at the dockside of the picturesque city of Nelson. Beau was within walking distance of his overnight motel accommodation. He grabbed his bags and said a heartfelt thanks and goodbye to each of his fellow kayakers. When he came to Jessie, he put his hands on her shoulders and gave her a kiss on the cheek.

'I've really enjoyed your company, Jessie, and I hope we see each other again one day.' She planted a long kiss on his lips and replied, 'That would be awesome, Beau. Make sure next time you come, you're single.'

They both chuckled and hugged, and Beau was relieved that there was no ill feeling between them. He picked up his bags and turned to find Ellen standing right in front of him.

'Beau, I can't tell you how much I've enjoyed spending this time with you. You're a very special man and I trust that your trip has given you the answers you seek.'

'Thanks Ellen, I've had an amazing journey and you've been a big part of that, particularly learning about your work. I know that our meeting is no coincidence. You've inspired me to search for my own direction in life.'

'Your own Empyrean quest,' Ellen said with a chuckle.

'That's it exactly.'

'I understand from Jacob that you're heading to Auckland,' Beau said, implying only a passing interest.

'That's right, I'm leaving tomorrow morning early on the bus to Picton to catch the ferry to Wellington. I'm on a flight to Auckland the following day.'

'I don't have a ticket yet for the flight or the ferry but if it's okay with you, I'd like to come along,' Beau suggested. 'I'm due to meet Cameron in Auckland in the next few days.'

'That would be great. I'd love to have a travelling buddy. I'll meet you on the bus at 7 tomorrow morning in the city centre then.'

She picked up her bags, gave him a peck on the cheek and walked off down the road. Beau watched as she walked away and contemplated the days ahead, excited about the prospect of spending more time with her and at the same time, questioning his own motives.

CHAPTER EIGHT
Opportunities Lost

Beau settled into his motel room and plugged in his mobile phone to charge it. Within fifteen minutes, his phone lit up with message after message. He checked his message bank and there were seven messages from his mother, three from his father and two from Liz. The messages were all similar. Beau, please call urgently, as soon as you get this message. What could be so urgent? he thought. He rang his mother first.

'Beau, thank God you've called! Are you okay?'

'Why wouldn't I be okay?' Beau replied, confused.

He noted that his mother was teary and asked, 'What's up Mum, what's wrong?'

'Has anybody spoken to you yet?' she asked.

'Spoken to me about what?' he said with an increasing level of urgency.

'Before I tell you, Beau, where are you right now?'

'I've just arrived at my motel in Nelson, Mum, why do you ask?'

'Are you alone?'

'Yes, I'm alone, for God's sake Mum, what the hell is going on?'

'Beau, I want you to sit down. I have something to tell you.'

'Fine, I'm sitting on the bed, what is it that you have to tell me?'

'It's about your brother.'

'What about Leon, is he all right?'

'Leon is dead, Beau.'

He sat silent for a moment trying to take in what his mother had just said. 'Leon is dead? What do you mean he's dead? How did he die?'

'He was found in his room in King's Cross. He'd overdosed.'

Beau tried to come to terms with what he was hearing, but it seemed so surreal. 'Who found him?'

'He was found by his roommate.'

'Did he…?'

'Commit suicide?' his mum interjected.

'Yes, commit suicide?' he asked cautiously, not really wanting to know the truth.

His mum choked back the tears and softly sobbed as she confirmed that he had indeed taken his own life, based on the autopsy which revealed the amount of drugs he had in his system.

'Autopsy, when did this happen?'

'It was a week ago yesterday, Beau. We've been trying to reach you.'

'I've got to come home straightaway,' Beau announced. 'When is the funeral?'

'That's just it, Beau, the funeral was today.' With a flood of tears, his mum announced, 'We buried him today. I tried to contact you. I've been trying since it happened.'

'I'm so sorry, Mum; my phone has been dead flat. We've been away from power and phone reception for the past week. I'd better come home as soon as I can get a flight.'

'If it's okay, I'm actually thinking of coming over to you. I could use the distraction of a trip and I just need to be with you whatever it takes.'

'Of course, Mum, I would love you to come here if that's what you want to do.'

'Scott will be with me if that's all right.'

'Of course it is. I would expect him to be with you. I would love to see both of you. I know it's difficult for you to talk about, but how was the funeral?'

'The funeral was incredibly difficult, Beau. There were hundreds of people there. Most of them who know your father came out of respect or obligation, I'm not sure which. There were a handful of people from Leon's current life in the Cross who showed up to pay their respects, and I'm grateful they did. Unfortunately, your father did not welcome them. I think he blames them for the lifestyle Leon found himself in.'

'If anyone should take the blame for Leon's death, it's Dad. He drove him away and he rejected his own son.'

'Don't be too harsh on him, Beau. He's from a different mould and he never understood why Leon chose the life he did. Deep down, he does blame himself, if you ask me.'

'How did Liz go at the funeral?'

His mum did not speak for some time until she reluctantly said, 'She was not there, Beau.'

'Not there? Why wasn't she there?' he asked with concern.

'She wasn't welcome, Beau. Your father and Kerry Weir have had the most terrible fight and I believe it's irreparable.'

'A fight? A fight over what?'

'That's not important for now, Beau.'

He sensed his mum was getting more upset by discussing it and so he left it alone.

'The most notable absence was you, and I know how much you would have wanted to be there.'

'Leon and I haven't been close for some years, Mum, you know that. I've tried to stay in touch with him as much as I could. He just kept pushing me back. I think he knew that I would do whatever it took to get him out of Kings Cross. At the end of the day, he just did not want to be rescued. I remember once when I intervened and had a drug support group take him to a safe house. He had all he needed there to recover and try to overcome his addictions. He looked at me one day and said, "Stay out of my life". It was in that moment I knew he was making a clear choice, even if that choice was self-destructive.'

'I know, Beau; I had similar experiences with him over the years. I found the best approach was to love him unconditionally. He would call me, perhaps once a month, just to let me know he was okay. He knew I wouldn't lecture him or try to intervene. I just wish he'd had the strength to call me when he was contemplating suicide. It was really weird. He'd been the best I've heard him in a long time when I last spoke to him. I've come to learn since that often when someone decides to end it, one of the signs is that they become calm and almost relieved that the torment will soon be over. It can lead to very confusing signs. We can talk more when I get over to you, Beau. Where will you be in the next few days? I need to organise flights. I can't wait to be with you as soon as possible.'

'I'll be in Auckland in two days, Mum.'

'That's it then, Beau; we'll meet in Auckland in two days' time. When you arrive and settle in, can you send me details of where you're staying?'

'I will. I'm so sorry I was not there for you, Mum. I'm just numb right now trying to absorb all this,' he sobbed.

'I've never wanted to hold you as much as I do right now, Beau,' his mum replied, sobbing with him.

Beau was very angry at his father for having driven Leon away from the family, and he could not bring himself to call him. *If I speak to him now, I'll rip his head off*, he thought. It was best to leave that discussion for later.

His next call was to Liz. The phone rang out and he left a message. He was keen to talk to her and get some clarity over the fight his mum had referred to. 'Liz, it's Beau, I've heard about Leon,' he said. 'Sorry I missed your calls. I've been off grid in a remote part of New Zealand with no reception. I understand your father and mine have had a disagreement. I would like to talk to you about it. Oh, and of course see how you're doing. I won't be back for some time. I'm extending my stay. Mum and Scott are heading over to be with me. Call me when you can.'

He hung up, desperate to find out what had transpired between the two lifelong friends. He wandered down to the corner liquor store, bought a bottle of wine and retired to his motel room. He felt so sorry for his brother Leon who had been lost for some time. He'd never come to terms with his sexuality, particularly given Jack's rejection of him. Beau had no doubt that his last days had passed in the seedy underworld of Kings Cross, largely due to feeling unloved by those who were supposed to be closest to him. He couldn't bear the thought of him alone and desperate in his final hours. *There's a message in that for me*, he thought, as he lay on his bed drinking wine straight from the bottle. *We're all just seeking to be wanted and loved*. His thoughts turned to his relationship with Liz. *Perhaps I really did drive her into Damion's arms*, he lamented.

The next morning, Beau woke and was startled to see the time. It was 7:30 am and he had clearly missed the bus to Picton. After his restless night, he had finally drifted off to sleep, exhausted, at around 3 am.

He made some frantic calls and managed to book a ticket on a bus for 9:30 am, calculating he could still just make it to Picton in time to catch the ferry to Wellington at 11:45 am. His anxiety heightened when the bus pulled into seemingly every bus stop along the way and he was convinced he would miss the ferry. At 11:30 am, the bus finally crested a hill and he saw the picturesque town of Picton nestled by the sea in front of him. The bus pulled up near the quaint commercial port where the ferry was preparing to leave. He raced towards it, expecting it to take off at any moment. With a bag over each shoulder, he raced up the gangplank to be greeted by a deckhand who was preparing to release the mooring lines.

'You're lucky you made it, mate. I saw you running down from the car park. On you get.'

Beau nodded in appreciation and struggled to the nearest seat where he collapsed, short of breath. He gathered himself before heading to the upper deck where he was relieved to find Ellen standing at the top of the stairs waiting for him.

'Beau, I thought you weren't coming,' she said, giving him a welcoming hug. 'It's so great to see you.' Immediately, she sensed something was wrong.

'You don't seem yourself today.'

'I got some bad news last night, Ellen. My brother Leon was found dead in his flat having overdosed on drugs.'

She explored his face in disbelief. 'Are you serious?' she said, grabbing his hands.

'Unfortunately, I am, Ellen. Deep down, I was concerned this would always be the outcome for Leon. He's been lost to the family for some years, rejected by my father due to his sexual and lifestyle preferences. He's been living as a male prostitute in Kings Cross. I've tried to stay in touch with him, but unfortunately, he rejected any attempts by the family, particularly my mother and me, to get him out of the situation.'

'I'm so sorry for you and your family. Sit down here. Can I get you a cup of tea or coffee?'

'A coffee would be great, thanks Ellen.'

Beau spent a good part of the trip across the Cook Strait chatting with Ellen about his brother Leon and his conversations with the family during the night. It was a relief to share with her how he was feeling. She was such a great listener and she had a beautiful empathetic way about her.

'My mother and her partner Scott are flying over to Auckland to spend a few days with me.'

'That's great, Beau. You need to be around family at these difficult times.'

'I feel as though I need to be around you as well, Ellen,' Beau confessed.

Ellen looked at him intently and smiled. 'I'll be there too, Beau, don't worry.'

She leant over and gave him a long, supportive hug and felt his tears as he embraced her. She held him for some time as he grieved deeply, knowing she was providing some comfort for him in the absence of his family.

Beau and Ellen had a night to spare in Wellington before they flew off to Auckland the next day. They decided to have dinner in the city that night and it became a celebration of Leon's life. Ellen bought a bottle of Champagne and tried to make the dinner fun and light-hearted. The evening was intertwined with funny stories of Leon as a young man as Beau reminisced about his brother. Ellen had the intuition to allow him to talk, knowing the healing power of sharing with others when grieving. Both were exhausted, still recovering from the physical exertion of the trip, so at her suggestion they turned in early.

'See you in the morning, Beau. I'll pick you up in a cab at around 8 am.'

'Great Ellen, sleep tight.'

They kissed each other on the lips for the first time and lingered just long enough for it to be more than a goodnight kiss. They looked at each other and with a grin, Beau turned and walked up the stairs of his apartment building without looking back.

The next morning, Ellen arrived on time. They shared a cab to Wellington airport and boarded a plane bound for Auckland. Beau was excited about meeting his mother later that day. I hope she's coping all right, he thought. He had never felt such a desire to be with her. After all, she had just lost her son and he knew how much she must need him right now. He also found himself thinking more and more about Ellen and how much he enjoyed her company. He was confused given she had displayed an interest the night before. However, today she was showing no real affection towards him. Is this just a deep friendship? he wondered. She always seems so pleased to see me. Perhaps I'm reading too much into it. She's obviously driven by her work and she may not have room for anything else. Beau fluctuated between these thoughts and then back to Liz. He felt guilty about wondering how another woman felt about him.

Beau booked into the same hotel complex where Ellen was staying. He booked a family suite with two bedrooms for his mother and Scott. He'd picked up his additional luggage and unpacked. He had no specific timeframe for how long he would stay in Auckland beyond that. After arranging to have dinner with Ellen and his family that evening, he waited for his mother to arrive with Scott from the airport. It was around 2 pm and the doorbell rang. Beau opened the door and saw his mother's angelic face. He fell into her arms. The two embraced for a considerable time, emotions overflowing, before Beau became aware that Scott was standing by, waiting to embrace him as well. Scott, who also had tears in his eyes, gave him a heartfelt hug.

'Mum, I can't tell you how glad I am to see you.'

'You look like you've lost some weight, Beau.'

He chuckled at the observation. Even at his age she was still mothering him. I guess it never stops, he thought.

The three sat around the patio overlooking Auckland Harbour admiring the cruise ship moored at the dock not far from their apartment balcony, and the many majestic sailing boats gliding across the harbour. An extensive marina lay off to the left where hundreds of boats were bobbing around waiting for their owners' attention. Beau, his mum and Scott spent the next hour sharing stories of Leon. He could not help but admire his mother's capacity to put perspective on life, even in her darkest hour. It was a great comfort to him that she was coping well, although obviously still in shock and grieving.

Beau changed the subject. 'I met a friend on the trip, Mum. He's taking me out on a yacht sailing the harbour for the day if you would like to join us? I'm sure he wouldn't mind. He's a lawyer here in Auckland.'

'That sounds wonderful, Beau. We'd love a day on the harbour. I know how healing the water can be for you and that sounds like a great way to spend some time. It truly is a magnificent harbour, isn't it?'

'Absolutely it is. They held the America's Cup yacht races here. By the way, I met a fascinating woman, an American. I've asked her to join us for dinner this evening if that's okay?'

'Of course it is, Beau. Any friend of yours is a friend of ours. I look forward to meeting her.'

'Her name is Ellen and she's a Doctor of Philosophy and a psychologist. She studies the history of human evolution,' he added.

'My goodness, I hope we can keep the conversation interesting enough for her,' his mother joked.

'She's a very down-to-earth lovely lady and quite the conversationalist.'

'I'm only joking,' she added. 'I'm sure she's delightful.'

After a pause, Beau asked the question that had been on his mind since she had called to tell him of Leon's passing. 'Mum, I need to know, what did Dad and Kerry Weir fall out over? Why weren't the Weirs, including Liz, at Leon's funeral? They've been an important part of our lives since I was born.'

She sat and looked at him for some time. Bowing her head, she took a deep breath and said, 'Liz has taken a domestic violence order out against you, Beau. She claims that when you came home from Hobart, you were drunk and struck her across the face in a fit of rage.'

Beau stared at his mum in disbelief. Shaking his head, he could not speak. Eventually, he blurted out, 'What the fuck?'

'We know the truth, Beau. You came to us that next day and told us what had gone down between her and Damion. I knew she was of low morals, but this is taking it to a new level, even for her.'

Beau was reflective. 'She will do anything to protect her name in the upper circles of society. I should have seen this coming.'

'You can't predict what people are capable of when backed into a corner, Beau. They will always surprise you.'

'What about Damion? He was there. He knows the truth.'

'He's been going along as usual. Remember, it's only her side of the story that's getting any traction. It spread like wildfire in her shallow community and they rushed to her side to support her. They would believe anything she fed them. She is after all the princess of the bunch.

'Damion came to Leon's funeral, as you would expect him to,' she continued. 'It was as if nothing was wrong. It was part of their strategy to put people off the scent. It backfired on them though. They had no idea that you had told your father what went down the night you came back from Hobart. Your father bailed him up and a very ugly and quite public argument took place where Damion pleaded his innocence. Of course, your dad would have none of it and unceremoniously kicked him off the property.'

Beau just sat there trying to take it all in.

'And what of Dad and Kerry?'

'As soon as your dad heard the rumour going around from one of his clients about you striking Liz, he drove straight over to Kerry's place. Obviously, he was furious and told Kerry about Liz and Damion. Kerry accused him of protecting you and said you were a chip off the old block. Then of course your father did exactly what he shouldn't have done. As I understand it, Kerry ended up on the driveway with a bloody nose. So that was that, the end of a lifelong relationship between two great mates. And sadly, it was all over a lie.'

'That's terrible, Mum. What a monumental mess. I'm so sorry you guys were dragged into all of this.'

'It's fine, Beau. It's not your fault. I'm sort of glad you found this out about her before it was too late.'

Beau sat bewildered and a little numb as his mum, changing the subject, spent the afternoon sharing the details of Leon's funeral. He had many questions he needed answered so that he could get a clear picture in his mind of the day. What was Leon dressed in? What was the coffin like? Was he cremated or buried? Who was at the funeral and the wake?

His mum was prepared for his questions and thought it important to fill in all the missing information he needed to know in order to feel a part of it.

Later that evening, Beau, his mother and Scott were seated at one of Auckland's better restaurants when Ellen arrived. Beau was taken by her beauty. She had obviously gone to some trouble as she was wearing makeup, a slinky black dress and high heels. He found himself wondering where she had got this ensemble from. She had been living out of a bag for years, trekking through remote areas. He was captivated by her every move as she approached the table.

She was obviously pleased at his reaction and prompting a compliment, asked, 'Do you like it, Beau? I picked it up this afternoon in the city.'

'Like it? I love it,' he responded, nodding his approval. He stood up and gave her a twirl and a big hug. Then he turned to introduce her to his mum and Scott. His mother rose from her side of the table and walked around to embrace Ellen in a hug reserved for special friends. They separated and seemed to gaze into each other's eyes for some time, acknowledging some form of ancient connection. Barbara broke the silence by saying, 'I'm so pleased to meet you, Ellen. I feel we have a lot in common.'

'We have one thing in common, there is no doubt,' Ellen said. 'We both adore your magnificent son.'

The two chuckled and Barbara light-heartedly added, 'He has his moments.'

Beau was stunned by Ellen's comment. Scott stood up from his chair and politely shook Ellen's hand. 'It's a great pleasure to meet you, Ellen. I understand you've been supporting Beau during a difficult time. We appreciate it very much.'

'Oh, I haven't done much, Scott, but thank you.'

They sat down and Beau and Ellen enjoyed sharing some of the adventures they had experienced during their trip. Beau encouraged Ellen to talk more of her work and philosophies on human development, which he knew would be of great interest to his mother.

'Mum is a bush psychologist, Ellen. She's the one we all go to in the family for advice.'

'Don't underestimate the wisdom that exists in families, Beau, particularly if it comes from someone as aware as your mother, based on what I've learnt from our conversations.'

'Why thank you, Ellen, I appreciate your comments. I'm just a simple person who has had an interest in people and why we do the things we do. I've never pursued it academically though.'

'Academia has its limitations,' Ellen said. 'I can assure you, I've learnt more from my life experiences and meeting amazing people from all over the world than I've ever done out of a book.'

'Interesting you should say that,' Scott said. 'Barbara and I initially got together after meeting each other on a retreat. I'm a writer focusing on most things to do with business. The real stories are the personal journeys of people, their sacrifices and motivations. That's where the intrigue and the human interest stories are.'

'I could not agree more, Scott. Most of my writing comes from my interviews with interesting people who are leaders of indigenous communities. It's fascinating to learn of their rituals and spiritual beliefs, tapping in to their wisdom, which is evident in the way they live day to day. Their beliefs have been passed down through generations and they're untainted by modern society. That's what I'm most interested in and what has driven me to be away for so many years travelling the world.'

'I would love to read some of your work one day, Ellen. Have you found the secrets to life yet?' she asked humorously.

'No, not yet, although I feel I'm closing in.' Ellen smiled. 'The one thing that has become increasingly evident to me is that we create more of our life's experiences than we know, and we are all connected to one another in some mysterious way. This is the one true constant in all my research.'

'We are simply energy after all,' Barbara added. 'Are we not?'

'That we are,' Ellen said, looking at Beau and smiling. 'That we are.'

As the evening ended, Beau kissed Ellen goodnight, as did Barbara and Scott. He promised to call her the next day to arrange a lunch before his mum and Scott returned to Australia.

'By the way, Ellen, Cameron is taking us sailing in the next day or so. Are you up for it?'

'Give me a call. I should be able to work it into my schedule,' she said with a smile.

Once Ellen had left, his mum asked, 'Where did you find her, Beau? She's an absolute delight. Beautiful, smart, funny, and I think she likes you,' she added with a grin.

'That's just what I need, more women and relationship issues, Mum. I'm here in New Zealand to try and get away from my troubles, not create more.'

'Just goes to show, you can't leave your problems behind, Beau, they will just follow you.'

Beau knew his mother was half-joking although there was some truth in her comments. The trip had given him space and time; however, his problems were still there.

*

Completely at home and exhilarated, Beau was at the helm of Cameron's beautiful fifty-foot yacht, *Synergy*, standing at forty-five degrees with the wind in his hair. A gentle fifteen-knot breeze was blowing down the harbour as the yacht glided through the deep inky-blue waters. Ellen sat beside him enjoying the clear blue skies and a perfect day chatting with Barbara and Scott. Cameron and his girlfriend Leah were on the foredeck changing the smaller jib sail for a larger headsail.

'Bring her up into the wind, Beau, and I'll drop this sail now,' Cameron said.

'Will do, Cam.' Beau steered *Synergy* up into the wind.

'That's perfect, Beau, you can lay her off again and we should get some more speed out of this bigger sail.'

'She's picked up already, Cam. We're cruising along at nine knots effortlessly.'

'That's great. You can head out towards the mouth of the harbour. That should be a great direction for us and it'll give us a good look at the rest of the harbour.'

Beau gestured for Ellen to take the helm, which she did without hesitation.

After mentoring her for a while, he commented, 'I see you've done this before.'

'I've had many sailing opportunities in the last five years in some very remote places. I must say, I've developed a great love of the ocean and so I grab any opportunity to spend time sailing. There's such peace and tranquillity gliding through the water under a gentle breeze. It keeps me in touch with my inner self.'

'I feel exactly the same way, Ellen. Sometimes, the clearest thoughts come to me when I'm connected to the boat and the water. In some strange way, it brings me right back to my centre, as if I've come home to myself.'

'Then you should trust that about yourself, Beau, and do it often. I find that most of us wander the Earth not grounded and not in touch with our inner knowing, our inner self, *doing* life not *living* life. When you find what brings you back to yourself, you should trust that knowing and make it a part of your life.'

'That's why Scott and I live perched on the side of a mountain, Ellen,' Barbara chimed in. 'We have this amazing sanctuary in the Blue

Mountains where I feel totally connected to all that surrounds me. For Beau and his father, it's always been the ocean.'

'Each to their own I guess, Barbara. It's definitely an individual thing. Your sanctuary sounds absolutely amazing.'

'We would love for you to come and spend some time with us, Ellen.' Barbara noted Beau's interest in her reply.

'I would love that too. It'll need to be on my next trip Down Under though. I'm heading back to the States in the next week or so.'

Barbara looked genuinely disappointed and saw that Beau looked at Ellen as if he was learning of her plans for the first time.

He had known she would be leaving, but not so soon, and he was confused, sad and elated all at the same time. He was grateful to be at this place at this time, enjoying a perfect day with his family and newfound friends. He could not help thinking, however, about Ellen and the potential for her to drift out of his life as quickly as she had entered it.

They enjoyed a magnificent day, which culminated in a beautiful fresh seafood lunch provided by Cam and Leah. As the day drifted on and the light began to fade, Cam guided *Synergy* into her mooring and tied up next to a magnificent old ketch, *Orpheus*, moored at the end of the dock. She was majestic, from a bygone era, beautifully restored and maintained. At a hundred feet long, she was imposing, oozing class and no doubt harbouring the secrets of many great passages past.

'Have a look at her,' Beau remarked enviously.

'Wow, that's *Orpheus*!' Ellen said. 'She's the yacht I'm travelling back to America on.'

Beau looked at her in disbelief.

'You're going back to the US on that?'

'I sure am. I've only seen a photo of her before this. She spends every second season out here in charter and then travels back to Florida to do a season there. Her owner lives aboard and he loves travelling the world. He gets passengers for a low fare to help him crew her to each destination. I heard about her from a friend of mine in Florida who travelled to New Zealand on her three years ago. I've timed the whole past year to make sure I'm here for her return journey. There are some remote South Pacific islands we'll pass on the way, which are of great interest to me.'

'That would be an amazing trip to do,' Beau said, lost in some distant dream of sailing the South Pacific.

'What's stopping you from going, Beau?' asked Barbara.

Beau turned and looked at his mother with his mouth agape.

'Are you serious? I can't just drop my life and wander off for months on end.'

'Can't you?' his mum challenged.

Beau stood and looked for a long time directly into his mother's eyes. He realised she was serious, and challenging him to explore the possibility without dismissing it offhand. Ellen sat quietly with a grin on her face.

'No, I can't. I mean, how would I make that happen? There would be so much to organise. What about the firm? I have this mess with Liz to sort out.'

He sat down next to Ellen and stared at *Orpheus*, at her sleek timber lines and wooden masts built in the tradition of the great ketches of the past. 'It would be great,' he said aloud, although talking to himself.

'If you want to make it happen, I'm happy to chat with the skipper,' suggested Ellen. 'I've Skyped with him a few times now and I'm aware that he's always looking for crew. With your background and experience, you would be a great asset on the trip.'

'You're all mad!' Beau said.

'Perhaps we are,' responded Barbara, laughing. 'Opportunities come and go in life. Very few people have the courage to seize them.'

With that, Ellen climbed onto the wharf and before Beau knew what was happening, she returned on board *Synergy* with a tall, lean, suntanned man in his late forties who had shoulder-length blond hair.

'Beau, this is Rick Connor, owner and skipper of *Orpheus*,' she announced.

'It's great to meet you, Beau,' said Rick in a broad American accent. 'I hear you might be thinking about joining our little venture back to the US?'

'Well, not really, Rick. I'm being coerced into it by this motley bunch.'

'From what I understand, you've done a fair bit of blue-ocean sailing. I could use a man like you on this trip. I have a young first mate, Bobby, who is with me all the time; however, he's lacking maturity. We're short on experienced crew. We need some additional skippering experience, particularly when the rough weather sets in. I'd appreciate it if you would seriously think about it. Part of the reason I haven't left yet is that I've been trying to recruit someone with experience. We're one sailor short of what is ideal to make this passage comfortable. Someone who can help skipper the yacht, take some shifts off Bobby and me and provide support if something happens to either of us.'

'Right, well thanks for the offer, Rick, I'll definitely give it some thought.' Beau was still in disbelief he was having this conversation.

'Let me know, Beau. If we're to catch the seasonal winds, we need to head out no later than first thing next Friday morning, so you've got five days to come on board. Great to meet you all.' Rick doffed his cap and returned to *Orpheus*, leaving Beau with much to contemplate.

'Beau, you'd be crazy not to take up his offer,' Cam said. 'I'd do anything to go on a trip like that.'

'Why don't you go then, Cam?'

'Over my dead body,' Leah replied quickly before Cam could answer.

Laughing and gesturing towards Leah, Cam replied, 'There's your answer.'

Beau looked at Ellen and perhaps for the first time, seriously contemplated the concept of dropping everything and embarking on the trip of a lifetime on *Orpheus*. 'What do you think, Ellen? Do you want me to come?'

'I don't think it's fair of me to answer that, Beau. You have a lot going on in your life and only you can decide what's best for you. Any comment I make may influence your decision and I don't want to do that.'

Beau looked at Barbara and inwardly cursed her for suggesting the idea in the first place. 'Why did you even mention the possibility of me going on the trip, Mum? You know how long I've dreamt of doing an extended sailing trip across the South Pacific.'

'Exactly, Beau, so why do you ask why I suggested it? One thing is for sure. It seems you're creating what you need in your life quite rapidly at the moment,' she commented as she turned and looked at Ellen. 'Most people don't understand that life's circumstances are born of their own creation. They ignore what is plain to see right in front of them. They choose ordinary instead of extraordinary and live a life unfulfilled, often following someone else's dream.'

Beau knew his mother was loading him up now given their conversation at her home in the Blue Mountains regarding his father's influence in his life.

The group said their goodbyes and Beau thanked Cam and Leah for a great day. He arranged to call Ellen the next day, without making any commitment about what he might do. He felt more confused than ever.

'Seems like you have a lot to consider,' suggested Scott as he put his arm around Beau's shoulder. Beau chuckled nervously and turned to take one last look at *Orpheus* before leaving the marina precinct.

*

'Have you heard from Beau?' Damion asked Liz as he handed her a cup of coffee.

'Not since he left a message on my voicemail. He was asking about the disagreement between Jack and Dad.'

'Disagreement? More like world war three,' he said, laughing. 'Does he know what you've done? The domestic violence order I mean?'

'He didn't seem to, although that was a while ago now.'

'Did he mention if he was coming home anytime soon?'

'No, he actually said he might stay for a while longer in New Zealand. His mum and Scott were heading over to spend time with him. He wasn't sure when he'd be back.'

'You're going to have to tell him what you've done and about us moving in together, Liz. The sooner we get this out in the open, the better for all concerned.'

'I know, babe, I'll tell him but it has to be face to face. I have to control his reaction.'

'He's going to be absolutely pissed at you, Liz. I must say, I just don't feel right about this concocted story.'

'I get that. You don't have the killer instinct, do you? How are you going to make it as a barrister?' she taunted. 'Promise me you'll back me up on this. You can't mention that you were here. The whole point is that he made up the story about you and me to cover up his abuse.'

Damion just nodded. He was sick to his stomach. There was no one else he would do this for. The things we do for love, he thought, knowing it went against every fibre in his body.

'Are you sure you're still keen for me to move in with you? Previously, you were concerned it was too soon. I worry that you're still concerned about what people will say about us after getting together so soon after your split with Beau. Those socialites you hang with.'

'They will all be supportive of me, don't worry about that. I'll see to it. I'm the abused woman. Everyone will understand that I took comfort in the arms of a lifelong friend. Don't worry. I can spin it so that we look like the victims here. There's probably not an influential person in Sydney who won't be appalled at what's been going on.'

'I guess so,' lamented Damion, compromised by his unconditional love for her. 'I do love this place, Liz, and I can't wait to live here with you.'

'I can't wait either, babe,' said Liz, snuggling into Damion's arms and curling up next to him.

'I worry what your family's reaction will be towards me though. Your father is a great friend of Jack's and he's going to be as pissed at me as Jack is.'

'After I called my father the other day, I'm sure that friendship is over. From what Mum said, they had a very heated discussion. In any case, I've got Daddy wrapped around my little finger. Don't worry about him. Mum is the one to worry about. I suspect she has some doubts about my story. Remember, she watched Beau grow up and knows him inside out. She was extremely fond of him and she's the one who brought us together from a young age. She was devastated when I told her. I saw the look on her face when I told her he struck me. She hasn't said anything though. She needs to believe my story in order to save face. She's so obsessed about having the perfect family in the eyes of the Sydney elite.'

'As long as we have each other, babe, none of that matters.'

Damion leant down and embraced Liz, kissing her passionately. Just then, there was a loud knock at the door. The pounding continued as Liz answered it. The imposing figure of Jack Sterling was standing in the doorway, looking extremely agitated. He demanded to know when Beau was coming back. Damion stepped towards Jack in a gesture of support for Liz. Jack, in his deep thundering voice, threatened, 'Stay out of my way, Damion. You're the cause of this monumental fucked-up mess!'

Damion knew the truth and could not defend the accusation other than to say lamely, 'I don't know what you're talking about.' He then took a step back, as most would when Jack was in this kind of mood.

Liz was crying now and pleaded, 'Jack, you don't know what I've been through.'

'Don't give me that bullshit. You've been a lying, conniving, spoilt little bitch your whole life. Don't forget, I know you. I've told your father as much. Now, when is Beau coming back?'

'I promise I have no idea when he's coming back. He left a message saying he might stay a few more weeks in New Zealand.'

'Well, he's not returning my calls. You're both responsible for driving my son away. He's needed here, for work, and his mother needs him.'

'Your relationship with your son has nothing to do with me, Jack. That's for you to sort out.'

Growing cocky, Damion said, 'I suggest you look at yourself if you want answers as to why he's not talking to you, and if you can't be civil, you'll need to leave.'

As he spoke, he stepped forward, as did Jack. 'You two fucking deserve each other,' Jack said, turning and leaving.

Damion slumped. 'Wow, that was intense,' he said, closing the door. He put his arms around Liz trying to calm her down. 'I guess he feels as though he's lost both of his sons at the same time. As much as he's a real prick, I feel a bit sorry for him. In any case, don't worry; you won't have to deal with him anymore.'

'We'll see,' Liz replied, looking concerned.

CHAPTER NINE
The Dilemma

Beau looked out of the window of the Qantas jet as it lifted off from Auckland airport. He turned to chat with his mum who was sitting next to him. Scott was in the aisle seat listening to their conversation.

'I still don't know what I'm doing, Mum.'

'What did you tell Ellen you were doing before you left this morning?'

'I didn't get a chance to talk with her. I went to her hotel room but she'd gone out for the day according to the front desk. She didn't answer her phone either.'

'I'm not surprised. She's a very ethical woman and she knows that it's not in your interests to influence you in any way at present. You still have a fiancée to sort out and a career to make some big decisions about. I doubt she'll discuss anything with you until you sort out the priorities in your life. Have you spoken to Liz recently?'

'I left a message on her phone a few days ago. She still hasn't called me back.'

'I doubt she's keen to talk to you, Beau. She made false accusations against you and you're the one person who knows the absolute truth.'

'There is another, Mum. Damion was there that night, although he would never admit it, the slimy so-and-so.'

'Have you spent much time contemplating your relationship? Despite what's gone on, is there anything you feel is worth saving?'

'Of course I've been contemplating it. I haven't slept much since all this has happened.'

'What are the thoughts that have kept you up, Beau?' his mum asked, digging deeper.

'I just can't believe my fiancée and my best friend could betray me like they did. And on top of that, for her to take out a domestic violence order against me, I don't even know who she is.'

'So, you've been kept up at night due to anger and resentment?'

'Well, wouldn't you be?' protested Beau.

'What about grieving the loss of her love and the potential loss of your dream of being together?' his mum challenged in an effort to bring some reality to his emotions and clarity to his feelings.

She had hit a nerve. Beau thought about what she had said. Was he actually rocked by their separation because of his love for her and the loss of their life together? Or was it more about the betrayal? Why wasn't he spending more time grieving the potential loss of his fiancée? He wondered what that told him about the depth of their relationship.

For the remainder of the trip to Sydney, there was silence between them all, even during the cab ride to the apartment where he was dropped off by his mum and Scott.

'Thanks for coming all the way to New Zealand, Mum. I really appreciate it. If I'd known I'd be back this soon, I would have come home to see you.'

'Don't worry about it, Beau. It was perfect. I also enjoyed meeting Ellen. The trip did Scott and me the world of good, even though it was rushed. I love you, Beau. You're my only boy now,' she said with tears streaming down her face, as she gently stroked his hair. 'Call me and chat when you have a chance.'

'I will, Mum.'

Beau gave his mum and Scott a lengthy and emotional embrace before watching them drive away, back to their home in the Blue Mountains.

He collected his bags and walked towards the entrance of the apartment with a sense of déjà vu. I wonder if that bastard is here, he thought, feeling the anger deep within. Reflecting on his mother's comments on the plane, he realised that he was more obsessed about Damion and Liz betraying him than he was about seeing Liz after the longest period they had been apart in many years. Interesting, he thought, as he climbed the stairs. Almost on cue, he could hear their voices coming from inside the apartment. Beau prepared himself for what he knew was inevitable. Damion and Liz together, in the apartment. The memories of the two of them entwined on the couch that fateful night came rushing back to him.

It was 2 pm on a magnificent day in Sydney. He put the key in the lock and saw the expansive apartment drenched in summer sunlight through its floor-to-ceiling glass walls reflecting off the glistening blue of Sydney Harbour. He walked across the living room towards the large patio. As if to confirm his knowing, he saw the familiar outlines of Damion and Liz sitting on the outdoor lounge facing the water. They were not yet aware of Beau's presence in the apartment and were laughing as they shared a glass of wine, with what appeared to be the remnants of lunch on the coffee table before them.

'Don't stop your fun on my account,' Beau announced as he entered the patio area and stood beside the couch facing the pair. 'It looks like you've been having a whale of a time.'

Liz was stunned and she stammered awkwardly, 'Beau, you're back.'

'That's right Liz, I'm back.'

'I thought you were away for another couple of weeks?'

'Seems to me we've been down this path before. Whenever I go away, Judas here just slips in to take my place.'

Damion looked ashamed and made no comment.

'There you go again, Damion, the disappearing man. You're the most gutless, spineless piece of work I've ever come across. That's right, piss off and crawl back to wherever you came from.'

Damion looked at Liz and shook his head. 'I can't leave you here with him, babe. He's clearly angry.'

'You're damn right I'm angry. By all means, hang around. I really would like to hear your story.'

'Beau, I have a domestic violence order against you. You shouldn't even be here.'

'What a fucking joke that is. I've done nothing but love and care for you our whole lives. How could you do this, Liz?'

'You gave me no choice when you went and blabbed to your folks. I told you we could work this through.'

'You had choices. But you took the path of lies and deceit to protect yourself.'

'I have a lot more to lose than you do, Beau. My reputation in society is all I have. You're talented. You've never cared what people think. You can get through this and rebuild.'

'I value my reputation as much as you do and I obviously value the truth more. I won't stop until I clear my name. Damion knows the truth,' Beau said, gesturing towards him. 'Or is he a part of this charade too?'

'He loves me, Beau. What more can I say?'

Damion stood sheepishly, remaining silent throughout the exchange.

'Nothing, Liz, you need say nothing,' Beau said. 'I'll get this overturned if it's the last thing I do. And you, you bastard,' he said, pointing accusingly at Damion, 'I'll put you on the stand as a hostile witness. Let's see if you're prepared to commit perjury and risk being disbarred. I'll destroy your career as a barrister by the time I'm finished with you.'

Damion looked at Liz, knowing Beau was right. He had more to lose than both of them if he kept up this charade. With a look of surrender, he pleaded, 'Enough, babe. This has to end. I've stayed silent, but I can't do this to him. You know how I've felt about this since you told me. He is, was, my best friend. I love you but I can't keep this lie going.'

Beau was stunned that Damion was taking a moral stand.

Liz, who had tears in her eyes, looked at Damion and knew in that moment that he was resolute. After what seemed to be an age, as she contemplated all options, she realised reluctantly that she could no longer continue with the lie she had set in motion. She turned and looked at Beau, then down towards her engagement ring. She twirled it around her finger as tears streamed down her face. Finally, she slid the magnificent diamond ring off and placed it in Beau's hand.

'So I guess that's it, Liz?' Beau said resignedly.

'Beau, I do love you and I'm so sorry I caused you so much pain. You know that's true. I'm just not in love with you. I'm in love with Damion and have been for a while. Please forgive me. I've made some poor decisions thinking everything was collapsing around me. Please try to understand. This was not planned, it just happened. I'm so sorry,' she repeated, sobbing uncontrollably. 'You and I have known each other since we were children. We've never been with other partners. You have to admit we're hardly passionate lovers. You're more like a brother to me. I just didn't think we were destined to spend our lives together as man and wife.'

Beau knew the truth of what she was saying. His animosity drifted away and gave way to his own truth. 'I've been doing a lot of thinking as well, Liz. I've been wondering why I haven't been as upset as I should be about the loss of our relationship. What's eating me up more is the betrayal by two of my closest friends and then the lie you told to cover it up. I think that says a lot about us and the type of relationship we've developed. We want very different things in life, Liz, and we've become very different people without even noticing it. I doubt we could ever make each other truly happy.'

Beau surprised himself with these honest comments from the heart. They appeared to release him in some way from the anger he felt and the undeniable realisation that they were not destined for a future together. Somehow, subconsciously, he had been pushing her away for a long time. It's probably not surprising that she fell into the arms of another, he thought. As the tears continued to flow, he reached for her and gave her a heartfelt hug. Then he grabbed her by the shoulders and held her at arm's length, looking into her eyes. 'We shared some great times, Liz, and I thank you for that.'

He leant forward and gently kissed her on the cheek. As they separated, Beau said, 'I truly wish you every happiness, Liz. I guess at the end of the day you were the brave one who took action and forced us to confront the truth before it was too late. I thank you for that. You've awakened me to the possibilities in my life, a life which on reflection has been operating on remote control, living to other people's expectations and not following my own dreams.'

'What are you going to do now, Beau?' Liz asked compassionately.

'Well, I think I have an interesting discussion with my father ahead, and then, who knows.'

Damion, still shattered by the loss of his friendship with Beau, added, 'Good luck, Beau.'

'Perhaps one day I'll experience the type of love that you must feel for her which made you betray a lifelong friend,' Beau said in response. 'For now, I just can't come to terms with it.'

Damion nodded, knowing there was no point in further discussion.

Liz did not try to defend Damion.

'I'll let my father know the truth, Beau. Perhaps he can repair his relationship with Jack. And then there's my mother…' Her voice trailed away.

'Liz, I'm going to leave that one up to you. After all, it's your socialite connections who feed off this type of scandal. It's best if you craft the message in a way that minimises the damage. Try the truth. It may surprise you.'

Liz nodded with a look of hopelessness, contemplating the difficult conversations ahead.

'I'll get Mum and Scott to come and grab the rest of my things and have them moved to their place, Liz. It may take a few weeks though.'

'That's fine, Beau. They can stay here as long as you need them to.'

'Thanks,' Beau said, grabbing his bags. Then he looked around the extensive apartment as if to etch the memory in his mind before walking out the front door for the last time.

He stood on the footpath and looked back at the apartment where he had spent the last few years of his life. He felt an unfamiliar calmness and knew that he was at last following his own path. No fiancée and nowhere to live. Oh well, he thought, laughing to himself, feeling freer than he could ever remember. He backed his car out of the parking space and headed towards his father's home. Beau had no idea what he was going to say to his father, probably because he was still struggling about leaving the firm after having spent his entire life around it or working in it. I have a well-paid, secure future ahead of me. I'm a very good lawyer. Am I really going to throw it all away? Is this just some sort of life crisis? Can I really walk away from it all? These thoughts kept spinning around in his head as he ran every scenario over and over. But I hate doing law, he thought.

One thing he knew for certain. No one turned their back on the great Jack Sterling and expected any level of compassion if they ever changed their mind. Jack had a great capacity to cut people from his life without emotion. Beau knew that being Jack's son would not exempt him from the same treatment. He had seen him do it to Leon at a time when his son had needed him the most.

As Beau approached his father's estate with its massive electric gates and security cameras, his anxiety increased. He found himself parked across the road just sitting, still deep in thought. He could hear his mother's advice echoing in his mind. Imagine each scenario into the future, Beau, and place yourself in that vision. One decision will feel light and the other heavy. Trust your knowing.

His final moment of clarity came when he tried to picture his life as a lawyer under his father's rule, and he felt heavy and depressed at the vision. He was not sure how long he had been there but noticed that the afternoon sun was low in the sky. As if a bolt of lightning had hit him, he felt a wave of urgency to follow his new path. That's it, it's over. I can't keep living in my father's world. I must find the courage to end it now. He drove forward and pressed the security voice activation on the gate and looked towards the camera. The gate slid open. He drove slowly up the long driveway which curved around in front of the house, its majestic pillars reaching up three storeys high. In all its grandeur, the house was a statement of Jack's success. As Beau approached the grand front entrance, the massive double cedar timber doors opened and he was greeted by Carla, his family housekeeper. She had lived with them since he was a boy.

'Beau, my precious Beau!' she shouted, excitedly dragging him to her ample bosom for a huge welcoming hug. 'Where have you been, my Beau?' she asked. 'Come in, come inside. I've been so worried about you. Your poor brother, it's so tragic. How are you?'

Carla had been a significant part of Beau's upbringing and more of a surrogate mother than servant. Of Italian heritage, she had a gregarious personality. 'Beau, have you eaten? You look so skinny. Let me prepare some food for you,' she offered, ushering him towards the kitchen. 'You need to eat something to keep your strength up.'

'No thanks, Carla, I probably won't be here for long. I just came to have a chat with Dad and then I'll be on my way.'

'He needs more than a chat, that father of yours. He's been so cranky lately. This morning I told him, "Snap out of it or I'll give you a good slap."'

'You would be the only one to get away with that,' Beau remarked.

'He doesn't scare me, Beau. He's all bluff and full of hot wind. If you knew my father, you'd know that yours is a pushover,' she said, laughing as she walked away towards the kitchen. 'At least let me get you a cup of tea.'

'Yes, fine thanks, Carla,' Beau called after her with a loving smile on his face.

No point in saying no anyway, he thought.

'Your father is in his study!' she yelled from some distance away.

'Thanks!' Beau called, and turned to walk down the long hallway with its elegant runner stretched out in front of him, running the length of the house. The home was of grand proportions and he fondly remembered running down these hallways as a boy, always in trouble for doing so, he recalled.

He tried to steel himself for what was about to unfold. Beau was now clear that law was not his destiny and he could think of nothing more exciting than to venture off into the South Pacific on a one-hundred-foot yacht. Particularly a yacht with Ellen aboard, he thought in a surprising admission. Beau had to acknowledge that he had some feelings for her although at this stage, he was not certain they were reciprocated. He stood at the closed door to his father's study, a place he knew well. Familiar feelings came flooding back to him of the many meetings in the study with his father, usually when he had done something to displease him. Perhaps a poor report card from school, or for some misbehaviour during the day. He felt like a young boy in his father's presence. I'm not a boy now, he thought. I'm a fully grown man with my own life to live. I can no longer live under my father's shadow doing the things he wants me to do. He clenched his fists to consolidate his resolve, then knocked firmly on the door.

'Come in,' came the familiar deep thundering voice from inside the study. Beau opened the door, closed it behind him and moved towards the grand desk his father had imported from England many years before. Solid mahogany with pearl inlays and large round turned legs gave the desk an imposing feel. The chairs in front of Jack's desk were much lower than his. This was deliberate. Jack liked his guests to be at a disadvantage height-wise. This was another one of his little power plays. Beau went around to his father's side of the desk and gave him a quick hug, which was superficial at best.

'Thank God you're back, Beau. Why the hell didn't you contact me? In any case, let's put that behind us. Have you been to see that conniving bitch of a fiancée of yours?'

'Yes I have, and it's over. She will withdraw the domestic violence order and let her parents know the truth. Damion finally grew a spine and said he couldn't continue with the lie. Not sure what she would have done otherwise, but she knew she was in a fight if she didn't set things right.'

'Well done, son,' Jack said.

'My reputation was at stake. I don't take that lightly.'

'Good then. Speaking of your reputation, now that you've got your little adventure out of your system, let's talk about getting you back to work. There's a mountain of cases to climb, one in particular I want you to handle personally. Con Materia, the New South Wales politician, called me a week ago. His daughter has been caught in possession of drugs and her case comes up in a few weeks. We'd have him in our back pocket if we can get her off. I want you to find a way and I don't care what it takes.'

Jack reached for the file on his desk and threw it in front of Beau.

'Dad, listen to me,' Beau protested as his father kept talking without even looking up from his files. 'Dad, for God's sake, listen to me for once. I'm not coming back to work.'

'Don't be ridiculous, of course you're coming back to work. You're a damn good lawyer and my successor. Under what possible circumstances would you not return to the firm? Your life is in your hands. Your future is laid out in front of you. Do you realise the opportunities that I've given you?'

'Dad, I appreciate everything you've done for me in my life. I know that you've only wanted the best for me. But you've got to let go. We aren't the royal family, for God's sake. There's no requirement for me to succeed you just because you took over from your father. I've had a massive realisation over the past few weeks culminating in an undeniable truth. I've been living other people's life choices, not my own, for most of my life. It's time now for me to make decisions based on my life's purpose and journey. The truth is, Dad, I hate law. I hate the hypocrisy of finding loopholes in the system to benefit guilty people because they pay a sizeable fee. That's not me.'

'Listen to yourself, Beau. You're not making any sense. Who put this nonsense in your head? Your mother, I bet!'

'Leave her out of this. She has nothing to do with my decision. The only thing she's ever done is encourage me to follow my own path. Something I should have realised years ago. I've just come from a discussion with Liz and we've decided to separate for good.'

'What are you saying? Have you gone stark-raving mad? All in one day, you're ending your commitment to marry Liz and resigning your career? I'm seriously concerned about you. Just stop and think for a moment. This fling between Liz and Damion will pass. You two are destined to be together. I know some people who can help you get your head straight.'

'Dad, the people you would send me to will only do your bidding. I'm thinking clearly for the first time in my life. I love you with all my heart and I always will, but I have to follow my own path now.'

Beau now saw something he had never seen before in his life. His father had sunk back in his chair looking defeated with a well of tears in his eyes. He was decidedly uncomfortable with his emotion and was struggling unsuccessfully to control it. Beau walked around to his father, grabbed him by the arm and helped him to stand. He wrapped his arms around him and held him tightly. At first, his father tried to separate. Beau held the hughard until he could feel his father surrender in his arms. It was as if their roles were reversed. They both started to sob uncontrollably. His father amid the tears declared, 'I feel as though I'm losing both of my sons.'

'You're not losing me, Dad. You will never lose me. You've been my hero my whole life and now it's time for me to find my own way out from underneath your shadow. I hope to make you proud.'

'I'm so proud of you already, my boy,' his father declared as he pulled Beau closer to his chest. Jack knew deep in his heart that Beau had followed his predestined path without question, out of respect for his father. Deep down, he was proud that his son was standing up for his own independent future, rather than staying trapped in the family legacy. 'I'm so sorry about Leon. I let him down badly and that's something I have to live with the rest of my life,' he said, barely holding back more tears.

Beau thought this show of emotion and declaration from his father was probably the first time in his life that he had truly got to feel the man behind the mask that was Jack Sterling. As they separated, they held each other by the arms and looked directly into each other's eyes. Beau saw a softness that was unfamiliar to him in his father's eyes. It was a look of pure love.

'Well, if you've made your decision and it's final, Beau, I guess there's no point in trying to talk you out of it. The truth is, I will miss you greatly working alongside me at the firm. The thought of not spending each day with you in the heat of battle breaks my heart. You're my best friend.'

'Exactly, Dad, and you are mine. Our relationship is changing. It's the end of our old relationship and the birth of a new relationship that can only grow stronger. The old relationship was destined for failure, probably creating resentment that could have lasted a lifetime.'

'I've done resentment and look where it got Leon,' his father said, shaking with emotion.

After finally gathering some composure, his father suggested they move to the large lounge chairs in front of the empty fireplace where they had shared many a night playing cards or scrabble.

'Will you join me in a glass of red wine?'

'Certainly,' Beau agreed enthusiastically, never one to pass on a glass of his father's wine.

Jack prided himself on the extensive wine cellar he had acquired over a very long period.

'I have a 1998 Grange Hermitage at perfect room temperature ready to go.'

'Wow, that's a $700 bottle of wine, are you sure?'

'If you're not going to be around to help me drink it in the future, then we might as well drink it now, son. When are you heading off on your next adventure?'

'That's one of the reasons I needed to see you tonight, Dad. I have the opportunity to embark on a passage across the South Pacific on a one-hundred-foot ketch called *Orpheus*. She's a classic, Dad. You would love her. She's leaving Auckland for America on Friday this week.'

'Wow, that soon? I'm a little envious of your newfound adventurous spirit. A part of me would love to have done something similar at your age but I guess I didn't have the opportunity or courage to leave my father and the Sterling legacy I inherited. I've missed out on a lot in building this life and sometimes the burden of leadership and responsibility can be restrictive rather than liberating.'

Beau knew his father's decision to follow the Sterling legacy was a choice; however, he felt he was finally having a truthful conversation with the man rather than the managing partner of Sterling and Finch. He had never seen him so vulnerable, speaking his truth without the façade. The pair sat together enjoying a truly world-class red, savouring every sip.

'Now, that is why it's worth $700 a bottle.' He was proud to be in a position in his life to afford such luxuries. 'What are you hoping to discover on this journey of yours, Beau?'

'Just recently, I've become excited about the prospect of understanding more about life's mysteries and seeking answers to some of the philosophical questions like, why are we here and what are we meant to be doing?'

'You're starting to sound like your mother with fairies at the bottom of the garden.'

Beau chuckled at his father's comment and followed with a further explanation. 'I met a fascinating woman in New Zealand call Ellen Hass. She's a Doctor of Philosophy and a psychologist who's travelling the world trying to link tribal history and the development of humankind to the ultimate quest for understanding human existence. She's searching for a bridge between our normal everyday life, our beliefs and behaviours, and the ultimate reason that we act and live the way we do. What I've realised, in spending some time with her, is that I have a similar desire to want to understand more.'

'Sounds like science-fiction to me, Beau.'

Beau knew his father would never embrace the concepts he was sharing. Jack often said, 'You're dead a long time staring at the lid so you may as well max it out know. When you're dead, that's it.' He had no belief in anything past the life he had.

'Well Dad, I have much to learn and much to discover. I'm probably not going to find my answers sitting in a courtroom.'

'You're more like your mother than I thought, Beau. All these years I've been trying to turn you into a hard-ass lawyer and you've harboured a desire to follow her journey into spirituality and all that unquantifiable bullshit.'

Even knowing the futility of it, Beau felt the need to defend his views. 'This is not airy-fairy stuff, Dad. Ellen explained that if you really look into some of the hard science that underpins our existence, like quantum physics, astronomy and pure mathematics, from the writings and discoveries of the greats including Einstein, Aristotle, Plato, Hermes, and many others, the explanations of our existence are there. I must admit to being completely fascinated by it and I can't think of anything else I would rather do. I guess you could say I've found an inspired path to follow and I trust my knowing that it's in my destiny to follow it.'

With that, Jack stood up in a gesture to end the conversation. Beau sensed he had lost interest in his son's newfound passion and had returned to his managing partner persona. He extended his hand to Beau to shake hands. Beau took his father's hands and pulled him towards his chest, wrapped his arms around him and hugged him once more. On this occasion, his father felt uncomfortable in the emotional embrace and firmly patted him on the back to bring the awkward moment to an end. Beau sensed the change in energy and said a heartfelt goodbye. 'I'll try and contact you as often as I can while I'm away, Dad; however, I'm not sure when that might be.'

'That would be great, son. You take care of yourself and don't forget to call your mother before you go.'

'Will do, Dad, I love you.'

Beau left the study and closed the study doors behind him. He felt overwhelmed by what had just transpired, reflecting on how vulnerable his father had been with him. As he walked back down the hallway, Carla grabbed him by the arm. 'What about your pot of tea, Beau? It's getting cold.'

'I have to go now, Carla. I won't have time for tea this evening, I'm sorry.'

'Then come here and give me a big hug before you go.'

Carla embraced him and he remembered all her hugs when he was growing up. 'You make sure you stay in contact, Master Beau.'

'I will, Carla, don't you worry. You'll be hearing from me real soon,' he said as he moved towards the door.

'I'd better,' she called after him in her familiar parental tone.

As he got into his car and drove down the driveway, he could not get the image out of his head of his father, as powerful and successful as he was, alone and broken, living an empty, loveless life.

After a few hours lost in his own thoughts while driving to the Blue Mountains, Beau drove up the steep driveway to his mother's home. He would spend the night with her and leave his car in the large shed at the back of the property. His mum and Scott greeted him at the door. 'I've got so much to tell you both.'

'Come on in, Beau, I can't wait to hear all about it.'

'I'll get you a glass of wine, Beau,' offered Scott, who took any opportunity to indulge.

'I've just come from sharing a bottle of Grange Hermitage 1998 with Dad.'

'I certainly can't match that, although I do have a very drinkable red that I can offer you.'

'That will be just fine, thanks Scott.'

Beau spent the evening sharing his insights with his mother and Scott and his amazing visit with his father. 'Mum, I want to thank you for helping me get to this point. Without you challenging me and giving me a prod, I doubt that I would be embarking on this journey tomorrow.'

'All I did was prompt you to examine your own truth. You're the one who has to decide your own path. I must say, I'm delighted that you've finally summoned the courage to confront your father and tell him what you need to do for yourself. That can't have been easy?'

'No, it wasn't easy, Mum, but a great gift came out of it. Dad became quite vulnerable and we shared a beautiful moment together as we embraced.'

'Oh, how wonderful for both of you, Beau. Your father has found it so difficult over his life to share emotion. To have a moment like that with him might open up a whole new level of connection.'

'I felt that already, Mum. In fact, it's quite sad that he's lived his life behind a stoic façade. He's pushed away love in order to maintain his bullish reputation, righteous and controlling. He admitted that he's missed out on a great deal.'

'That's a massive admission from him. Your father very rarely lets his guard down. It's one of the reasons I couldn't stay in a relationship with him.'

'I know, Mum. You're such an open loving person.'

'She sure is,' Scott chimed in, putting his arms around Barbara and giving her a short but passionate kiss.

The next morning, Barbara drove Beau to the airport to board an international flight back to Auckland. After a teary goodbye, he entered customs and turned to watch his mother walk away, not knowing when he would see her again. After settling in to the departure lounge area, he decided to call Ellen. He had not spoken to her since he'd left New Zealand a few days earlier. Why didn't she call me to check if I was joining her on the voyage? he wondered. With some trepidation, he rang her number. He was disappointed to get her message bank. Why isn't she answering? Damn, I desperately need to know if she still wants me along on the trip. Beau thought for a while and decided, no, I don't need to know. I'm going on the trip regardless. We are friends and that is all we are. I don't need to get into another relationship so soon after Liz. He berated himself for placing too much emphasis on how Ellen felt about him. He boarded the plane and for the next two hours, thought about the massive life changes he was undertaking. Have I gone mad? he contemplated, laughing to himself. So what, I will definitely have an adventure. His mind continued to drift to thoughts of Ellen, picturing her smile and recalling the great times they had already shared. Take it slowly, he counselled himself. If it's meant to be it will unfold in good time.

Beau landed at Auckland airport and after clearing customs, tried Ellen's number again.

'Ellen, it's Beau.'

'Beau! It's so great to hear your voice. Where are you?'

'I'm standing outside the International Airport in Auckland,' he said, unable to contain his enthusiasm.

'Really, so you're coming on *Orpheus?*'

'I sure am, Ellen, if Rick will still have me?'

'Rick is going to be so excited that you can make the trip. I think he was resigned to the fact that we would have to get underway without you. What about Liz, Beau? What have you decided about her?'

'Liz and I have decided to go our separate ways, Ellen. In fact, she was the one who raised it first. She's in love with Damion and that phase of my life is over.'

'That must have been incredibly difficult for you?'

'Yes and no. I guess on reflection we haven't had a close intimate relationship for many years. It's amazing how life goes by and the changes are so gradual, we don't notice that things are deteriorating until we look back in hindsight.'

'I'm glad you're joining us.'

Beau was delighted to hear the sincerity in her voice given the fears he had been harbouring. 'Not as glad as I am, Ellen. This is a dream come true for me. I've pictured this passage in my mind over and over again since I was young and first took to the ocean on a yacht.'

'This trip is no accident, Beau. The more you understand universal law, the more you'll realise that everything that comes to you, good and bad, is created by you. You manifested this journey over many years of intent. If you had given into your fears, you would have stayed stuck, looping in a relationship and a career you did not want.'

'Wow, I never thought of it like that. I can't wait to see you,' Beau said, hoping he did not sound too desperate.

'Come down to the boat as soon as you can, Beau. We leave first thing tomorrow morning.'

As Ellen hung up the phone, Beau went over the conversation in his mind, examining every inflection in her voice. She sounds excited that I'm coming, he thought. Then, when she hung up, it was a bit matter-of-fact. He spent the cab ride to Auckland Harbour running over the conversation in his mind, then dismissing it, only to revisit it.

'Come aboard, Beau,' Rick said in his American drawl, smiling broadly. 'So glad you could join us.'

He climbed the small ladder to the deck and the welcoming sight of Ellen met his gaze. She had obviously gone to some trouble to look nice for his arrival. She was wearing a very flattering sundress in bright tropical colours. He was secretly glad that she had made an effort and hoped that it was for him.

'Hi Ellen, you look wonderful,' he said as he embraced her.

'Beau, I've missed you,' she said, whispering in his ear during their embrace.

The two separated and looked into each other's eyes. There was no doubt now in Beau's mind that there were feelings between them and that they were reciprocated. He gave her a quick peck on the mouth to test the theory. He was not disappointed, as Ellen equally engaged in what was unmistakably a kiss with more intent than casual friends. Beau, deciding to play it cool, separated with a welcoming smile.

'I've so much to talk to you about, Ellen. I'm so excited about this trip.'

'I feel we have come together on this ship for a reason, Beau.'

'So do I,' responded Beau. 'Why didn't you call me though? I wasn't sure whether you wanted me on the trip or not.'

'I said before you left that I was not about to influence your decision regarding your career or Liz. I felt over the days before you left that there was a growing attraction between us and I didn't want to influence you in any way.'

'You would have to be the most ethical person, along with my mother, that I've ever come across,' Beau said with a smile.

'I'll take that as a compliment,' Ellen responded, returning the smile. 'Come below and I'll show you your accommodation,' she said excitedly as she turned towards the hatch.

'Right behind you,' said Beau, equally enthusiastic. It was as if they were two kids on the first day of school holidays.

Beau was allocated a hammock and a locker in the vast area below decks which, no doubt in days gone by, had been used for cargo. He noted that Ellen had a small cabin aft on the port side she shared with another girl. 'There are fifteen guests on board of varying ages and nationalities, including you now, and four crew,' Ellen advised as he placed his limited luggage under his hammock. 'I haven't got to know any of them yet.'

'On a long sea journey, I'm sure they'll all have an interesting story to tell,' Beau commented.

He made his way back on deck and was met by Skipper Rick, who introduced Beau to his first mate Bobby who looked like he was in need of a good meal. He was a scrawny youth, perhaps twenty-five, with scraggly blond sun-bleached hair and a skin colour consistent with a life in the sun. He did not appear too welcoming, nodding unenthusiastically and extending his hand.

'Bobby, it's great to meet you. I'm looking forward to sharing this experience,' Beau said.

'Just keep your eyes open, listen and learn and you'll be fine.'

Interesting response, Beau thought. Maybe he feels a little threatened by Rick's comments regarding my experience in ocean sailing.

'I'm just here to learn, Bobby, and I will appreciate anything you can show me.'

'Good then,' Bobby responded, shutting the conversation down. The rest of the afternoon, Beau familiarised himself with the ship. He had never been on an old ketch like *Orpheus*; however, the principles of sailing were the same. He followed the path of the ropes, the blocks, the sheets, and the sail tracks and before long he had a pretty good working understanding of the rigging and sails. He was looking forward to setting sail in the morning and experiencing the great ship at full sail. She was truly a majestic vessel, well-equipped for a deep blue-ocean passage.

As dawn broke the next day, and with a light breeze from the east, the deep throb of *Orpheus*' diesel engines signalled her departure. She slowly pulled away from the dock with nineteen souls aboard. Beau could not help but marvel at the sight of the city of Auckland as it faded into the distance. It finally disappeared behind them as they headed down the harbour towards the harbour mouth and open water.

The sun, now bright in the morning sky, created a shimmer on the swell as far as the eye could see, and Beau reflected on the massive life decisions he had made in the past week. It seemed surreal that he was standing on the deck of this historic ship, heading off on a new adventure.

CHAPTER TEN
The Passage

The big ketch cruised along, the increasing ocean swell rolling endlessly towards her. The day was pristine, still warm at this time of year. The cloudless sky blended with the blue ocean, giving the eerie feeling of an endlessly shifting horizon ahead. This would be a familiar sight over the coming weeks and months as *Orpheus* headed northeast on its course to the Panama Canal via the Cook Islands. Ellen would be exploring her work further in the Cook Islands. There were fifteen islands in the group, spread over thousands of kilometres of ocean.

Beau looked around the boat; all passengers and crew were on deck enjoying the magnificent day, soaking up the sun after leaving the New Zealand mainland. In scanning the group, he noticed that they were predominantly young, apart from a group in their forties to fifties. He thought their presence an unusual sight and wondered about their story.

'What a day, Beau. How good is this?' commented Ellen as she joined him at the bow. Beau was enjoying the familiar rise and fall of the swell and the distinctive salt air filling his nostrils as the salt spray mist drifted lightly on the wind.

'This is as good as it gets, Ellen, and there's no place I'd rather be.'

'Me either. I've been looking forward to this for a long time. There are really only a few short stops on our trip to the United States. The Cook Islands will be a great break for a week or so and then after a stop at Rurutu, we'll be off towards the Panama Canal and our final destination in Florida.'

'A lot of ocean miles between here and there,' Beau remarked. 'No doubt we'll get to know these people very well over that time.'

Ellen looked around the deck of *Orpheus* and noted the various groups gathered enjoying the day. 'Any time you confine a group of people to an environment like this for any length of time, you're definitely going to find out a lot about them, Beau,' she said.

'In all honesty, Ellen, it's one aspect of the trip I'm really looking forward to. Learning more about understanding people and why we do the things we do. I was fascinated by your ability to get to the core of what was going on with people on our South Island tour.'

'I'm happy to share what I know, Beau. We have plenty of time to kill in the coming months. There's lots to observe right here on *Orpheus*. I do my best to ask questions, show an interest and try to understand people. People love to talk about themselves. It allows me to chat with them in a way that opens them up to me more. I try to understand their perspective and speak to them in a way that they feel heard.'

'That makes sense. How do you do that?'

Ellen chuckled. 'Patience, Beau, patience. We have a whole trip ahead of us.'

Rick approached Beau and tapped him on the shoulder.

'Time to earn your keep. Can you take the helm for the next four hours? She's on autopilot, so stay in overview and make sure there's nothing approaching.'

'Will do, Skipper.'

'Is it all right with you if I take her off auto-helm and steer her myself to get the feel of her?'

'Do what you want, Beau. You're in charge when on the helm.'

'Great, thanks Rick.'

'Bobby and I are going to sort out a duties roster, organise the provisions and make sure everyone is settled in. No free rides on this trip,' he said, smiling. Beau took the helm from Bobby, who gave him last-minute instructions as if to imply Beau was a novice. Beau smiled, took her off auto-helm and felt the energy of the wind working in sync with the sail setting and the design of the hull, gliding the hundred-foot ketch at six knots through the water.

'She's not fast, but she's certainly grand,' he commented to Ellen as he immersed himself in that familiar feeling of becoming one with the vessel.

Rick kept a watchful eye on Beau and quickly became comfortable that he had an experienced yachtsman at the helm. He noted how he reacted to wind shifts before they impacted the boat, thus maintaining boat speed. It was an innate skill honed over many hours at the helm. He smiled to himself and nodded his approval, a gesture that did not go unnoticed by Bobby who seemed to follow Rick around, constantly looking for acknowledgement.

That evening, Beau sat down to a meal prepared by the passengers on kitchen duty, one of whom was Ellen. Rick sat next to him and handed him a roster. 'While this may change, Beau, I want you to do two four-hour shifts a day on the helm. From what I saw today, you're more than capable of shifts alone, which will allow Bobby and me to share the helm duties equally with you.'

'Love to, Rick.'

Beau noted that he had the 5 am to 9 am and the 5 pm to 9 pm shifts.

'Bobby has it covered tonight so you can start from tomorrow.'

Rick stood, tapped Beau on the back in appreciation and left him to finish his meal. Afterwards, Beau took a quick stroll on the deck before deciding to retire early. He stopped by the galley to thank Ellen and her fellow cooks for a beautiful meal; however, she was busy in the clean-up process so he offered a quick goodnight to all and retired to his hammock. The next Beau was aware, he felt Rick's hand on his shoulder.

'Wake up Beau, it's your shift. It's 5 o'clock. Time to take the helm.'

Bleary-eyed, Beau rolled out of his hammock and immediately moved towards the steep stairs leading up to the deck. Bobby was at the helm.

'Thanks Bobby, I'll take her for a while,' he offered, stepping into the helm position. Bobby stepped to the side and allowed Beau to take the helm, giving him clear instructions as to the wind conditions and sail settings. He continued to stand next to him for some time as if to critique Beau's performance.

'Try keeping her nose up, Beau, you're sliding downwind a little. With this strong southeaster behind us, you'll need to fight her tendency to slip downwind. That's why she's off autopilot.'

'Thanks for that Bobby, I'll keep an eye on it,' Beau responded, allowing the young man his dignity.

Beau marvelled at the rising sun in the east, just above the horizon, and the beauty of the deep blue open ocean in the half-light. From the helm position, there was a good ninety-foot of ketch in front of him with two massive wooden masts filled with sails. Is there a greater sight on Earth? he thought. He placed *Orpheus* on auto-helm as the wind subsided, a modern addition sailors of the past could only have dreamt of. Relaxed and in control, he sat back on the navy-and-white striped cushioned bench seat behind the helm which gave him the perfect vantage point. From here he could access the satellite navigational equipment, steerage and a traditional compass. He was constantly checking the satellite navigation with the compass readings. He also had charts available, although in open water there was little to go on other than the stars at night. Beau was a skilled celestial navigator.

The morning drifted by without incident and he enjoyed his time alone. Just after 7:30 am, Ellen came on deck with a serving of scrambled eggs and bacon. They sat together on the helm seat and enjoyed the sound of the waves slapping the side of *Orpheus*, her wooden planks echoing the thud as she gently pierced her way through wave after wave. It was a sound that Beau had become very familiar with over many years and it served to reaffirm his love of the ocean. The sun was now up and Ellen sat back soaking up the warmth and the calming radiance it provided as time seemed to drift by without relevance.

Their serenity was interrupted by Rick who was ushering people onto the forward deck where they were seated in a big circle.

'Beau, put her on auto-helm and come and join us,' he requested. Then he announced loudly, 'Right then, it's time to get to know each other. This is a time-honoured tradition on *Orpheus*. What I would like each of you to do, one at a time, is to introduce yourself and tell us something interesting about you. Something you would like to share with the group that tells us a little about who you are and why you're here with us on *Orpheus*. I'll start,' he said. 'I'm Rick, skipper and owner of *Orpheus*.' He gestured to his beautiful ship. 'She's my life, my home, my mistress, and everything in between. I've undertaken this exact journey on six separate occasions, spending every second season in Florida then Auckland. I'm not married and never have been.' Rick looked across at Amy, the thirty-something American lass sitting on his left. I wonder what's going on there, Beau thought as they exchanged looks.

'It's one of the pleasures of my life to be able to share this beautiful ship with you all,' he continued. 'Without you onboard, I would not be able to do what I love. I've worked on boats all my life in the Florida area, mostly on prawn trawlers.'

With that, Rick looked to his left and Amy, without further prompting, started. 'Hi, I'm Amy, thirty-six, born in Houston Texas. While some of Texas does have a coastline, I'm from the farming districts and I didn't see the ocean until I was twenty-two years old. This is my third season on *Orpheus* and my role as stewardess is to make sure all of you good people are well looked after.' She smiled then gestured to her left.

'I'm Bobby, the first mate on *Orpheus* and second in charge,' he said, looking deliberately at Beau. 'I'm twenty-three years old, from America, and this is my third trip to New Zealand and back. I'm single,' he stated, looking in the direction of a young girl who appeared to be in her teens. That's also interesting, Beau thought, noticing she had returned the look, blushing. He's either laying some groundwork, or perhaps there's some history there.

Bobby looked to his left and Beau started.

'Hi, I'm Beau, thirty-two, a lawyer from Sydney. I've recently broken up with my fiancée and quit my position at my father's law firm to embark on this adventure.' Beau sensed the raised eyebrows and a few comments in hushed voices amongst the group. 'I know,' he said, as if to head off their judgement. 'It sounds extreme but sometimes life takes a turn. I have a passion for blue-ocean racing and I've successfully completed many Sydney to Hobart yacht races. I grew up around boats and there's no place I would rather be right now than here with you all. I'm privileged that Rick has asked me to assist him to sail *Orpheus* to the US. Thanks for the confidence, Rick,' he announced, nodding to the skipper.

'Hi, I'm Ellen, thirty-three from Florida in the US.' She smiled as she said her age and looked at Beau, knowing that she had purposely not divulged it to him in the past. 'Respect your elders,' she whispered to him and chuckled before she continued. 'I'm a psychologist by profession; however, my real passion is philosophy, human dynamics and the mysteries that prevail over this life of ours. I've spent the past five years travelling to remote parts of the world and this is the last leg of my journey. I hope to get to know each and every one of you over the course of our adventure together.'

The rest of the introductions around the circle flowed quickly as Reg, who seemed to be the elder on board, and Jean, a frumpy woman, introduced themselves as a married couple from New Zealand in their late fifties. They had recently lost their entire life's savings in an investment scam and had just decided to take off on what little money they had left. Then there were four backpackers who had met up when travelling Australia together: Trudy, a twenty-four-year-old from Canada, an attractive blonde who was on a twelve-month gap year following the completion of her law degree; Beth, a twenty-six-year-old medical student from Denmark; Gerhard, a Swiss engineer, twenty-four, very tall and lean, who had travelled for the past eight months through Indonesia, Australia and New Zealand; and Joel, with a broad cockney accent, twenty-three. He was a university dropout, slovenly in appearance with dreadlocks, who was visiting New Zealand on a twelve-month visa from the United Kingdom. John, the thirty-two-year-old Australian, introduced himself as a recently divorced, unemployed mining contractor who just needed to get away from the drama that was happening in his life. Jenny, a forty-eight-year-old oceanographer from New Zealand, had a specific interest in making the trip to test some theories she was working on regarding ocean currents and the health of reef systems in the Pacific. Dan was a nineteen-year-old college student from New Zealand studying building design. He was Jenny's son and his mother had invited him on the trip to assist her in gathering data for her research. Brad, a forty-five-year-old divorcee from Australia had lived aboard boats most of his adult life. He was an IT expert and a self-confessed nomad. There was Grant, twenty-nine, who had recently been discharged from the New Zealand Army after ten years serving on two tours in Afghanistan. This trip was an escape from society where he had struggled to fit in following his retirement from active service. Laura was a thirty-four-year-old Australian, unmarried and travelling with Sue, thirty-two, also Australian. They appeared to be romantically involved based on some earlier interactions. The pair had recently sold their cafe on the Gold Coast in Queensland, Australia after ten years of hard slog and decided it was time for adventure. Finally, Gail, eighteen from Auckland, New Zealand had been invited on board just a week before by Bobby. She had just finished a year of working as a hairdresser after graduating school the year before. The exchange between her and Bobby was not lost on Rick.

'Thank you to everyone for participating,' Rick announced as he looked towards Bobby, who was doing his best to avoid eye contact. He knew full well Rick's rules around any personal involvement with paying passengers. 'Now that you've formally introduced yourselves, please don't be strangers. We're confined here on this vessel for the best part of two months or more and your trip will be much more enjoyable if you get to know each other. As you're aware, I've given you all specific roles to perform while you're on board. Those rosters will change and you'll get a chance to do different things. I ask that you engage in these tasks with enthusiasm. This is a low-cost passage for a reason. It's a working holiday. The last thing I want to say is the most important, so listen up. I'm Master and Commander on this ship. I have final say on all things that affect the souls on board. This is a responsibility I take very seriously. It's not a democracy. Do I make myself clear?'

To a person, there was acknowledgement of Rick's statement and it was clear to everyone on board that they were in a hostile environment and that Rick was the one they would turn to for his experience and judgement when needed. With that, Rick stood and as he was leaving he turned back towards the group. 'If for any reason something should happen to me, Beau is the next in line as skipper of the vessel. He has a wealth of experience in charge of ocean yachts.' Rick looked directly at Bobby to ensure his message was heard, then left to check the navigational instruments and cast his eye over sail settings. Beau could feel the seething energy of Bobby directed right at him. He knew that there was no way Rick could leave charge of the vessel to Bobby given his age and obvious lack of leadership. It was also clear to him why Rick had waited to secure a more experienced backup skipper before he embarked on such a long sea passage. What would he have done if I'd decided not to come aboard? he wondered.

As the passengers began disbursing, Bobby and Gail were in a heated discussion. Beau noticed, following the morning meeting, that Rick seemed to be upset at Bobby for inviting the young girl on board. Perhaps he knew him well enough to question his motives. This could be interesting, he thought as he joined Rick at the helm.

'Thanks for your comments and the vote of confidence, Rick. It means a lot to me.'

'Well thank you, Beau. I meant every word of it. I can't thank you enough for agreeing to join us at such late notice. As you can see, we're a bit light on experience, particularly when it comes to leadership.' Rick was gesturing towards Bobby.

'I don't think I'm his favourite person right now, Rick.'

Rick chuckled to himself and repeated the message he had given to the passengers a moment before. 'I take the responsibility of all the souls on board very seriously. I could not leave *Orpheus* in Bobby's charge so once again, thanks. With you on board, it takes a great weight off my mind. I would have had no option other than to hire a qualified skipper to join the passage if you had decided not to come with us. Bobby lost his father at a young age and I guess he sees me in that role. He's constantly trying to please me and prove that he's capable of command. It's my fault for allowing him to live on board for so many years leading the nomadic lifestyle that we do. It hasn't been great for his maturity and development. He doesn't know it yet, but this will be his last trip with me on *Orpheus*. He has to go out and start making a life for himself. He will never be in control of his own life if he continues to live here in my environment.'

Beau thought about Rick's comments and how relevant they were to his own life. 'I know exactly what you mean,' he said, shaking his head. 'At my age, I'm just now breaking away from my father's influence for the first time.'

Rick nodded, acknowledging Beau's words and patting him on the back as if to suggest he should not be so hard on himself.

The day drifted by under clear blue skies and on a gentle rolling ocean as the passengers and crew went about their daily chores. They were all settling into shipboard life where often mundane tasks were critical to survival. Scrubbing decks, tending ropes, cooking, cleaning, and of course relaxing on deck seemed to fill the time. Ellen arrived on deck and sat next to Beau on his now favourite bench seat at the rear of *Orpheus*. He sat for hours at a time marvelling at the great ship before him as she glided through the pristine ink-blue ocean.

'Right Beau, it's time for your first lesson in human dynamics. What, in your observation, do you think is going on for Bobby?' she asked in a challenging but light-hearted manner.

'Ah, Bobby. I have to say upfront, Ellen, that I have some inside information about him from Rick. Apparently, Bobby lost his father as a young boy and has adopted Rick as his surrogate father.'

'That fits perfectly with his behaviour, Beau. Have you noticed how he follows Rick around like a loyal dog wanting to please his master? People will do anything to feel loved. That's the essence of most human behaviour. He's seeking Rick's approval in the absence of his father's approval so that he gets to feel loved, albeit by a surrogate father. In a way, his father abandoned him even though he passed away. People still feel abandoned regardless of the reason they are left alone.'

'Did you see the look he gave me when Rick announced I'd be the next in line as skipper?' Beau asked.

'You be careful of him, Beau. Don't underestimate what people will do when what they believe to be their rightful position is taken away, and so publicly. Don't be surprised if he tries to find a way to discredit you in Rick's eyes. He's still very immature and you need to expect him to act that way.'

'I totally agree, Ellen. I'll keep my eyes open when he's around.'

The night watch was a peaceful one for Beau in calm weather, with *Orpheus* cruising along at five knots. Beau was conscious of Ellen's earlier comments about Bobby and noticed he was lurking around the foredeck. Bobby was not aware that Beau could see him. Normally when not on watch, he would not miss an opportunity to sleep or catch up with Gail, who as a young girl, seemed to be struggling to make any friends on board other than Bobby. No doubt, Bobby liked it that way. At second glance, Beau noticed that Gail was in fact with him. Perhaps they're trying to grab some quiet time, Beau thought. Distracted by increasing wind gusts, Beau tended to new settings on the helm. He was concerned that they might have too much sail up for what looked to be a front appearing on the horizon off the starboard bow, heading towards them. He shouted out to Bobby, 'Hey Bobby, can you give me a hand?'

'You're the superstar. You work it out. I'm on a break.'

It could be a long voyage, he thought. Leaving the helm in the safekeeping of autopilot, Beau ducked below deck to organise some help with the sails. Rick was in his cabin looking over some charts of the Cook Islands.

'Rick, there's a blow coming and I recommend we get some sails down.'

'Okay Beau, I trust your judgement. Let's grab Bobby and two of the other men. It's always a difficult task in the dark to get them down so we'll need a few hands on deck.'

'Bobby is already on deck with Gail, Rick. I saw them earlier. He seemed reluctant to help when I asked.'

'Did he?' responded Rick, clearly disturbed. Just as Beau and Rick climbed up the steep steps to the deck, the unmistakable sound of a girl screaming could be heard in the blustery conditions. Rick looked towards the foredeck and in the darkness noticed a struggle occurring.

'Come with me Beau, quickly.' Rick moved urgently towards the disturbance.

Bobby and Gail were lying on the large sail bag at the front of *Orpheus* in an embrace; however, Gail was clearly not a willing participant. As Rick and Beau got closer, it was quite clear that she was half undressed and Bobby had her slight frame pinned beneath him. He was oblivious to Rick and Beau's presence when they reached him and dragged him off the young girl. Gail was sobbing and the fear in her eyes told a story. Bobby was also taken by surprise and he struggled with Rick who had both Bobby's arms behind his back and his strong forearm around his throat.

'What the hell do you think you're doing?'

'She wanted it, Rick, I swear she did. She led me on.'

'You're a fucking liar, Bobby, you sleazy little prick. Keep the fuck away from me,' Gail screamed, sobbing uncontrollably.

'Beau, take her below and get one of the female passengers to look after her, preferably Ellen.'

Beau helped the young girl cover up and supporting her to stand, he escorted her below, closely followed by Rick who still had a stranglehold on Bobby. He threw him into his cabin and locked the door.

'Grant, guard that door and don't let him out under any circumstances, do you understand?'

'What has he done, Rick? What's going on?'

'I haven't got time for questions right now. Just do as I ask please.'

'No problem, got it covered Skipper,' said Grant in his military tone.

Rick returned on deck where Beau had already organised a few men to assist with reducing sail area. Again, he saw the benefit of Beau who had just taken command in a difficult situation, and he had the boat sorted.

'Leave it to me up here, Skipper. I'm sure you want to deal with what's happening downstairs.'

'Damn right I do, Beau, thanks.'

Rick went to check on Gail who was in deep conversation with Ellen. 'Is it okay if I come in?'

Ellen looked at Gail who nodded in agreeance.

'Are you okay, Gail? Did he harm you?'

'Not really,' she said, still crying through her words. 'Thank you so much for coming to my aid when you did. He wouldn't stop.' She was crying uncontrollably again.

'First and foremost, I have to ask. Do you want to lay charges? I can keep him confined until the next landfall and have him arrested if that is your wish.'

'No, please don't. I don't want to make a big thing of it. I guess he had different expectations from mine. He said I owed him for getting me on *Orpheus*. He said it was time for me to pay up.'

'Did he now?' Rick said in utter disgust.

'He befriended me on the Auckland dock one day after I had admired the yacht. He took me aboard and promised he could arrange a passage to the United States for a very cheap price, no strings attached.'

'Well, it seems that there were a few strings you may not have been aware of, Gail. He gave me some sob story about you needing to get to the US to see your estranged mother, which is why I agreed to the reduced fare.'

'That's not true, Rick. I guess I was naïve.'

'That's okay. Rest up and I'll chat with you in the morning. Anything you need, just ask.'

Rick deliberately did not talk to Bobby that night. He organised shifts at his door to ensure he didn't attempt to knock it down. There was nowhere for him to go in any case.

The next day as dawn arose, Beau was at the helm as usual when Rick joined him.

'I have a problem, Beau. I needed Bobby to help man the watch on this voyage. I can't leave him confined the whole way.'

'You have to, Rick. He attempted rape.'

'That depends on Gail and what she wants to do about it.'

'Regardless, she must feel safe on board, Rick. That's our first responsibility.'

Ellen arrived at that moment.

'How is she this morning, Ellen?' asked Rick.

'She's fine. A little shaken. A part of her feels guilty for allowing it to get to that stage.'

'I guess that's normal,' Beau chimed in.

'It's very normal for women to feel that way, Beau, however, they shouldn't. At no stage did she lead him to believe she would have sex with him. She's actually repulsed at the thought.'

'She seemed very flirtatious though,' added Beau.

'She's eighteen. Of course she's flirtatious. She's experimenting with that energy. It's not an open invitation for a man to rape her though.'

'Of course it isn't, Ellen, you're absolutely right. Some of these young men, however, get mixed signals and have difficulty in turning off the fire when it's lit. In saying that, as you say, no is no. That's it!'

'Does she want to press charges, Ellen?' asked Rick seriously, showing his willingness to follow through if necessary.

'She definitely does not want to, Rick. She wants the whole thing to go away.'

'How will she be with him around the ship?' asked Beau.

'I've decided he'll only be allowed out of his cabin twice a day for an hour at a time, supervised. That's my decision. He must take responsibility for his actions. As you suggested, Beau, we don't want Gail feeling that she has to watch out for him all the time. I'll offload him in the Cook Islands and arrange for his passage home to the States. He's lost his right to be on board. In the meantime, I'll attempt to get an experienced helmsman in the Cook Islands for the rest of our passage. Rarotonga, the capital, should have some options for us given they're a seafaring nation. In the meantime, Beau, it's just you and me to share the load. I'll do three four-hour shifts and you can slot in by doing an extra four-hour shift as well if you will.'

'Of course Rick, whatever you need.'

CHAPTER ELEVEN
An Inevitable Union

The days blended as they left many nautical miles behind them, making good time towards the Cook Islands.

Ellen, in her gentle disarming way, had got to know most of the passengers on board. She shared her observations with Beau over many enlightening conversations, giving him a greater understanding of the human dynamics at play and people's motivations. She had developed quite a connection with Amy, Rick's thirty-six-year-old Texan partner. She had established that Amy was very much in love with Rick and had found her home on *Orpheus*. She had a lovely open honest way about her, no doubt the product of honest, loving parents, who had raised her on a large cattle property in the heart of Texas. Often, these wide-open spaces and honest hard-working environments reflected in the personalities of those raised on the land.

Ellen had noted that Trudy, the twenty-three-year-old Canadian, had taken a shine to Beau and used her recent graduation from law as an excuse to chat with him often. Ellen did not feel in any way threatened and found the young girl's obvious attempts to interact with Beau quite amusing. Trudy was a very attractive young woman and used all of her flirtatious skill to go after what she wanted.

Jenny, who was on board to explore coral bleaching in the Cook Islands, was rarely seen. She spent hour after hour in her cabin reading and researching. Young Dan, her nineteen-year-old son, had struck up a friendship with Gail, who seemed to have recovered from her ordeal rather quickly and showed a distinct interest in him in return.

Ellen commented on the resilience of youth and the carefree way in which they went about their lives. 'When did life get so serious?' she said. The three young Europeans and Trudy, the Canadian, seemed to be a group clearly linked by the excitement of travel and adventure.

Laura and Sue from the Gold Coast had struck up a friendship with Reg and Elaine who found common ground in sharing their various challenges in business over many years. Beau was fascinated by how quickly people with common interests found each other and created a bond.

*

Beau was lying on his bunk after a long morning shift at the helm when Beth walked up to him with her arms full of what looked to be her gear.

'Are you all right?' Beau asked inquisitively.

Just as he spoke, Ellen climbed down the steep steps and Beth turned towards her with a smile.

'You're in my bunk, Beau, get out,' Beth demanded playfully.

'What are you talking about? This is my bunk.' Confused, Beau looked towards Ellen to see if she had any idea what was going on.

'You two are driving me mad. You're entwined in some sort of dance of denial around each other when it's obvious to everyone else that you desperately want to be together. That's right, you want to be with her and she wants to be with you. There, I've said it. Now pack up your gear, Beau, and move into the cabin with Ellen for all our sakes.'

Beau, with a look of shock, examined Ellen's reaction to Beth's comments. Ellen was smiling and she took a step towards Beth and gave her a big hug.

'Well, if it's okay with you and more importantly with you, Beau? I would love to share my cabin with you.'

Beau was flushed with embarrassment.

'Is it really that obvious?'

'Obvious, are you kidding? You guys can't walk past each other without exchanging a longing gaze.'

Beau welcomed the humorous way in which Beth related their interactions and laughed nervously to cover his embarrassment. After hugging Beth, Ellen helped Beau from the hammock, placed her hands on either side of his face and pulled him towards her for a long, passionate kiss.

'That's better,' Beth exclaimed. 'Now we can all relax and stop walking around the elephant in the room.'

Beau gathered his belongings and helped Beth move the last of her stuff out to his bunk area.

'We really appreciate this, Beth, giving up your cosy bed for my hammock.'

'The hammock looks kind of cool. I'll be fine.'

Beau entered his new shared environment, sat on his bunk and reached for Ellen's hands. He looked her in the eyes and with welling emotion, declared, 'I'm not really good at this relationship stuff, Ellen. I've only ever had one real partner in my life, and look how that ended.'

'You have more love to give, Beau Sterling, than you could possibly know. I'm not sure that Liz knew how to love you in the way you needed to feel loved. It's early days and I don't want to get ahead of ourselves, but I would be lying if I said I didn't have some developing feelings for you. I want to explore where we can take this.'

Ellen moved slowly closer to him, inviting him to kiss her but holding back enough to see if he would respond. They moved towards each other and then hesitated, each waiting for the other to make the first move. Then, simultaneously, they embraced and kissed passionately. Beau broke the moment, saying, 'I guess I better go and check to see if Rick needs me.'

'You're not getting away that easy,' Ellen said with a smile.

She dragged him towards her and fell back on her bed, bringing him down on top of her.

'You're right, bugger Rick,' he said, kissing her and fumbling for the buttons on her blouse.

Simultaneously, he dragged his shirt off above his head and threw it to the floor. Beau could not remember ever experiencing the level of passion he felt in that moment, as Ellen undid his belt buckle and slid both of her hands down to his naked buttocks. She pulled him towards her forcefully, and made a rhythmic grinding motion. He felt her moisture between her legs as she passionately kissed him. His firmness incited her more and she struggled to remove her shorts and pants. As he kissed her neck from her shoulder to her earlobes, it seemed to ignite her passion more. She arched her back and writhed underneath him in an unrestrained display of longing. Beau caressed her soft, full breasts and traced his tongue around her nipples, feeling their erectness displaying an eagerness for more. She responded by sucking his nipples hard, leading him to the border of pleasure and pain. As she reached down and freed him, stroking him, he felt like he was going to explode with anticipation. He entered her gently, slowly and rhythmically thrusting deeper and deeper, increasing only as she responded in kind. He kissed her passionately and both of them became lost in the ecstasy, entwined in a newfound deep emotion for each other, taking their intimacy to a new level. They moved in unison, building tension to a point beyond which they could no longer endure. Beau was mesmerised by Ellen's contortions beneath him. He gave himself over and surrendered to the rush flooding his body as he released completely, lost simultaneously in the moment of her complete surrender. It was an experience of utter unity unlike any he had ever had before. As they lay in each other's arms in the glowing aftermath, Beau had a reflective moment. For an instant, he thought about Liz. Interestingly, his thought was one of finality, knowing that a chapter in his life was closed forever.

*

Rick was at the helm of *Orpheus* as they approached the harbour entrance to Avatiu, Rarotonga. Waves broke either side of the manmade breakwater protecting the only safe harbour. The entrance was best negotiated at high tide and Rick timed his arrival perfectly at around 10 am. Rocky, coral-encrusted outcrops appeared to be just below the hull; however in reality, they were some five metres below the crystal-clear emerald water. The brilliant sunlight helped with navigation as they moved closer to their anchorage point, where the crushed coral ocean floor shallowed to only three metres. The island paradise beckoned, with its white beaches framed by the lush green vegetation that dominated the island landscape.

The harbour was small and Rick only planned to anchor for a short stay to drop off passengers and reprovision. He had been in contact with the coastguard to determine a suitable replacement for Bobby.

He had also organised a flight back to the United States for Bobby, via Los Angeles to Florida, which was leaving the following day. Bobby pleaded with Rick to change his mind and allow him to continue on the voyage. Rick remained steadfast in his decision to relieve Bobby from his position as first mate, not only because of his actions, but to provide him the push he needed to seek his own path in life. Gail had also decided to disembark at Rarotonga and to his mother's dismay, so had young Dan who had suffered from constant seasickness on the trip to date. His greater motivation, however, was the connection he had developed with Gail and his desire to join her on the return trip to New Zealand.

The voyage from Rarotonga to the Panama Canal was approximately ten thousand kilometres, a passage of potentially eight weeks depending on the winds. They were planning to spend some time in the surrounding islands to accommodate Jenny who had arranged, as part of her passage, to do a few days of diving on the surrounding Cook Island reefs to measure the extent of coral bleaching. As an oceanographer, she had been to the area ten years earlier and was keen to take new readings for comparison. This work was directly related to global warming and the extent to which increasing temperatures were damaging the planet's natural reef systems.

Rick was well versed in the provisioning required for this journey based on the numbers on board and his many trips over the years. Rick, Beau, Ellen, Grant, and Jenny boarded the tender for a trip to town to gather provisions and meet with their new crewmember, Kulani, who had spent years working commercial vessels out of Fiji. At the age of forty-five, he was an ideal, experienced addition to the crew and after past weeks, he would be a welcome relief to Rick and Beau who had spent many long hours at the helm. A native of the Cook Islands, he would also be of great assistance in getting the best produce for their stores. On board the tender was a disgruntled Bobby. They would come back for Gail and Dan later to avoid any last-minute awkwardness. Jenny had already said a teary goodbye to her son Dan, as he would be heading straight to the airport. They'd had a heated disagreement the previous day over his decision to leave with Gail.

The tender pulled up to the wharf near the south wall where they disembarked. Beau, Ellen, Grant, and Jenny left Rick and Bobby alone, sensing a difficult separation after so many years together on board *Orpheus*. As much as Bobby had let Rick down by his actions, Rick felt a great sadness in saying goodbye to the young man who had been a part of his life and a surrogate son over the past few years. Bobby had tears in his eyes as he pleaded one last time for Rick to change his mind.

'Rick, I beg you, please let me stay with you, at least until we get to the US.'

'No Bobby, it has to be this way. It's time for you to carve your own path and get out from underneath my wing. I've taught you all I can and I've allowed you to stay too long. You've lost touch with reality, living the nomadic life we do. Just be grateful that I'm not handing you over to the authorities right now to face charges.'

'I'm grateful Rick. I know I fucked up, but you have to let me stay. I love my life on *Orpheus*. She's my home and sailing with you is all I want to do.'

'If you have a passion for life at sea, Bobby, then you'll find your way back to it, but not on my ship.'

Rick, with a heavy heart and still angry, handed over an airline ticket, placed $US500 in Bobby's pocket and then turned and walked away.

He returned immediately to *Orpheus*, and picked up Gail and Dan to take them to the town wharf where they would catch a cab to the airport. Their flight back to New Zealand was leaving later that day. Standing on the wharf, Rick felt a wave of guilt come over him. This crime happened on my watch, he thought. 'Once again Gail, I'm so sorry about what happened. I feel I've let you down terribly. Bobby was my responsibility. I did not act on the signs soon enough. I should have known the little grub would try something after the first day I saw you together.'

'Please don't be hard on yourself, Rick. You and Ellen were really supportive, and I'm grateful that you kept Bobby away from me.'

'Are you sure you're right to travel?'

'Absolutely, I have my new bodyguard with me,' she said, placing her arm through Dan's.

Dan smiled like an adoring puppy and nodded in agreeance as they picked up their bags and walked off the wharf and into the terminal building. Rick watched them walk away. We sure are interesting creatures, he thought, smiling as he wandered down towards the street markets to catch up with the shore party.

Kulani was a fascinating man and quite worldly, having worked extensively through Australia, New Zealand and the South Pacific. He'd had his children young, and they had now grown up and moved away from home. His wife, La-ana, worked in the markets selling fresh produce from their small crop farm in the hills. Kulani was a seafaring man who had spent most of his life following in his father's footsteps. He was away from home for long periods, often as a skipper for hire, ferrying sailing vessels from Australia, New Zealand and Hawaii to the Cook Islands and back. Wealthy people would pay to have their vessels sailed to these exotic places where they could fly in, spend a month on board, and fly home. He was well versed in the way of his ancestors and had a depth of knowledge passed down through generations. Ellen, in particular, had some interesting conversations over lunch in meeting him. Rick was more than impressed with his sailing pedigree and relieved that a seaman of his skill and capacity would be joining the voyage.

Jenny, keen to utilise Kulani's knowledge of the local Cook Islands group to assist in her oceanic studies, asked him, 'Your knowledge of the local islands will be invaluable to me, Kulani. I'm looking forward to learning of your experiences of the surrounding reefs and the health of the reef system. Has it changed much in your view over the past twenty-five to thirty years?'

'In some parts yes, in others no. I understand concerns about our planet temperatures rising and coral death as a result. Perhaps certain cultures are contributing to changes on the reef; however, I have stories passed down going back five hundred years which talk of the white death. I can't help but believe that the reef system is a living organism and like all living organisms, it's both dying and regenerating constantly. It has happened before and it will happen again. After all, the whole of life is a cycle. We would be very naïve and arrogant to believe we are the only impact. There are still active volcanoes in the Cook Islands and French Polynesian chain, some beneath the ocean. I believe these underwater eruptions spewing molten lava and debris into the currents would affect anything in their path.'

'Yes Kulani, there is never one cause, I agree. In fact, one of the reasons I'm fascinated by your homeland is the unique natural geological phenomenon. I've been studying the effects of recent activity in the area and its effect on the reef system. The Cook-Austral chain extends to the northwest for two thousand kilometres from the Macdonald Seamount, an active submarine volcano, to the island of Aitutaki. The scattered islands were born from volcanic activity over time. There is little else above sea level.'

'So what reef systems are you interested in exploring?' asked Ellen, wanting to head to Rurutu as soon as possible.

'Rick has agreed to take me to Aitutaki, Ellen,' replied Jenny.

'That's correct, Jenny, I did,' replied Rick, rolling his eyes.

'At a cost I might add,' Jenny joked, smiling broadly.

'In any case, we will do a casual sail up through to Aitutaki Island, which is about a hundred and forty-two nautical miles to the north. There we will spend about five days so that Jenny can do her research. After that, we have a seven to eight-day sail to Rurutu, where Ellen needs to go. A beautiful place, I believe, with excellent snorkelling and diving.'

Kulani seemed agitated listening to the discussion.

'So you're heading through the Argo Seamount region to Rurutu, Rick?' he asked.

'Yes Kulani, that's the plan. Ellen has important work there and I agreed to take her. It's the only reason she's on this passage with us.'

'That's right, Kulani. I had arranged this part of my journey with Rick almost twelve months ago. It's extremely important to my work.'

Unexpectedly, Kulani got up from the table and walked outside the restaurant, shaking his head.

Rick joined him outside and asked, 'Are you okay?'

'I did not know when I signed up for this passage that you were planning on travelling through the Argo Seamount region.'

'What is your concern, Kulani?'

'It is a forbidden area, Rick. If you choose to go there, the gods may not let you pass.'

Rick was sensitive enough to Kulani's traditions not to challenge his concerns by labelling them as superstitions.

'Many of my ancestors have died there in raging storms and giant seas.'

'I understand the weather patterns can be unpredictable in the area, Kulani. I also understand that at this time of year, it is not unusual for severe weather patterns to develop in the South Pacific. But *Orpheus* is built for severe conditions and she's survived for seventy years. I trust my ship and my crew. Besides that, Rurutu is a tourist destination these days, albeit a remote one.'

'You do not understand, Rick. Those people fly in there. In our beliefs, the open ocean in a two-hundred-nautical-mile radius around Rurutu is the region where Ranginui and Papatuanuku, known as Rangi and Papa, reside. They are direct descendants from the source, ancient creators responsible for the origins of our world. You cannot go there uninvited or you will perish. My ancestors told of mystical islands rising up from the sea, sending rafts and oceangoing canoes onto hidden reefs, never to be seen again. Only a few ever returned to tell of their plight.'

'I can understand those old legends, given the nature of the region. There are underwater volcanoes only twenty metres below the surface. However, nothing has erupted or arisen out of the sea in that area for thousands of years, Kulani.'

'This is something beyond anything you can comprehend or control. I know what I know Rick. If you travel through that area, the realm of Rangi and Papa, you are in the hands of the gods.'

'I need to know now, Kulani. Will you still help me get these people safely to Florida?'

Kulani looked away from Rick and looked towards the sky. He drew in a deep breath, exhaled and said, 'I am a man of my word. I have made a commitment to you and it is my honour at stake. Also, it is too late to find another replacement. For that reason, and against my better judgement, I will embark on the journey with you, Rick. I implore you, however, to reconsider travelling through the realm of Rangi and Papa.'

'I will speak with Ellen about it, but because I committed to take her there, I can't promise to change course,' Rick replied. Then he gathered the group together and set about organising the provisioning.

'What is the matter with Kulani?' Ellen asked.

'I'll talk to you all when we're back on the boat. He has some spiritual beliefs and concerns about the area around Rurutu in French Polynesia.'

Provisioning was a huge task and it took them the best part of four hours to assemble a stockpile of fresh fruit, vegetables, fish, meat, tinned food, and fresh drinking water for the long journey ahead. After a night at anchor in the harbour with *Orpheus* fully provisioned, Beau, Rick, Ellen, and Jenny sat down over breakfast to discuss their proposed destinations. Rick explained Kulani's concerns about travelling through the Rurutu region.

'I completely understand his concerns, Rick,' said Ellen, more than interested in the topic. 'I've heard of these myths and legends before and to some extent, they're part of my research and the reason I'm travelling to these waters. Rangi and Papa that he spoke of are considered in the Polynesian religion as the Father Sky and Mother Earth of all creation. He would not want to enter their realm for fear of displeasing them. The area he describes is the same as my great friend Cappy told me stories about when I was a girl. Cappy spent his life at sea. Now, perhaps these are all coincidences based on mythology. You know how old seafarers like to spin a yarn,' she said with a chuckle. 'It's not a coincidence, however, that I'm completing my research in these waters.'

'He's deadly serious, Ellen. He asked me to try and convince you not to insist that we travel through that region.'

'Rick, I don't want to abandon my work because of someone's superstitions, as much as I respect them. I believe there are important answers to my research to be found there.'

'I totally understand, Ellen. I've committed to take you to Rurutu as it's sort of on the way to the Panama Canal. In any case, a few days detour for us won't make a lot of difference. I made a commitment to you and I cannot justify changing our plans based on his fears.'

'Great then, it's settled, Rick,' said Beau, 'we stay with the original plan and head off this morning.'

Beau put his arm around Ellen as she watched Rick approach Kulani on the foredeck.

Kulani looked at Rick deep into his eyes and said, 'Tapu.'

'Meaning what?' replied Rick.

'It's sacred and forbidden. I need to go now and ask for forgiveness to assist with our safe passage.'

CHAPTER TWELVE
Voyage to the Forbidden Realm

Rick guided *Orpheus* out through the entrance of the safe harbour, past the harbour walls and into the open turquoise waters. He and Beau had charted a course to Aitutaki, about a hundred and forty nautical miles to the north. A consistent southeast trade wind assisted *Orpheus* as she gently rolled over the slight swell.

Beau approached Rick, who said with a broad smile, 'I bet this beats sitting in an office in some glass tower somewhere, Beau?'

'You're damn right it does, Rick. It doesn't pay though,' he chuckled. 'Then again, I'm learning there's more to life than acquiring material wealth.'

'There sure is, Beau. I believe you have to be resourceful enough to live a comfortable life to cover the necessities, which no doubt is different for each of us. For me, it's always been about my freedom. Choosing how I spend each day, living my life in a way that fulfils me the most.' Rick took a deep breath of clean ocean air and took a moment to acknowledge the life he had created for himself.

'Well, you've certainly done that, Rick. It's interesting that you mention freedom. I was so lost in the grind that I've only recently realised I've never really been free. My father's obsession with winning dragged me and everyone around him into his game. Your lifestyle seems perfect for you though, Rick.'

'Sure is. I can't see myself ever doing anything else.' Then he added with a knowing look, 'It seems to suit you pretty well too, Beau.'

Beau nodded and with a wry smile agreed, 'Yes, it does.'

Beau took a moment to appreciate the open ocean, with clean fresh air to breathe, content that he had made the right choice in leaving his old life behind. *Orpheus* sailed effortlessly through the day and into the evening. Beau took his watch at the helm and noted Kulani had taken up a vigilant position at the bow. I wonder what he's doing, Beau pondered. He seems to be quite agitated and unsettled. Does he really believe in the myths he spoke about? In thinking about it, Beau remembered that Matiu, the Maori elder in New Zealand, had spoken of similar gods they had worshipped. Celestial beings of pure light, ascended to the earthly plane to give wisdom and guidance.

Kulani kept a diligent watch on the horizon as they proceeded into the night and when he took a shift from Beau, he did not say much.

'Are you okay, Kulani?' asked Beau, concerned.

'No Beau, I'm not. I have no first-hand experience in the Argo Seamount, but where the ocean is alive, the gods' displeasure often leads to death. I've seen the fear in the eyes of those who have survived to tell the tale.'

Beau patted Kulani on the back in a gesture of understanding and left him at the helm. He went down the steep steps below deck and joined Ellen and Rick in the galley.

'We prepared some hot seafood soup for you, Beau. Sit down and relax for a while,' Ellen said.

'I just had another rather disturbing conversation with Kulani. He's still completely obsessed about the Argo Seamount region.'

'Of course he is, Beau,' Ellen said. 'He's been brought up with stories from his ancestors. They're real to him and who knows, perhaps we should not be too dismissive.'

'I'm certainly not dismissive of his beliefs, Ellen. In fact, I was recalling our meeting with Matiu in New Zealand. He and his son spoke of similar gods they had worshipped.'

'That's right, Rangi and Papa, celestial beings that come from the source of all creation. They've been consistently described to me in all my travels over the past five years. One of the reasons I've sought out different Polynesian descendant cultures is to gather more understanding of their beliefs around Rangi and Papa. That's why Rurutu is so important.'

'Who knows? Maybe we'll meet them,' Beau mocked light-heartedly as he tucked into his soup.

'Careful what you wish for, Beau.'

*

Deep down, however, Ellen did not get caught up in the myths about these so-called gods. She did, however, have a fascination for the wisdom of those who had relayed the many stories about them. Not the least of whom was Cappy, who had captured her imagination all those years ago. Ellen was careful about whom she shared her beliefs with. She had studied all the religions and the great scholars of history over her life to try and unlock the secrets of the Universe. She believed that many of them were descendant prophets, accessing a level of knowledge and wisdom that could only come from some inspired place, a connection to a higher realm. These thoughts had driven her search for years, and she could not help but think there was at least some substance to the notion that evolved prophets had existed throughout time. Jesus was a prophet based on Christian beliefs from the Scriptures. The Dalai Lama, Muhammad and Buddha could all be considered evolved prophets, as they had delivered messages that transcended their time. The great ancient Greek philosopher, Hermes Trismegistus, the purported author of a series of ancient sacred texts, underpinned the foundation of many religious philosophies. Ellen was always fascinated by the great minds like Einstein, Plato, Da Vinci, Isaac Newton, and Galileo, all of whom had unquestionably unlocked previously unknown secrets of universal laws way beyond their time that had led to a greater understanding and awareness. Others, like Gandhi, Mandela and Mother Teresa, had changed the world. The questions about how these great men and women had possessed wisdom and understanding beyond their time had intrigued Ellen all her adult life.

*

The next morning dawned with a magnificent sunrise, smooth seas and a light ten-knot southeaster. Beau was dutifully on watch checking course settings and ensuring *Orpheus* was performing to her best under the conditions. Ellen was snuggled up next to Beau half-asleep.

'Are you awake yet, sleepyhead? Don't miss this amazing sunrise.'

Ellen made a muttering sound and struggled to wake up from her drowsy state. 'I'm awake, I think, just give me a minute.'

Ellen and Beau had been inseparable since they had declared their feelings for each other. Beau could not remember a time when he had been so blissfully happy. With a broad smile, he hugged her tight and kissed her on the forehead. She snuggled in closer and hugged him back.

'You're an unexpected surprise to me, Beau Sterling.'

'Why is that?'

'Well, I didn't expect to find love on my journey. In fact, it was the last thing on my mind.'

'Ah, so I caught you off guard then,' Beau replied, chuckling. 'Love was the last thing I expected to find as well, Ellen. I was only supposed to be going on holiday to New Zealand to get my head straight...and here I am.'

'Sometimes we have to let go of everything we know in order to create space for the new. Letting go, in my experience, is one of the most difficult things for us.'

'That's sure true for me, Ellen. I'm a living example of spending years stuck, hanging onto a life that was not right for me.'

Beau stood up and noticed land on the distant horizon. 'Go and tell Rick there's land ahead, Ellen. If I'm not mistaken, that should be Aitutaki.'

Jenny had just arrived on deck.

'That's Aitutaki all right. I remember it from my last visit ten years ago.'

Rick had come on deck and he now took the helm and guided *Orpheus* towards the southwest of the island and a small break in the barrier reef. They anchored off the entrance, as *Orpheus* was too large to enter.

'What's the story of the island, Jenny?' asked Rick.

'The Polynesians first settled Aitutaki around AD 900. Captain William Bligh called in here in 1789. Just seventeen days later came the infamous mutiny on his ship the *Bounty*. These days it's a favourite destination for European holiday-makers. There is, however, an unexpected side to the island not normally associated with the typical image of islanders,' Jenny warned. 'They've been conservative Christians since the first missionaries arrived in 1821 and they dress accordingly. It's not considered polite, even for men, to show too much bare skin in public. Based on my previous experience here, it's important to respect their wishes and culture by not wandering around as we would at the beach back home without a shirt or in a bikini.'

The tender was lowered and the first of the passengers, six in all including Beau, Ellen and Kulani, headed towards the pristine lagoon bordering the main settlement. As was their beautiful custom, locals in traditional dugout outrigger canoes paddled towards the shore party, treating the visitors to a traditional welcome. The women were beautifully adorned in colourful dresses with flowers in their hair and leis of frangipani flowers around their necks.

The days drifted by gently for all the passengers except Jenny, who meticulously measured reef bleaching, comparing her records to those of ten years previously. She spent a great deal of time in the water, diving on wide areas of the surrounding reef from the tender of *Orpheus*. Beth, Gerard, Joel, and Canadian-born Trudy asked if they could accompany Jenny and support her in her work, at the same time exploring the reef with all its colours and tropical fish. They were fascinated to learn from Jenny how adaptable the coral was to water temperature changes. She explained how the coral expelled a species of symbiont algae living inside the coral. Through its innate intelligence, the coral adopted the host symbionts which were more resilient to changes in water temperature. This process was essential to their survival and had been going on since the dawn of time. Jenny had discovered that much of the bleaching she had recorded a decade earlier had improved, and the coral had not only recovered, it was thriving. She explained that coral flourished in water that was constantly around twenty-nine degrees centigrade.

'Most bleaching is a temporary shock to the reef system, not a death sentence,' she explained. 'It can be caused by our planet warming, underwater current temperature changes, pesticides washed into the ocean, and long-term historical climate cycles. The recovery can vary and a decade can often make a big difference to the health of the reef system. We should be very mindful of our effect on our reef systems while at the same time, not dismiss the natural occurrences that have been going on for millennia.'

Her new students were captivated by the complexity of the massive living organism of the reef, and by Jenny's passion for it. They were in awe of the labyrinth just beneath the surface of the ocean, hosting all manner of fascinating life forms, most of which they had previously been unaware of. Their time with Jenny created a lasting impact on each of them and broadened their horizons.

Kulani stayed on the island with relatives and introduced some of the passengers on *Orpheus* to the locals and their culture. As a boy, he had spent a good deal of time on the island. Reg and Elaine from New Zealand had become close to Lara and Sue from Australia and they enthusiastically accepted Kulani's invitation to visit some of the villagers in their homes. Beau and Ellen spent long lazy days swimming in the lagoon and intimate sunset walks on deserted beaches. They were enjoying the simple pleasures of life, such as feeling the crushed coral sand between their toes and watching the gentle waves racing up the beach and then retreating. They mainly kept to themselves and took the opportunity of escaping the confines of *Orpheus*, enjoying some uninterrupted time, indulging in each other and their newfound relationship which was deepening by the day.

Rick, who had become somewhat of a loner over the years due to his chosen lifestyle, preferred to stay on board *Orpheus*. He seemed to revel in the constant checking and rechecking of the workings of the old ship. It gave Beau a great deal of comfort knowing how fastidious Rick was when it came to *Orpheus*. She was truly his life's work, and his connection to the boat was beyond simple ownership.

On the last day at Aitutaki, after Jenny had collected all the data she required, all crew and passengers boarded *Orpheus,* excited about the next phase of their journey. All except for Kulani, who after their brief stay on Aitutaki where he was able to be more of himself amongst his extended family, became quiet and reserved, as if to steel himself for the journey ahead.

'Rick, before we take off on the next leg of our journey, I must ask one last time. Please reconsider staying away from the Argo Seamount region.'

Rick was distracted by the beautiful tones of combined voices singing on the foreshore, accompanied by the blowing of conch shells blending into the symphony. Kulani's relatives had come down to farewell *Orpheus*.

'What are they singing, Kulani?'

'It's a prayer to the gods. They are praying for our safe passage.'

Rick looked at Kulani and placed his hands on his shoulders.

'Don't worry, my friend; the ocean is my home. I'll make sure we get to America safely.'

Rick saw a look in Kulani's eyes which, he had to admit, made him feel uneasy. He patted him on the back, turned and instructed the crew on watch to raise the sails and head out towards the west side of the island before turning east towards their plotted course to Rurutu.

CHAPTER THIRTEEN
Beyond the Mist

All on board *Orpheus* settled in for the five-hundred-nautical-mile journey to Rurutu, a five to seven-day sail provided the winds remained favourable. Beau took his turns at the helm, which he increasingly looked forward to as he became more in tune with *Orpheus* and her subtleties. Ellen, when she was not on other duties, often joined him, partly to keep him company and partly to make sure he stayed alert during the long night shift. They made good time on the first two days due to a twelve to fifteen-knot southerly. The sails were fully hoisted and *Orpheus* powered along at a steady seven to eight knots. Life on board was generally harmonious.

On the evening of the fourth day out from Aitutaki, the horizon filled with green-black clouds rolling in from the south. Rick had been keeping an eye on the barometer; a low-pressure system had formed and was heading their way. Kulani glanced towards Rick and gave him a look as if to suggest the gods were about to bring down their wrath on the unsuspecting ship, bobbing around like a small cork in a giant ocean with the only landfall some two days away. Rick took the helm from Kulani and called for all hands on deck.

'We need to reduce sail now! Beau, take two crew up forward and drop the mainsail as quickly as you can. Kulani, grab two others and reduce the sail on the aft mast. Leave only the smaller jib sail rigged. This is going to be one hell of a blow. Don't worry, Kulani, I've been through much worse before.' Rick's broad smile seemed almost to challenge the elements.

'So have I, Rick, but not in these waters,' Kulani replied, looking back towards the oncoming front with fear and dread in his eyes.

Within minutes, the smooth seas had turned into steep waves with rolling foam tumbling down their deep-green face as *Orpheus* crashed through trough after trough. The old wooden boat creaked and groaned as the ever-increasing swell battered her hulls. Beau noticed the frightened look on many of the passengers' faces and took it upon himself to assure them that they were safe and in good hands.

'You can't take an open-water passage like this halfway across the world and not expect a bit of weather!' he shouted above the now raging wind. '*Orpheus* has been through much worse in her seventy-year history, I'm sure.'

He had just finished his reassuring speech when without notice, the ship rolled violently on its side, having been hit by a rogue wave, bringing green water over the decks. These waves were often twice the size of the prevailing swell and seemed to come from nowhere. Those not hanging on securely were washed off their feet and hurled violently across the deck. Jenny struck her head on the base of the aft mast and Grant quickly grabbed her as the ship righted herself.

'I want everyone below decks now except for Beau and Kulani!' Rick commanded. 'Beau, I'm going to need your help on the wheel. We have fifty knots of wind on the stern and I can't hold her alone.' Beau raced back to the helm and stood side by side with Rick as they fought to hold her on course, running directly away from the wind. This was taking *Orpheus* well off course, however, it was the safest option and their destination was the least of their concerns for now.

'Kulani, keep an eye on the rigging. Some of those ropes are about to let go. See if you can secure them before they do!' Rick yelled, his voice being whipped away by the violent winds. With Kulani's ocean experience, he did not need much direction. He was already moving to lash down loose objects and retie ropes to ensure the rigging remained intact. Another huge rogue wave smashed against the starboard side of *Orpheus,* making her heel over on her side again, and everything that was not tied down surged from one side of the ship to the other.

'We have to slow her down, Beau!' Rick yelled, his voice barely audible over the roar of the wind. 'We're surfing down the face of these waves at fifteen knots. We'll bury our nose if we don't do something. Kulani, help Rick with the helm. I have to put a drogue out to the stern.'

Rick unpacked the parachute-like drogue and a hundred feet of strong rope. After setting it up, he dropped the drogue over the back of *Orpheus* and the parachute filled with sea water, eventually reducing the speed of the old ship. Kulani was shaking and had become paralysed with fear, lost in a nightmare of impending doom. He gazed towards the oncoming seas with glazed eyes as if expecting to meet his displeased gods rising out of the sea with the next rogue wave, ending *Orpheus* and all souls aboard.

Rick grabbed him by the shirt and pulled his face in close. 'It's just a storm, Kulani. You've been through many just as bad before. Pull yourself together. We need you to focus right now.'

Rick's intervention snapped him back to reality and he grabbed the wheel again and helped Beau who was struggling on his own.

The passengers below were tending to minor injuries and an increasing number were becoming seasick. Brad excelled in this hostile environment, having experienced severe seas before. Interestingly, his brash manner gave way to a caring concern for his fellow passengers and he endeared himself to them. Ellen, in particular, thanked him and could not help but reflect that everybody had an endearing side. Sometimes, it was just a matter of finding it under the masks people wore to keep them safe. There was an inner toughness and kindness to Brad that she knew she could rely on, even given his crusty exterior. Grant was tending to Jenny's wounds, bandaging her head which was bleeding heavily.

'How is she, Grant?' Ellen asked.

'She will be fine. She has a slight concussion. I just need to get the bleeding under control.'

She smiled at Ellen reassuringly, noting her concern. The storm raged for three hours and the ship took a pounding, rolling on her side many times. Rick seemed to thrive in the environment, almost excited at the challenge. He was a true ocean spirit, Beau thought to himself. As the moon came up over the horizon to the east, the winds abated, as did the sea. Beau stayed on the helm, now manageable by himself, while Rick checked for damage. Beau smiled at Kulani and placed his hand on his shoulder.

'Thanks, man. You were there when I needed you and I really appreciate it.'

'Perhaps our prayers have been answered, Beau.'

'I'm sure they have, my friend.' Beau pulled the big man towards him in an embrace reserved for those who had survived adversity together. Kulani, after their embrace, looked towards the heavens and clasped his hands together in a gesture of gratitude to the gods.

At daybreak, Beau arrived on deck for his morning shift on the helm. He was greeted by a dense fog and almost no visibility.

'Where did this come from, Rick?' he asked, straining to see anything ahead.

'I have no idea, Beau. It's been like this for the past few hours.'

'But we're nowhere near land.'

'We're still two days from land and at this pace, probably more. We're hardly moving. The wind has completely dropped out.'

'Is there anything showing up on the satellite navigation?'

'Nothing at all, and I don't expect there to be in the middle of nowhere. The maps show we're still a hundred and fifty nautical miles from Rurutu.'

'Strange to say the least,' Beau said. 'Do you want me to take the helm?'

'I think I'll stay with it for a while longer. At least until we clear this thick fog.'

The rest of the passengers and crew straggled on deck over the next hour and all were fascinated with the slow drift of *Orpheus*, seemingly being carried along in a cloud.

'It's hard to maintain steerage in this light breeze,' Rick declared to Kulani who had arrived on deck, looking around in disbelief.

'I've never seen anything like this in all my days at sea, Rick.'

'Not sure I have either, Kulani,' Rick declared, looking perplexed. 'I've heard of sea fog, but it's rare and usually comes from a cold wind off warm waters. We have almost no wind and it's anything but cold at this latitude especially at this time of year.'

The eerie quiet seemed to unsettle everyone, particularly Kulani.

'Can we start the engine and get out of here, Rick?' suggested Kulani urgently.

'I think we will have to,' replied Rick. 'We're not going in the direction we need to. This fog cloud seems to be dragging us along with it, away from our plotted course.'

With that, Rick fired up the big diesel engine and steered *Orpheus* back on their desired course. The motion of the ship surging forward seemed to pierce the fog for an instant, but then she became engulfed again.

'That's weird, Rick. We almost came out of the fog and then it engulfed us again, as if to keep us within it,' Beau said.

'That's impossible, Beau. Let's not get carried away with imaginings. Go up to the bow and keep a close watch for any other vessels in the area. There's nothing showing on the radar, however, some smaller local fishing vessels may not carry radar equipment.'

Beau reacted instantly and with Ellen, stood watch at the bow. They could not see anything, and the only sounds reaching them were the slow chug of the diesel engines and the bow wave peeling off either side of the hull as it pierced the glassy water.

Just in that moment, Beau thought he saw something ahead. 'Did you see that, Ellen?'

'See what, Beau? You're making me edgy.'

'I swear I saw breaking water ahead.'

'You're going stir-crazy, Beau. There's nothing out here. You're as bad as Kulani. We're in the middle of nowhere. The nearest land is days away.'

They looked at each other in disbelief as a rush of energy came over them, flooding their being.

'Did you feel that?'

Ellen nodded, acknowledging the unexplained phenomenon, grabbing her arms to check if the cold rush against her skin was real.

Beau, with increasing alarm, again announced, 'There, I saw it again. A reef off the port bow, one hundred metres ahead!'

With a newfound urgency, Beau shouted from the bow, 'One hundred degrees to port, Skipper. Reef, dead ahead! Turn one hundred degrees to port.'

Rick was not reacting. It was as if he was in another world, oblivious to the warnings.

'Skipper, there's a reef dead ahead!'

Beau knew he had no time to run the twenty metres to the helm position. The fog cleared ahead once more and Beau was pinned by the impossible vision of a large island, five hundred metres in front of him. The fringing reef was almost on top of them, with waves breaking over it. He looked over his shoulder to see a huge swell peaking, ready to break. Ellen grabbed Beau's arm as they braced themselves for the inevitable collision. The tumbling white foam from the following wave hit the side of *Orpheus* and picked her up like a wayward surfboard, propelling her sideways, out of control and onto the reef. The timber made a sickening sound as it cracked under the pressure, piercing a massive hole just above the water line where she lay over on her side. Beau shook his head to regain his senses and looked back at Rick, now shocked into action and quickly assessing their situation. It was fast becoming life and death. *Orpheus* was taking in water where her side was lying on the reef in a metre of water.

'I'm not sure if the tide has peaked yet. We could be washed off the reef and into deep water!' Rick yelled to anyone within earshot. 'We have no choice. Abandon ship!' he shouted as he moved around the deck, trying to be heard over the pounding surf. 'Abandon ship, abandon ship!'

Beau helped Rick untie the tender from its secure position on deck and launched it over the side. Kulani was now kneeling on the deck, which was leaning over at a forty-five-degree angle, chanting. Beau grabbed him by the shirt and barked instructions at him.

'Get up and help the others. We need to get everyone off the ship and into the life raft now. Move it!'

With fear in his eyes, Kulani followed the instructions as if in a trance.

'Get below and make sure everyone is out from down there.'

Kulani just nodded, bewildered by their predicament.

Rick knew the ship would not sink, at least for now. She was stuck firmly on her side on the reef; however, if the water continued to rise, she could eventually slide off the edge of the reef and disappear into deep water. Rick and Beau were quickly gathering fresh water and some simple provisions to take with them, not knowing when they might be able to return to the ship.

'Bring that spare sail as well, Beau. We may need it for shelter.'

The trip to shore proved difficult. Rick navigated the tender, with Grant and Brad on the oars. Beau waited on board *Orpheus* with the remaining seven, including Ellen, Kulani and the four young travellers who were all busy gathering essentials, only to be vetted by Beau.

'Leave that behind. It's not a priority!' he yelled at Gerhard, who was carrying a large camera.

'This is all my photos of my past eight months of travelling. I'm not leaving it behind.'

Beau snatched the camera from his grasp. 'Go and look for items that will save our lives. If we can't eat it or use it for shelter, it stays. If we're able to, we will come back for the rest,' he commanded, leaving no room for negotiation.

Annoyed, Gerhard returned below to help Ellen scavenge for tinned food and gear that would be useful for their survival.

Rick and Brad quickly returned with the raft after leaving the others on the beach.

'We found a passage through the reef, Beau. It's about two hundred metres away and there's a deep channel that leads to a safe lagoon.'

'Great work, Rick. We've got a heap of gear here to load that I think will be important over the coming days.'

After loading all the gear and the remaining crew and passengers, Beau stepped off *Orpheus* and looked back at the stricken ship lying on its side. 'I sure hope this is high tide around here, Rick,' Beau commented as the raft pulled away.

'If it's not, she will break up and be washed off the reef as the tide comes in. We will have no chance of salvage then.'

Beau looked at Rick and noted the fear on the faces of everyone in the raft, each contemplating the possibility that they might truly be marooned in this hostile place.

However, Beau noticed the beauty of the island as they approached it. The water was the familiar turquoise of these parts, which never lost its magic for him, almost like a jewel glistening, framed by the white sand of crushed shells and corals. There were steep cliffs on either side of the beach which seemed to lie at the entrance of a large gorge. Already in survival mode, Beau noted a creek flowing from the gorge out into the ocean, relieved that there might at least be fresh water. It was also apparent that the island, with a massive crater rising up to around a thousand metres some twenty kilometres away, emitting thick volcanic ash, had been created by an underwater volcano. The lush vegetation around the flatlands that surrounded the steep walls of the mountainous crater tapered off gently until they reached the dramatic cliffs on the coast, falling vertically over two hundred metres to the sea. The closer he got to the island, the more he realised that it was brimming with life. Birds made a racket on their arrival, disturbed by their new visitors. He could not help but feel the island was almost prehistoric and it seemed to emanate a forbidding energy. They came to a halt in the shallow waters of the beach. The others were there to greet them and shed tears of relief as they hugged one another in the knowledge that they were safe, at least for now.

In the hours that followed, the group made a large makeshift shelter using a sail from *Orpheus* strung up over a log suspended between two trees. The young Europeans took on the role of establishing a fire and a stockpile of wood. There was indeed fresh water emanating from the stream that flowed from the gorge Beau had spotted earlier. Rick kept a vigilant watch on *Orpheus* on the reef. He was particularly concerned about the rising tide.

'Looks like the tide is retreating,' Beau observed as he sat down next to Rick on a rock ledge overlooking the reef.

'I think it is, Beau. I must say, I'm incredibly relieved. It would appear that we hit the reef right on high tide. As you can see, it's completely exposed now and *Orpheus* is sitting high and dry. I believe we can do some temporary repairs, which may be enough to float her on a king tide and bring her into the lagoon for further repairs. I don't want to give any false hope to the others though. The damage seems to be just above the water line when afloat. It gives us a much greater chance of making her seaworthy.' Rick's emotion welled up, having contemplated the worst for his beloved vessel and home.

'Just let me know whatever I can do to help, Rick,' Beau offered, placing his hand on his shoulder. 'If we're going to be here for a while, we need to explore whatever this place is and find out what food source we can secure.'

'I agree, Beau. We should organise a meeting tomorrow morning in the clear light of day and discuss a plan to get off this island. Where the hell did it come from? It just seemed to jump up out of the ocean,' Rick said, confused, as he turned and left to tell the others of their plans.

Ellen walked up to join Beau looking out over *Orpheus*. He looked at her in a way that suggested they were thinking the same thing.

'I know what you're thinking, Ellen. Let's not get carried away. There must be some logical explanation for how this island got here and why it's not on any charts.'

Ellen did not respond. She just looked around in wonder. Could this be the mystery island Cappy had spoken of when she was a girl? she wondered with excitement. It all seemed so unreal and impossible.

CHAPTER FOURTEEN
Journey Through the Unknown

As they sat in a group around the morning fire, Rick outlined the plight of *Orpheus*. 'We have a remote chance of salvage. We have to pick the right tide and do some interim repairs on the damaged hull to try and get her into this lagoon. If we can do that, we have a chance to repair the hull enough to set sail again.'

'I think we need to split up into two groups,' added Beau. 'One group will remain here and support Rick with *Orpheus*. The other group will set off and explore the island. We don't know if we're alone or how long we may be here. We don't know what food source we have available to us. We can salvage a lot of supplies from the ship, however, at this stage we're unsure of the water damage. Don't forget, the supplies are mostly stored below deck in the bowels of the ship. It could be totally underwater.'

'Beau is right,' said Grant. 'I volunteer to head off with the exploration group. I have over ten years of army experience behind me and it could be invaluable.'

'Does everyone agree with this plan?' asked Rick. 'If not, speak up now.'

The group, still in a semi-daze, nodded in agreement and seemed glad to be led by anyone with a plan.

'Okay, so let's work out who stays here with Rick and who comes with me to explore the island,' suggested Beau. 'Kulani, I would like you to join us in case there are indigenous tribes here. You may be able to assist in communicating with them.'

'No way, Beau, I'm not going out there,' he said. 'We're not supposed to be here. I tried to warn you. We have intruded into the sacred realm and the gods have brought us here for punishment. If we venture out there,' he said, pointing towards the large volcanic rim at the centre of the island, 'we will not come back.'

'Okay Kulani,' replied Beau in the knowledge that there was little point in discussing the matter further. 'Rick will need your help in any case getting *Orpheus* repaired and into the lagoon.'

'I would also like to keep Brad with me given he has some boating experience,' said Rick. 'The repairs are going to be hard work chopping down trees into planks. I'm going to need some youthful energy too.'

Gerhard, Trudy, Beth, Joel, Sue, and John all agreed to stay with Rick and Amy to help with *Orpheus*.

Beau took aside his group, which now consisted of Ellen, Grant, Jenny, Reg, Jean, Joel, Laura, and himself.

'Okay, listen up,' Beau instructed, leaving no doubt that he was taking command. 'I don't know what we're going to find out there,' he said, pointing towards the thick wooded forest. 'Based on what we can see from here, it's likely we could be away for at least one night and two days. We need to stick together, and move at a slow but steady pace, ensuring everyone keeps up. Reg and Jean, as our elders, you need to speak up if you're struggling.'

They both nodded.

'Grant, you stay at the rear and make sure no one gets left behind.'

'Sure thing, Beau.'

The group split up with their allocated tasks to gather some essential items including water and food. Beau left to chat with Rick and discuss their plan.

'Rick, I don't know what we're going to find out there.'

'I know, Beau, and that's why I want you to take this.' Rick reached below some blankets he had salvaged from *Orpheus* and handed Beau a double-barrel shotgun with a dozen cartridges. Beau looked at Rick in a way that suggested he was only just realising the gravity of the journey ahead.

'I guess if we don't go we'll never know,' he said, trying to break the mood. 'We'll be heading off within the hour, Rick. I plan to be back in time to assist you in getting *Orpheus* afloat and into the lagoon in a few days' time.'

'That's great, travel carefully. It will be at least a couple of days before we can do a temporary patch on that hull. By my calculations, based on the moon cycles, we should have a king tide within three days which may be enough to float her off the reef, if we're ready in time.'

'We'll be ready,' offered Beau, shaking Rick's hand firmly.

Beau and Ellen, together with the other six in the group, set off around 9 am in bright sunlight towards the huge gorge that was their only apparent option, given the large cliffs that surrounded the beach. They had secured enough provisions and water for a few days and they carried them in makeshift packs made from torn sail canvas. Beau led the way and Grant, as agreed, took up his position at the rear. They entered the gorge, which had steep craggy rock walls rising a hundred metres on either side. It became obvious that they would find it difficult to locate a safe place to ascend to the upper fields. The freshwater creek ran through a tropical grove with sandy beaches on either side. It was lush with coconut palms, ferns and massive trees towering along the bank of the creek, creating a beautiful shady place. It was suitable for a more permanent camp, Beau thought, not wanting to alarm the others by declaring it.

As they trudged through the soft sand, he scanned the far reaches of the gorge at least half a kilometre into the distance. He could hear a massive waterfall which seemed to cover the entire cliff at the very end. Alarmingly, there appeared to be no way out of the gorge. Over the next hour, they traversed slowly towards the imposing wall that signalled the end of the gorge and their options. Jenny suddenly let out a scream, drawing the group's attention to the thick scrub at the edge of the beach. Emerging from the undergrowth was a large lizard, some two metres long. It moved slowly but purposefully towards them without fear, like some prehistoric relic from the past.

'What is it?' shouted Ellen as it kept coming towards them.

'It looks like one of those Komodo dragons from Indonesia,' said Grant, stepping protectively in front of the women. All of a sudden, there were three more, all larger than the first. Their long tongues were flicking outward, as if to taste what was to come.

'This does not look good,' Beau said, urgently ushering the group towards the creek.

'And neither does that,' said Grant, pointing at the sky.

A large flock of huge black ravens with metre-wide wingspans were clearly interested in their presence. They were circling lower and lower, anticipating the possibility of a fresh kill. The forest became increasingly noisy, with small monkeys leaping through the trees over one another in ever-increasing excitement. Beau ushered the group along the bank of the creek, constantly monitoring the dangers from all sides with the predators closing in.

'I think we're on the wrong end of the food chain here,' he said.

Grant stopped occasionally to throw fist-sized rocks at the lizards to slow their progress as the group tried to negotiate the soft sand underfoot. He kept Reg and Jean in front of him as they struggled to keep up with the increasing pace. They reached the end of the gorge and huddled close to the cliff face, saturated by the spray from the waterfall thundering next to them. With seemingly nowhere to go, Beau noticed a cave behind the pristine waterfall, which seemed be pouring over the edge of a large rock pool two hundred feet above.

'Quickly, in here!' he yelled over the increasing noise, while the lizards and the excited monkeys moved closer and closer, seemingly conspiring to trap their prey in a well-rehearsed move, offering no room for escape.

As they huddled together in the cave, it seemed their pursuers were not so keen to follow, put off by the force of the water creating a curtain in front of them. 'That should hold them up for a while,' Beau said, relieved to get a moment to contemplate their next move.

'I'm not so sure about that!' yelled Grant, throwing rocks at one of the larger lizards now entering the cave.

The others joined in throwing stones to drive the massive creature back outside, at least for the moment. Beau kept the loaded shotgun by his side at the ready. He scanned the cave for their next move. 'There's our way up, Ellen,' he said, pointing towards a rugged pathway just visible in the dim light. 'It's steep but I think we can make it. It seems to lead to the upper rim.'

Beau could not help but consider that the pathway was there for a reason. Someone or something uses that path, he thought to himself.

It was a good twenty minutes of steep, slow, upward progress before most of the group reached the upper rim of the gorge. They looked down towards the entrance of the gorge in the far distance and could see what could only be members of Rick's group following the creek towards the grove.

'They're probably looking for timber, Ellen. I hope they don't travel too far into the gorge and receive the same greeting we did.'

Ellen, out of breath, scaled the last metre to the top of the rim.

'We're too far away to warn them.'

Reg and Jean had fallen back a hundred metres or so, closely flanked by Grant ensuring they trod carefully on the loose rocks. A fall now would be fatal. 'How are we going to get back to the others, Beau?' Ellen asked.

'I can't be worried about that now. Our only option is to go forward. It's about five hundred metres to that forest line. Beyond that, there seems to be at least five to seven kilometres of thick forest before we reach the bottom of the volcanic rim.' Beau scanned the open area before him. 'There doesn't appear to be any sign of life in the fields before the forest, which is a good sign. By the same token, there doesn't seem to be any food either.'

'Let's keep going,' suggested Ellen, who kissed him on the lips with a loving look and started moving briskly towards the forest.

The others had all reached the top of the rim and they fell into line, following Ellen and Beau across the fields. They arrived at the edge of the thick forest and instantly, Ellen felt an uneasy presence. Only two hundred metres inside the forest canopy were well-trodden paths that led left and right.

'Looks like we have a decision to make,' said Jenny.

Without alarming the others, Beau exchanged a look with Grant. The tracks confirmed his concern that they were not alone on this island. Without further consultation, Beau took the path to the left, shotgun at the ready, and the others followed a winding sandy path through the forest without question.

Before long, he stopped and Ellen asked, 'What are you stopping for, Beau?'

'Can you smell that?' he asked.

'Smell what?' replied Ellen.

'Smoke, I'm certain I smell smoke.'

The others heightened their senses and looked around the forest.

'Yeah, I smell it too,' agreed Jenny.

Beau grabbed the shotgun and raised it to his side in a position he could fire quickly if necessary.

'The rest of you stay here. Grant, follow me,' Beau gestured, setting off cautiously.

They followed the path for a further five hundred metres until they came to the edge of a clearing.

'Get down, Beau,' Grant urged in a hushed voice, grabbing him by the shoulders. The two lay quietly in the thick foliage just before the clearing.

'Do you see that?' Grant whispered.

'What do you think they're doing?' asked Beau.

'I don't know, but it seems like some sort of ritual. The way their bodies are painted, spears at the ready, dancing around the fire. They seem to be in a trance-like state.'

'I hope it's not us they're excited about,' Beau said.

'Look, there. The warriors are carrying someone out from a large thatched hut.'

As they lay quietly on the forest floor, Beau and Grant witnessed six tribal warriors carrying a captive, who was violently struggling to get free, towards a large flat rock which resembled an altar. He looked terrified and he was screaming in an unknown language, which only seemed to excite his captors more. They placed the man's body on the altar and held him by his arms and legs. Without delay, a heavily decorated warrior, who looked to be a chieftain due to his larger headdress, emerged from what appeared to be the main hut carrying a primitive axe made of stone. After dancing around the fire in circles for a few minutes and chanting, he approached the captive. With the aim of an expert, he removed the head of the man lying on the altar in one swift stroke, causing blood to flow everywhere, covering the men holding down the captive and exciting the whole tribe, who looked to the heavens and chanted in unison.

Beau gasped in horror and Grant covered his mouth firmly. He was shaking uncontrollably as Grant, with the experience of two tours in war-torn Afghanistan, lay half across him to restrict his movements.

'Beau, quietly and without any sudden moves, I want you to start crawling backwards. Be careful not to make a sound.'

Beau turned and looked into Grant's eyes. He saw the steely gaze of the war veteran and heard the certainty in his instruction. He nodded and very slowly, started to crawl backwards until he felt that he was deep enough in the forest to be safe from view. Grant tapped him on the shoulder and quietly rose to his feet, pulling Beau with him. In a crouched motion, they headed back down the trail only to come face to face with poles just off the pathway, which had previously gone unnoticed, containing the skulls of past victims. Beau let out a gasp. Grant turned around towards the clearing to see the tribesmen now peering into the forest towards them. The chieftain was shouting instructions as the men of the tribe scattered, grabbing spears and axes.

'Time to run, Beau!' shouted Grant and they took off towards the others.

Grant grabbed the shotgun from Beau, who handed it over without protest, and knelt down on one knee. He fired at the first warrior in pursuit, dropping him in his tracks. The rest of the tribesmen stopped suddenly and could not comprehend what they had seen. They gathered around the fallen body in bewilderment, picking up his limbs and dropping them in disbelief.

'This is our chance, Beau. Quickly, go, let's go!'

'What the hell was that, Beau? We heard a shot!' exclaimed Ellen.

'No time to explain. We need to move, now!'

Jean was frozen in terror. Grant grabbed her by the arm. 'We have to go and quickly,' he commanded, pushing her in front of him.

The others followed down the sandy path, brushing aside the thick foliage encroaching on their path. They arrived at the intersections which led back to the gorge they had just escaped from. Without hesitation, they took the only alternative path, leading away from their pursuers.

Grant stopped and again turned, bent down on one knee, took careful aim, and fired a shot at the leading warrior, bringing him down with expert marksmanship. This time, they were halted for only a brief moment before they leapt over the body and kept coming. The pace was taking its toll on Reg and Jean who were struggling to keep up. Grant caught up with the group again, to find Jean bending over in complete exhaustion.

'I can't go on, Reg. Leave me here and go on without me.'

'There's no way I'm leaving you here. You have to keep going. If you stay, I stay.'

'No one gets left behind,' Grant said as he grabbed Jean under the armpits and dragged her up, supporting her weight. 'You can always find something in you to push further and harder than you believe possible. If you don't move now, you'll most certainly be captured and undoubtedly killed. You know that Reg wouldn't leave you to that fate alone.'

'That's right, Jean. I'm staying with you no matter what happens,' confirmed Reg. With a resigned look, Jean took one step and then another and started to move in a half shuffle down the path. Reg supported her on one side and Grant the other, and they made progress towards Beau and Ellen who were lagging behind the others, keen to assist if necessary.

'She will do it for Reg but not for herself.' Beau shook his head.

'Says something about her self-worth,' said Ellen.

'Come on, we have to keep moving,' urged Grant, who had rejoined them with Reg and Jean in tow.

They eventually caught up with the others who were halted in front of a large lagoon surrounded by a steep rock wall.

'The track ends here,' said twenty-three-year-old Joel in his broad cockney accent. 'We're trapped.'

'Where to now?' asked Jenny, trying to avoid sounding panicked. As they looked around the lagoon, Jenny noticed the subtle movement of water swirling downwards through the rock wall.

'That water is going somewhere, Beau. It's moving either through a crack in the wall or through an underground cave.'

'We haven't got a second to waste,' urged Grant, throwing the shotgun to Beau. In an instant, he disappeared beneath the surface of the dark and forbidding water. It seemed like he was gone for an age while the warriors kept closing in. He resurfaced and gasped, 'There's a way through an underwater cave to the other side. I've seen it. Come quickly!'

Beau urged the others into the water, only to be confronted by Joel.

'I can't swim,' he muttered, shaking his head. 'I never learnt.'

'You don't need to swim, Joel. Just hold your breath and Grant and I'll tow you through.'

'I can't,' he protested, pulling away from Beau's grip and backing away from the water's edge. The warriors were now nearing the clearing as Joel looked behind him and then back at the forbidding dark water of the lagoon, sensing an impossible decision. With wide-open eyes, trembling, he allowed himself to be dragged forward by Grant and Beau. Beau took one last shot at the warriors without aiming and missed, slowing them temporarily. By the time they entered the water, the rest of the group was gone. They made their way to the far wall of the lagoon some twenty metres away, sensing the swish of the spears entering the water next to them. Grant let out a cry of pain as a spear pierced his left shoulder.

'We have to go under now!' declared Beau, as he led a count of three, two, one and dived below the surface. Grant quickly followed, dragging Joel under with him. The cave entrance was two metres below the surface. They pulled themselves through the narrow opening and along the cave wall for about five metres. Grant covered Joel's mouth and nose as he panicked and struggled. Using the rock wall as leverage, he moved towards the light and finally emerged from the cave. As they broke the surface of the water, they found themselves eerily in an identical lagoon on the other side. Joel surfaced coughing and spluttering and was dragged to the shore where the others had now gathered.

'Did you feel the resistance as we came to the exit of the cave?' Ellen asked Beau.

'I thought it was just my imagination. It felt like a wall of heavier water. As I pushed through it, I could feel it pass over my whole body like a wave of energy. What do you think it was?'

'I don't know, Beau. It felt similar to that feeling we experienced on *Orpheus* just before we hit the reef.'

He nodded, agreeing, but bewildered by the phenomenon. They scanned the walls of the lagoon in silence, fearing that their pursuers would follow and soon break the water's surface as well.

'I'm not sure where we are or how we get back, but at least we've shaken off whoever those people were for now,' declared Beau. The group was slumped on the sand in near exhaustion.

Grant, lying face down on the beach, was being attended to by Jenny and Ellen. The spearhead had not fully entered his shoulder. With a veiled grunt, he bore the agony while Ellen helped Jenny gently remove the spear. Ellen tore off the sleeve of her blouse to cover the wound, as if she had done it many times before. 'Five years living in the islands, you get very resourceful,' she said, noting Beau was looking on.

'It would seem so,' Beau acknowledged.

'Okay, let's move out.'

The command came from Grant who was on his feet ready to go, dismissing the pain and moving off down the track leading into the jungle.

'I'm not sure if the shotgun will be of use to us anymore, but I'll bring it anyway,' said Beau, picking it up and tucking it under his arm.

The group moved cautiously through the jungle of thick tropical trees. Colourful birds sang loudly from the upper branches. Fragrant flowers were growing on vines entwined in the trees.

'This feels like a different place altogether from the other side of the cave,' commented Jenny, 'although it's exactly the same in some ways as well. It almost has a welcoming energy.'

'I know what you mean,' agreed Ellen. 'The fresh tropical fruit on the trees, the abundant flowers, and it seems sunnier and brighter somehow.'

Beau led the group down the track, cautiously scanning ahead, concerned that the afternoon would soon turn to night. Grant was as vigilant as ever at the back of the group, looking behind constantly to ensure their pursuers had indeed finally given up the chase. As the afternoon closed in quickly over the jungle canopy, Grant chose a small clearing as a camp for the night and set about erecting makeshift shelters out of logs and branches. The others followed his lead and before long, they were settled in with a fire going to keep unwanted visitors at bay.

The night was long and humid, as Beau and Ellen lay together on a makeshift bed of palm fronds.

'This island is full of contrasts, Beau. We're surrounded by incredible beauty, but it's so unpredictable. And what's with that cave? We seemed to pass through to a different place energetically; however, it looks exactly the same as the other side. Here, it's so beautiful and calm somehow. For some reason, I don't fear this place. Not like the horrors of the gorge and those warriors.'

'I know what you mean, Ellen. I wonder what today has in store for us. My main concern now is getting back to the others. Obviously, we can't go back the way we came.'

'No, not if we can avoid it,' agreed Ellen, shuddering at the thought of what lay on the other side of the underwater cave.

CHAPTER FIFTEEN
A Choice of Two Paths

None of the group slept much on the damp undergrowth, still shaken by the bizarre events of the day. As the first light of dawn filtered through the jungle canopy, they were up and ready to press on to wherever the trail took them.

'Well, let's see what interesting adventures are in store for us today,' said Grant, wincing and feeling his left shoulder.

'It seems to have closed over well,' confirmed Ellen, inspecting the wound.

Grant nodded as if it was no big deal, ushering the others to get moving.

'I wonder how Rick's group is going with getting *Orpheus* into the lagoon for repairs?' pondered Ellen aloud.

'He's a survivor, Ellen, and a very capable man. If anyone can get her seaworthy again, he can. For now, we can only go forward.'

Beau led off down the path, concerned that the shotgun was of no use now. What would they do if they met with more hostile locals? Ever prepared, Grant had spent much of the night making spears whittled with his army knife, which was never far from his side. He handed the men one each as they filed past him.

'Use it if you have to. Don't hesitate,' he urged.

'Don't worry, I won't,' responded Reg, grabbing the weapon firmly while ushering Jean in front of him. Grant had come to respect Reg. There was an inner toughness in him which he knew he could rely on when it mattered. He'd demonstrated it yesterday, revealing a calm strength in the face of imminent danger as he supported his wife. Jenny walked up to Grant and grabbed a spear from his hands.

'Can't let you fellas have all the fun.'

Grant smiled and slapped her hard on the back in acknowledgement.

They travelled for a good two hours and the volcano emerged larger, a thick white plume billowing from its summit. Its forbidding presence was now casting a shadow over the forest, and its walls gradually became steeper to almost vertical near the rim.

'I would not want to be around when that thing erupts,' said Joel.

'Most of the islands in this region were created through volcanic activity rising up from the seabed, Joel,' Jenny explained. 'In saying that, this one isn't even on the map.'

'Based on what we've seen so far, it's like no world I know,' Joel said, nervously scanning the landscape around them.

The group marched on for another two hours through the thick jungle, each of them on high alert. They were edging closer to the giant wall of the volcano as the sand track gave way to rich volcanic soil, dark and fertile. Jenny knelt down, sifting the soil through her fingers. 'The farmers back home would kill for land like this. You could grow anything on it. Perhaps we'll find some root vegetables for supplies. Of course, there's as much fruit as we want but it wouldn't last long in this heat.'

'This little trip of ours has turned into one of survival, so forget the shopping list,' said Grant.

'I agree. Our priority is to get everyone back safely reunited with the others. That's all that matters now,' Beau said.

As the group moved further down the track, they were halted by Grant holding his hand in the air. 'Quiet! Everyone be very quiet!'

'What is it?' asked Beau, joining Grant at the front of the group.

'Look there, ahead in the clearing.'

Beau was taken aback by the sight of young children playing noisily in the open fields about two hundred metres ahead of them.

'Everyone stay here and keep off the track. Stay hidden under the thick foliage until Grant and I come back to get you. No matter what you hear, do not follow us.'

Beau and Grant moved off quickly but silently in a half crouch towards the clearing. This village had a very different feel from the warrior village they had previously stumbled upon. There were women sitting around in groups weaving baskets. Others were tending the fields where rows of lush green crops had been carefully planted and lovingly nurtured. A group of men obviously returning from a hunt were entering the village from the opposite direction, carrying a large wild boar strung upside down on a log by the feet.

'What you think, Grant?'

'Certainly feels very different from our last encounter.'

'I agree. But I doubt they'd have encountered white Europeans like us. I'm not sure we'll be welcomed with open arms.'

'You could be right. What do you think we should do?'

'There appears to be no way forward other than through their village. The jungle is too thick to try and go around it, and we're certainly not going back from where we've come, unless we have no other choice.'

Just as they were discussing their options, Grant noticed something unusual. Walking out to meet and greet the hunters arriving back to the village was an unmistakably Caucasian male. He looked to be about sixty years old.

'Do you see that, Beau? There, on the other side of the compound.'

Beau looked towards the man greeting and congratulating the hunters. He had long hair and a white beard, and his skin was tanned from years of exposure.

Beau and Grant rejoined the others and shared their discovery.

'Do you think they're dangerous?' asked Jean.

'It's hard to know,' replied Grant. 'If we walk in there with our spears, we're not going to get a warm welcome. I'm sure of that.'

'There's no doubt about that,' agreed Ellen. 'I'd like to take a look for myself. I've lived amongst islander people for five years and I believe I've the best chance of assessing if they're hostile or not.'

Without waiting for group consensus, Ellen moved off down the track. She returned within a few minutes.

'They appear to be typical of many of the island tribes I've met. There are warriors, but in my view the village seems to be a peaceful farming culture. If they believe we're not a threat, we may be able to get to communicate with the old man and convince him that we're lost and need help.'

'That could be very risky,' said Grant.

'I understand that, Grant. Do you have a better solution?' She waited for a moment and when he did not reply, said, 'I thought not. I believe our best chance is for me to go alone. As a solitary female, I don't pose a threat to them. You need to trust me on this.'

Beau and Ellen looked at each other.

'You can't go alone, babe,' Beau pleaded.

Before he could say more, Ellen said, 'This is our best chance. We're wasting time. If we're discovered here as a group, it may turn out to be much more confrontational. I'll come and get you once I've convinced them we represent no threat. If I don't come back, well, I guess you'll need to find another way.'

'I don't like this idea,' Beau said, shaking his head. 'We should stay together.'

'I agree with Beau,' Grant said forcefully.

'Thanks for your concern, Grant, and believe me, I wish there was another way. But I'm confident they're a farming community, very different from the last tribe we encountered.'

With that, Ellen gave Beau a brief hug and a reassuring glance before cautiously moving off down the track towards the village.

'She's determined when she wants to be,' Beau said.

'Damn right she is,' responded Grant, as they took up a position closer to the clearing to watch her progress.

Ellen entered the clearing and within a short distance, she encountered a group of young girls singing and dancing in a circle on the outskirts of the compound. She began singing in a similar style to emulate them. One young girl smiled and reached out her hand in an invitation to join in the game. She joined the circle and danced briefly before a woman from the tribe noticed the intruder and immediately ran towards the children. Ellen smiled at the woman and approached her tentatively, still holding the child by the hand. She handed over the child in a non-threatening gesture and the woman grabbed the child into her arms and pulled away from Ellen with fear in her eyes. The disturbance prompted others to approach Ellen slowly and inquisitively. First, other women and then some of the men followed. They did not appear to fear her; rather, they were intrigued to find such an unusual visitor to their village. They spoke in a dialect she was not familiar with.

Before long, she was surrounded by a rowdy crowd. Beau and Grant looked on, increasingly alarmed.

'We can't just sit here and do nothing,' Beau said.

Just then, an American accent cut through the noise.

'Do you speak English?'

Startled to hear a familiar language, Ellen turned to the voice and locked eyes with the man Beau and Grant had spotted earlier. He walked towards her, instructing the crowd in their language to let him through.

'Why yes, I do,' she replied with a smile, trying to project a calm and engaging presence.

'Sounds more like American to me,' replied the man, laughing.

'As does yours,' she responded, joining in the joke. 'My name is Ellen.'

'Um, I thought I might have lost that southern twang years ago. Apparently not. I'm Aaron. It has been some time since I've used English.'

'We were shipwrecked,' Ellen explained.

'Of course you were, my dear. That is the only way to get here,' he said dismissively. 'How many of you are there?'

'There are eight of us here and eight back trying to repair the ship. We thought we would explore the island for provisions as much of our stored food was destroyed, submerged in the ship's hull.'

'Well, there is ample food here,' the old man gestured, looking around at the crops. 'Not sure it would keep for long once harvested though.'

The rest of the tribe seemed to lose interest once they realised there was no threat.

'They seem surprisingly accepting of me being here,' she noted, pointing towards the tribespeople.

'You're not the first from the outside world to reach this point, my dear,' he said nonchalantly, turning and walking towards the compound.

'Would it be all right if I bring the others in as well?' she asked respectfully.

'Of course, the more the merrier,' he offered without even looking back at her.

Uncomfortable, and hoping the tribespeople would be as casual as he was, Ellen quickly made her way back to Beau and Grant. They returned to the group together.

'No weapons,' she announced, looking specifically at Grant and anticipating some resistance.

He reluctantly put down the gun and the others ditched their spears in the undergrowth. The group cautiously entered the compound and, to their surprise, no one took much notice of them.

'Welcome to you all,' came the greeting from Aaron with his arms open. 'Our home is your home.'

The group looked at one another in amazement.

'Yes, hi,' offered Beau, extending his hand to Aaron.

'How do we do this again?' laughed Aaron in his jovial manner, shaking Beau's hand vigorously. 'Come on in,' he invited, ushering them into a large hut with a stone circle at the centre. A fire was being attended to by a diligent tribesman.

'As hot as it is, these people insist on continually burning a sacred fire,' he said. 'This is Chief Alika. He is the guardian of the tribe.'

The chief extended his arms to the sky and muttered words in a chant. To their surprise, in broken English, he said, 'Welcome to your tribe from my tribe.'

He then sat down at the edge of the circle and gestured for the group to do the same.

Inquisitive because of her research, and intrigued at his ease amongst the native people, Ellen knew that Aaron would have a wealth of knowledge about the island and its people.

'How long have you lived here?' she asked.

'Um, let me see. I arrived here as a seventeen-year-old boy on a ship just like you. So, I'm not sure how old I am now. Must be well over sixty-five, I reckon. So perhaps fifty years, give or take,' he said, as if it was yesterday.

'Have you not wanted to leave?'

'What, leave all this? Are you kidding? Not a chance. Had the opportunity a few times. Nothing back in the States for me now,' he dismissed, stoking the fire.

'So, if you were shipwrecked, how did the others leave here?' asked Beau, hoping for some insight into their plight.

'Well, the good ship *Majestic* landed on that reef out in front of the gorge. This island came out of the fog from nowhere and before we knew it, bam! We were on the reef.'

'Sounds familiar,' whispered Grant to Joel.

'Wait a minute, did you say the *Majestic*?' interjected Ellen.

'Yep, the *Majestic*, why?'

'That was the ship Cappy used to talk about,' she said, turning to Beau with excitement.

'Cappy. Did you say Cappy?' asked Aaron.

'Cappy, yes. He was a dear friend and neighbour of mine back home and he used to tell tall tales of great adventures. He said it was aboard the *Majestic*.'

The old man sat with a stunned look on his face, mouth open. Eventually, he looked directly at Ellen and with tears in his eyes asked, 'Is he still alive?'

'He was when I left the States five years ago, although he was very old then so I don't know.'

'Cappy was my mentor and the captain of the *Majestic*. He was on this island with me for two years before he decided to leave. He was inspired to get back and share his learnings with the world.'

'Oh my God, that's amazing! The old bugger was telling the truth all the time. All of those grand stories and I thought he was just entertaining a young girl. There was always a profound message in his tales though. I guess as I got older, I stopped believing in them, but his wisdom always remained with me.'

'Well, who would believe you now if you went back and told them about this place? When people are ready, they will hear the message. I'm sure he helped many people with his wisdom learnt from his time here. He wanted to share it, which is why he made the sacrifice to leave. And it was a sacrifice. This place is paradise for those who seek the truth.'

'Who doesn't want to find paradise?' asked Jenny.

'In my experience, most people,' Aaron replied. 'They're trapped by their fear and they stay stuck in their own version of the world, rather than taking a leap into the unknown.'

'Haven't you stayed stuck on this island?' asked Jenny, shrugging her shoulders. Her directness made the others uncomfortable.

'Stuck? Who, me?' he asked, laughing. 'I have led a blessed life of constant expansion here. For that, I am eternally grateful. It's not where you are that determines your evolution as a soul. Most people are stuck even though they're racing all over the world, endlessly seeking a false nirvana. I've found my purpose here.'

'You're sounding like Cappy now,' commented Ellen.

Aaron smiled, touched her arm with genuine appreciation and thanked her for the compliment.

'I, for one, want out of here,' said Joel. 'We've been pursued by reptiles and attacked by hostile natives. No paradise here.'

Aaron looked towards the chief with a knowing glance. They had seen many like this before.

'How do we get back to the ship from here?' asked Grant, bringing the conversation back to more urgent priorities.

'Ah yes, the ship. Well, that is an issue. If she hasn't broken up on the reef by now, and assuming she can be refloated, the ship has no other way to make landfall except through a narrow passage in the reef.'

'That's the lagoon we entered after we struck the reef,' Grant said.

'That would be it,' Aaron acknowledged. 'She can only enter the lagoon once a month on a king tide, which by my calculations of the moon's cycle should be in a day or two. Now, I wish I could give you an easier path back to her, however I can't. The only path back to your ship is the way you came. There are sheer cliffs that surround the entire island except for the gorge. There is no other way.'

They all looked at one another, defeated by the reality of their situation. Jean started to cry and was comforted by Laura and Reg.

'Well, if that's the only way back then that's the way we will go,' said Grant emphatically. Then, trying to rally the group for the arduous trip back the way they had come, he said, 'Let's go. I've been planning for this very contingency and have an idea on how we can slip past the dangers we faced on the way here. The edge we have now is that we know what to expect. That will give us a fighting chance. If we can get through the cave just before sunset, we can move quietly under the cover of darkness to the top of the gorge undetected. Then we can quickly get through the gorge just on daybreak by following the creek and be back to the others by early morning.'

'Yeah, great,' responded Jenny. 'That's if the lizards are in a good mood and have other plans for dinner.'

'Do you have a better idea?' challenged Grant.

Jenny slowly shook her head, acknowledging the obvious. There was no other option.

'We only have a few hours left to get back through the cave with some daylight,' Grant continued. 'Otherwise, we'll waste a whole day. We can't risk another altercation with that hostile tribe, which is almost certain in broad daylight.'

'I can't go back through the underwater cave,' announced Joel, looking forlornly at the ground. 'I just can't do it. I'll find another way.'

'There is no other way.' Aaron was looking compassionately into Joel's eyes.

Joel looked fearful and hopelessly defeated. 'Then I'll stay here. I'll drown if I try to get back through that cave.'

'Others before you have been exactly where you are now, facing the same decision,' Aaron said. 'But staying here through fear is not a valid reason to stay. Even though you are here as a group, individually you've created this moment. It's an experience you've created to expand yourself for your ultimate higher good. There is something huge for you all in the decisions you are about to make. If your destiny is to leave, then overcome your fears and go. Follow your path.'

Ellen looked at Aaron with a sense of wonder, drawn to him. He has enormous wisdom, she thought. His message seemed to come from some higher inspiration.

In a moment of complete certainty, she looked at Beau and said, 'I'm staying. I've been looking for this place my whole life and I know there's something here that I must explore. Don't ask me how I know. I just need to trust my intuition.'

Beau looked at her with his mouth open. 'Are you serious? You don't know what life here would be like. What if you never get off this island?'

'Cappy did and so can I, when the time comes.'

'Don't be insane,' interrupted Grant. 'No one gets left behind and that includes you, Ellen, and you, Joel.'

Grant grabbed Joel firmly by the shoulders. 'Look at me, Joel. Do you trust me?'

Joel looked up slowly with fear in his eyes. 'Yes, I trust you.'

'I got you safely through the cave before and I will do it again.'

Joel nodded reluctantly and surrendered to Grant's certainty.

'Then let's get going. All of us, now, before it's too late to get through the cave.'

Ellen turned to Aaron.

'Would I be welcome to stay here with you?'

'Of course, my dear. We are an open community and you're welcome to join us for as long as you desire.'

Beau walked up to Ellen. 'You're serious, aren't you?'

'Yes, Beau. I believe this is the end of my five-year search. I've found what I've been looking for after all these years travelling the South Pacific. And most of that time, I wasn't sure of what I was looking for. There's no way I'm going to walk away without exploring what drew me to this place. I would feel incomplete, wondering for the rest of my life if I had missed an opportunity to discover my destiny.'

Beau placed his head in his hands, trying to comprehend the gravity of what she was saying.

'We've only just found each other, Ellen. We have our whole life ahead of us. I thought it would be together!'

'I know, Beau. Trust me. You would not want to be with me if I abandoned my dreams. It would be a hollow life. Stay with me, Beau. I know we've found each other for a reason. Think about your journey and all that has transpired to bring you to me and to this place at this time. You're searching too, aren't you?'

'Well, yes I am, I guess. But this was not in my plan, that's for sure.'

'We've created this amazing opportunity together, Beau. To do something incredible and step into the unknown. I want to do it with you.'

Beau looked at Grant, who was now clearly losing his patience. 'She's flipped, Beau, lost her marbles. Leave her here. We have to go, now!'

Ellen was crying and holding Beau in her arms, kissing him as if it were their last kiss. He stepped back from her with tears welling in his eyes.

'I have a responsibility to Rick and the others, Ellen. I can't just abandon them. I must try to get them off this island and safely home.'

'What about your responsibility to yourself, Beau? When are you going to prioritise what you want in your life? It seems to me that you've always been the one responsible for everyone's life but your own.'

Her comments were pointed and they hit a raw nerve in Beau.

'I'll always love you, Ellen.'

'Right, we're on our way then,' announced Grant.

One by one, each of them gave Ellen an emotional hug and said their goodbyes. Numb and lost, Beau looked back at Ellen longingly and the tears rolled down his face. Then he moved off down the track and into the thick forest once more.

Beau and the group made good progress back to the underwater cave.

'I'll go last with Joel,' commanded Grant, closing down any possible discussion. He was mindful that if Joel had an issue, it might lead to others being too scared to go back through the underwater cave.

'I'll go first,' offered Beau, trying to distract himself from the wrenching feeling of leaving Ellen behind. Again, Beau was torn between his sense of responsibility and the life he was longing to live. *What have I done? Will I ever see her again? But I have to get these people safely off this island and back to their loved ones*, he constantly reminded himself.

It was getting dark when Beau leapt into the water and swam over to the rock wall just above the cave. With a huge breath, he dived deep and entered the cave. Time seemed to stand still and his mind wandered to thoughts of Ellen. The pressure in his chest and his need to breathe brought him back to the reality of urgently needing to reach the exit of the cave and surfacing for air. It was longer than he remembered and his lungs were exploding as he dragged himself out of the cave and swam for the daylight. He broke through the surface, gasping for air and taking in some water, spluttering and coughing while clinging to the rock face trying to recover. *I have to keep my mind on the job*, he thought.

Over the next ten minutes, except for Joel and Grant the rest of the group made it safely through one by one. They waited for a further ten minutes with increasing anguish.

'That's it. I'm going back through to see what the hell is going on,' Beau said.

With that, he dived into the water and with more determination and focus this time, emerged on the other side to find Grant consoling a distraught Joel at the wall above the cave entrance.

'What going on?' he asked.

'It's all good, Beau. We're right to go, aren't we Joel?'

Joel had terror in his eyes and he was shivering uncontrollably.

'It's almost dark, Joel. We have to go now,' said Beau. 'You two go first and I'll follow.'

Joel started to shake his head. 'It's all right. I'll stay here and go back to the village.'

'Then Grant and I are staying too,' Beau said emphatically.

'That's right. You stay, we stay,' said Grant.

Joel looked at each of them in disbelief.

'Leave me here, for God's sake.'

'No one gets left behind,' Grant declared. 'Let's go, now!' Grant started breathing deeply.

'On the count of three, we go. One, deep breath, two, deep breath and three!'

Grant grabbed Joel by the hand and dived deep, dragging Joel behind him. Beau followed closely and they pushed and pulled him through the narrow passage. Joel's panic was escalating, and he was out of breath when they broke the water's surface.

They all gathered on the beach to recover and discuss their next challenge. Somehow, they must slip past the warriors and hopefully, they could do so under cover of darkness as Grant had planned.

They made it back to the fork in the track without being detected. As they were entering the open field, they came face-to-face with two warriors returning from a hunting trip, carrying a wild pig tied to a log. Without hesitation and knowing that their silence was imperative, Grant attacked the men who were startled at the sight of these strange intruders. Grant used his knife to take the first man out instantly. The second warrior ran straight past them and took off down the path to his village, but Beau followed and tackled him from behind. They struggled, with Beau trying to keep him silent, but the man's cries had alerted others in the village and Beau, separating himself, ran back to the group.

'We have to go, now. They're coming!'

No longer concerned about their silence, they ran towards the gorge. It seemed much further away than they remembered, particularly now that the entire village was emerging from the jungle some fifty metres behind them. Reg and Jean were lagging dangerously behind but Beau kept them moving. As they reached the top of the gorge, Grant wasted no time in ushering them down the steep track, leaving only himself and Beau behind.

'Go Beau, now.'

'Not without you.'

'I'm coming. I just want to make sure you all get down the track and to safety.'

Beau started down the track and turned in time to watch Grant easily take care of the two warriors who had led the charge. He disarmed the first in one movement and used his spear to take down the second.

'Right, that'll buy us some valuable seconds, Beau. Go, go!'

As they reached the halfway point, it was obvious that they were no longer being pursued. They reached the base of the cave and relative safety.

Beau looked around at the dishevelled group who were in fear of their lives. He knew that had he not returned with them, some of them would not have made it this far. This, however, did not relieve the immense grief he felt at having left Ellen behind.

CHAPTER SIXTEEN
Island Life

Aaron guided Ellen to a mudbrick hut with a thick thatched roof on the outskirts of the village compound. She was still in a state of shock, constantly looking back towards the jungle and expecting Beau to appear at any moment.

'This will be your new home for as long as you're with us. It hasn't been used for some time. Feel free to make it your own.'

'That is incredibly generous of you, Aaron. I hope I'm not putting anybody out of their home?' Ellen said.

'No, not at all. We eat as a group shortly after sundown. Wild boar is on the menu, spit roasted. Highly recommend it. You're most welcome to join us. I'm sure you're hungry.'

Lost in her thoughts, Ellen took a while to respond. 'Yes, um, I would love to join you,' she said, not wanting to insult her new host even though food was the last thing on her mind.

That evening, Ellen joined in the feast with at least forty others from the village. It seemed that the young families had eaten together earlier and taken the children off to another fire on the outskirts of the compound where they were sharing stories of mythical creatures, tribal history and past great deeds. Ellen had noticed that while the tribespeople spoke in a common language, there was a smattering of English and Spanish.

Trying to force herself to make conversation, she said, 'Their language is interesting, Aaron.'

'It's a combination of all the influences that have come to this place over a long time,' he replied. 'Feel free to use English with them. Even the young are taught to speak in English, although they don't get to practise often.'

Over the next couple of days, Ellen tried to adapt to village life. She spent her days in the sun tending crops, getting to know others in the village and helping with village life where she could. Each day at around 3 o'clock, there was a brief thunderstorm which provided ample water for their crops to flourish. Aaron allowed her space to settle in and checked in with her every now and then. Lost without Beau, she asked herself if she had made the right decision. She had never felt so deeply in love before and her emotional pain was a massive weight, affecting her whole being and dominating her every thought.

*

The days were long for Ellen without Beau and she felt as if she was just going through the motions, completing her chores and hardly interacting with others in the village. Late on her second day in the village, Ellen was sitting on the ground in the open field pulling weeds from around the crops, deep in her thoughts, when she noticed Aaron leaning up against the main hut. He had a huge knowing smile on his face. She turned instinctively in the direction he was looking and to her complete astonishment, saw Beau emerging from the jungle track, running towards her. She closed her eyes in disbelief and took a second look as if to test her own reality. Tears of elation flowed down her cheeks. Beau was beaming, but he also had a look of desperation on his face. He could not cover the fifty metres to Ellen quickly enough. She stood and ran into his arms and they embraced for an age, kissing passionately, declaring their love for each other.

What...how...but you said...' stammered Ellen, still kissing him frantically.

Beau, with a loving smile, cradled her face and stared into her teary eyes.

'By the time I got to the top of the gorge, I knew I could not go on without you, Ellen. It has taken me two days to get back to you. The warriors on the other side of the underwater cave chased us across the open field to the top of the gorge. We made it down into the cave below where they could not follow, and that's where I left Grant and the others.'

'Anyway, you're safe and you're with me now,' she said, concerned only with the present and the feel of his strong arms around her.

Aaron, observing their emotional reunion, nodded knowingly to himself. He had never doubted that Beau would find his way back to her.

Ellen had a new lease on life and excitedly showed Beau around the village. Everything now felt completely right with world. The chores she had been struggling with became a joy.

After a week or so, on one of Aaron's visits to their hut, Ellen and Beau took the opportunity of asking him to share his knowledge of the island.

'This island seems to hold many mysteries,' Ellen said.

'Ah yes, that it does, my friends. The island has many hidden facets to it. For a start, this is not the only village on the island. In this province alone there are eight other villages, many larger than this one. At times we are in conflict with them. When we are at peace, we travel to another village and trade with them. Some of our group move from village to village and take a partner. The couple then move into the village of their choice, just as you do in your world with neighbouring cities, states or countries. Some villages are aligned to our way of life and others less so.'

'Are they all as civilised as this one, or is that your influence over your time here?'

Aaron laughed at the suggestion. 'I would like to think that I had some influence, given I've spent most of my life in this village and on this island. The truth is, they were much as they are now when I found them all those years ago. There have been many travellers, such as you and I, who have found their way to this place. Some have stayed and some have moved on and left the island. Some have died trying, due to the choices they made. Some live in the other villages because they fit better with the culture and philosophies of those villages.'

'What has kept you here for all these years then, Aaron?' Beau asked.

'I'm known as the gatekeeper, or guide, for people such as you. I've said before that each of us has a destiny created by our own beliefs. Most are not ready for the expansion this island has to offer. They either try to leave or move to the other villages to live out their lives in this realm. Most are caught up in fear and a longing for the world they left behind, even though they are looping around and around in that world, doing the same things and getting the same outcomes. That is the way of us all, most of the time. It's especially significant, however, when we are ready to take the journey to a new realm of evolution as a soul.

'Your powers of creation have brought you to the brink of an awakening to the laws that govern our existence,' he continued. 'You have a knowing that your destiny is linked to what you may discover here. Trust that knowing.'

'Forgive me for saying so, Aaron, but aren't you hiding away from life here, looping yourself in this place?' Beau said.

'Don't be so rude!' exclaimed Ellen. 'Sorry, Aaron, he's a lawyer!'

A broad smile came over Aaron's face.

'That is a fair question, Beau,' he acknowledged. 'The difference is that I've found my purpose in life here. My role is to guide you, just as I have others, to the next realm. I know that I have a destiny to fulfil here.'

Ellen sat with tears of gratitude welling in her eyes, excited by the possibilities available to them and the knowledge that her long search had not been in vain.

Beau tried to comprehend what was being said. Was this guy some sort of spiritual guru? Or were they just the ravings of a madman after a lifetime of being trapped here? He had to admit Aaron sounded rational. Ellen had inspired him to leave everything behind and embark on a path of discovery himself. *For now, what have I got to lose?* he thought.

'Well, Aaron,' Beau said, breaking the silence. 'I don't know what to say. Where to from here, I guess?'

'Ah, patience, my friend, all in good time. When you are ready, I'll guide you, unless you're not. That is all for now.'

Aaron stood and without further comment, left the hut.

The next month drifted by without incident and Beau was beginning to wonder if this was all there was to life on the island. Ellen was fascinated, having visited other tribes in the valley with Aaron, noting the different cultures and traditions and at times experiencing a different energy. Some were not so welcoming and she was glad to leave. Some had an aggressive underlying energy and she felt uncomfortable and always on guard, glad to move on quickly. The various tribes seemed to tolerate one another and when it was advantageous, they traded produce and livestock. Interestingly, English, while not spoken day to day in their own communities, was understood by most. They behaved and socialised like any culture in a developing third-world economy.

One evening after sunset, there was a disturbance on the edge of the compound. Beau and Ellen ran from their hut to discover one of the young hunters had caught a neighbouring tribesman stealing chickens from the enclosure. Other men arrived to help secure the thief as he struggled to get free. Aaron joined them, looking concerned.

'This is how it starts,' he said, shaking his head.

'How what starts?' asked Beau.

'Our warriors will detain him for a trial tomorrow. If he's found guilty, which he obviously is, he will be put to work in this village as a farm labourer.'

'For how long?' asked Beau, interested in their form of justice.

'It can be for a few months or more, depending on his past transgressions.'

'That seems entirely reasonable to me. I thought you were going to say they would lop off his head or some similar barbaric punishment.'

'No, these people are more evolved than those of your first encounter on the other side of the lagoon. They are from a different realm. We value life here and have law and order. We are a more civilised and enlightened community!'

'What is your concern then?'

'His tribe will not accept his incarceration. They will come after him. They will punish him themselves for being the perpetrator of this incident, but they will not accept another tribe detaining him. This is how tribal wars start. We haven't had an incident for a year or two. This will not be good. You, Beau, would be expected to fight if necessary. It's not safe here now. We must go at first light. In any case, I sense you are both ready. It is time for me to guide you to your next destination.'

'Where are we going?'

'Tomorrow, you will see.'

*

As the soft light of sunrise filtered through the trees, Aaron appeared at the entrance to Beau and Ellen's hut.

'What do we need to take?' asked Ellen, having no idea of what lay ahead.

'Nothing but water,' replied Aaron. 'You'll have everything you need where we are going. Let's get underway. We have a two-hour trek to the base of the volcano.'

'The volcano! We're not going near that thing, are we?' asked Beau, alarmed. 'It's still active, isn't it?'

Aaron turned without responding and started walking towards the trail leading from the village. They walked past the man detained the previous night, kept in a bamboo enclosure with two guards diligently watching him.

'No doubt the village that he's from would have missed him by now. It will not be long before they come for him,' Aaron noted.

'Won't your people miss you, Aaron?' asked Ellen.

'No, I often come and go for long periods. I live amongst them; however, I'm not one of them.'

They walked for hours and the massive volcano loomed ever closer. Beau was becoming increasingly concerned the closer they got.

'When was the last time this thing erupted?' he asked.

'Not while I've been on the island. Most probably the day it rose from the ocean. It doesn't mean it won't today, though. At times we have tremors, so there's still a lot going on in that crater,' responded Aaron with a slight grin.

Beau shook his head with concern and looked at Ellen who was smiling also, enjoying the mind games while trying to contain her own doubts. Eventually, they arrived at a vertical wall with no obvious path forward. Beau looked at Aaron. 'Great, where to from here?' he said almost mockingly.

'Through there,' Aaron said, pointing to a crevice that was almost undetectable. It was a slim gap in the wall travelling up about thirty metres at a slight angle, barely wide enough to fit through sideways.

'I'm not going through there,' Beau said. 'I won't fit.'

'Don't be a girl,' Ellen responded, smiling even more now as she moved towards the narrow crevice that Aaron had already disappeared through. She looked back at him where he was standing with his mouth open, dumbfounded.

'It's like the underwater cave, Beau. Sometimes you have to face your fears,' she said, giggling to herself.

He looked back towards the track from where he had just come and, shaking his head in resignation, reluctantly followed Ellen into the wall.

'I can't stand tight spaces,' he said, his words echoing through the crevice. His mind was racing and a wave of panic came over him. Sweat trickled down his forehead and he could feel the rock pressing on him both back and front.

'Keep moving,' came the faint voice of Aaron, who was now disappearing further into the crevice.

Beau, his heart pumping, finally began to slowly edge sideways through the wall as his fear of being left behind overtook his claustrophobia. They were climbing, and he picked up his pace to try and catch up with Ellen, desperately not wanting to lose touch with Aaron. It seemed an age, although probably only three minutes had passed before he emerged in a massive underground cavern where he joined Ellen. Aaron had already moved ahead to the far side of the huge expanse. It was three storeys high to the cavern roof with only a sliver of natural light emanating from the crevice from which they had just emerged.

Aaron gestured for them to follow a narrow path leading around the wall of the cavern. It was a well-worn rock floor, winding upwards. They made their way along the path, constantly trying not to look down as they climbed ever higher until they were almost at the roofline. Aaron again squeezed through a narrow gap to a smaller cavern and then onto a ledge which, to their complete horror, traversed the rim of the crater.

'We are inside the volcano!' Beau said in disbelief.

'Be very careful here. Focus on the trail not the pit,' Aaron urged them.

Frozen with fear, Beau and Ellen were standing on a metre-wide ledge looking into a pit of red and orange molten lava swirling far below. The heat was immense on their faces as they stared down, mesmerised by the constant movement of the lava, almost drawn to its beauty.

'Keep moving quickly, both of you,' Aaron urged. 'We want to spend as little time traversing this ledge as possible. You can easily be overcome by the heat and fall in. You would not be the first.'

Beau knew he was not kidding. Eventually, after some fifteen minutes of intense concentration, they traversed the volcanic rim and seemed to arrive back where they had started. Beau looked at Ellen and shrugged in a gesture of confusion as they passed through what appeared to be the identical chamber they had passed through before. As he entered the small chamber, convinced he was back where they had begun, Beau could feel a familiar wave of energy, a resistance. Like a physical pressure on his skin, ever so slight but unmistakable. He pushed through it and turned to Ellen. 'Did you feel that?'

'Yes. It was exactly the same feeling we experienced when we came through the underwater cave.'

'We seem to be going around in circles,' Ellen said to Aaron.

'It would appear so, however, not everything is as it appears,' said Aaron without stopping.

They returned down the identical track to the floor of the cavern and back into the crevice, and emerged a few minutes later at the cliff face in front of the wall where they had started.

'Are you having us on?' demanded Beau.

'Easy, Beau,' Ellen intervened, trying to calm him down.

'Look up there,' Aaron said, gesturing towards the sky above the steep wall of the volcano. The entire mountain top was bathed in a soft light, unlike anything either of them had ever seen before.

'Did you notice when you came through the lagoon and appeared on the other side that it was exactly the same as where you had just come from?' asked Aaron.

'Well yes, we did, although it felt energetically different. It was an amazing coincidence.'

'Coincidence? No, it is no coincidence. It's difficult for you to comprehend, I know. We've travelled to a different realm, a different space/time continuum.'

Ellen looked at Beau in amazement. 'I've studied these phenomena in theory but we can't experience such an event, can we?'

'You just did. That's enough of the questions for now. We have some climbing to do.'

Aaron led them up a steep path that wound higher up the outside wall of the volcano. The air became cooler and the cloudless sky seemed to beckon them onwards. Finally, they crested the peak and a large plateau emerged in the distance. There was a village on the plateau far below, bustling with people. The whole plateau was bathed in brilliant sunlight, creating a picture-perfect scene as if from some fairytale. They stopped for a moment to take in the wonder of this place.

'Look Ellen, you can see the distant coastline. This is truly a magnificent place, Aaron. Do the other villagers come up here?'

'No, they're stuck in their restricted world. They don't know it exists. It's not part of their reality. They're not ready to transcend their known existence. The path forward is not even apparent to them. They honour fear over the unknown, and so they choose the known where limited expansion exists. Each of us evolves at different times and only those ready to discover the next level of truth about our existence transcend to the next realm.'

Ellen looked at Beau and felt the emotion welling within her. 'Is this where Cappy spent his time?'

'Yes, Ellen, it is. Cappy was here in this village before he got the calling to return to the world as you know it and help others on their path of discovery. You, it would seem, are one of the chosen ones.'

Ellen's heart was filled with immense gratitude. Thank you for your love and guidance, old friend, she acknowledged, reaching for Beau's hand as they continued along the summit ridge towards the path leading down to the village.

CHAPTER SEVENTEEN
Realm of Discovery

The path wound along the ridge above the village, past a large crystal-clear lake leading to a massive waterfall. The thunder of the water was deafening as it fell hundreds of metres down to the plateau below. It formed a stream that meandered through the fields near the village, then flowed into another lake at the far edge of the plateau before cascading off the edge, directly into the ocean far below.

'Wow, look at that,' exclaimed Ellen. 'It's like a scene from a fairytale. Everything is so pristine and clear and illuminated by the sun drenching the entire plateau. The grass is so green and the sky's bluer than I've ever seen it. This place has a beauty unlike anything I've experienced in all of my travels, Beau.'

'It's incredible, babe.' Beau hugged her, feeling their connection that was deepening into love.

The path down to the village passed under the waterfall many times as it wound its way down the steep descent. The misty spray from the enormous volume of water cascading down felt refreshing after their long day on the trail and seemed like a fitting cleanse before they entered the village. As they walked across the open fields with the towering rim of the volcano now behind them, and the magnificent expanse of the ocean in the far distance as a backdrop, the three of them made their way to the edge of the village. Ellen and Beau expected the local inhabitants to greet them cautiously as before. What they experienced was unexpected and they were stunned, looking around in bewilderment. It was as if all the countries of the world were represented, the people surrounding them as if they were conquering heroes.

'Welcome, welcome you made it, congratulations.'

There were pats on the back, hugs, smiling faces of all colours and nationalities, and voices speaking in many different languages. They were swept up in the melee.

'Just enjoy the ride,' suggested Aaron who was also in the middle of the huddle, which was moving slowly towards a large central town square surrounded by stone buildings. The crowd moved slowly back still chanting, leaving the visitors in the middle of a large circle of fifty or more people.

'What happens now?' asked Beau.

'Now we get to meet Cielo,' answered Aaron, smiling and trying to contain his excitement.

The crowd parted, and a striking woman with a captivating presence glided into the town square and stood tall and regal in front of them. She was lean, ethereal in appearance, and she had olive skin, broad shoulders and was an imposing hundred and eighty centimetres tall. Despite her height and broad shoulders, her raven-black hair flowed down her back suggesting she embraced her femininity. She was wearing a colourful silk wrap that wound around her waist and her chest and over one shoulder. She showed little expression on her beautifully sculpted, strong face with high cheekbones and a small square chin. She emanated inner strength. She looked at Beau and Ellen directly in the eyes, penetrating right into them with her clear, emerald-green eyes as if to examine every minute part of them.

Then she smiled and turned to Aaron, taking his right hand in hers and holding the palm of his hand to her heart and hers to his, embracing him affectionately. 'You've done well, my friend.'

She turned to Ellen and Beau and said, 'I'm Cielo. We've been waiting for you.' She walked to Ellen and embraced her in the same way, and then did the same with Beau. Beau felt a rush of pure love through his body as she separated from the embrace and held his shoulders. She looked him in the eyes again, and then back at Ellen, saying, 'Please join me in the Great Hall.'

She turned and with the grace of a catwalk model, glided back across the square to a large stone building with huge solid timber double doors adorned with intricate carvings. Stunned by her magnetism and held captive by her imposing presence, Beau and Ellen followed without question.

It was late afternoon and the sun was gradually sinking low in the west, softly tinging the clouds pink and orange and creating an eerie half-light. Many others from the community flooded into the Great Hall. Cielo was in the middle of a large circle with a small circular stage raised at its centre. There was no seating. Everyone sat on the floor facing Cielo, who sat cross-legged on the raised stage.

'Will we get to talk with her?' Beau asked Aaron, excited about what was to come.

'We will. Just observe for now. There will be plenty of time. This is a simple ceremony that we do every day as the sun sets, giving gratitude for all that is.'

Beau looked at the stage where Cielo was gazing towards the ceiling, some ten metres above them. In that moment, the afternoon sun reflected through the centre of the dome-shaped roof, which was sealed by a glass prism. As if on cue, a beam of light poured into the room and directly onto the stage, illuminating it and Cielo like a spotlight. Cielo stood, arms stretched above, reaching towards the prism of light.

'I acknowledge and give gratitude for all here who are present and, in particular, to our new arrivals. May you find what you are looking for. Bring forth all the universal wisdom that resides in us and beyond, to heal those who have come to seek love and guidance. May they see the divine perfection in their triumphs and their adversity, leaving only pure love pervading their spirit.

'Join hands now. One by one around the circle, announce one thing you're grateful for to the person either side of you, starting on your left.'

There were over a hundred and twenty people gathered in the Great Hall and the process flowed effortlessly. Genuine gratitude was expressed by all present, with tears of joy evident on their faces.

'I've never felt such a loving and connected energy in a room like this,' Beau said to Ellen.

'I haven't either, Beau.' Ellen was clearly moved by the experience.

At the end of the ceremony, Cielo stepped down off the stage and walked to Beau and Ellen. She offered her hand to help Ellen stand, and Beau followed. She placed her hands on Ellen's shoulders and looked her directly in the eyes in a genuine connection, saying nothing. She then placed her hands on Beau's shoulders and connected with him in the same way. The love they felt pouring through them was overwhelming. Ellen had tears of pure joy streaming down her face. 'But I don't even know you,' she said, not understanding what she was feeling.

'I've known you since the dawn of time,' replied Cielo, smiling and leaving the hall.

Aaron guided Beau and Ellen out of the Great Hall to a stone house on the edge of the square. There were at least half a dozen people tending to the home, sweeping floors, scrubbing benches, stocking shelves, and making up beds with clean blankets.

'This is where you'll be living,' motioned Aaron.

'Why are these people helping us?' asked Beau.

'You're a welcome member of our community now. Everything is shared and everyone helps each other.'

Beau looked at Ellen and shrugged his shoulders. 'Thank you, Aaron. Thank you so much for guiding us to this place.'

'You guided yourself through intention. I'm just a conduit. That is my role and my purpose. Tomorrow I'll leave you and head back to the village.'

'You're not staying with us?'

'No, I must go back and wait for the next enlightened souls who find their way to the island.'

'Travel safe, my friend, and we shall see you again,' said Beau.

'That you will, Beau.'

Ellen and Beau looked around their new accommodation, touched by the lengths that the community had gone to to make them feel welcome. There was a refrigerator, a butane gas cooker, a full pantry, and fresh hot bread on the counter.

'Can you believe this, Ellen?'

'I'm trying to take it all in. I've never felt so welcomed.'

There was a knock at the door.

'Hi, welcome. My name is Sebastian and it is my honour to show you around.'

Sebastian appeared to be in his mid-forties. He had a strong Spanish accent, was lean and suntanned and had jet-black hair and a goatee. He stood tall and proud.

'Thank you, Sebastian, we would be grateful to have you guide us around.'

'Come then; let me show you your new environment. Please feel free to ask any questions. I'm sure you have many.'

They followed Sebastian out of the stone hut, noticing the many houses of a similar construction and realising that the village was built in a certain pattern. The Great Hall at the centre was surrounded by huts similar to theirs. They spanned outwards in ever-increasing circles, with seven laneways radiating out like seven spokes on a wheel.

'Is there a purpose to the layout of the village, Sebastian?' asked Beau.

'Everything has a purpose, Beau,' replied Sebastian, not stopping to expand on his answer.

As they reached the outskirts of the town, Beau estimated that there would be at least fifty stone huts similar to theirs.

'There appears to be no school or courthouse or any other administrative buildings, Sebastian.'

'That is correct, Beau. The Great Hall at the village centre is the only place for the community to meet and all matters, including education for children and adults alike, are conducted there.'

'What do all of these people do with their time?'

'They are like any community. Some are bakers, some are builders and some are teachers of our children.'

'What about Cielo? Is she the leader of the community?'

'We don't think in terms of leaders and followers here. Cielo has access to great wisdom, wisdom beyond the rest of us here. For that reason, she holds a special place amongst us.'

'Where did she get the wisdom from?'

'All in good time, Beau. All in good time.'

On the outskirts of the township, lush fields were planted with all manner of crops. There were also pens with pigs and fowls, cows grazing in the fields and goats perched high on the ridges surrounding the village.

'I noticed we have gas and power in our hut.'

'Yes, we are completely sustainable. We have butane gas made from pig secretions. And tomorrow, I'll take you to the turbines at the base of the waterfall which generate much of our power. Water is in abundance here, as you can see. The energy from the turbines is stored in massive battery banks. We also harness power from the sun, the source of all life.'

Beau was captivated by their ingenuity. As they circled back around the village to arrive at the entrance to their hut, Ellen expressed their gratitude for his informative tour and warm welcome.

'I'm just across the square in that stone hut with the red door if you need me. Please do not hesitate to call for me if there's anything you require.'

'Before you go, Sebastian, what is your role here in the community?'

'To put it in terms with which you will be familiar, you could call me the mayor of the village, although it is an honorary position. A chosen obligation if you like.'

'Okay, I see. So you were elected?'

'Elected,' Sebastian laughed. 'Yes, well, I guess I was elected through the law of attrition. You see, apart from Cielo, I've been here the longest.'

'The longest? If I may be so rude, how long have you been here?'

'Time is not relevant here, however, based on your normal calendar, I guess it would be close to fifty years or so.'

'Fifty years? That's not possible. You can't be more than forty years old!'

'I'll be seventy-five in March this year, by your time,' announced Sebastian with a grin as he turned and walked across the square towards his house. 'I'll see you in the morning.'

Beau smiled at Ellen and shook his head. From what they had experienced in the short time since they'd arrived, there was clearly something beyond their meagre understanding prevailing over this place, he thought.

They had the most peaceful sleep they could ever remember and awoke as the sun streamed through their open window. Ellen set about making their breakfast.

'How did you sleep?' asked Sebastian, inviting himself in.

'Good morning, Sebastian. Beau and I were just finishing up some breakfast. Wonderfully, thank you.'

'That's great. Today will be a big day. Cielo is keen to meet with you and start your sessions.'

'Sessions?'

'Yes. She will meet you in the Great Hall as soon as you feel ready.'

'What are these sessions that you refer to, Sebastian?' asked Beau.

'They are the beginning of your awakening. It's nothing for you to be concerned about. Have you noticed the openness and unconditional love that exists within the community here? That is because they have worked tirelessly to free themselves from the unnecessary burdens they carried around for most of their lives until they found this place. We are all still peeling back layers of conditioning and changing our beliefs around issues that constrain us. These sessions will help you to do the same.'

'Well, we will be delighted to meet with her as soon as we're ready, Sebastian, thank you.'

'She will be waiting for you in the Great Hall,' Sebastian repeated, then he turned and left as quickly as he had come.

'I'm fascinated and intrigued by what lies ahead,' Ellen said to Beau.

'But what do you think it's all about?' Beau asked.

'I wouldn't worry about it, Beau. Based on my experience so far with the people here, I'm looking forward to meeting with Cielo.'

Beau nodded unconvincingly as they cleaned up and prepared for their meeting.

They entered the Great Hall, noting it was completely empty apart from Cielo sitting on the raised platform, bathed in a beam of sunlight. Her eyes were closed and she appeared to be in some form of meditative state. Without looking up or opening her eyes, she acknowledged Beau and Ellen's presence. 'Welcome to you both. Come up here and sit with me.'

They sat opposite Cielo. She reached forward and held each of them by the hand. 'I'm sure you have many questions.'

'Well, yes we do, Cielo.'

'We are an open book here. Please feel free to ask anything you wish.'

Beau hesitated before asking, 'What is this place? How long has it been here? What is its purpose?'

With a knowing smile, Cielo answered, 'These are the three questions most commonly asked by all newcomers, not surprisingly. I'll cover some foundational knowledge in our first meeting today, but we will have many such daily meetings. To start with, you're in the village of Polaris, on an island of the same name. It's more widely known as a mythical legend in some cultures. A lost land in the middle of the Pacific Ocean. As you can see, it's very real to you in this moment. It has been here since the dawn of time and will always be here. Its legend as a lost land stems from those who have spent a lifetime seeking it without success. It only appears to those who are ready to discover the truth that resides here. Its purpose? Its purpose is to unlock a new level of awareness for the chosen few who seek it. Most people are unconscious, travelling through life unaware of the magnificence that surrounds them. Perfection that exists in everything, the grand design if you will, at least to the extent we can comprehend at a low level of evolution. It takes an open mind and an open heart to embrace all that Polaris has to offer. It has also been referred to as one of the pathways to the Empyrean, the source of all creation.'

Ellen sat wide-eyed and looked at Beau in stunned silence, hanging on Cielo's every word. He nodded as if to acknowledge Ellen's lifelong search which had led her to this place. He was in a haze of disbelief, trying to comprehend what appeared to be incomprehensible.

'I will, when the time is right, reveal universal laws that govern our existence. This knowing flows from the collective knowledge that exists in the fourth and fifth realms. I'm just a soul on my own journey, as you are. Please do not see me as anything more than another soul who has been down the path you are on, a common path for us all in our evolution. A teacher, just as you needed in primary school preparing you for high school. There have been many teachers presented to you over the course of time. We've tended to either kill them because their views threatened the power structure of society, or hold them up as gods, the creators of all things. It is true they are part of creation; however, they are only a small part. The source, or the Empyrean, as the ancients described it, exists at a level beyond all comprehension. No one, past, present or future, who resides in the lowest realms of existence here on Earth can access it. Each of us only has access to the realm we are currently connected to. At the earthly level, it's a bit like a toddler trying to understand quantum physics. To get there, you have to build the foundations of understanding. That is our purpose on Earth. To build a level of understanding that allows us to eventually escape the physical world and shed ourselves of these earthly bounds. I can assure you, it's a quest worthy of your energy.'

'I like the physical world,' Beau blurted.

'That is normal, Beau. Our ego is attached to our physical identity. Part of our challenge in elevating our vibration to higher frequencies is to shed the ego, our obsession with a singular identity and our attachment to all things physical. We should still embrace these things while we are here to experience them. It's just that when we are held captive by them, we stay stuck, looping in unproductive life cycles. We are all on a journey, an exciting discovery of ourselves. All else is a mere fabrication in the complex web of existence, designed to provide exactly what we need to confront us for the sole purpose of our individual expansion. The mind is perfectly designed from the moment our soul enters the body to create unique perspectives on life, forming our views, prejudices, beliefs, and fears. Is any of this making sense to you both?'

'It's the most beautiful explanation I've ever heard of life. Deep in my knowing, I believe I've always known this to be true for me, Cielo,' responded Ellen.

'That is because you're beginning to trust your knowing, Ellen. You're communicating with your higher self. That is what led you here in the first place. Nothing is an accident. I see that you're familiar with Polaris, or at least with the legend that surrounds it.'

'Yes, I've studied the constellations. Polaris is a star known as the North Star or true north. It's a symbol of polarity and balance, equality and synchronicity.'

'Brilliant, Ellen, exactly.'

'How did you know that she was familiar with Polaris?' asked Beau, intrigued by Cielo's intuition.

'I see past your words, Beau. I see your pure energy, which reveals everything I need to know.'

A little intimidated, Beau wondered if she could read his mind and everything he was thinking. 'What are these sessions we've been told about, Cielo?' he asked awkwardly.

'While you've physically arrived here, this is a gateway. You can only continue your journey to a higher realm and all that it has to offer once you're clear of the constant chatter and emotional noise burdening your minds. If you remain bound by the constraints of the physical world, lost in the emotional turmoil that is the foundation of the lower realms, you will continue looping there. These animal traits cloud the ever-present messages of the higher mind and soul. You cannot access the next realm of evolution until you gain mastery over these basic instincts that all of us have, which are perfectly designed as feedback to guide our higher mind, but not to hold onto as an identity. You both have unresolved emotions, and I will work with you to dissolve their control over you. That is our priority for now!'

'Surely you're not suggesting that we need to get rid of all our emotions?'

'No Beau, I'm not suggesting that at all. Emotions are an essential part of our feedback mechanism. They exist to pinpoint areas within us that are out of balance. Just as a warning light in a car indicates something that is not working, emotions are our soul's warning light. We are not meant to hold onto emotions. We are meant to trace them to the source of our unrest and resolve them. Most diseases suffered by mankind stem from unresolved emotions. Have you noticed when you're infatuated, angry, grieving, or engaged in some unrealistic fantasy that you're thrown off-centre? You're unable to make clear choices. That is because your higher mind, your soul's voice, is masked by the animal level choices that exist in the earthly realm. Mankind seeks to embrace every pleasure and avoid every pain. This obsession creates a dense vibrational energy that distorts the clear messages our soul and higher mind have access to. Any time you perceive a positive without a negative, or vice versa, you'll bring into your reality an event that will evoke the polar opposite emotion to bring you back to your true centre.

'As Ellen explained, Polaris, true north, is the place of polarity and balance, equality and synchronicity. This is called equilibration. You'll notice a significant difference in your peace and calmness and your capacity to access your higher mind once you deal with emotional issues. Once you master equilibration, you'll want to experience the physical world in a different way. You'll embark on each new day with wonder in your heart and gratitude for the perfection of creation.'

'What about love? Isn't that an emotion? Surely you don't suggest we remove our unresolved emotions around love?'

'Love is not an emotion, Beau. Love is the essence of who we are. I'm not talking about infatuation. Infatuation is an emotion. Our unresolved emotions around infatuation are wrongly labelled as love. Pure love cannot be dysfunctional. It's something very different. The people in this village are all at various stages of equilibrating their emotional state. I'm sure you've already noticed they exude grace, wisdom and love which is all that the higher mind and soul are. In essence, all that you are. The path to awareness and evolution is through quieting your emotional chatter and allowing connection to your higher mind and soul. Once you cleanse your unresolved emotion, we will move on to some revelations about our existence and creation, to the extent of my humble understanding. I have limited knowledge, limited by my current evolution as a soul. There are vast expanses and evolutions beyond my meagre understanding.'

She paused. 'But I sense that your minds are full right now, trying to absorb this information. We will start tomorrow morning, first with you, Ellen, as I sense you are readier. Beau, you've come on this journey inspired to this point by Ellen who has been searching for many years. I sense that you've been searching as well. However, your search has recently been inspired by dramatic events. If you prove not to be ready within yourself, it will be revealed and you'll be asked to leave.'

Ellen looked at Beau with a concerned expression. Cielo would not hesitate to banish Beau if he was not ready for the next level of expansion.

CHAPTER EIGHTEEN
The Sessions

As Beau and Ellen entered the Great Hall the following morning, Cielo was waiting with two men and a woman. Beau recognised Sebastian, who gestured for them to come forward and sit opposite them. He then introduced Ava, Lionel and Nickolas.

'These are my most trusted healers and they will be assisting us today,' Cielo announced.

Beau and Ellen nodded in acknowledgement.

'Before we begin, I must ask you, Ellen, given we will be revealing some deep and personal information, are you comfortable with Beau in the room?'

'I'm happy to leave,' interjected Beau.

'That won't be necessary, Beau. I would like you to stay.' Ellen reached for his hand.

'Wonderful, no secrets then,' declared Cielo. 'In any case, there is nothing any of us has done or not done in our lives that is deserving of judgement from others.'

'How so?' asked Beau.

Cielo thought for some time, as if to contemplate whether to take his question further. 'Is it all right with you, Ellen, if we explore Beau's question first? I think it is important.'

'Absolutely, Cielo, please continue.'

'Let me ask you, Beau; what is a human trait you believe you would never display and yet you would judge others for?'

'That's easy; there is no way I would kill someone. I do not believe in taking the life of another, so I can state without hesitation that I would never do that.'

Cielo looked towards Sebastian and nodded. He moved quietly into position and was simultaneously joined by Nickolas, Lionel and Ava. In an instant, they grabbed Ellen and dragged her to the centre of the Great Hall, holding her down on the floor. Sebastian produced a large knife and held it tight against her throat, with aggression and madness in his eyes. Cielo looked at Beau who was standing with his mouth open in shock. She reached for a large knife sitting just behind her. She stood and walked towards Beau, placing the knife in his hands. 'We're about to find out. Sebastian, in thirty seconds, I want you to slit her throat.'

Sebastian nodded as if he would enjoy the process. Ellen struggled beneath the weight of her three captors with terror in her eyes. She was crying uncontrollably, wriggling back and forth in an attempt to set herself free.

'What the fuck are you doing?' shouted Beau. 'Let her go now!'

'We will not let her go, Beau. You have twenty-five seconds left before we slit her throat.'

Beau paced around, screaming, 'You people are fucking mad!'

Ellen's terror increased as she felt the pressure of the cold steel blade of the knife against her throat.

'Beau, for God's sake, help me!' she pleaded. 'Help me; they're going to kill me!'

'Let her go! Let her go right now!'

'We will not let her go, Beau. Ten, nine, eight…!'

'Stop right now, you fucking maniacs!'

'Six, five, four…'

'Stop now, or I will…'

'Or you will what, Beau?' asked Sebastian, still appearing intent on ending Ellen's life.

'I'll fucking kill you, that's what!' he screamed, holding the knife above his head in a violent outburst and moving in close to Sebastian ready to strike.

Just as the tension in the room reached a climax, Sebastian and the others let Ellen go and helped her to stand. Beau's face was red with rage and he was shaking uncontrollably as he turned and looked at Cielo.

'What the hell was all that about?'

'What I'm interested in, Beau, is what would you have done?'

Beau looked at Ellen, who was trembling. He realised he had lost complete control of any rational thought and, still shaking, he bowed his head and dropped the knife to the floor. He looked up slowly and said angrily, 'I would have killed him.'

'So, if it meant his life or hers, you would have killed him? Three minutes ago, that was not even remotely possible for you.'

Beau nodded, trying to contemplate what he now realised he was capable of.

'Exactly, you would have killed him. Let this be a lesson. We are all capable of murder under the right circumstances. There is no trait that exists in the human realm we do not all possess and are all capable of exhibiting. That is why judgement is such a useless pastime, but regrettably, it is practised by most. Think of it this way: unless you've walked in my shoes, you'll never truly understand my motivations. Based on your values, you are capable of killing in order to protect what you hold most dear. We all are.'

Beau was shaken. He walked towards Ellen, who was being held and acknowledged by Sebastian, Lionel and Ava for her bravery. He pulled her towards his still heaving chest. She collapsed into his arms and he held her for a long time.

'I actually thought I was going to lose you,' he said.

'These are not ordinary sessions,' Cielo declared. 'They will be confronting at all levels and they are crafted to get to the core of issues decisively.'

'Well, you certainly achieved that,' said Ellen, now laughing through her tears.

'Take a moment and gather yourself, Ellen. We will begin sessions again in fifteen minutes.'

Beau and Ellen walked outside the Great Hall into the sunlight. 'This is intense, Ellen. Are you sure you want to continue?'

'I'm sure, Beau. I believe they have a pure intention and you must admit that was an effective way to convince us about judgement, don't you think?'

'Effective, yes, it was effective all right,' laughed Beau, still shaken. 'That has to be the most impactful lesson I've ever had.'

'So, let's not judge their methods. Clearly, these people are here for our benefit.'

Beau nodded although he was still stunned by the experience.

They returned to the centre of the hall where the elders were waiting.

'Are you feeling okay to continue, Ellen?' asked Cielo.

'Yes, I am, thank you Cielo. I thought you were a peaceful loving people.'

'Love moves in mysterious ways, Ellen. Sometimes, tough love is the most appropriate love. I want to ask you, what have you been searching for these past years?'

'I guess I've been seeking more understanding about the meaning of life.'

'Ah yes, the meaning of life. A very broad goal, that is for sure. But if you were to narrow it down, what within you do you hope to heal through this process? What is missing and unresolved in you?'

Ellen thought for some time and emotion gradually welled up within her. She looked down, struggling to maintain her composure.

'That thought right there, Ellen. Where did you go just then?'

Ellen slowly looked back up at Cielo. 'I was thinking about my father.'

'Fine, your father. Tell me about him.'

Ellen's lip quivered as she tried to gather herself.

'How old are you in the memory you have right now, Ellen?'

'Nine, I'm nine years old.'

Beau sat silently, not game to move, fascinated by the intensity of the situation.

'What is your father doing?'

'He is packing his bag.'

'He is packing his bag. Okay then. Why is he packing his bag? Is he going somewhere?'

Ellen responded, barely whispering, 'Yes, he's leaving home.'

'He is leaving home. Leaving home on a trip?'

'No, he's leaving home for good,' Ellen spluttered through her hands, covering her face. Her whole body was convulsing with pent-up emotion.

'Will you get to see him again?' asked Cielo.

Ellen could not answer. She simply shook her head.

'So that was the last time you saw your father? It is what you just recalled in your memory?'

Ellen nodded yes.

Cielo motioned for Lionel, a man who appeared to be about thirty-five years old, to sit in front of Ellen.

'Ellen, I want you to look up. Look at this man sitting here in front of you. In this moment, this man represents your father.'

Ellen slowly raised her head and wiped away the tears. The little girl in her, desperate to see her father, looked deeply into the eyes of the man in front of her. She could see and sense her father as if he was actually there. Something she had imagined a thousand times before.

'Ellen, it's me, your father,' Lionel said softly, with pure love and a longing to connect with her. He reached for her hand and asked, 'How have you been, my beautiful girl?'

She refused his advance, reacting, 'How do you think I've been, you bastard? Alone and lost, that is how I've been.'

'I'm so sorry, my darling. I've missed you so much. Can you forgive me for leaving?'

'Forgive you? Have you any idea how difficult our lives became when you abandoned us?'

'No, I don't. I'm so sorry I was not strong enough to confront my demons and stay in your life. I've thought of you every day of my life.'

He held his hand out to her and with love in his teary eyes asked, 'Come to me, Ellen, my beautiful girl.'

Ellen sat stuck in her anger and disappointment, unable to move.

'You can't just come into my life and ask to be a part of it,' she challenged him. 'You left us alone, to fend for ourselves. I used to cry myself to sleep every night.'

Cielo moved in closer and placed her hand on Ellen's shoulder.

'You must have a lot you want to ask him, Ellen. He is here, now. Ask your father what you've always been yearning to ask him. He is sitting right in front of you. Go ahead, ask him.'

Ellen looked at Lionel, then at Cielo. Turning back to Lionel, she said in a soft, fractured voice, the voice of a little girl, 'Why did you leave me, Daddy? Was it my fault? Didn't you love me anymore?' By now, she was sobbing uncontrollably.

Cielo placed her hand on Ellen's shoulder again. 'Now, I want you to swap places with your father.'

Slowly and silently, Ellen exchanged places with Lionel.

'Now Ellen, I want you to become your father. That's right, feel exactly what he would feel. Lionel, you are now Ellen. Ask again.'

Lionel repeated Ellen's words with the same tone and inflection in his voice. 'Why did you leave me, Daddy? Was it my fault? Didn't you love me anymore?'

Ellen sat for an age looking at Lionel then back at Cielo.

'I want you to go deep inside yourself, Ellen. I want you to access all that you know about your father. Everything you've blocked, everything you know to be true. The answers you seek are right there inside you. Become him in every sense. Trust your knowing.'

Ellen slowly turned back to Lionel. She could feel her father and all that had been going on for him at the time he left. It was a knowing that came from deep within her. She became him in every way. 'Of course I love you, my darling. I've thought about you every day of my life since I left.'

Leaning forward, Ellen reached out and held Lionel's hands. She looked deeply into his eyes and with tears streaming down her face, said from the heart what she had always known deep down to be true. 'Please hear me when I say it was not your fault. How could it have been your fault, you were just a little girl.'

Looking down, Ellen examined her inner thoughts and, with absolute certainty, delivered her truth as to why her father had left. 'Ellen, you were too young and you were unaware of the truth,' she said, as if channelling her father.

'I was an alcoholic and a drug addict,' she continued. 'I had been that way for a long time before you were born. I could no longer trust myself with you or your mother, as the alcohol made me violent. I thought it was best if I left you and your mother's lives for good. I thought you would be safe and happy without me in your lives.'

Ellen looked at Cielo, stunned by the truth of why her father had left. She was quivering uncontrollably.

'You see, deep down you've always known the truth,' explained Cielo. 'Your father loved you so much that he left your life believing it was the most loving thing he could do for his daughter. Swap places again.'

Ellen and Lionel returned to their original places and sat knee to knee.

'Hold hands. Ellen, this is your father sitting in front of you again'.

Lionel repeated word for word what she had just revealed. Ellen internalised the truth of what she had always known. She shook uncontrollably as the cells in her body holding onto all of her pent-up anger towards her father reordered themselves.

Cielo asked, 'If you could have one thing from your father right now, what would it be?'

She held out for some time before eventually saying, 'I just want to be held.'

She reached for Lionel then and fell into his arms, crying uncontrollably. He cradled her like a small child, and she sobbed and sobbed for a long time. He stroked her hair and acknowledged her the whole time.

Cielo motioned for Beau and the others to come in close. They gathered around and formed a huddle as Lionel cradled her. Ellen felt the love of her father pouring through her just as she had wished as a little girl. Cielo broke into a hum, a tune with a resonance Ellen had never experienced before. It was a harmonic that went right through her, reaching every cell in her body. After around fifteen minutes had passed, Cielo asked, 'So Ellen, what have you learnt?'

Wiping away her tears, Ellen looked at Cielo and replied, 'I know in my heart that my father always loved me. Even though he caused me great pain in abandoning me, I know now he did it for me.'

'Your father was a broken man. You knew this deep down, when you revealed your truth. I believe that now, with your new perspective, if you searched your repressed memories you would recall incidents of his violence when you were a little girl.'

Ellen nodded. 'Yes, there's no doubt my upbringing was full of tension and although I was protected from the worst of it, he was very volatile and Mum wore the brunt of it.'

'It never ceases to amaze me how much the truth lies deep within each of us but we choose to honour the emotional trauma rather than our own knowing. Do you feel a little bit lighter after expressing that emotion and understanding where it comes from?' asked Cielo.

'Absolutely,' said Ellen, who was now giggling with relief.

'I want to take this one step further,' Cielo said. 'To put it in context, emotions exist only to serve as a signal that we are off-centre. Most of us carry unresolved emotions in our bodies, causing distress and depression. Depression is suppressed, unreleased emotion, pressed down like a great dark burden within us. It's normally capped by unreleased anger. In essence, it's the gap between unrealistic expectations and the truth of our life existence. If we create expectations that can't possibly be fulfilled, then we inevitably become depressed. Expression is one of the keys to releasing depression. The other is to understand the reasons those emotions become locked in the first place. What are we being unrealistic about? Where have we set up a fantasy that can never be fulfilled? You pined for the love of your father and wished him back in your life. You expected him to walk through the door one day.'

'You're absolutely right, Cielo. I did expect him to walk through the door every day.'

'It was never going to happen, was it?'

'No, I can see now that his way of loving me was to stay away.'

'So you carried a level of depression through life based on an unrealistic expectation.'

'I wish I'd met you years ago.'

'All you've done, to this point, is release some locked emotion and gain a level of understanding as to why your father left you. The next level of your healing will be to change your entire perception, your belief system. But that is enough for now,' Cielo announced. 'Let's have a break and enjoy a meal together. This afternoon, I want to take this to another level.'

Beau looked at Ellen, wondering what could possibly be next.

Ellen was chatty over lunch. 'I feel that a huge weight has been lifted off me, Beau. However, I know there's more to this. I can't believe the truth was within me all of my life, yet I carried that trauma around unresolved like a dark veil hidden from others. I guess I wore a mask to hide it, projecting a carefree image. It wasn't until it was exposed that I realised how much it was affecting me.' She paused. 'Beau, are you listening to me?'

'Sorry, babe, I guess I'm just really reflective right now. Watching you go through that has brought up a lot of emotions for me.'

'What sort of emotions? What do you think they mean?'

'That's the problem, I just don't know. I'm churning up inside and I feel quite ill.'

They walked back to their hut and, sensing he needed some space, Ellen left him in a state of deep contemplation and self-analysis. She returned to walk back with him to the Great Hall.

'Welcome back. Please join our circle,' invited Cielo as the afternoon sessions started. The four elders were standing in the centre of the room and Beau and Ellen joined them and closed the circle.

'Join hands. I want to acknowledge these amazing people and give gratitude for their journey of healing. May our intuition and insight flow through us in a collective energy of connected souls as we join together with a pure intent of accelerating the healing of those who have come to seek illumination.'

The energy flowed through Beau's body as it had done when they first met Cielo. It was an intoxicating rush that brought tears of gratitude to his eyes. He looked at Ellen and she was obviously affected also.

'I've never felt more accepted and unconditionally loved,' Ellen said, acknowledging each of the elders in turn.

Cielo said, 'Ellen, I want to take your healing from this morning and create a change of state within you. This healing is based on a principle that is taught by only the most evolved. Although it is a universal principle that exists everywhere, it remains a mystery. It's there in plain sight, yet, as a people, we choose to remain in a mist of confusion and uncertainty. This is one of the fundamental building blocks of all creation, yet the world at large looks everywhere but the obvious for their answers.'

Beau was looking at Ellen, confused but excited.

'Do you realise that everything that exists does so from a duality of positive and negative? The creation of our existence can be traced back to the division of a single cell. When we split the atom, we discovered that cause and effect were involved. We are in a constant state of simultaneous creation and destruction. Nothing is ever gained or lost.'

'In that case, we must be immortal?'

'Well, Ellen, we are not immortal, yet we are eternal. We are simply energy. The basis of all known matter in every corner of the Universe is energy, including us. The soul is a being of light. Scientists have labelled a photon 'wave particle'. Past great masters have called it the hidden face of God. We are one and the same. Inseparable. To understand creation, it helps to study the collective knowledge of past masters. Einstein concluded that the Universe is created and destroyed every ten to the power of forty-three seconds through an endless oscillation between wave particles. All things, including us, are made of fine-grained, strongly interacting positive and negative particles, all neatly balanced out.'

'Okay, I get the link, but how does it have any relevance to our day-to-day lives?'

'Our mind, with its incoming ideas and outgoing thoughts, is also composed of, or associated with, vibrations of electromagnetic light wave particles. Our mind tunes in or tunes out by increasing or decreasing the frequency of vibration of these light wave particles.'

'So, are you actually suggesting that my thoughts can be detected by someone else?'

'Have you ever thought of someone and, in that instant, they have called you or contacted you in some way?'

'Of course I have.'

'How do you think that may have happened?'

'I haven't thought about it.'

'Let me use an example. A mobile phone's electromagnetic waves can be transmitted at the speed of light around the world in one seventh of a second. Our thoughts and our mind's vibrations are beyond our capacity to understand in terms of connectivity. Most people feel free to ignore any human law whenever that seems to serve their purpose. It's universal law that ultimately governs Earth and its inhabitants. These laws have existed since the dawn of creation. They are unveiled as we discover, bit by bit, pieces of the puzzle that we had not seen before. There is nothing new that exists.'

Ellen looked at Beau, knowing they were in the presence of knowledge beyond what they knew.

'Who are you?' Ellen demanded, looking directly at Cielo.

'That will require further explanation, Ellen. All in good time. In this moment, I'm interested in continuing your healing. Based on what

I've described, do you understand that everything is in perfect balance at all times? That includes you and your emotions, given we are just particles of light-emitting wave particles of energy.'

'Yes, I think so,' she stuttered, looking at Beau who shrugged his shoulders.

'So it follows that if you're experiencing a negative energy, there must be an equally charged positive energy in perfect balance at the same time?'

'Well, yes, however, there was nothing positive about my father leaving me.'

'Nothing positive,' repeated Cielo. 'Um, okay. Did you not under-stand what I just explained about equal energy existing simultaneously? There had to have been a positive to your father leaving, Ellen, based on universal laws. You have become identified with your so-called trauma. Most people walk around oblivious to being trapped in a one-sided perspective about things that have happened to them. Their past gives them a story, an excuse about who they are. It's scary when you peel away all excuses in life. Don't be too hard on yourself though. It's part of the reason we are enduring this lifetime. One of the greatest discoveries in human nature is that you can change your life by changing your perspective and attitude of mind.'

'How can I change my perspective. If it happened to me and I was the one who lived through it, isn't that my perspective?'

'Can you recall, as best you can, what it was like in the home with your father there?'

'It was volatile. Since this morning, I've recalled much more about my life back then.'

'Volatile. Okay, then what was it like after he was gone?'

'If I'm honest, it was calm and predictable and loving. My mum gave me much more time.'

'And once your father left, who became the father figure in your life?'

Ellen thought for a moment. 'No one that I can recall.'

'Think harder. We are always in perfect balance. You felt abandoned by your father, the father energy, in that moment, but there must have been someone with father energy supporting you. Who became the father figure in your life at the exact time your father left? Think hard, they were there. Who was it?'

Ellen sat for a long time, shaking her head, struggling to come up with anything, then in a flash of realisation it came to her. 'Oh, that's right, Cappy! He lived next door. He came over all the time. Even when Dad was still there, he used to come over to check on us and make sure we were all right. If I'm truthful, he was fathering me for many years by filling the void left by my father's life choices. I guess, now that I think about it, he was a surrogate father to me. He would tell me stories. Whenever I wanted an older male's point of view, he was always there for me, even as an adult.'

'He would have been a great influence, Ellen. After all, he spent some time amongst us here. Nothing is lost. Energy is not destroyed, it transforms. Your father's absence brought to you a surrogate father in Cappy. So there are no coincidences, Ellen. You've been on a path since you were a young girl, created by you, but you were not aware of it.'

'It would seem so.'

'Let's take this further. We've established that life at home improved significantly. We've established that you had a father figure all along, even though he was not your biological father.'

'Yes, I did,' stated Ellen, still amazed she had not seen the obvious.

'What if I told you that your higher mind came into this world knowing exactly what your soul needed for you to expand? And that you created every experience that has happened to you? Let me ask you. Have you pushed away relationships in your life to make sure they did not leave you first?'

Ellen looked at Cielo as if she was mind-reading, and then she looked at Beau, almost embarrassed.

'Yes, that's exactly what I do. It has cost me many relationships. As soon as I had strong feelings for someone, I would do something to push them away.'

'We come into this life with pure intent to manifest situations perfectly designed to set up patterns and beliefs that give us exactly what we need in order to evolve greater awareness. What do you think yours was, Ellen, given what happened to you as a young girl?'

Ellen thought for a moment and the answer was evident. 'Have my father abandon me?'

'Exactly, Ellen. We set up these events in our lives in the form of trauma and adversity and sometimes, positive situations like excessive abundance. All of these creations will bring forward, over time, the opposite energy to return you to balance, into equilibration, if you're aware enough to see the perfection. So Ellen, why did you create these experiences?'

'I guess I was just testing how much they loved me. My dad left me and I thought he loved me, so why wouldn't my partner leave me? If I was horrible to them and they loved me enough, they would stay. It was a test, I guess. I sure pushed some of them to the brink just to see if they would love me enough to stay with me.'

'That is exactly why you did that, Ellen. And in the process, when they inevitably left, because you ramped it up until they did, you would get to be right. Your false story about who you were due to past trauma, the abandoned victim, would be vindicated. "See, they always leave me." It validates the victim in you and you stay stuck, looking for the next relationship to do the same thing, never really understanding why you did what you did, or worse, blaming the other person in the relationship. People with emotional pain like this get very good at subconsciously selecting partners who will, eventually, leave them as well, just to validate their pain.'

'Oh yes, I've done that with most of my partners,' Ellen conceded, reaching for Beau's hand. Then she sat for a long time, shaking her head. So many wasted years doing the same things, she thought. 'Hold on. I'm confused. If we're always balanced, why do we need to set up these life experiences? Surely they're not necessary?'

'That is incredibly insightful, Ellen. We can only truly know ourselves once we've experienced all parts of ourselves and integrated them. The path to higher realms is to experience life in all its glory and disappointments, to own and integrate every part of ourselves, every human trait, which brings together all our opposite sides, therefore increasing our vibration. Through this process, we understand that we are all one and the same. We can remove all judgement of ourselves and others so that only love, gratitude and wisdom remain.'

'I'm a psychologist. Why couldn't I see what I was doing?'

'We rarely see our own dynamics, Ellen. I intuit that you're very insightful about others.'

'She sure is,' interjected Beau, looking now at Cielo with a growing curiosity. Eventually, he could not contain himself. 'How do you know all this stuff? As Ellen asked before, who the hell are you?' he insisted.

Cielo looked at Lionel, Ava and Nickolas.

'Sometimes, Beau, to be in service to others, in the interests of increasing awareness and elevating the vibrations of all mankind, we choose to come back and share our wisdom with those who are ready to hear it.'

'Come back? Come back from where?'

'We are from here just as you are; however, some of us have evolved beyond the physical world to another realm of pure energy, closer to the source. To come back into a physical body and live with the restrictions that come with that is a supreme sacrifice for us. It is, however, a chosen obligation. We are here to serve and assist those ready to vibrate at a higher level and ascend.

'That is enough for today. We are nearly ready for our sunset ritual when the entire village comes together to give gratitude and share wisdom in support of others. Take some time, clear your heads and we will see you at the sunset ritual. Then, tomorrow, we will meet again for sessions. Then, Beau, we will see if you are truly ready to integrate here or not.'

Beau looked at Ellen with concern. She smiled at him and with her newfound certainty, hugged him.

'You're here for a reason, Beau,' Cielo stated, noting his uncertainty. 'You should embrace all that this place has to offer. You created every event that has led you to this place. You're still writing the script. What do you want it to look like?'

Still feeling ill and reflective, Beau reached for Ellen's hand as they left the Great Hall and wandered into the late afternoon twilight.

He became increasingly unsettled as the afternoon drifted on.

'I just don't know what's wrong with me, Ellen. I feel like escaping this place even though I know it's amazing and healing.'

'You're feeling a high level of anxiety, Beau. It's normal. Usually, people run from the feeling. It indicates that something big is about to be revealed, and you know it will be painful emotionally to re-experience it. I see it in therapy all the time. This is exactly when you should walk towards it and not away from it, as most people do. Confronting your past is where the real healing begins. In amongst all that pain and hurt is the chance to come to terms with the past, let go of what is holding you back, and come out the other side, free from the shackles that have bound you for years.'

'It still scares me though, Ellen.'

'If it was easy, everyone would do it, Beau. That's why so many of us travel through life with unresolved emotional baggage and live a restricted, unfulfilled life as captives of our fear.'

'How are you feeling after your sessions?'

'It's difficult to describe how calm and centred I feel. My thinking is clearer and I'm at peace within myself. Not elated and not fearful. If I was to describe it, I'd say I feel integrated, resolved and content, harbouring no secrets or fears. I can't believe how the burden of my father leaving had become a cloak that shrouded me every day of my life and affected my relationships so much. It wasn't until it was removed that I realised how big a burden I was carrying. It was not so much expressing my anger that released me, although it did feel good to get it out, it was more the understanding of why I suppressed the emotions of him leaving and the effect it's had on my life with other relationships. Once Cielo explained the balance of energy, both positive and negative, that was always there in every emotional situation, it led me to re-evaluate my life after all these years. I'm simply blown away by the relief and freedom it's given me. I've been constantly labelling things that have happened to me as good or bad. To understand that they are neither good nor bad and that they are both, simultaneously, is a revelation. I can see it clearly now as if a veil has been lifted, and the intricate workings of the world and all the interwoven, interconnected parts.'

'Wow, I could do with some of that, Ellen.'

'That is exactly why you must confront your fear and take this unique opportunity while it's here. Without clearing your past and understanding how it relates to your life, I don't believe you will see the perfection. So, Beau, if not now, when?'

'You're right, Ellen. I wish I could do it right now.'

'Tomorrow is your time, Beau. Try and get some sleep tonight. Tomorrow, you need to be ready to give everything you've got. You'll need to be completely vulnerable and honest if you are to achieve your ultimate breakthrough. That seems to be the key to a great outcome.'

Beau nodded reflectively, searching his life for what might come up as his big breakthrough. Deep down, he knew it would have something to do with his father, however, there was much more beneath the surface he had suppressed, feared and failed to confront.

Beau and Ellen embraced the sunset ritual that evening and enjoyed connecting with the others, giving gratitude for being on Polaris and having the opportunity to seek the wisdom that resided in this magical place.

Ellen woke in the early hours of the morning and Beau was not beside her. She hurried out of bed and heard movement in the bathroom.

'Beau, are you all right?'

There was no response. As she entered the bathroom, she found him slumped over the toilet. She rushed to his side and comforted him as he repeatedly convulsed into the bowl.

'I don't know what's going on, Ellen. I feel as though my whole stomach is turning inside out.'

'You're churning inside because of emotions that have been bottled up for most of your life. The thought of confronting in the next few hours whatever's going on for you has brought them to the surface. I think it's a good thing,' she assured him, helping him back to bed.

Beau did not sleep for the remainder of the night. Ellen spooned him as he lay in a foetal position, shaking, dreading the new dawn and what tomorrow might reveal.

CHAPTER NINETEEN
Beau's Awakening

The next day dawned as beautiful as ever. The mountain village was drenched by the morning sun, creating comforting warmth and a glow brighter than anything they had seen. The sky was clear and the air so fresh it smelt sweet.

Beau had a glassy look in his eyes as he and Ellen entered the Great Hall. Cielo was waiting with Sebastian, Ava, Lionel, and Nickolas from the day before. Sebastian introduced a younger man named Matthew and a middle-aged man named Harrison. They were welcoming, exuding the same calm, certain energy. Cielo welcomed them all and gestured for them to sit as she led a universal expression of gratitude. Beau was fascinated to watch as tears welled in her eyes. She was clearly overcome with gratitude. The others, in varying degrees, followed her with an earnest expression of their own.

'May we have access to universal wisdom and love as we come together with the purest intention of healing the newest member of our village, Beau.'

The ritual was quick but intense and the group all took a deep breath to return to being present in the room for the next phase. Cielo reached forward and held both of Beau's hands, looking deeply into his eyes.

'Beau, it's your time. You've been in a state of emotional turmoil for the past twelve hours. What is underneath all that emotion?'

'How do you know that?' Beau asked almost accusingly.

Cielo did not respond. She held his stare and waited for an answer.

'I don't know.'

'Yes you do, Beau.'

'I'm trying to understand it, where it comes from. All I can come up with is the hold my father has had on me during my whole life.'

'Let's explore this a little further. What are you feeling right now, in this very moment, with regards to your father? If you could describe it, what colour is it?'

Beau sat looking down at the floor, searching for an answer. In a soft voice he responded, 'Black, it's black.'

'Okay, that's great, Beau, it's black. If you could describe the texture of your emotion, what would that be?'

Again, Beau continued to look down while he searched his feelings, trying to understand it without knowing what it was.

'If I had to describe it, I would say it's like sump oil, thick and sticky, as if it's all over me.'

'Great, so it's black, thick and sticky like sump oil all over you. If you were to relate that to your father, Beau, what does this black, thick, sticky sump oil have to do with him?'

Beau sat for some time, shifting uncomfortably as he sat cross-legged on the floor. Cielo sensed a wave of emotion rising within him and, just as he looked up at her, tears welled up in his eyes.

'I feel as though he's smothered me, controlling every part of my life since birth. He was the coach of my football team, he pushed me with schoolwork, he was always reminding me that I'm the heir to the Sterling dynasty and have a responsibility to ready myself for the inevitable.'

'What is the inevitable, Beau?'

'The inevitable is that I will assume the role of managing partner of Sterling and Finch, one of Australia's foremost law firms. And the unwritten inevitable is that I will produce a son and heir to replace me.'

Ellen looked at Beau, surprised, given he had never mentioned this aspect of his relationship with his father before.

'How have you reacted to this lifelong pressure, Beau?' asked Cielo.

'It's one of the reasons I'm sitting before you now,' replied Beau. 'I confronted him a couple of months back when I left Australia to come on this trip. I met with him in his office at our family home and told him that I no longer wanted to be a lawyer, nor did I have any desire to take over the family business.'

'It sounds to me, Beau, like you've already taken a huge step towards breaking one of your lifelong patterns. That pattern was giving your power away to your father. I have no doubt the breaking of those shackles has helped you to vibrate at a higher frequency, leading you to Ellen and ultimately here, to Polaris.'

'I had not thought of it that way. I guess so, Cielo.' Beau smiled at Ellen, who was nodding approvingly.

'I want to take you back to your childhood, Beau. I understand that your father was obsessed about your legacy within the family, particularly given he fulfilled what he saw as his obligations a generation before you. But his controlling of you seems to be more than this. How early in your childhood do you recall your father becoming so smothering?'

Beau rubbed his face with his hands, trying to clear his mind.

'I want you to look at the floor, Beau. Put both hands palm down on the floor. Look at them and take yourself back. Imagine those hands are the hands of a five-year-old boy, a six-year-old boy, a seven-year-old boy.'

Just as Cielo mentioned the seven-year-old boy, new raw emotion filled every part of his body and he started to shake his head.

'What is going on for you right now, Beau? You're seven years old. Where are you?'

He hesitated and kept shaking his head, trying to avoid the painful memories. 'No, it's nothing,' he said, still shaking his head.

'Beau, you are seven years old. Where are you?'

He took a deep breath and, as if he had been transported to another time, revealed, 'I'm at my best friend Curtis' house.'

'Why are you there, Beau?'

'He lived a few blocks away from our house and I used to go there in the afternoons after school because Mum and Dad were at work.'

'Okay, so you're at your friend's house. Who else is home?'

Beau sobbed with fear and bowed his head. He began to shake, saying, 'No, no,' moving his head from side to side. 'There is no one else.'

'Beau, there is someone else there. Who is it? Don't be afraid. We are here for you. Who is in the room with you?'

'I just wanted him to stop. Please make him stop!'

'Make who stop, Beau? Who is with you at your friend's house?'

'It's Curtis' father. He's coming into the room again. Please tell him to go away!'

'What is he doing, Beau? Is he in the room yet? What is he doing?'

With absolute terror in his voice, Beau answered, 'He's taking his belt off again and yelling, "Drop your pants, both of you, right now! Bend over the bed and get what's coming to you, you naughty, disgusting little boys."'

'Is Curtis beside you?'

'Yes, we're holding hands and crying, screaming, "Stop, please stop!"'

'And what's happening now, Beau?'

'He's strapping us violently, again and again with his belt.'

Shaking uncontrollably, Beau could hardly utter a word as he relived these dramatic childhood moments.

'So, he's finished strapping you with his belt, Beau. What's he doing now?'

Beau did not answer. Shaking, he rolled over on his side into the foetal position, rocking back and forth. Ellen was stunned and terrified.

'What do we do now, Cielo? We can't leave him like this.'

Cielo was calm and centred, and she nodded at Ellen. 'This is perfect, Ellen. This is exactly where he needs to go.'

Cielo leant gently over the top of Beau and whispered in his ear. 'Is the black, thick, sticky sump oil all over you now, Beau?'

'Yes, it's all over me.'

'It's a dark energy pinning you down, Beau. You've been carrying it around with you all your adult life. You need to face it, Beau, right here, right now. What's happening to you now, Beau? What is Curtis' father doing now?'

Beau was rocking back and forth, lying on his side, shaking.

'Just get him off me, please, tell him to stop!'

'What about Curtis, Beau? Is he still there?'

'Yes, he's on top of Curtis now. Curtis is screaming and I can't help him. Oh my God, I can't help him, I can't help him!'

At that moment, Cielo signalled to Lionel and the young man, Matthew, to move into position. Matthew lay down next to Beau.

'Beau, Curtis is lying beside you now. He's calling out to you, Beau. What are you going to do?'

Lionel had taken off his belt and was simulating beating the young man who had taken on the role and actions of Curtis. Then, he pinned him down as if to force him into a sexual act. Beau could not stand to hear Curtis screaming for help.

'I can't do anything, Curtis, I can't. He's too strong.'

'Help me, Beau, please help me. Get him off me!' screamed Matthew, emulating Curtis' terror.

In that moment, something snapped in Beau. With the strength of ten men, he flew from his position on the floor and, in a split second, smashed Lionel from the side, rolling around on the floor, wrestling with him. Lionel was protected by the other elders, who were guiding the process without Beau being aware. After a considerable struggle, Beau ended up straddling him, sitting on his stomach, pinning his hands to the floor.

'You'll never touch him again, you sick bastard!' Beau screamed, his face only inches from Lionel's. 'It stops now!'

Beau forcibly held Lionel to the floor, symbolically regaining his power over their tormentor, and cried the pent-up tears of many years.

Lionel lay there submissively, not making eye contact, as if defeated. Some minutes passed. Eventually, as Beau's energy and anger subsided, Cielo gently grabbed him by the shoulder and said, 'It's okay, Beau. You've wanted to do that for a long time, haven't you?'

Beau took a very deep breath and, exhausted, looked at Cielo, 'Yes, I have.'

Cielo motioned to Ellen.

'Ellen, I want you to take Beau outside into the fresh air. Take some deep breaths and enjoy the sunshine. Afterwards, have something light for lunch and be back here for the next phase. We've released some stored emotion and brought the trauma to the surface, which is useful. However, we are yet to deal with the mind. Recalibrating his belief system will create more permanent healing. Before you go, it's important that Beau understands that Lionel was not Curtis' father. He was playing a role. I don't want any residual energy remaining unresolved towards the elders. So Beau, listen to me, this is Lionel. He is not Curtis' father, and this is Matthew, not Curtis.'

Beau, with love and gratitude in his eyes, stepped forward and hugged both men. He appreciated what it must have taken for them both to adopt roles such as that of a sexual predator, so foreign to who they were as evolved souls.

'I don't know how you can do that so convincingly.'

'That is easy,' responded Lionel. 'We've all been that person and committed similar offences against others throughout the passage of time. Remember, there is no trait that is not inherently a part of us. The key to removing all judgement is to own that we have, at some time during our long journey, been capable of such atrocities. As appalling as it may seem to us at each stage of our evolution, we would not be who we are today without our past experiences, both as a victim and as a perpetrator. This is how we gain polarity in our energy field, thus increasing our vibration. It's all part of the master plan and the only pathway to accessing higher realms.'

Beau nodded numbly. Ellen, reeling from the revelations of the past few hours, nodded and without a word, escorted Beau out of the Great Hall.

Ellen and Beau sat alone during lunch and Beau did not speak a word. He was lost in his thoughts, occasionally breaking down, integrating the massive confrontation of his hidden trauma that had been revealed. He occasionally shook uncontrollably, releasing waves of suppressed energy. Ellen intuitively knew to give him his space and allow him time to put everything into perspective. She had not spoken a word to Beau by the time they returned to the Great Hall for the afternoon session.

'Welcome back,' Cielo gestured to them.

Beau was now more aware and present as he returned to his body. Ellen smiled at Cielo, indicating that he was okay and ready to continue. Cielo repeated her ritual of looking towards the light streaming through the roof of the Great Hall, giving gratitude for the flow of collective wisdom and healing that was about to take place.

'Welcome back for the next phase. To release stored energy and emotion in your body, taking back the power you gave away all those years ago, is healing and important. The lasting change in your vibration only comes from changing your belief system. It comes from understanding that you created this traumatic set of circumstances over an extended period of time for your soul's greater purpose.'

'I have to stop you right there, Cielo. You have no concept of what I went through. That abuse went on for three years.'

'I understand, Beau. However, what I would like to explore is, why? Why did you bring this into your reality?'

'Why would anyone bring this into their reality? It's ridiculous to suggest that someone would go through this level of suffering of their own volition. It was just the depraved act of a sick man and we were the victims. End of story!'

'Did you hear anything that Lionel said just before you left this morning's session, Beau?'

'Well, sort of, I think so.'

'I thought not,' she replied. 'Okay then, let's go further with this. Beau, I need to ask you, what happened to Curtis?'

'Why is that important?' Beau asked disdainfully.

'Because I believe you have another unresolved emotion that you're not talking about.'

'It's over and done. Time to move on, it's as simple as that.'

'Curtis. Beau, what happened to him?'

Beau avoided eye contact with Cielo as Ellen moved closer, holding him, sensing there was something big he was suppressing. He slumped and was choked up with emotion before he finally announced, 'He committed suicide. There; are you happy? He killed himself and I couldn't do a thing about it. I wasn't there for him.'

Ellen kept holding Beau as he revealed the true depth of his trauma.

'You're feeling guilty? Is that right? You could not prevent his abuse and beyond that, his eventual suicide?' Cielo prompted.

Beau could not speak as he bowed his head and just sat, supported by Ellen, not capable of holding his own weight.

Cielo had peeled back every layer of his wounded soul, leaving him bare and exposed. Beau lost control of his emotions, continually muttering the words, 'I'm sorry Curtis, I'm so sorry I wasn't there for you.'

Cielo allowed Beau to cycle through his emotions. After some considerable time, she placed a hand on his shoulder and looked him in the eyes. 'What age was Curtis when he took his own life, Beau?'

'He was fifteen years old.'

'Were you a part of his life at the time that he took his own life?'

'No, my father had moved our family to a new home. I hadn't seen him for five years.'

'So you had no way of knowing that he had drifted into such a level of despair, causing him to take his own life?'

'No, I had no idea. I found out about his suicide from an old school friend some years after it happened.'

'How long have you been blaming yourself for Curtis' death?'

'Since the day I found out about it. I should have been there; I should have known he would take his own life. It was his father, for God's sake. How could he do that to his only son?'

'He was obviously a very disturbed man, Beau, and as a young boy, you could not possibly have changed the situation.'

Beau sat in silence for some time, shaking his head, coming to terms with the deep secret he had held inside him since childhood.

'Beau, I need you to listen to me right now, this is very important. When did your father find out about the abuse?'

Beau took a breath, looked Cielo in the eyes and said, 'Only after it had been going on for a few years. I broke down in the kitchen one evening because I refused to go back to their house after school, as planned. Dad demanded to know why and pressed me until I started crying, completely distraught. I told him what had been going on. He demanded to know why I hadn't told him earlier. Curtis' father was a very violent man and a drunk. He had knives and a gun in the house, which he would bring out to threaten us. He told us both that if we said a word to anybody, he would not only kill us but our families as well.'

'And what did your father do about it, Beau?'

'He told me that I wouldn't be going back there ever again and that it would be taken care of. I have no idea what my father did, although I do know what he's capable of. He knows powerful people in powerful places, some ex-clients in the underworld. We moved to a new home a month later and I never saw Curtis again.'

'And what about your mother, Beau. How did she react?'

'Dad made me swear never to tell her. I guess he wanted to spare her the anguish.'

'Did you notice that your father's protection and smothering of you dramatically increased following this incident?'

Beau looked thoughtful as a new and insightful realisation came over him. 'Come to think of it, he was very different after that. He wouldn't let me go anywhere by myself. He never missed picking me up personally from school, and I used to go back to the office with him until it was time to head home. Every school holiday, I was required to work at the firm filing documents.' As the memories came flooding back, he continued, 'Wow, that's right. I just realised. He signed me up as part of his sailing team at around the same time. We sailed every Saturday in the regattas around Sydney Harbour. He also took on the coaching role of my football team. It was as if I was attached to his hip from that moment on.'

'So, Beau, you can see that your father, suffering his own guilt over not protecting you, overcompensated from then on. He made sure that you were never left unprotected again.'

Beau sat with a stunned look on his face, the full awareness of what Cielo had said flooding through his body.

'You're absolutely right. I would have done the same thing if I were him. As a father, he must have felt incredibly inadequate and lost.'

'Yes, and he's spent the rest of his life making it up to you. You see, his motive was love for you, Beau. It was never to rob you of your potential for your own life. He just got lost in his world of overprotection and nurturing of you by staying close to you, which has continued until this day. To our parents, we are always children in need of parenting regardless of how old we become. No wonder he wanted to keep you in the family firm. The dynasty was just an excuse.'

Beau had tears in his eyes, but for a different reason. All his resentful energy towards his father had dissipated. Now, he only felt understanding, pure love and gratitude for him. He wished he could be by his side right now to hug him and tell him how much he loved him. 'Yes, I do see all that now,' he said, with a new perspective on his father's role in his life.

Cielo ended the session with another gratitude circle and Beau could not wipe the smile off his face. He had never felt so free. He held onto Ellen at every opportunity, thanking her for her strength, love and guidance, his heart full of love and gratitude.

'You see, most of what we lament as victims are emotions we store, often for a lifetime, based on hate that comes from a lack of understanding of the benefits of any given experience. I need to ask you, Beau: because of the trauma you experienced, there must be an equal and opposite benefit to you and your life's purpose? You attracted the trauma into your life to launch you towards something greater for the good of humanity. I want you to think for a moment. What did you go on to do as a result of your experience as a seven-year-old boy?'

Beau thought about this and then, as if a lightbulb had flashed in his mind, his eyes lit up and he responded, 'Pro bono. I've been a champion of the legal rights of abused children. I've devoted a great deal of my time, without seeking financial compensation, to ensure that these victims have their day in court. I can't believe that I've never made that direct connection before. I guess I was never really looking for a benefit in amongst my pain and suffering.'

'Most people don't, Beau. But your contribution to society is directly attributable to your traumatic experience. That is the sort of lifelong inspirational work that can come from such adversity. If you look deeply enough, you find that the balance is always there.'

Beau and Ellen looked at each other, amazed at how, in just three hours, his life could be so liberated. He felt light and full of love and gratitude without the heavy dark energy that had prevailed over him for decades. The mask of his strong and stoic demeanour had been stripped away. There was no longer a need for him to be anyone other than his authentic self.

'So Beau, how do you feel about Curtis' father now?'

'He is still an asshole, Cielo. However, I now see his role in shaping my life and giving it some purpose in the bleak and negative environment that is practising law.'

'I guess that's all we can ask for at this stage, Beau. In time, you'll shed a tear of gratitude for his role. I will leave you with this. What if he had agreed to come into this world and be a part of your creation, your experience, to give you exactly what you needed in order to grow and expand? What if he did this, even though he knew he would destroy his own life and be persecuted in the process? Would that not be the ultimate act of love for another?'

'That would be the ultimate sacrifice, wouldn't it?' he conceded, nodding his head.

'Yes, it would. That is all for now.'

Cielo closed her eyes and privately gave gratitude for the healings that had taken place.

As they left the Great Hall, hand in hand, Beau commented, 'It really is true, isn't it, Ellen?'

'What's true, Beau?'

'Cielo always says, "If we change on the inside, the world changes on the outside." Nothing in my outside world has altered, just my perspective of it and the realisation of how it has served me. With that awareness, everything looks different.'

Ellen thought for a moment. 'You know what, Beau? I'm only just getting it. Perhaps the Universe exists on the inside, in our mind and soul, and the outside is just a projection of our own creation; part of the journey we've chosen for our evolution?'

Beau had already turned his attention elsewhere and did not respond. He was lost in the carefree feeling of having the burdens he had learnt to live with every day lifted. He felt truly liberated and was marvelling at the unique beauty of the plateau. It was as if he was a young child, seeing it for the first time, the orange glow of sunset providing a perfect conclusion to a day he would never forget.

CHAPTER TWENTY
The Hidden Truth

The following weeks and months passed quickly. Beau and Ellen continued to attend weekly sessions, peeling back layer after layer of stored emotions and breaking entrenched belief systems that had been hampering their freedom and their capacity to live an authentic life. Time had no relevance in this magical place, where the community banded together with love and respect for one another, giving daily gratitude for the blessings and life lessons that were bestowed on them.

Ellen passed the days helping tend to crops and spending time with the elders to learn as much as she possibly could. She had spent years searching for something that she had been told by many was only a myth. Now that she had found it, her passion was to become an effective part of the village, contributing to their daily life, immersing herself in the culture and serenity. She became obsessed with Cielo and her wisdom, soaking up every piece of knowledge she could.

Beau helped around the village with building maintenance and daily chores. Each day, just before the sun set, they walked the two kilometres along the path to the edge of the plateau and sat looking out at the distant ocean. Curiously, Beau thought, no ships or boats ever passed by. Three months had passed quickly.

On one of their evening walks to the edge of the plateau, they felt Cielo's presence behind them.

'How have you settled into village life?' she asked.

'We both love it here, Cielo,' answered Beau. 'Every week that goes by we become clearer and closer to each other and ourselves. The peace we feel is something we've never experienced. We've been waiting for the most appropriate time to ask: where does all this come from? Where does your wisdom come from? The common answer around here is, "All in good time." Don't you think it's time we were provided with some real answers?'

'Yes Beau, it's time you both knew more about Polaris.'

Cielo sat down beside them. She stared out over the ocean and was silent for what seemed an age. Eventually, she spoke.

'During your sea voyage, you found your ship surrounded by a mist. That mist is the veil that hangs over each of us, perfectly designed to keep us blinded until we are ready for the truth that lies just beyond it. Once you were ready to see past the mist, you were guided to Polaris. Ellen, you and your desire to seek answers to your evolution as a soul in your lifetime has led you to this place. Beau, you too have, in your own way, been seeking answers. Facing your fears with your father and his expectations propelled you into a search for yourself, and you found Ellen.

'The others with you on your journey onboard *Orpheus* were merely players in your quest. That is why, when the time came to choose a path forward or back, they chose to return to their known existence. Regrettably, this is the response of most of humanity when it comes to choosing between advancing into the unknown or remaining stuck in a restricted world, regardless of the pain they endure daily. You'll recall that just before you arrived in Polaris, you passed through what would have felt like an energy field.'

'Yes we did, in fact Ellen and I mentioned it to each other. It first happened when we cleared the mist and the island revealed itself. It happened again in the underwater cave, and then in the volcano.'

'What you experienced was the crossing between one realm to the next. This island is a physical example of what exists in your world; however, the realms are hidden there and not clearly identified as they are here, on Polaris. Here, we reside in our own dimension, not visible to the outside world, unless the chosen few bring it into their reality, just as you both have. All the realms between realm one and realm four coexist simultaneously; however, people only connect to the realm they resonate with. We each have access to the realm that matches our energetic vibration, and we always maintain a heightened awareness of the realms below us that we've travelled through over time.

'We have no access to the realms above until we are clear, emotionally, from what has held us back and we can see clearly the positives and negatives of those events. It's only when we truly see them and have absolute gratitude for all our experiences that we can resonate at a frequency that connects us to a higher realm. That requires evolution and awareness at the soul level. When you left the beach, you passed through realm one, which was dominated by reptiles. Each of us has evolved through each of these realms, in our own individual and timeless journey, as we make our way back to the source of all creation. We still have reptilian traits and can revert to them in stressful situations. Fight, flight or freeze is a good example. These are pure reptilian instincts that stem from endless years of survival strategies and that serve in life-threatening situations. When you climbed up from the gorge and onto the plateau, you walked the trail through the jungle. Did you notice that the people there were a primitive culture, steeped in violence, worshipping anthropomorphic gods?'

'Yes, we came close to losing our heads and becoming one of their trophies.'

'They exist in realm two. At times we can, as humans, be violent and revert to these realm two traits. Curtis' father, Beau, was residing in realm two. That is why we cannot judge him for what he did not know. We've all been there ourselves in some form. Although in the present we can't recall past experiences, they are part of our soul's innate intelligence and evolution. We've committed similar atrocities somewhere in our past. We would not have evolved to this point without experiencing them both as perpetrators and victims.'

Beau and Ellen were lost in wonder, trying to integrate every word Cielo was saying.

'You encountered a resistant energy again as you traversed the underwater cave and entered the lagoon on the other side. That is the moment you entered realm three. More advanced and evolved people live in realm three. Aaron, as the gatekeeper, recognised your readiness to seek the next level of awareness. That is why he guided you here, to provide you with access to the learnings and wisdom within realm four. As the ultimate creator of your own existence, you've brought this island, and all it has to offer, into existence. Realm four is the last stage of human evolution in a physical sense. While there are many realms above realm four, your physical body is not required in any of them for your soul's continued evolution. You're pure energy and light.'

Beau sat motionless, as if time stood still, knowing that what he was hearing came from an inspired place. It resonated with his own truth. 'How do we access this level of knowledge when we leave this place?'

'You'll realise, if you leave here, that you always have access to higher realms and always have had, provided you continue vibrating at a frequency in tune with them. That requires you to use your emotions as feedback in each situation. The more centred you are, the higher your vibration and the quicker you will return to a calm, centred state when life events throw you off-centre. If you choose to remain reactive, holding onto emotions in a depressed, unliberated state, these animal level instincts will keep you stuck in the illusion for as long as it takes to set yourself free.

'No one promised that the evolution of the soul would be easy. Most of us are chasing the unattainable and we live in constant disappointment, looping in a world of judgement, greed and grief and seeking external validation, feeling there is no way out. At times, we will slip back through unresolved emotion into the lower realms and suffer the same torment; however, we will know the way back. We can consciously choose to *ignore* what we've learnt, but we cannot *unlearn* what we've learnt. This entire island is not a part of the physical world, although it's presented to you in this way to make it easier for you to comprehend. It has always been here and you've always had access to it.

'Time is irrelevant in the higher realms. Have you ever left your conscious thoughts behind and in a daydream state, found the answer to a problem that has plagued you? It usually happens in a contemplative state when you are alone.'

'Absolutely I have, many times!' replied Ellen.

Cielo looked at Beau. He was deeply searching his memory.

'I have also, come to think of it,' he said, starting to piece together his understanding.

'That is your higher self, accessing the higher realms.'

They tried to absorb this profound wisdom and then Ellen broke the silence. 'Somehow, I have an inner knowing that what you've shared has always been my belief, as if it were obvious, although I've never heard it as clearly as in this moment. Almost as if I was asleep and now I'm awake.'

'We are all knowing beings, Ellen, and wisdom resides in the fields of energy within the realms. After all, we are simply energy in a different form, always building and destroying. Even at a cellular level, we constantly renew. So yes, you've always had access to this wisdom whenever your energy field was ready to resonate with it. It's just that most people don't know how, because they're not searching for anything other than their daily survival, looking to strive and improve their material wealth in the hope it will bring them happiness.'

'What of the others on *Orpheus,* Cielo? What became of them?'

'They are players in your dreamlike state, Ellen, and even though they were a part of your journey here, they have no knowledge of it and are still drifting in a shroud of mist unaware that this island even exists. You've been here three months, in our timespan. However, time has stood still for them. In their experience, they have not left the ship and you are there with them. You're both here and there, and everything you experience here will have happened in an instant. Time and space are an illusion, Ellen. I can see you are still struggling with this concept. Let me give you an analogy. When you dream, the people in your dream seem very real, do they not?'

'Well yes, at the time I'm dreaming they are very real.'

'If you came across someone in your dream, do you think they would have any recollection of their involvement?'

'Well no, they have no idea because it's my dream, not theirs.'

'Exactly, Ellen. It is your creation, not theirs. Dreams are a powerful source of testing the realms, higher and lower, providing our subconscious with more information. The dream state is part of our higher mind's exploration. Through dreams, we can test the boundaries without our conditioned response constraining us.'

After some considerable time searching to understand, Beau asked, 'So are we in a dream here?'

Cielo replied with a smile, nodding, 'Yes, in a way, you are.'

'What about you? You're clearly from realms beyond here.'

'You may recall that I mentioned some of us choose to come back to the physical world and help others on their path of discovery. As you continue to evolve, you'll understand that there is no greater purpose for any soul than to be in service to others. That service can manifest in many forms. It may be to teach a skill, provide knowledge in some aspect of life, feed the homeless, or unlock the mysteries of the Universe to enable you to move to the next phase of your evolution. I've been where you are now and, in essence, we are one, not separate. We emanate from the same source.

'I've heard you refer to creation as the Empyrean, Ellen, which is of ancient Greek foundations. I use the term myself. Whatever people call it, they are referring to the same thing, the source of creation. Whatever I can do to help others vibrate at a higher level and ascend the realms, helps raise the collective awareness of all. There is no greater honour. When my time is done here, I will no longer reside in the physical world.'

'Does everyone have to come through Polaris to ascend to higher realms, Cielo?' asked Ellen.

Cielo laughed. 'No Ellen, this is your creation. Different souls have different paths to higher realms. This is yours.'

Beau and Ellen, with hearts full of awe, love and gratitude, stood and hugged Cielo, feeling her magnificent pure energy and light flood through their bodies. As they separated, and without a word, Cielo turned with that grace of movement that always fascinated Ellen and glided back down the long path towards the village. They were left to bask in the magnificent sunset with its orange tinge glistening on the distant ocean, each lost in contemplation.

*

The next morning, they awoke excited. 'I can't wait for today's wisdom circle, Beau. It's a shame it's only once a month during the full moon cycle. I wish we could have them more often. To have the mysteries of the world revealed with such clarity helps make sense of the hidden order of things.'

Beau reached for Ellen and held her in a loving embrace. They shared tears of gratitude as they reflected on the privilege of finding Polaris.

They were late to the Great Hall. The gratitude session again commenced, with each person expressing in three words something they were grateful for. Ellen loved the connection and intimacy that this simple, beautiful process provided. It always ended in connecting with the person either side of them.

Once the session began, Beau, who up until then had only been an observer in the wisdom circles, decided to jump straight in with a question he had always wanted to know the answer to. 'Cielo, what happens to us when we die?'

Cielo looked at him with a smile. 'Ah, the immortal question, Beau. What took you so long?'

The elders were giggling amongst themselves. They knew all newcomers would eventually ask.

'We never truly die, Beau. It's not possible, as we are energy, and energy is never gained or lost. As the saying goes, from dust to dust. We are, in essence, pure electromagnetic light wave particles. We simply transcend from one form to another. When we choose to create a physical experience, we separate from the many to the one. That is our journey here on Earth. When we transcend from the physical world, our journey is back to the many, the collective mass of energy in the realm we resonate with. The basis of all matter is energy, which, at our still basic level of understanding, is an intangible, light wave particle that science has labelled a photon. At my level of realm connection, I do not have access to what makes a photon, the basic particle of energy. It has been described by some as the God particle, or the essence of everything.'

'You mentioned God. Is there a god?'

'You're really on a roll today, Beau,' Cielo quipped, and the elders chuckled. 'It is a very individual question. God is just a term for creation. It has many interpretations and has been misused and misrepresented over the course of history. Primal peoples worshipped the sun, the moon and animals. In the last two thousand years, we've made God in the image of man, an anthropomorphic God. We have, over history, given our power to a higher entity. It makes it easier to blame, abdicate responsibility and keep us helpless. That helplessness has prompted those who take advantage of fear and insecurity to create a vengeful God. Religion controls the masses through indoctrination, keeping people stuck, worshipping something of man's own creation. These religious doctrines are more alike than they are different. That is because they all derive from the same documents produced by man over time, claiming they are the word of God. What better way to gain power and influence? That is not to say there are not inspired teachings in these religions. There are. My knowing, however, is that we are all part of creation; God, if you want to call it that. Each of us, as a part of creation, possesses the power of creation. In fact, everything that happens to us is our own unique creation, for the ultimate evolution of our soul, in the pursuit of our ultimate return to the source. For me, Beau, **GOD** is the **G**lorious **O**rigin of the **D**ivine. You can make your own interpretation.'

'So, what they teach in the Bible and other Scriptures is not true?'

'Societies need rules, Beau, and these doctrines contain very specific guidelines. They are there to keep people under the spell of the promise of eternal salvation. You do not need salvation. You are an eternal energy. You cannot be destroyed; only your form will change. You're a perfect creation, determining your own path. That is not to say that many of their guidelines are not worthy of following, so long as you do so because it resonates with your own internal knowing and not out of fear of some retribution.'

'So there is no hell?'

'Hell is a state of mind on Earth, Beau. When you give away your power and abdicate your existence to others, you do the same things over and over, get the same outcomes, and believe you have no control over your destiny. That is a place you might call hell. Liberation of your soul to higher realms does not come from someone else giving you permission. It only comes from growing awareness, embracing your experiences and seeing the perfection in all things. Only then can you vibrate at higher frequencies and access a higher state of being.'

'What is this perfection you speak of, Cielo?' asked Ellen, absorbed by the concepts.

'Our mind, with its incoming ideas and outgoing thoughts, also comprises or is associated with vibrations of electromagnetic light wave particles. Our mind tunes in or out by increasing or decreasing the frequency of vibration of light wave particles. Our capacity to do that will determine the extent to which we see the perfection in any situation. Let's use the example of a spinning top. The faster it spins, the more centred and upright it becomes. If one side is black and the other side is white, at some point they merge to appear grey, completely equilibrated. So, is the spinning top black, white or grey? At its highest frequency, there is only one perspective. It's perfectly merged and integrated. That is what we are trying to achieve with our minds. When the top slows down, there is density. If the top speeds up, there is awareness. What if your mind could see both sides of an event at infinite speed, blending black and white, and negative and positive emotions, which could be synthesised and synchronised into an unconditional awareness called love? You would, in that moment, weep tears of gratitude for the perfection that is our existence. I mentioned the photon before, the God particle, the divine essence and the frequency of infinite oneness. It's always in perfect synchronicity, both sides in perfect balance. That is all we are, so our journey is to maintain that state of being. The lower your vibrational frequency, as in the top spinning slowly, the more you differentiate and are separate, like the black and white side of the top.'

'Oh right, I get it!' said Ellen. 'So what you're saying is our journey in the physical world is to see the perfection in any situation, that nothing is ever gained or lost. Everything is always in perfect balance, just like a magnet with opposite poles. The more we can see that both sides exist simultaneously, the higher our vibration?'

'Exactly, Ellen, there is no pleasure without pain, no infatuation without resentment, no one side to any equation. One-sided equations can't exist. It would not only defy the laws of physics, it would defy the laws of creation. All of consciousness, including ours, is as an observer. Emotional reactions bring about an eventual opposite reaction in us, perfectly designed to bring balance to our energy, increasing our vibration, whether perceived or not at the time. If we ignore the opposite energy and stay out of balance in our perceptions, dense like a slow spinning top, our soul and mind will continue to create situations to bring us back to centre over time, until we can acknowledge both polarities and increase our vibration again. There is perfection in the system, and its feedback to our higher mind eventually leads us to a higher vibration. We can't lose. The world is full of people, however, who seek to take advantage of us by promising one-sided fantasies. We are drawn to these fantasies because they appeal to our realm two animalistic tendencies of seeking pleasure without pain.'

'Surely though, there are some situations that are too horrific to have an upside?' asked Beau.

'Let me ask you, Beau. At the exact time you were being abused, who was energetically supporting you?'

'No one that I'm aware of!'

'Someone was supporting you at that exact moment. Who was it?'

Beau thought for a moment.

'Well, Curtis was definitely supporting me.'

'Yes, he was. He was right there in the room with you. He loved you in that moment of despair, just as you loved him. Sometimes, we can't imagine where the support is coming from. It might be from the other side of the world, from your mother, your father, a sister, or a friend. It's always there in equal energy, in that exact moment, I can assure you. Energy does not dissipate; it just takes alternative forms and it is always perfectly in balance. That is why it's impossible to be incomplete as a soul. Nothing is missing. As we travel through the lower realms, we are constantly searching for that which is not actually lost, unconditional love, which, in essence, is our pure state of being. It's part of the grand plan in order for us to know ourselves. It's our own creation, perfectly designed to bring forth challenges for us to overcome. Eventually, the gift, on the other side of the equation, will be evident, balancing our perception, thus elevating our vibration. How many times have you looked back years later at a traumatic situation or major problem and seen the benefit of it as it has played out in your life? If you can grasp this universal law and apply it in any situation, it will liberate you and elevate you. It's like seeing through the matrix to the underlying order of things. The answer will also give you direction as to your life's purpose, to what you're meant to be doing with this life. Beau, did your abuse as a child have an upside in finding some purpose?'

'Well, yes, I guess so. I went on to do volunteer work assisting other abused children. It was the most rewarding thing I've ever done.'

'Right, so did you see it at the time?'

'No, not at all. I only saw it when you pointed it out recently.'

'Okay then. How long were you trapped in a self-imposed prison of negative emotion, grief and anger that kept you stuck all these years?'

Beau thought for a moment. 'At least twenty-five years.'

'Do you feel, since understanding the other side of your abuse and how it served your life purpose, that you've been released, that you've shed the emotional burden you've carried all those years?'

A huge smile came across Beau's face as he realised the extent to which he had been liberated. 'Yes, Cielo, I'll be eternally grateful for the peace you've brought me. It has made me realise that I must devote my life to assisting others in their journey through life. What I didn't realise was that I had already moved into my purpose by helping others, that is, representing abused children as a lawyer. I just did not see it at the time. I had found my purpose through my trauma.'

'What about your father, Beau?'

Tearfully, Beau responded quietly and contemplatively, 'I've spent most of my life judging my father, holding him away and blaming him for my lack of direction. I now understand why he did what he did. He loved me so much in his own way.'

Ellen looked at Beau and held his hand, acknowledging how far he had come.

'Judgement is interesting, Beau. We only judge others because we deny that we have the same traits in ourselves that we despise.'

I still can't forgive Damion though, Beau thought.

'Where did you go just then, Beau?' Cielo asked.

Beau snapped out of his fleeting thought and looked at Cielo.

'Oh, um, I was just thinking about my best friend who betrayed me by having an affair with my fiancée.'

'Betrayed you?' Cielo asked in a way that prompted Beau to regret the thought, wondering where this would now lead.

'Well yes, he did betray my trust.'

'How long had this been going on, Beau?'

'If I'm honest with myself, looking back, they had been seeing each other for some time. I just did not see the signs.'

'Did not see them or did not want to see them?' Cielo challenged.

'If I'm completely honest, I probably pushed them together through the lack of energy I was investing in our relationship.'

'So part of you had left the relationship energetically?'

'I guess so. We had been friends all our lives, and I'd never been with anyone else. I guess we both needed to experience more of life and we felt trapped.'

'And how has Damion's so-called betrayal benefitted you now, Beau?' Cielo asked, smiling at Ellen.

Beau looked at Ellen, reached for her hand and said, 'It has given me the greatest of gifts.'

'So, can you see that, at a subconscious level, you created Damion's intervention in your relationship? It was perfect for your expansion. You just could not recognise it at the time.'

Beau sat, nodding his head and feeling emotion well up inside him.

'What are you feeling now, Beau? What is that reaction?'

'I guess I feel love for him,' he said, still trying to reconcile this new emotion. 'If he was here now, and I can't believe I'm saying this, I would want to give him a hug and tell him I forgive him.'

Cielo nodded in acknowledgement. 'You're getting this fast now, Beau. By the way, there is nothing to forgive. He did exactly as the three of you intended. We are always creating, whether we know it or not.'

Beau had a huge smile on his face. Feeling love for Damion, he said, 'I can't believe how free I feel. I guess I've been carrying this around as a massive burden since it happened.'

'Yes you have,' Cielo acknowledged. 'The important learning, as we gain more understanding, is that all of us have the same traits and we are all capable of the same actions. What we despise in others remains unhealed, or unowned, in ourselves. Every one of us, on our own journey at our own pace, has demonstrated every trait and that is why, once we see the perfection in all things, we gain tolerance for the ignorant and enhance our ability to lose all judgement over others. After all, we've all come through the same process.'

'I'm not sure I would have cheated on my best mate with his fiancée though, Cielo.'

'If Ellen had come into your life prior to Damion acting on his feelings with Liz, are you saying there is no way you would have fallen in love with her, given where your relationship with Liz was at?'

Beau looked at Ellen, who was now smiling at him, and he felt his heart melt with a love he had never experienced with Liz.

After kissing her passionately on the lips, he turned to Cielo and conceded, 'Okay Cielo, you win. I should have remembered my first lesson when you nearly had me stabbing Lionel to save Ellen. I guess I'm capable of anything given the right set of circumstances.'

'Sometimes we need to take you to the edge to demonstrate what we are all capable of, Beau.'

Cielo moved towards Beau and acknowledged him by placing her hands on his shoulders, looking him in the eyes. He again felt immense gratitude. The whole room stood as Cielo looked towards the sunlight streaming through from above. She expressed gratitude for the healing and brought the session to a close.

*

Almost two years had passed, and Ellen and Beau had become well entrenched in village life.

Ellen approached the clearing near the foot of the waterfall where Beau, shirtless, was chopping wood for fires. Smiling, she was taken by his muscular arms flexing as he struck the log accurately time and time again, shattering it into kindling.

'Confucius says, "Before enlightenment I chop wood. After enlightenment, I chop wood,"' Beau said, returning her smile.

She was laughing as she embraced him. Beau took in the pristine scene of the cloudless blue sky and the waterfall thundering nearby.

'How could anyone want or need more than this?' he said.

'Time seems irrelevant here, Beau. It seems like only yesterday that we walked down this path with Aaron.'

'Thank God for Aaron. I often think of him and the sacrifice he makes by residing in the lower realm as a gatekeeper.'

'That is his chosen purpose, Beau. He fulfils his purpose by being of service to others.'

'What is your purpose, Ellen? What do you believe you should be doing with this life?'

'That question has been occupying my thoughts more and more often lately, Beau. I keep thinking of all the people out there who are oblivious and in pain, living in fear and searching for the unattainable: pleasure without pain, gain without loss. The truth will set them free, Beau, and I'm feeling a responsibility to share what we've experienced here on Polaris. That is what Cappy did for me and I'm eternally grateful.'

'I must admit, Ellen, I've been missing my family and I feel an increasing need to talk with my father again. There's much healing to do there. As for me, I've achieved a sense of total peace and gratitude for my past and feel that I've released him from any guilt he may be carrying. In saying that, I can't imagine living back in the so-called 'real world', leaving the life we have here. In any case, we have no idea about how to leave. I've never seen a ship pass by here. Even if we made our way down to the lagoon again, what is the point when there is no one there?'

'I asked Cielo over a year ago, and she just smiled and said, "You need to create it. First, you have to believe you can." So I guess what she was saying is that the key is our intent and absolute belief in our ability to create our present and our future. Until now, neither of us has wanted to leave, so we've been creating exactly that outcome.'

'How insightful you are, Ellen.' The familiar voice of Cielo came from behind them.

'Where did you come from?' asked Beau, startled to see her there.

She just smiled and continued. 'You can leave here at any time. You simply need to set a clear intention, for however long it takes, and create the outcome you want without wavering in your belief, just as you did when you created your journey here.'

'The truth is, I don't know if I want to leave,' responded Ellen.

'So, there is your creation, Ellen. Until you have certainty, a clear and absolute intention, you'll never create an outcome other than uncertainty, keeping you stuck. Remember, you're always creating. If you're uncertain, then you're creating uncertainties. If you have no deep-down desire to leave, then that is your creation.'

Cielo smiled, turned and left as quickly as she had arrived.

'She has this capacity to simply appear when she's needed,' Beau noted, shaking his head as he went back to chopping wood.

The talk of leaving stayed in the back of their minds in the weeks that followed. Neither of them raised it again; however, it was occupying their thoughts. During breakfast one rainy morning, the waterfall thundering in the distance, Beau's silence got the better of Ellen.

'You seem distracted, Beau. What's on your mind?' she asked.

'I'm fine, babe. I guess I can't let go of the thoughts I had of home and leaving Polaris.'

'I've been giving that a lot of consideration myself. I believe my experience here, and what we've learnt, has to be for a reason. I can't help but feel a calling to share it with others. I want to inspire others, just as Cappy did for me. How liberating would it be to share the truth? What an amazing contribution, and legacy, it would be to help others to understand what we've learnt here. Imagine if they could feel the elation we feel in not carrying unresolved guilt, grief, abandonment, and all the other negative emotions that sit inside us, ultimately causing disease. Imagine if they felt unconditional love for themselves and others, and constant gratitude for their creations, both challenging and supportive, knowing that both are for their soul's evolution.'

'You certainly have found your passion, Ellen. I can see how inspired you are. I've thought about the same thing. I believe I met you for a reason and I've been on a parallel journey with yours. I also feel there is much to do with the remainder of my life, inspiring others to the possibilities. So what do you want to do?'

'Firstly Beau, I want to spend my life with you,' she shared, moving close to him.

They embraced and kissed, immensely grateful for having found each other. As they separated, Beau said, 'And I with you, Ellen.'

She nodded, looking deeply into his eyes, smiling and at the same time wiping away some tears.

'So what do you think, Beau? Should we leave Polaris?'

He held out for some time, teasing her, shaking his head as if he was struggling with his decision. Then he said with a broad smile, 'I think we should, Ellen.'

She smiled, elated that they were on the same path. They hugged again and felt inseparable in that moment. Two people in love, inspired by a united vision and determined to be in service to others.

CHAPTER TWENTY-ONE
Back to the Future

Each day, following their decision to leave Polaris, Beau and Ellen spent at least an hour in the morning and an hour each evening sitting and meditating overlooking the distant ocean. They were trying to create something outside of themselves that would facilitate their return to the world they had left behind some years earlier. As the weeks went by, they became increasingly frustrated. Each day passed, similar to the one before, and they could not see a way to manifest their intention to leave.

'This is not working,' lamented Beau at the end of another hour of deep meditation.

'Perhaps we're focusing on the wrong intention?' Ellen suggested.

'That's an interesting observation, Ellen.' Again, the unmistakably silky voice of Cielo flowed over them as if it had drifted in on the breeze. They looked around to find her sitting on a rock only a few metres away.

'We've been focusing intently on getting off the island, Cielo. We're trying to coordinate our thoughts to manifest a ship entering the lagoon.'

'It seems to me that you're focusing on the *how* and not the *why*. By focusing on the *how*, you're missing the very essence of creation. If you focus on the *why* and return to your inner knowing, your soul's inspiration and purpose, you'll align your energy with universal intention. There lies your secret to manifestation. This is a solo journey. Each of you must find it within yourself to source your own creation.'

Cielo again rose and wandered off down the path to the village, leaving Beau and Ellen to contemplate what she had told them. They looked at each other as if a light had been turned on.

'Of course, Ellen, that's it! We've been going about this all wrong. This isn't a journey we need to plan like a trip to some distant destination. This is about tapping into our essence, our own internal knowing at the higher mind level. Cielo has mentioned this often, but I feel as though I've only just heard it for the first time.'

Excited, Beau and Ellen returned to the village and joined in the gratitude ceremony with a clear vision, understanding their new intentions to manifest the life that each was inspired to lead. In the weeks following, they regularly sought counsel from Cielo.

'You've both come such a long way since you arrived here in Polaris,' Cielo acknowledged. 'Now is your greatest challenge. You will recall that, at the very beginning, I mentioned that you are here to learn to create. Clearing you of the unnecessary burdens you carried emotionally only gets you ready for the next phase. We are always creating unconsciously for our own evolution that which is designed by our higher mind. However, to create something from the conscious mind, we must be centred, vibrating perfectly in tune with universal vibrations for a clear, unwavering intention. As I said, this will be an individual journey. Only when you set a clear intention, focusing on creating the life you wish for yourself, will you manifest it. This will require an ever-increasing level of detail, an internal vision flowing through your mind like a full-length movie, seeing the colours and smelling the scents, walking through and interacting with those you want in your life. Just as you've created your experience here on Polaris, you'll need to create every detail, every aspect of your new existence. Where you are, what you will be doing on a day-to-day basis, the smells, the environment around you, and the impact you'll have on the many people you will encounter and potentially inspire. The more you can project yourself into this life, with absolute certainty, the more likely you are to manifest it. If you're not clear, you're likely to manifest something other than your ideal creation. Many people live a compromised life, stuck in a creation that comes from an unclear intent. Fear or historical wounds still govern them so that at their core, they do not believe they deserve what they truly wish for, leaving them looping, and without the knowledge or capacity to escape their own creation. They are yet to learn the difference between conscious and unconscious manifestation. If they do not believe they have any influence over their future, they are right. You'll hear them speak of a world where things happen *to* them. That is their journey for however many millennia it may take to realise that they always had control over their destiny.

'Ellen, this island. Does it look familiar to you?'

'I said to Beau, as soon as we landed here, that this is the place I saw in my dreams. The place I imagined all those years ago when Cappy told me stories of his time on a magical island. It's the place that I've been searching for, not even knowing if it existed.'

'Exactly. You manifested it, and your constant obsession in finding it brought it into reality. There lies the way forward for you both,' she said, standing and leaving them to contemplate what she had shared.

Beau and Ellen spent the following weeks focusing on their futures, honing their ideal lives with increasing detail. Of course, part of this ideal life was to journey together, sharing the love they had found in each other. Another month came and went; however, they did not experience the same level of frustration as before. They were just going about their lives with a knowing that they were creating their future, and could let go of the frustration of *when* this would happen. As their individual visions became clearer, they were more excited and inspired about the life they were each creating. Ellen, in particular, often shared great detail with Beau about her vision. She had an unquestioning knowing that she was on track to manifest the life she was inspired to lead.

As the morning sun streamed through their bedroom window, Beau awoke and rolled over towards Ellen to embrace her as he did every day with a loving hug and a passionate kiss. It was one of his favourite times of the day, filling his heart with love for her and her love for him. On this particular morning, Ellen was not lying next to him as she usually was. He called out for her. 'Babe, are you okay?'

There was no answer and he became uneasy. Fear came over him and he quickly got dressed and headed out to the streets of the village where others were now going about their daily chores.

'Have you seen Ellen?' he asked as he walked amongst them. 'No,' was the common response. He kept walking through street after street. No sign of her.

Perhaps she's gone to the Great Hall to see Cielo, he thought, moving quickly in that direction. The Great Hall was empty and his fear increased into a mild panic. Beau moved quickly along the two-kilometre path to the edge of the plateau, where they had sat most afternoons watching the sunset. No sign of her there either. Where could she be? he wondered. It was unusual for her to leave the hut without telling him where she was going. Beau walked back the two kilometres to the village and out the other side, towards the giant waterfall, which was another of their special places. He called her name over and over without response. With increasing urgency, he ran back to the centre of the village and saw Cielo entering the Great Hall.

'Cielo, wait please, I need to speak with you.'

'Certainly Beau, come on in and join me.'

'I don't have time, Cielo. I just need to know if you've seen Ellen.'

'Come inside and join me, Beau.'

Beau knew that it was futile to insist on a response from her and so he followed her into the Great Hall. Cielo took her time and sat cross-legged on the raised centre pedestal, in her usual place. 'Come and sit beside me, Beau. Here, sit right next to me.'

'Cielo, I can't find Ellen anywhere. I've been out to the edge of the plateau. I've searched the waterfall and the forest. I've been through most of the streets in the village and asked everyone I've come across. No one has seen her.'

Cielo sat in silence and just looked deeply and knowingly into Beau's eyes.

Eventually she asked, 'So Beau, what do you think has become of her?'

'I don't know. I was hoping you could tell me. I'm getting very concerned.'

'I want you to place your hand on your heart and search deep inside for the love you have for her and her for you. Can you feel her?'

'Yes, of course I can. She's always in my heart.'

'Do you recall our many discussions around energy? It only changes form, it's never lost.'

'Yes, I do recall that, however, I'm not sure how this relates to Ellen missing right now?'

'If you knew that she had gone to the next village for a visit, and would be back to be with you this evening, would you miss her?'

'Well, no, I guess I wouldn't, not like I am at present not knowing. But I would know that she was okay.'

'So you're honouring your fear because she's not physically present with you now, when you know that she is pure energy that cannot be dissipated. She is always present, always with you. It's your obsession with the physical world that creates fear around loss, Beau. It's no different when people pass over from the physical world in the transition we call death. Their energy is never lost. What we *crave* in another is only relevant in the physical world. They are pure energy and love, always, just as they are when they are physically with you. That cannot die.'

'I do understand that, Cielo, however, it's a very difficult concept to live with while we are still here in the physical world. The fact is if she was not around, I would definitely miss her greatly.'

'Of course you would Beau, and I'm not suggesting that you shouldn't. I'm just asking you to lose your fear around any form of loss of Ellen and her essence, while fully understanding your need for her physical presence.'

'So, are you trying in a roundabout way to tell me that she has died, Cielo?'

Cielo smiled and reached for Beau's hand, holding it as she looked into his eyes. 'I've been waiting for this day for some weeks, Beau. Ellen's capacity to manifest and create her future is extraordinary, while yours is still developing. Ellen has transitioned to her new life. After all, isn't that what you were both trying to create?'

'Of course it is, Cielo. I did expect that we would create it together though.' Beau was suddenly very emotional.

'Who's to say you haven't created that life together, Beau? From what I've witnessed, I believe you have. You need to maintain your certainty around your own life's creation to manifest it. Fear will be your greatest barrier to success. This fear is what keeps most in the lower realms, looping around and around, rather than creating a life full of love, gratitude, wisdom, and purpose.'

Beau nodded and could see that Cielo was guiding him. As difficult as it was, he had to stay with his individual intention of creating a life filled with purpose; a life together with Ellen.

'You believe that Ellen's life manifestation includes you, Beau, as her life partner?'

'Of that, Cielo, I have no doubt.'

'Then so it shall be, Beau, so it shall be. Your greatest challenge is to focus on your internal guidance regarding what you should be doing with your life. With or without Ellen, what is your purpose? Go about your life here in the village with certainty and assurance and without time limits. It requires an unwavering belief that you will create the life you desire, all in good time. If you truly believe it, without reservation, only then can it manifest. The time it takes for you to get to that place of pure and unreserved belief becomes irrelevant.'

Cielo stood and hugged him, pouring all of her love and intention into him, then she turned and left him alone in the Great Hall.

Beau sat for some time in his grief, lost in his emotions, wondering if he would ever see Ellen again. He wanted to believe he would be with her. However, his doubt and fear crippled him. He wanted so much for it to happen right now. Days passed and he spoke to no one. He spent his time lost in his chores, sitting for an age at the edge of the plateau, looking out to sea as they had done together most days. He could not get over his doubt and fear that he would remain here alone and without Ellen.

Months of grieving passed and Beau's desire to learn to manifest became an ever-increasing priority. He noticed that he had begun to spend more time thinking about his purpose and what he wanted to do with his life. One full moon, during the wisdom circle with everyone from the village in attendance, he raised the issue of creation. 'I love Ellen unconditionally. However, I know now that she's not my purpose. I have a burning desire to share with others what I've learnt here. My awakening is that I've always been most inspired when I'm in service to others. My work with abused children at the firm, and my mentoring of younger staff over the years, has been the most rewarding part of my life. I recall days where I would take underprivileged kids out sailing, to teach them confidence and about the beauty of nature. Those days changed them and even more, they changed me. This is the type of work I've been preparing for my whole life and Polaris has been the pinnacle of that journey. I'm ready to go back and continue my life's calling.'

Cielo rose and walked to him. She held him by the arms and looked right into his soul. 'Beau, this is the first time I've felt your energy purely congruent with your life's purpose, connected to universal energy. When these energies align, anything is possible. It's the very essence of creation, the path of least resistance. People will come and go in our lives. That is not to say we don't love them unconditionally. Regardless of our love for and connection to them, children included, others can never determine our life's journey. That can only come from an inspired place within you and it is greater than any one person. The irony is that when we let go of misaligned priorities, we leave space for real intentions. Only then can we truly create our intended life's purpose. You'll recall when you arrived here that I warned you might not be ready for the fourth realm and the universal wisdom it has to offer. That was because you were infatuated with Ellen, who was truly on an inspired path and came here through her own creation. You were only granted access because you had made significant sacrifices and had walked away from a secure life to find your true path. You had begun your quest for the source of all creation, the Empyrean as Ellen would say. It's an endless journey of evolution entirely beyond our understanding. All we can do is take one step at a time in the right direction and open our knowing to the guidance that is there for all to see, when we are ready to receive it. You allowed your inner knowing to guide you and Ellen was just part of your journey to get you here. Only when you let go of the *how* and got in touch with the *why* did you arrive here in your own right.'

Beau felt as if he were bathed in pure light and he experienced a calm certainty, a new level of understanding and freedom.

'I feel like I've just arrived at a new existence, Cielo.'

She smiled and the entire village rose to surround him, as they had done on the first day Beau and Ellen had arrived.

'You have, Beau. Welcome,' she announced. They all waited in turn and hugged him, as if for the first time, acknowledging him one by one.

'Welcome Beau, we've been waiting for you.'

Beau drifted off to sleep that evening, exhausted, and for the first time, he was not obsessed about Ellen and how much he was missing her. While his thoughts wandered to his love for her, he knew she was not separate from him. Whenever he closed his eyes and focused on their love for each other, she was right there with him. His focus became more about envisaging a life supporting others to release their anxiety and the historical wounds that held them captive. He felt at absolute peace with his own existence, as if he were wrapped in a light of pure joy. His clarity around this new existence was dominating his every thought and he could see and feel his life in absolute detail, as if he was walking through his own movie, living it now, in the moment.

Beau was startled by a large hand on his shoulder. The familiar voice of Kulani brought him back to reality.

'Beau, Rick has been screaming at you, asking if you can see anything beyond the mist!'

Beau thought for a moment and sensed the thick mist around him. He was back on *Orpheus*, at the bow. His body filled with a rush of pure love and excitement as he felt the soft loving hand of Ellen pulling him towards her, and then she was kissing him passionately on the lips. She beamed and said, 'Welcome back. You'd better answer the skipper before he sacks you as first mate.'

She could not contain her excitement as Beau realised where he was. He smiled back at her and then, with a jolt of concern, looked urgently through the breaking mist for any sign of the island or of crashing waves on the reef. There was nothing but a calm, pristine ocean ahead.

'All clear ahead, Skipper!' he hollered to Rick at the helm. The mist cleared, revealing a stunning blue sky.

The breeze sprang up from nowhere and Rick gave the order, 'Hoist the mainsail and let's get underway! We've wasted enough time drifting around here!'

'Hardly a waste of time I would say,' Beau said, smiling at Ellen and pulling her into his arms.

www.ingramcontent.com/pod-product-compliance
Lightning Source LLC
Chambersburg PA
CBHW020829260626
47169CB00003B/902